Annie's Stories

ANNIE'S STORIES

CINDY THOMSON

TYNDALE HOUSE PUBLISHERS, INC.
CAROL STREAM, ILLINOIS

Visit Tyndale online at www.tyndale.com.

Visit Cindy Thomson's website at www.cindyswriting.com.

TYNDALE and Tyndale's quill logo are registered trademarks of Tyndale House Publishers, Inc.

Annie's Stories

Designed by Beth Sparkman

Edited by Erin E. Smith

The author is represented by Chip MacGregor of MacGregor Literary Inc., 2373 NW 185th Avenue, Suite 165, Hillsboro, OR 97124

Scripture quotations are taken from the *Holy Bible*, King James Version.

Annie's Stories is a work of fiction. Where real people, events, establishments, organizations, or locales appear, they are used fictitiously. All other elements of the novel are drawn from the author's imagination.

Library of Congress Cataloging-in-Publication Data

Thomson, Cindy, date.
  Annie's stories / Cindy Thomson.
    pages cm. — (Ellis Island)
  ISBN 978-1-4143-6845-0 (sc)
1. Young women—New York (State)—New York—Fiction. 2. Irish—New York (State)—New York—Fiction. 3. Fathers and daughters—Fiction. 4. Storytelling—Fiction. 5. Self-realization in women—Fiction. I. Title.
  PS3620.H7447A56 2014
  813'.6—dc23   2014001580

Printed in the United States of America

20   19   18   17   16   15   14
 7   6   5   4   3   2   1

In fond memory of my father,
Lloyd "Pete" Peters,
who wore many hats during his lifetime,
including that of a whistling postman.

Acknowledgments

DURING THE PROCESS of writing *Annie's Stories*, I gained a keen awareness of how much I had to be truly thankful for. God is good, all the time, and I realized that even during the times I struggled with aspects of this story, the goodness of my Creator still blanketed me, reassuring me that, as Annie learns in the story, good always wins out. I realized that this was the important truth I needed to remember along my storytelling yellow brick road. I'm thankful God still teaches me to remember what I have no excuse for forgetting at times.

I'm grateful that so many of the modern-day survivors of Magdalene Laundries shared their stories online so the world could see that it's possible to step out on the other side of oppression and work to see that wrongs are acknowledged and not repeated. May God continue to guide and heal all those affected.

I've been blessed to have many helpers travel this road with me.

I'm thankful for my editor Stephanie Broene, whose grace, kindness, discernment, and interest in my characters and their stories has blessed me so much. My editor Erin Smith's incredible talents helped this story in immeasurable ways. All the folks at Tyndale House are such outstanding people to work with, and I'm grateful for each one.

Thanks to Chip MacGregor for continuing to believe in my storytelling.

Many people supported me with their prayers during the writing process, and I'm a firm believer that the most powerful thing we can do for each other is pray in earnest. Thank you, Etna UMC prayer group and my Writer Sisters.

A long list of fellow writers blessed me with their insights and brainstorming, including Nicole O'Dell, Cara Putman, Lisa Samson, and Rachel Hauck. A huge thank-you to Rachel, who not only helped me think through some difficulties I was having with the plot, but also called me and prayed over the phone.

For my research I used many of the same resources I acknowledged in *Grace's Pictures*, but it's important to mention again the Ellis Island Foundation and to suggest that readers with ancestors who passed through Ellis Island, and anyone interested in this era, visit www.ellisisland.org.

Thank you to Sandra Thomson and Susanne Fox for your advice regarding the German words in the story. If there are any errors, they are mine alone.

My heart swells with gratitude that God has blessed me with family. I love them all near and far and want to acknowledge the support of my mom, Golden Peters; my mother-in-law, Eileen Thomson; my sister, Beverly Wallace; my handsome sons, Dan, Jeff, and Kyle; and my beautiful daughter-in-law, Kelsey. So many friends all over the world have encouraged me as I worked on this story. Thank you all. Without my cheerleaders, this task would be beyond daunting.

And to my husband, Tom, whose support and love never wavers. Thanks for allowing me the time to write and for accompanying me on so many research trips and book signings, and for giving me the inspiration for Annie's sweet tooth. My writing journey would not be nearly as much fun without you!

And finally, thank *you*, for reading and for reaching out on Facebook and other sites and through e-mail. If we haven't yet met, please visit my site, www.cindyswriting.com, to find out the many places where you can find me. I enjoy hearing from readers, and this story is truly for you!

PS—Subscribers to my newsletter have the opportunity to read one of Annie's stories. Please sign up at www.cindyswriting.com.

No matter how dreary and gray our homes are, we people of flesh and blood would rather live there than in any other country, be it ever so beautiful. There is no place like home.

L. FRANK BAUM, *THE WONDERFUL WIZARD OF OZ*

1

SOMETIMES THE SMALLEST THINGS ignited memories Annie Gallagher would sooner forget. This time all it took was a glimpse of a half-finished tapestry Mrs. Hawkins had left on her parlor chair: *Home Sweet Home*. Annie pressed her palm against her heart, trying to shut out the realization that she was far from home—and not just because she now lived in America.

In a few days it would be her birthday, but she wanted to forget. Birthdays held no significance when your parents had gone to heaven.

For most of her life Annie had traveled with her father, a *seanchaí*, a storyteller from the old Irish tradition. She had learned the age-old stories of the great warrior Cuchulain and the tragic tale of a cruel stepmother in "The Children of Lir." She learned of kings and monks and lords and wild beasts. But when night came and he tucked her into whatever straw cot they had borrowed for the night, he told her tales that were just for her—Annie's stories, he called them. Now that her father was gone, those stories were all she had, her only connection to a place, intangible as it might have been, that she called home.

She held on to them, brought them out from time to time to remind her she'd once lived in someone's heart. Without that, she feared she might plunge again into darkness.

Annie approached the breakfront cabinet gracing the wall opposite a substantial parlor window that looked out to the street. She opened the door, revealing her special lap desk. Suddenly her father's voice lived again in her mind.

"Look here, Annie lass," her da called one day from his mat by Uncle Neil's hearth. Neil O'Shannon was her mother's brother, and he hadn't wanted Annie and her father in his home, but her father—who was just as dismayed to be there but had found no other open hearth in that sparsely populated countryside—had been too ill to move on.

Annie had just come inside from gathering seaweed on the shore. She set her reed basket on the table and came closer. Da held a box of some sort.

"See here. 'Tis a writing desk—pens and even paper inside." He opened the box and showed her how the top folded into a writing surface.

"I've never seen anything like it." Annie rubbed her hand across the inlaid design on the edges. Swirls, flowers—so beautiful.

"I should write down your tales for you."

"Which ones, Da?" She examined the ink pot. Full.

"Why, Annie's stories, darlin'. Those that are yours. I won't be here forever to tell them to you."

She shook her head. "Don't talk like that, Da. And don't you know, I won't be forgetting them."

"Don't suppose you will. But I'll write them just the same. I'll add some drawings. You'd like that, so."

She had not thought he'd done it, not until after he'd passed on and Father Weldon helped her find those pages, those precious hand-scribed stories, the day he'd rescued her from that evil Magdalene Laundry, a prison-like place for young girls who had committed no crime except being homeless and unwanted.

She sat down on the piano stool in Mrs. Hawkins's parlor as the memories flooded her mind like a swarm of midsummer gnats. She heard Father Weldon's voice. "Hold on to the good memories. The Magdalene Laundry you were in does not speak for the church, child. There are those who are compassionate, even within its walls, but they allow fear to overshadow what's right. I implore you to focus on the good now, the good you have seen among my parishioners. And know that God will provide," he had said.

Perhaps Father Weldon had been right about the laundry. The church wasn't evil. Sister Catherine and a couple of the other nuns seemed to care. But Annie was sure God had not been in that laundry. God couldn't be bothered, she'd realized.

"Don't give Neil O'Shannon a second thought, child," Father Weldon had told her, his eyes soft. "Your father was a remarkable man. You have your memories now, don't you?"

Painful memories she could not forget. Not so far.

Her sorrow had begun on a day in January in the year nineteen hundred, the day they'd buried her father.

"A wanderer is only at home in the hearts of those who love him."
Annie had heard her father say this, and now that he was gone, Annie had no place in the world. She had been born of a great love between two people separated by hatred, as tragic a tale as Romeo and Juliet.

She had heard the story from her father many times. Annie's parents had fallen in love, but the O'Shannons did not want their daughter to marry a Protestant, especially a *seanchaí*. But they'd done it anyway, run off to Dublin, where an Anglican minister married them. A month later, while her father and mother traveled on the road to Limerick, Annie's mother's family tracked her down, locked Annie's father in a cowshed, and then stole her mother away. After some time, her father found her mother, but tragically she died in childbirth, and from then on, it had only been Annie and her father.

Now, just Annie.

"Marty Gallagher was a magnificent storyteller," the priest had said to those gathered in the churchyard. "Not only could he recite entire Shakespearean plays by memory, but he told his own tales as well. Many of you gathered here were privileged to be entertained by him."

A man she didn't know—but was told was Mr. Barrows from Dublin—had approached her after prayers were said. "My deepest sympathies, Miss Gallagher."

She thanked him, but his condolences seemed to slide right by. There was nothing anyone could have said to make that better.

"The entire world will mourn his passing." He extended his black umbrella over his dipped head and backed away.

People say all kinds of odd things when someone dies. Paying respects at a funeral was fine and good for that man, whoever he had been. He'd gone back to Dublin and carried on. But Annie? She was only twenty years of age, and her life spread out before her now like a long, lonely highway spilling into distant hills beyond where the eye can see.

It was what had happened after the funeral that had led to her imprisonment in that unspeakable place.

She rose now, shut the door to the breakfront, and wiped it down, though she'd noted no dust. Glancing out the front window at the pedestrians populating Lower Manhattan's sidewalks, she observed men carrying large black satchels. Businessmen.

Not a *seanchaí* in the lot, she supposed. If she ever married, it would be to someone who appreciated the power of a story.

Sighing, Annie brushed her feather duster along the windowsill and the glass globes of the oil lamps. How she'd come to be the housekeeper at Hawkins House was by chance, a stroke of incredible luck, to be sure. Father Weldon had sent her there.

"I will arrange for a woman named Agnes Hawkins to take you in. She and her charity supporters are opening a home for girls in New York, and she needs a housekeeper to help her get started."

"Why would you do this for me, Father?"

This man, a British priest in the west of Ireland, was such an oddity. Even Da in his storytelling could not have created such an unlikely rescuer.

"I had great admiration for your father, Annie. He was a fine man, God rest his soul. Being a storyteller, he wandered, going from place to place to do his work. In a small way I'm like he was. I am in a foreign land. My sister, the woman who will take you in, is as well. But God directs our paths. We don't always end up in the places we'd imagined. I'm to see you get away from here safely and begin life anew with hope."

Annie knew as well as winter follows autumn that God had not directed her. If he had, he never would have allowed her to end up in that horrible laundry. Without her father, without God, Annie was adrift on a dark, choppy sea. She'd hoped living in America at Hawkins House would lead her out of the nefarious hole she'd been plunged into since her father died, and it had been a fortuitous beginning. Mrs. Hawkins was nice, and Annie truly was grateful to her. But her father had said home is where the people who love you are, the people who truly want you. He had not said home was where people were just nice to you.

Annie had been fortunate to come here, indeed. However,

everyone knew luck ran out. There were many chapters of Annie's life yet to be written. No one in Ireland had believed Annie capable of directing her own destiny. But now? Now she needed to make her own way without Da . . . and without even God's help.

2

STEPHEN ADAMS often wondered about the people who wrote the letters he delivered. They came from distant lands like Ireland, Germany, Russia, and every once in a while from as far away as Australia. Stephen had never been anywhere but New York. Born and raised. So were his father and mother. As far as he could tell, his ancestors had all been born in the city, back to the original Dutch planters perhaps. But he didn't really know. No one did. The only thing he knew for sure was that none of that old immigrant money had been passed on in his family, and he was the only one left. His parents—God rest their souls—along with his brother, who had died last year in a construction accident, were buried in Cypress Hills over in Brooklyn. Oh, he had some cousins here and there, but none had stayed in touch, and if they had, Stephen would have to keep making excuses for his father's death. He was glad not to have to do that.

These folks on his route? Many of them had no family in America, and they'd pressed on, making do, striving for better. Their stories were inspiring. Stephen could press on too.

"Howdy, Mr. Adams!" Matty, one of the kids he often saw on his route, greeted him.

"Hi there, fella. Have breakfast today?"

The kid shrugged and kicked some pebbles with his too-small shoes. "I'm not hungry. Ma gave me a bit a coffee in my milk."

"Today?"

"Not today."

Stephen reached into his mailbag and pulled out the apple he'd brought for his lunch. "Take this then, for later, when you get hungry."

The boy beamed. "Thanks!"

Stephen continued down the street, whistling one of his favorite Irish ballads and thinking about the folks he would likely see today.

Hawkins House was one of his favorite stops on his mail route because Annie Gallagher was the housekeeper there. He made sure to stomp heavily on the front stoop. As he'd hoped, the front latch opened. He held out some letters. "Morning, Miss Gallagher. Got a letter from home for you and a postcard for Mrs. Hawkins. Seems her nephew and his wife have been to Coney Island again."

"You must be mistaken." Her face turned pasty. "Not a letter for me."

He held it up. "Miss Annie Gallagher. It's from County Mayo, Father Joseph Weldon."

"Father Weldon wrote to me? He writes often to Mrs. Hawkins—he's her brother—but this is the first I've received."

He reached into his bag. "I almost forgot. Got a new boarder, don't you? A Miss Wagner?"

"We do."

He waved a long envelope in front of his face. "Seems there is plenty of news, judging from how thick this is." He handed the letter to Annie. Their hands brushed for just a moment.

Her face reddened and she pulled at her sleeves. She looked down, seeming to study Kirsten Wagner's fat letter, which made the other one look malnourished.

He hesitated, whistling "The Stone outside Dan Murphy's

Door," a tune he'd learned at the Irish dance where he'd hoped to see her. Some of the girls there had said she attended on occasion.

She cocked her head to her shoulder. "An Irish tune, and you a true Yankee?"

He stopped, wondering if he'd offended her. He did not want to scare her off. He'd try something else. "Say, I heard the kids over on Bowery acting out a story—*The Wonderful Wizard of Oz*. They were pretty good. A lion, a scarecrow, a man made of tin. Have you heard of it?"

She smiled, her teeth like pearls. "I have, though I've not seen a copy myself. I must look for it next time I stop at Bourne's since so many people recommend it."

Good. He'd at least engaged her a bit. "I shall do the same." Now he didn't know what else to say. "Well, I suppose I'll be going now."

"Thank you, Mr. Adams."

"My pleasure. Always good to see you, Miss Gallagher." He spun on his heels. "Enjoy!"

Annie closed the solid wood door carefully and leaned against it a moment, holding the letters to her chest. Since she'd arrived, the only news she'd had was what Father Weldon wrote to Mrs. Hawkins about. She glanced down at the writing that spelled her name and then looked up to see Mrs. Hawkins moving toward her.

"I thought I heard you talking to the postman. What has he brought?"

Annie and their boarder Grace McCaffery lovingly referred to the woman as the Hawk because of her keen senses. And here she was to ask questions just as Annie pondered what receiving the letter meant.

Annie put on a pleasant posture. "Seems your people have been frolicking at Coney Island again." Annie waved the postcard at her.

"Oh, bother. My Harold's sister's boy and his wife. They spend more time gallivanting than being gainfully employed. Give me that foolish thing." Mrs. Hawkins snatched the card from Annie's fingers and examined the drawing of a carousel. "The writing is too small for my eyes. What does it say, love?" She handed it back to Annie.

"It says, 'Wish you were here. Love, James and Caroline.'"

She shook her head. "What else has the postman brought?"

"A rather large letter for Kirsten Wagner."

The woman took both letters from her hands before Annie realized it. "You received a letter from Joseph. I do hope it's not bad news."

"I . . . uh . . . I don't know, Mrs. Hawkins."

The woman patted her arm. "There, there, love. You are a long way from that horrible place, and you have wonderful memories of your father to cherish. Focus on those. You are here now as you should be." Mrs. Hawkins began straightening her framed botanical prints that lined the walls of the hall.

Annie smiled, trying to muster the confidence her employer had. She glanced back down at the letter. Perhaps her uncle Neil had died and Father Weldon felt it was his responsibility to let her know. She lifted the thicker piece of mail, pondering whether or not to leave it on the entry table. Annie had been away on errands when Kirsten first arrived at Hawkins House a few days ago. She didn't know what instructions she had been given. "If I leave Kirsten's letter on the mail tray, will she know to retrieve it?"

Mrs. Hawkins pointed toward the silver tray lying on the entry table. Her prized Paul Revere piece, she called it. "I will make sure she knows it's there, love."

Annie retreated to the quiet of her room in the back of the house. The tenants lived upstairs, but she and Mrs. Hawkins had separate rooms at the end of the downstairs hallway near the kitchen, and her room was her sanctuary.

She stared at the envelope with the postage stamp bearing an image of the British monarch. She opened it and slowly unfolded the letter.

Dear Annie,

I hope this letter reaches you posthaste. I want to tell you that your cousin Aileen was married last spring, and sadly her husband, Donald, was lost at sea this summer.

Oh, my. Annie would not have wished that on the girl, despite what she'd done to Annie. Aileen had gotten married far younger than most, and to suffer this while no more than a teenager?

Aileen misses you, and so we are sending her to New York on the Teutonic. Please meet her and take charge of her. We are counting on you. Trust me that I saw no alternative. Please inform my sister to expect her.

Yours truly,
Fr. Joseph Weldon

Annie refolded the letter, rubbing her temples with her thumbs. So they had already sent Aileen to America. Aileen, one year younger than Annie, was in Annie's estimation a mollycoddled, intolerable child. Obviously Donald's family had not been prosperous enough to take Aileen in. Pity, but Aileen O'Shannon here? After what she had done by pointing a finger at Annie when Annie had been innocent? Uncle Neil had believed his only daughter over the niece he barely knew when Aileen had accused her of carrying on with Johnny Flynn—a complete mistruth that had prompted Neil to send Annie to the nuns. Oh, how Annie had hoped to put that whole chapter in the past.

Annie opened the letter again and reread it. She had not missed anything. There wasn't much there. Angry tears burned at the corners of her eyes. The O'Shannons were no more family than the robins pecking at the wee herb garden out back. If they even had hearts, Annie had no place in them.

The sound of paper crinkling under her fists surprised her, but she gave in to it and wadded the letter into a tight ball. Grabbing the bed warmer on the floor, she opened the lid, tossed the paper in, and drew a match from the tin box bolted on the wall near her door. Her first efforts to strike the match failed, and tears streamed down her face with her frustration. When she finally coaxed a flame, she lit the paper on fire and watched as it sank into a hot ball and then wafted into black ashes.

When her father had fallen ill, they happened to be near Neil's farm. Annie had thought there might be some mercy in the man she'd never met. She'd been surprised to discover the O'Shannons had not known she had been born alive. Neil had thought both his sister and her baby had passed away. Annie would later understand why her father had kept the truth from Neil, who had turned out to be a self-serving and pernicious man. Back then, though, Annie had been stunned to discover that Neil and Cora were about to shut Annie and her father out into the cold until Annie's father offered them what little money he had left. Once Da passed on, Neil had said he had no obligation toward Annie. Why, now, should he expect Annie to feel any duty toward his daughter, especially after the lie her cousin had told?

Annie squeezed her eyes shut. It must be bad over there for

the O'Shannons to resort to this. But truly Annie didn't know if she could forgive Aileen, that wee impetuous lass.

Mrs. Hawkins questioned her over dinner. "Tell me about that letter, love. Was it about your relatives?"

"It was. My cousin's husband has died."

"Oh, I am so sorry, love." Tears sprang to her eyes and she fingered her silverware. "And her so young. I do hope she has something to remember him by." The woman continued to stroke the handle of a table knife, one of the belongings she'd kept from her marriage after her husband, Harold, passed on.

Annie nodded and rose to pour more tea.

"Was there anything else in the letter?"

"I am afraid so."

"What is it, love?"

"My cousin Aileen. Father Weldon says to tell you to expect her on board the *Teutonic*."

"She's coming to live with us? How wonderful for you."

Mrs. Hawkins did not understand that this was awful news. Aileen was coming and Annie would be expected to "take charge" of her. However selfish it might be, Annie had planned for her position at Hawkins House to precipitate a new life, away from folks like the O'Shannons.

Mrs. Hawkins folded her chubby hands on top of the table. "I know what concerns you about this, love."

"You do?"

"Indeed. Aileen reminds you of where your uncle put you, but trust me, nothing of that sort will happen to either one of you girls."

"Thank you, Mrs. Hawkins." The woman *had* been kind. Annie reminded herself that Mrs. Hawkins had been forced to take her in because of her brother's bidding, and therefore could not truly care about her, at least not as much as her father had. He'd said home was in the hearts of those who loved you. Annie had to build her place to belong from scratch, without anyone's help. And now she would have to ensure that her cousin's arrival did not thwart her plans.

Before bed she consulted her account book from the Emigrant Savings Bank, where she deposited the pay Mrs. Hawkins gave her. After four months of saving most of her income, she had $81.54. She tapped a pencil to her lips.

"You are good with the books," her da had said.

She had kept track of all their expenses, and Da had told her when times were rich and when they were lean. He'd said his family left him an estate that he sold before meeting her mother. The earnings had kept Annie and her da on the road, doing what he loved—meeting and greeting folks and entertaining them. By the time Da died, however, he told her there was not much left.

"There's not been time to work properly," he'd complained.

She'd asked him if the estate funds were depleted, but she never got an answer, as sick as he was. That had to be the truth, though. No couriers came by, no farmers carrying cheques like they'd done in the past. Da had registered his whereabouts on their travels so that their money would find them. They had never been dirt-poor like so many others, not until he got sick.

She sighed as she thought about it. His inheritance had run dry just as he took his last breath. A man like Marty Gallagher deserved much more. His legacy should be remembered with a memorial or a statue . . . No, something more fitting to a storyteller. A house filled with stories. A magnificent library with a brass plate over the door naming the building after him.

She'd received her own education from a diverse group of

hedge-school masters—those traveling scholars who taught on their own terms rather than conform to the government's state schools. While the name dated back to a time when the men's religious affiliation caused them to resort to teaching outdoors under hedges and taking their wages in barter—the way her father essentially had done—Annie and her father were pleased the masters still traveled about and had welcomed her. And her education hadn't been inadequate, despite what many Irish folks thought about a woman's limitations. Those roving instructors trained her to read and calculate numbers, and she was pretty good at it. Her da had taught her to love stories and learn from history. Stories had filled Annie's head and delighted her soul for as long as she could remember. Her love of books and learning had never left her. What might seem impossible in Ireland surely was possible here. Why couldn't a woman in America establish such a place as a memorial library, so?

But now she had to earn her own money. She would need a new coat come winter, and she had set aside twenty cents a week for that expense. Some of the Irish lasses she'd met told her to buy her coat on time and make regular payments, but she would not do that. Her da had taught her to pay in full when she purchased anything, and to owe no man even a farthing. Just because her savings were accumulating more slowly than she wished was no reason to dismiss that advice. She would not rent the building that would bear her father's name because then she'd be at the mercy of a landlord. She would purchase her own property. She had been considering something like this for some time, even though she'd discovered she needed a minimum of one thousand dollars for a proper-sized structure. In just over four years she would have enough, but could she endure Aileen for that long?

3

A FEW DAYS LATER Annie noted the new boarder's letter still lying on the silver tray.

"She comes home from work so late I've not had the opportunity to tell her about it," Mrs. Hawkins said. "But thank you for bringing it to my attention because she is home at the moment." Mrs. Hawkins moved toward the kitchen, her black heels clicking on the floorboards. She paused and returned to Annie. "Written in English, wasn't it?"

Annie glanced at the mail. "Truly. Our postman is as American as President McKinley and wouldn't have delivered it otherwise."

The woman winked at her. "Oh, but he is much more handsome, wouldn't you say, love?"

"I . . . uh . . . well . . ."

Agnes Hawkins closed her eyes, pursed her lips, and shook her head. Then she asked for the letter, which Annie handed her. The woman turned it over and smoothed the paper with her thumb. She held it toward the light coming in from the kitchen window. "I'm thinking that the whole thing might be in English, and I would be surprised if our Kirsten could read it. The country folks in Germany must be more educated than I realized."

Annie felt her mouth drop open. "I'm not going to open it to find out."

Someone coughed from the back stairs.

Unsure how long Kirsten had been observing them, Annie tried to obscure the fact that they had been nosy by collecting the letter from Mrs. Hawkins and handing it to the petite German girl. The thin blonde with the hard-consonant dialect of the Germans, with no apology for her illiteracy, pushed it back toward Annie. "I cannot read it. You will tell me what it says, *ja?*"

Mrs. Hawkins folded her hands in front of her. "We don't mean to pry, love. Just surprised someone would write to you in English."

"You do not pry." She gave her wee head a dismissive shake. "My brother wrote it, Mrs. Hawkins. I never learned to read, in German or any other language. He went to school and learned English. He probably thought someone would read it to me." She shrugged her shoulders.

Annie could not contain her curiosity. She had not yet had the opportunity to learn more about this girl. "Where did you learn to speak English?"

Kirsten licked her thin lips. "I learned . . . My father thought I should know. He knew only a few words and although he did not believe his daughter should go to school, he thought I would one day emigrate. Things in my country . . . the times are hard. So he sent me to work at our neighbor's farm. The neighbor's wife, when . . . *als ein kleines Mädchen* . . . uh . . . a little girl, lived in America. She was sent back to marry and stayed, but she teach me, *ja?*"

Annie nodded to show she understood. "There are schools for immigrants, at night. You could learn to read."

Kirsten shook her head. "I work now."

"And your brother? He is in Germany?" Annie asked.

"Uh, *nein*. He is in America."

Mrs. Hawkins, seeming to want to rescue Kirsten, who still struggled a bit with the English language, held up a finger to interrupt. "He is working far upstate, Annie. Helping with the construction in the state capital, didn't you say, Kirsten?"

The girl bobbed her blonde head.

Kirsten was just the kind of lass Annie hoped to help with her new library—someone alone and needing skills, especially the ability to read. Even though it did not seem she wanted any help beyond having her letters read to her, Annie hoped she'd be interested later.

From the front parlor the mantel clock struck four. Mrs. Hawkins shooed the girls toward it. "Go on and read it, Annie."

When they entered the large room where they spent their leisure time and entertained guests, Annie watched as the new girl moved to the edge of an upholstered chair like a down feather on a breeze. She seemed so weightless a brisk north wind might have blown her off her feet. As sad as this girl seemed, Annie couldn't help but wonder what might have happened to her before she came to live with them. Had the darkness threatened to swallow her as well?

Annie chose the sofa in direct line with the chair and slid a fingernail underneath the seal on the letter.

Kirsten narrowed her crystal-blue eyes in Annie's direction. "It is from Jonas, *ja*? Does it say from Jonas?"

Annie laid the letter in her lap. "Are you sure you want me to read this to you?"

"I would not trouble you, Annie Gallagher, if it were not necessary. Please, go on."

"If you would, just call me Annie."

"*Ja.*" The girl lifted her chin in Annie's direction.

Annie directed her gaze to the bottom of the paper. *Your loving brother, Jonas.* "Aye, 'tis from your brother, Jonas."

Kirsten sat straighter. "I knew it was so. *Gut, gut.*" Her balled fists resting in her lap seemed to suggest she wasn't as pleased as she tried to sound. "Please read, Annie."

Annie inhaled and began.

> *"Dear Kirstie,*
>
> *Your brother has been busy. I miss you, but I am happy you are in a comfortable place. No matter how hard I work pounding nails into lumber beams all day, I will never forget to pray for you and wish you well."*

Annie swallowed hard before taking a breath to continue. They were only words on paper, true, but a rush of warmth ran up Annie's neck to her chin as she stared at the script. These words were not meant for her, yet they touched her deeply. So kind, so gentle, reminding her of her father. Kirsten was loved. The tongue is never too far away from the heart's intentions. Words reveal the character of a man.

Annie cleared her throat as though a tickle had interrupted her. Then she continued.

> *"Please let me know you are settled in safely. I do hope my contacts did not lead you astray and that this boardinghouse is taking good care of you."*

Annie glanced up to see Mrs. Hawkins standing in the doorway.

"Jonas found Mrs. Hawkins's place for me, and I'm working until we can be together again," Kirsten explained. She turned toward Mrs. Hawkins. "He inquired and found the minister of your church, *ja*?"

"That's correct, love. Reverend Clarke recommended us. I will get us some tea. You go on."

"Thank you." Annie turned back to Kirsten. "Well, 'tis fine to know we have a good reputation," Annie said. "I hope your stay has been acceptable."

"*Ja.* Very much, thank you. I especially enjoy this day. I do . . . an errand for Mr. Watson. He is my supervisor. So I am dismissed from work early today, *ja.*"

Kirsten worked at a shirtwaist factory, having taken the job the first day she arrived.

Annie bit her lip but couldn't hold back her tongue. Reverend Clarke had said one should measure one's words. She just had to release the commentary waiting on her lips. "Your brother is quite educated to be writing in a foreign language, so."

Kirsten sighed, lacing her alabaster fingers together in her lap. "I suppose he is."

The male in the family got the education, like Kirsten had said. Annie picked up the page again, hoping she hadn't embarrassed the girl. All the Irish immigrants Annie had met at the dances, even those who spoke the native Irish language, could read and write English, at least well enough to get along. But that wasn't true of all new immigrants. Annie could do so much for them, perhaps even save those without loved ones from falling into despair.

She pasted on her best smile and focused again on the letter. She spoke aloud what she read—various bits of news about Kirsten's kin back home. When she got to the last paragraph, she read silently first to herself and then blurted, "Oh, I think that's good news for you."

Kirsten's cheeks bloomed pink. "What?"

"He wants to come see you." She read on.

*"I wish to live in Manhattan myself. There must be
plenty enough construction work close by."*

Kirsten's face paled. She waved a palm at Annie. "Oh,
he has *gut* job. He should stay at it, *ja.* Stay where there is
work." She bit her lip. "In the capital of New York. He works
there, *ja.*"

Annie nodded, not understanding why anyone would
choose to be separated from someone who truly loved her. She
turned back to the letter.

*"I expect to have enough for a train ticket soon and will
settle things up here by October. Please ask if there is room
for me at your boardinghouse."*

An amused gasp burst through Annie's teeth just as Mrs.
Hawkins tottered into the room with a tray of china cups and
a tin pot of tea. "Who needs a room, dear?"

"Do not worry," Kirsten said. "I . . . I will tell my brother the
house is for women only, with your help, Annie Gallagher. You
will help me . . . write a letter, *ja*? He will not come here, *nein.*"

"Your brother? How wonderful that he's coming to the city."
Mrs. Hawkins deposited the tray on the round tea table by the
window. "There is an adequate house two blocks north. Let me
check on that. When will he arrive? Is he staying on? Does he
have a job here?"

Kirsten squirmed on the chair as though she sat on pins.
"Perhaps October. But maybe he will not come. Please do not
do anything yet, Mrs. Hawkins."

"Annie's own cousin is expected soon from Ireland. How
nice for you, lovies."

Annie tried not to grimace as she folded the letter neatly
back into a square and handed it to Kirsten. Lovely for Kirsten

perhaps, but not for Annie. She began to help Mrs. Hawkins serve tea.

"We will tell him where to stay and where to get work. Could you reply to him, Annie?"

Annie turned to catch a glimpse of the young boarder. Kirsten's stare darted between Annie and Mrs. Hawkins. "Certainly. If Kirsten would like me to."

The German girl rose to her feet, the top of her head just brushing Annie's shoulder. "He should know that he cannot come here. We should mail it soon. Could you do it today, Annie?"

"Let's do it now, so."

Annie approached the tall breakfront bookcase on the far side of the room and removed her father's writing box from behind one of the glass doors. She brought the box to the sofa and lifted the lid. Withdrawing a sheet of paper, she laid it on the slanted writing surface. Then she carefully pulled open the tin inkwell cap. As she inspected the steel nib of one of her pens, she felt Kirsten's stare. "I'll be ready in a moment, but please do not speak too quickly or I won't be able to keep up without blotting the paper."

Kirsten's pale brows arched. "You have . . . *die Stifte* . . . uh, such fine . . . writing instruments. You must be an accomplished . . . uh . . . scribe."

"Me? Only the fortunate recipient of my father's writing desk."

"Did he do much writing?"

Mrs. Hawkins had seated herself in her overstuffed damask-covered armchair, the one everyone knew was reserved for her. She wrinkled her forehead as she slurped from her china teacup. "Do tell, Annie. I have always wondered myself."

Annie rubbed her fingers over the side of the box, admiring

23

the inlaid pale wooden design of intertwining vines as she had done a hundred times in private. "He told stories, mostly. That was his profession. I believe the only ones he wrote down are the ones I have in this box."

Mrs. Hawkins reached for one of her oatcakes. "What kind of stories are they?"

"Children's stories. Tales about rabbits and mice and such. He used to tell them to me aloud, like Irish folks do. Then when he got sick, he wrote these down . . . before he died. . . ." Her voice caught without warning.

Mrs. Hawkins rose and brought her a cup of tea. "There now," she said when Annie had swallowed a bit of the weak tea the woman was so fond of. "You don't have to tell us if you don't want to."

"I . . . uh . . . I was just going to say he wanted me to have a tangible link to our time together." And that was all she now had.

"Why, isn't that lovely."

"I didn't know he'd written them down until later. Father Weldon—that's Mrs. Hawkins's brother," she told Kirsten. "He found them in a secret compartment in the writing desk."

Mrs. Hawkins tapped her fingers together. "I did not know that. Can you show us?"

Annie ran a hand along the back edge until she heard a click. Then she opened the lid and revealed the compartment.

"Isn't that amazing, love?"

"It is. If they hadn't been concealed there, my uncle would have stolen them."

"Why?" Kirsten asked.

"He was just that mean. He took the wee bit of money my da had left, which had been stored in this desk, but not in the compartment. My father must have believed these stories were more valuable than money because he had to have removed the money from the hiding place to make room for these papers. On his deathbed, my father told Father Weldon where to find them."

Kirsten brushed a napkin to her lips. "Your papa? He was . . . published? Books? Newspapers?"

"Oh no. Like I said, he *told* stories, you know—entertained folks. These on paper, they are just tales a father told his daughter."

Mrs. Hawkins set her cup down on the table. "Well, he certainly had a beautiful lap desk. I have always admired it."

Annie held her pen over the paper. "Thank you. Kirsten, please begin."

The girl instructed Annie to introduce herself as the scribe of the letter and to tell Jonas that when he came, there would be another boardinghouse willing to take him in. And not to worry. Kirsten was adamant Annie put that in, and Annie thought it was quite considerate of her.

When Kirsten closed the correspondence, Annie left the letter lying on the writing surface to dry and returned to her tea. The task hadn't taken too long after all.

The front door opened and closed. Annie glanced up. "That would be your roommate Grace, returning from work."

Mrs. Hawkins rose and held up her hand. "See to your leisure. I'll see to the meal."

There were only two boarders at present: Grace, who was a nanny and maid for a widower and his children in Midtown, and now this wee German lass. And soon Aileen. Annie expected more boarders in the future. And then she might not have leisure time. "Thank you." She sipped her tea for a few minutes and then returned to the writing box and carefully carried it to a side table near Mrs. Hawkins's chair, mindful not to disturb the drying letter. "I'll come back shortly and ready the letter for the postman," she said to Kirsten.

"Oh, love," Mrs. Hawkins called out before she could leave. "I left a gift for you on your bed."

"A gift?"

"I believe it is your birthday, isn't it?"

Annie was sure she hadn't mentioned that. She had tried not to think about her birthday arriving without a gift from her father. "How did you know, Mrs. Hawkins?"

The woman swatted the air. "Oh, you must have mentioned it sometime."

"I . . . uh . . . That was not necessary, Mrs. Hawkins. How kind of you."

"I wanted to, love. I overheard you and the postman discussing a book you'd like to read. I happened to be in the bookshop and they had it. Do you know the papers say the editions of that book have been selling out almost as quickly as they come off the presses?"

Annie put a hand to her jaw just in case she was gawking. "Thank you, Mrs. Hawkins." Annie could not comprehend what had motivated this action, but she was more than delighted. No one other than her father had ever been so thoughtful. The woman's hawk-like senses at work again.

Mrs. Hawkins beamed at her. "Hurry along now."

Annie rushed to her room and found a book with a green cover waiting for her. She snatched it up and felt the weight of it in her hand. She'd seen thicker books, but *The Wonderful Wizard of Oz* was not at all as abridged as she had imagined. She set the book on the mahogany desk. Flipping it open, she noted brilliant illustrations similar to the spectacle-wearing lion on the front cover. How remarkably the book was colored. What a valuable gift this was. Her father would have loved . . . She blinked back the thought. She did not want the emptiness in her heart to shadow this moment. She rubbed her hand over the surface of the book. Stories always revealed more than most folks realized. She could not wait to discover this one's meaning.

As Annie read about Dorothy's house landing on the Wicked Witch of the East, someone knocked on her door. "Come in."

Kirsten entered, wringing her hands in her skirt. "I just wanted to thank you for writing my brother for me."

"You are welcome." Annie wanted to get back to the dreamworld of the book. She had visions of brightly dressed Munchkins frolicking in her head.

Kirsten did not leave. "I was wondering if I could ask another favor."

Annie only had one hour before dinner, and she had to find out more about the good witch in the story. A good witch had to be more interesting than Dorothy's gray Aunt Em and Uncle Henry.

"That dance you are going to. Tomorrow? I am usually working, but I will ask to leave early, like the Irish girls do . . . and I was wondering if I might go with you."

Annie would not mind doing things for Kirsten that she would soon begrudgingly have to do for Aileen. "Certainly. Be ready at half seven. That's when the driver comes."

"You do not mind?"

"Not if you don't. 'Tis an Irish dance. You know that?"

"*Ja.* If the *gut* people of Hawkins House go there, it must be a place I should like to go too. I . . . uh . . . I want to be with *gut* people, you know."

"'Tis a bit of fun for sure. You are most welcome."

"I will be ready." She nearly bounced out the door.

Annie shut the door behind her. If only she could stay in Oz, where dreams were real. Unlike Dorothy, she could never hope to go home again. She stared at the book lying on her bed. Just because someone gives you a gift doesn't mean there is love, and like Da said, home is where the people you love are. Grace's employer was generous, but the Parkers were no more Grace's family than Mrs. Hawkins was Annie's.

As Annie struggled with those logical thoughts, she wasn't sure she'd convinced her heart. She walked over and stroked the pages of the gift. Her very own book, and a new copy at that. If it could be true that Hawkins House could be Annie's home . . . but nay. Her genuine home only existed now in her dreams.

4

STEPHEN HAD NOTHING to look forward to this evening but a good book. He was almost finished with Jules Verne's *Facing the Flag* and had brought it to work to read during lunch. He pulled the novel from his bag as he approached his apartment building, musing to himself that if there was ever a way to read while working, he'd absorb a greater number of books. Wouldn't that be grand? Books while he walked. Authors like Verne were always coming up with fanciful inventions of the future. Imagine some type of recording device like a phonograph that could capture someone reading aloud and was small enough to be transportable. Stephen was always reading in the *Times* about H. G. Wells's quirky futuristic ideas. He wondered if Wells or Verne had ever thought of that.

Stephen practically tripped over his landlord, who met him inside the entry door. Stephen's apartment was located up a flight of stairs inside the building. The offices of Davis Publishing were on the ground floor just to the right of the entry, and Alan Davis owned the entire building.

"Adams." The portly man tipped his head.

"Davis. Fine day, wasn't it?"

"What's that you're reading, son?"

Stephen handed the book to him. Alan Davis squinted at

the cover. He flipped through the pages, noting Stephen's bookmark near the end. "Did you enjoy this?"

"I have, yes. I didn't know much about ships and submarines before reading this. And the way the governments were all vying to keep a weapon capable of massive destruction from being produced by a mentally unsound man. Fascinating."

Davis handed the book back. "Verne. Quite the imagination, hasn't he?"

Stephen shifted on his sore feet. "Well, actually most everything he proposes seems viable."

"Hmm. What else have you read lately?"

"I've reread some Dickens. Some George MacDonald, a few of those serials by that Redmond fellow—a Brit, isn't he?"

"I think so. Mysterious lad, though. No one knows much about him, except that he's passed on now."

"Pity."

"Yes." Davis pulled on his lapels the way college professors tended to do when they were about to say something scholarly. Stephen had become a thorough observer of human idiosyncrasies while working his route. Davis smacked his lips before he spoke. "Here's something the average postman wouldn't know. Redmond used a mark on every manuscript, to identify his work. Apparently the fellow was a bit of a traveler, and verifying that a manuscript was truly his became problematic, so he used a secret design only publishers knew about. Even after he had an exclusive publishing agreement, the practice continued."

"That so? You've seen it?"

"I have, over at the club. Walter Page showed it to me."

Stephen scratched his head. "Why does that name sound familiar? Who is he?"

"A new partner with Doubleday. You probably read about him in the papers."

"I suppose so. Doubleday published Redmond?"

"No. Don't know where he got it. Those old boys in the club, they collect such artifacts, and now that the author has left this earth, some wealthy gent will probably pay good money for that paper."

"Hmm. What do you publish?" Stephen had always wondered, but the opportunity to ask had never presented itself before now.

"Dime-store novels and a few British reprints." The man puffed out his chest. "But we're looking to make some major acquisitions in the near future."

Stephen had no idea what he meant. "Sounds splendid."

"Have you always liked to read?"

"Since I was a boy. Reading took me places I could never travel to. Reading was . . . You know, sometimes kids prefer to live in an imaginary world rather than the real one."

"Good that children enjoy reading. Parents buy books for kids who like to read."

"Uh, yes, that would delight a publisher, I would imagine."

"Suppose you'd spend your money at the bookshop, if you had it to spend."

Stephen lacked a natural proficiency for managing money, although he did try. And with little discretionary income to spare, he needed to pay close attention to ensure his paycheck covered his necessary expenses, something he was not very good at. Leave it to Davis to point that out. "Books are hard to come by. A friend who owns a diner lent me this one. I should finish it tonight so I can return it. If you will excuse me, I am going to retire. Nice speaking with you, Davis."

"Of course. Good evening, Adams." The man lifted his hand and then turned back to his office, where he accessed the stairs to his own apartment.

Stephen unlocked his door and entered his dark, cold home. He pulled the string near the door, which lit the room from an overhead fixture. Being in a building where there were offices meant he had electric lights, and he enjoyed that benefit, especially since there was no one there to warm things up for him after a long day at work. The furnishings he'd purchased were sparse and well used, but he didn't care for a lot of furniture anyway. Cluttered up the space.

He hung his coat on a row of pegs behind the door and plopped down on his lumpy sofa. This place would not do for a wife. Women liked pretty trappings, flowered fabrics, and ornate lamps and mirrors—things his mother had once used to decorate the apartment he grew up in. He'd left it all behind when . . .

He rubbed his eyes. He could not have kept any of it, not with the memories. His brother, Hank, hadn't wanted to take anything because he roomed with other men and had no space of his own. If Stephen were able to make a home with someone, he would have to buy new things. How much did they cost? He didn't need much for himself, but having a family would require more than he currently had. He looked around his apartment and tried to imagine it filled with children and a wife. Laughter, singing, board games, and all sorts of toys—he would not mind how crowded that would be.

First, however, he needed to lift the burden that hung on him like a concrete anchor. It was his responsibility to bear the cost of three burials: his mother's, his father's, and not long ago his brother Hank's. He disliked owing the undertaker but bore his lot alone because he had to. Unfair, but what in life was fair?

His arms felt cold and empty. To embrace someone, not just shake the hands of acquaintances, would bring life back to his heart. He enjoyed reading books about families and could, through the pages, imagine being a father himself, a good one, the kind of man God intended fathers to be. He patted the old black Bible on the spindly end table next to him. The greatest commandments were to love God and to love others.

Show me how.

He added the novel to his pile on the end table and picked up the evening paper he'd brought home. He ignored the news columns and turned to the advertisements. Life insurance, telephone service, ladies' garments—all expenses he didn't now have but hoped to take on when he had a family. Skirts and gowns cost nearly fifty cents apiece.

He tossed the paper aside. The tune he liked to whistle came back to him as he prepared a meal of cold chicken from his icebox and sweet buns baked a few days ago by his neighbor.

After he ate, he opened the small box where he kept photographs of his family. In one, taken during a time when his father had been employed, his mother stood with her hand on his father's shoulder while he sat stiffly on a stool. Stephen perched on his father's knee and Hank held on to his mother's hand. His mother had thick, red hair, and she was so young in this photograph. He didn't remember his father ever having such a bright expression. He gazed at the faces of those people who were blissfully unaware of what their future held.

Stephen's eyes went to the brooch pinned at his mother's throat. He dug into the box and pulled out the piece of jewelry. He reached for the handkerchief in his pocket and rubbed the tarnished silver filigree that surrounded the enameled heart. One day he hoped to give this to his love. If something as disastrous as his father's lost savings ever befell Stephen, he would not crumble from it. He would never abandon a wife and children. Such cowardice, if it ran in bloodlines, could be extinguished, he hoped, with effort and prayer.

5

When the driver arrived Thursday evening, Annie, Kirsten, and the other boarder, Grace, climbed into the wagon bed. It was worth the inconvenience of riding in a farm wagon rather than in a carriage if it meant a crowd would fill the dance hall. Annie tried to attend whenever she could, if for no other reason than to allow the music to send her back to a happier time. *Keep the good; discard the bad.* Her father loved music and was always whistling one of the old tunes. Annie loved the throng. The dance reminded her of neighbors in Ireland gathering in the evenings for music, *craic*, and dancing. It was as close to the memory of her father's mass storytellings as she could get.

"You've brought a new friend," Emma called from somewhere within the sea of black skirts.

Annie made her way over to the friend she'd met at one of these dances as smiling lasses pulled aside their shiny boots to let her through. "A new boarder from Hawkins House," she explained. "This is Kirsten Wagner."

"I'm Emma. So pleased to meet you."

"*Ja.* And you." Kirsten was so shy she didn't meet Emma's gaze.

Emma reached for Kirsten's hand, then turned back to Annie. "Gerry's band is playing." Emma held a gloved hand to her lips.

Annie bent her head toward Emma. "I know you're sweet on him. May the most you wish for be the least you get, Emma. And all happiness to follow."

"Ah, so. But there's another lad, an Italian, who's nice too. So many handsome young men in America, and what about you, Miss Annie? Sure and you'll never find a husband if you don't start looking."

"A husband? I'm an independent woman, don't you know?" She said it in a jesting manner, but she did mean it. She'd have to make her own way. Men as noble and caring as her father had been were rare. Out there, somewhere, there had to be a path to guide her to a better place, a place she'd travel to alone. Father Weldon had spoken of it when he blessed her.

Before he sent her off on the ship, he had asked her to rise. His hand hovering over her head, he blessed her in the way of Saint Patrick with a prayer of protection: *May the strength of God pilot you. May the wisdom of God instruct you. May the hand of God protect you. May the Word of God direct you. This day and forevermore.*

Direct her where? If only he had told her how to find it, but find her way home she would, somehow.

At the dance hall, Annie led Kirsten to a crowd of other maids as Emma tagged along. Kirsten could find friends here. After a few introductions Annie directed her to the refreshments table and watched as she sipped on a glass of ginger beer.

Grace joined them, wiping fizz from her lips with her fingers. "I love my job, but I'm so happy to have some time off."

"*Ja,*" Kirsten agreed.

"Even without your betrothed?" Emma teased.

"He works nights," Grace explained.

Annie marveled at Grace's transformation. She'd come over a frightened immigrant, like so many, and now after a time of courtship, she was getting married and moving into a home of her own. Happiness comes to some. Others have to go after it.

Kirsten's sullen expression spoke of some kind of unmentioned heartache. Annie tried to engage her. "You have a fine job, don't you, Kirsten? Make lots of money?"

Kirsten slid her boot in an arching motion in front of her. "I do fine."

Grace smiled at her. "And you're not changing nappies, either."

The sounds of a fiddle and accordion covered any further conversation.

"Let's dance." Emma pulled Annie away.

Annie caught a glimpse of someone she thought she recognized. Near the door stood a man in a dark suit twirling a cap between his hands. Curly black hair and pensive posture . . . Was that the postman? An all-American lad like him here? He did seem to enjoy Irish tunes, but she could not get a clear enough view to be sure it was him.

Emma led her closer to the band, probably to get a better look at the fellow she was fond of, and when Annie glanced back, she no longer saw the stranger. It probably hadn't been the postman.

The room bulged with men and women in black and brown clothing, but the music was a thriving, glorious kaleidoscope. It wasn't until after the third reel that Annie realized Kirsten was sitting alone. Taking pity on the girl, Annie left the center of activity and joined her on the outskirts. They exchanged smiles and Annie was about to ask if she was enjoying herself but decided to ask about Kirsten's brother instead.

"He is a very fine gentleman, Annie."

"He sounded quite kind, I mean from the sound of his words in the letter." The girl hadn't lost all connection with her home since her brother cared about her.

"You would like him if you truly knew him." A distracted expression filled Kirsten's eyes.

"Truly?"

The girl's face brightened. What had she been thinking just a moment earlier? "Everyone likes my brother. No reason they should not."

"Oh, I'm sure you're right, darlin'. I suppose I was thinking everyone's a matchmaker these days. Emma's afraid I'll be a spinster."

"You? With your *gut* looks?"

"You flatter me."

"I would wish for hair as wavy as yours, and the color of a sunset, Annie."

"A sunset? Thank you, Kirsten, but your hair is lovely too."

"*Ja.*" She twisted a strand around her index finger. "Did you post the letter yet?"

"First thing tomorrow."

"You wait and see. He will send a quick reply." Again the words sounded hopeful, but Kirsten's demeanor did not match.

"He is very devoted to you."

Kirsten's face drained of color. She glanced toward the door and turned back to whisper. "There is someone . . . I do not know, but it seems someone is following me."

Annie looked around. "I don't see anyone, so."

"I know." She flagged her hand. "Nothing. Must be nothing." She excused herself. Annie watched as she wandered over to a group of giggling lasses. They enveloped Kirsten and Annie soon lost sight of her.

The girl was so new to America she had likely not become accustomed to the crowded city, if such a thing were possible. Or perhaps, like Annie, she had tried to escape the pains of some miserable happening.

On Friday misery did descend, but not in a manner Annie or anyone else could have expected.

"People on the trolleys are saying no one is safe if the president cannot attend a public gathering like the Pan-American Exposition without fearing for his life," Grace exclaimed as they sat around the silent piano.

Mrs. Hawkins shook out the evening newspaper, but the words still stuck to the pages. The president had been shot. "Buffalo, where it happened, is a long train ride north," Mrs. Hawkins said. "Still in the state of New York." She nodded at Grace. "They should have had well-trained men there, like your Owen, protecting the president."

Grace's face reddened. Annie hoped there was more than one good man in New York. But this shooting proved that evil men lurked everywhere, even in music halls in Buffalo. If God was not with the president, then how could Annie ever expect he would protect her?

Mrs. Hawkins stared at the paper again. "The *Times* says the assassin was a man named Czolgosz, an anarchist, who lives in Cleveland."

Grace stood and gazed out the window. "There is no answer for why these things happen."

Annie knew Grace had to be thinking of the sorrow the Parker family had endured. She turned to Mrs. Hawkins. "How do you suppose—I mean, surely Reverend Clarke has mentioned something, some way to overcome evil and injustice? Can nothing be done but just endure it? If the American president can be harmed like this . . ."

"Jesus told us, love, that in this world there will be tribulation, but he has overcome the world."

The woman seemed content with that. So did Grace. The thought that one must wait for Jesus to return unsettled Annie.

Inaction only led to injustice. Annie longed to retreat to her book, where surely following a yellow brick path led to better things.

Move on, Dorothy. Find your way home.

Mrs. Hawkins took a sip of her evening tea and kept reading. "Thankfully it looks as though President McKinley will recover. The king of Italy last year. And now this. Oh, dear God."

Two days later, with the city still abuzz over the assassination attempt, Annie sat with Grace and Mrs. Hawkins in their usual pew at First Church. Kirsten should have been off work like everyone else, but her boss insisted she return on Sunday mornings to catch up on whatever had not been finished that week. Annie thought about the lass while the choir sang.

When the choir finished, Reverend Clarke approached the lectern, looking grave. Annie tried to listen, but Kirsten and her brother were still on her mind. She pondered why Kirsten was so restrained and skittish. Within the mass of people in Manhattan, Kirsten surely couldn't believe there was someone watching her with more than mild curiosity. When Annie realized how inattentive she'd been, she gave her head a shake and tried to focus on the man's words.

All she managed to catch before he concluded with prayer was a sort of poem that he recited. The words seemed to dance in her head like music:

> *There in my Father's home, safe and at rest,*
> *There in my Savior's love, perfectly blest;*
> *Age after age to be, nearer my God to Thee.*

Then everyone rose and sang from a hymnal. Annie blinked back tears. She missed the rest she'd had in her father's presence, and she never knew when some turn of phrase would set off her grief. Thankfully Annie could usually rein in these emotions. She did not want to share her grief with anyone and was grateful she had the length of the hymn to regain her composure. This moving-on business was arduous.

A week later the newspaper's reports proved wrong. President McKinley would not recover. Annie didn't know him, of course—had not read anything in detail about him in the newspapers since she'd arrived—but somehow she felt that he'd been a good man like her da. Secretly she feared that without President McKinley to lead them, the United States might slip into the orphan-like nothingness where she was.

After supper that night Grace and Mrs. Hawkins began talking about the sorrowful passing of President McKinley. "I do believe his family will suffer from losing him, as will the entire country," Grace said.

Mrs. Hawkins sighed. "I suppose we all empathize with their grief, don't we, girls?"

Although Annie understood it, she did not want to discuss it. She could not control her tears as it was. She rose to serve tea and occupy her thoughts.

"Oh, that dear man's wife," Mrs. Hawkins exclaimed. "As a widow myself I know the pain."

Grace placed her hand gently on the woman's arm. "I'm sorry."

Mrs. Hawkins could easily be moved to tears, as she had been when Queen Victoria died. Annie wished she had an excuse to quit the room because she hated seeing others in this kind of misery. It made hers all the worse.

"New York's own Theodore Roosevelt shall now be president," Mrs. Hawkins said.

So the country was not left without a ruler. "Will he be a good leader, Mrs. Hawkins?" Annie knew there were disreputable folks in positions of authority, such as the doctor in the Magdalene Laundry. The thought sent a spasm down her arms.

"I believe so, love. He did some good works here in this state."

"That's admirable, so." She bit the inside of her cheek as she fought to keep bad thoughts away. *Focus on the good.*

Grace picked up her camera, which for her was as precious as Annie's stories. She began winding a roll of film. "A pity Mr. Roosevelt had to take office in this manner."

The Hawk exhaled. "They say the president's last words were from a Christian hymn."

"Truly?" Annie poured tea.

"It's right in the newspapers, love. It's been widely reported. In fact, bands will be playing the hymn during his funeral procession."

Annie sat back down. She welcomed the distraction from talking about the pain of being left behind. "Do you know this dirge?" She had not yet learned all the American hymns.

The Hawk swallowed hard. "I do indeed. The words were penned by an Englishwoman. I read that the poor now-departed president recited some lines on his deathbed. I don't know which lines, but this is what I remember." She cleared her throat. "'Nearer, my God, to Thee, nearer to Thee. E'en though it be a cross that raiseth me, still all my song shall be, nearer, my God, to Thee.'"

The woman choked back a sob, and Grace embraced her.

Annie thought the words sounded familiar. "How does the tune go, if you don't mind me asking?"

Mrs. Hawkins sipped her water and then answered. "I do not mind at all, love. It is a beautiful hymn."

When she began to hum, Annie knew she had heard it recently. "We just heard that at church, now, didn't we?"

Both Grace and Mrs. Hawkins sighed. "I don't remember singing it for some time," the elder woman answered.

"Oh, but I was sure—"

"Those exact words and that tune?"

"Well, I think so. It all sounds so familiar."

Grace stared down at her camera's viewfinder as she spoke. "Perhaps Reverend Clarke mentioned the hymn at some time, Annie."

Annie conceded this and collected the teacups to return to the kitchen, the tune playing out in her head as clear as an Irish church bell.

6

WHEN STEPHEN PICKED UP his deliveries on Monday, the mail sorter called to him.

"I think this one probably goes on your route."

"Thank you, Minnie." He hurried over to the dark-skinned woman and collected the letter. "Say, how do you like the new job?"

When Minnie smiled, her whole face brightened. "I am so blessed, Mr. Adams. My mama never dreamed her girl child would be working in an office building for the United States government."

"I understand, but things are different these days. Nearly four decades since the end of the War between the States, and finally things are improving. And please call me Stephen."

"In New York things are different, yes, Stephen. And I'm a blessed woman." She motioned for him to come closer and whispered, "Living in New York is mighty dear, you know? The cost of everything . . . um-hum, I am not in the South no more."

"Yes. What my landlord charges for rent uses up the majority of my monthly income."

"My husband, Leonard, is running an investment you might

be interested in." She pointed a finger and gave her wrist a twist. "Whatever you give him, in one week he'll give you back 10 percent more."

"Is that right? Your husband knows something about the stock market?"

"Um-hum. He's worked for an investor for ten years, more or less an errand boy, but he's a smart one and he has ears. Met him right after I came up here to live. Been married a month now, and he's a good provider. He knows things, inside talk that can make a lot of money. Got himself fifteen depositors already. Want a part? All it takes is a dollar to get started."

Stephen considered this. Besides needing money for his future hoped-for family, he had debts to repay due to his family members' funerals. He'd asked God for help. What if this was the answer?

He pulled a one-dollar silver certificate out of his pocket and gave it to her. If he lost it, he'd know better the next time. But if Leonard could invest it and bring Stephen a profit, Stephen just might pay off his debts faster. He'd sooner trust an investor than a bank, after what happened to his father.

She quickly stashed the money away. "Now don't be talking about this. He's not opening it to all folks just yet."

"Minnie, this doesn't involve the US mail, does it? Because inspectors don't tolerate—"

"Don't you worry about that. I'm planning on keeping my job. You can trust my Leonard."

"I don't know. Maybe I shouldn't—"

"Shouldn't what? Look, Stephen, if it don't make money for you, he'll give you the dollar back. You lose nothing. Give it a chance and come see me at the end of the week, all right?"

Stephen left the office feeling uncertain. She'd said no risk, though.

Whistling as he went, he tried to forget about it and focus on his duties.

During his lunch break, Stephen sat in the Battery and opened a can of cold beans. He'd paid his rent, but he'd only made a small payment to the undertaker. He'd make up for that soon. He watched some children play tag and tried to imagine his meal was really a hot shredded beef sandwich instead of cold navy beans. It really wasn't so bad. He had just enough money left to eat at Giovanni's on Saturday night, and that thought would keep him going the rest of the week.

When he stood to pitch his can into one of the new sanitation department waste receptacles, he realized he needed to notch another hole in his trouser belt. His lack of funds was causing him to lose weight. As he walked away from the park, he noted some kids playing there, four boys ranging from about six years of age to about twelve. They should be in school, but no one would insist on it, he knew. He wondered if any of them were hungry. He knew as a kid he often was, but he had nothing to give any of them now, and that made him sad.

Stephen hurried to take the trolley for a couple of blocks. The drivers allowed a uniformed postal worker to ride for free and save a few steps.

When he jumped aboard the trolley, he was surprised to see Mr. Archibald Murray, the undertaker. "Mr. Adams, I hope you were not in the park because you lost your job."

"No, sir. Just lunch break."

"I see." The man pushed back his high-grade stiff hat to give Stephen a semiconcerned stare. "I am reminded, Mr. Adams, that—perhaps financially anyway—matters have not been pleasant for you of late."

Stephen glanced around, noting a few faces from his mail route. "Shall we refrain from talking business on the trolley, sir?"

"Indeed. I'll send a man round to your house in a week or so, someone the likes of . . . say, Jim Jeffries?"

"The boxer? What the devil—?"

"That's right. Heavyweight boxing champ of the world. I know his brother. I know people, Adams. Don't make me resort to . . ."

"No need, Mr. Murray. I haven't reneged or anything."

A lady in an oversize Gibson-style hat cleared her throat and held a gloved hand over her mouth. The undertaker gave her a quick glimpse and then looked back to Stephen. "Well, I am a sympathetic man. One must be, in my line of work, you understand." He leaned in to whisper, "But I'm not overly patient when someone's loved ones were buried over two years ago, son."

"I know. I'm sorry."

"Just make up the difference this month. Can you do that?"

"Yes." No Giovanni's this week. He might be his father's son, but he was determined not to become the failure his father had been. Stephen paid his bills, mostly, and slept well. It was just the undertaker's debt he had not yet cleared, but the rest he kept up with. If God ever blessed Stephen with his own family, he would never send his son out to beg on the streets.

Stephen got off the trolley and kicked a can as he walked. During the last decade of his father's life, the man had held a dependable construction job. That was when Stephen got hired on at the post office and things improved. Stephen might have even been able to put his sad childhood behind him if it weren't for what was to come. As soon as life dealt Stephen's family a nasty blow—his mother grew ill with some kind of rapidly advancing cancer, and the bank failed and took his father's life savings with it—instead of fighting back, his father had turned into a jellyfish.

No one but Stephen, Reverend Clarke over at First Church, and Mr. Murray knew that Stephen's father had died not from heart failure, as most people believed, but by his own hand. Stephen had not even told his own brother that a few weeks after their mother passed, their father hanged himself with a belt behind the family's tenement. Mr. Murray had been discreet. Stephen was grateful.

As he passed one of the letter boxes he attended to, he noticed a man banging his fist on it. He spoke without looking at Stephen, his collar pulled up to cover most of his face. "Do you have the key, son?"

"I'm the postman."

"Open it. I am on official business."

"Unless you have replaced the postmaster, I cannot. It's not time—"

The man turned slightly, his back toward Stephen. "You don't understand. Someone . . . That is to say, I put something in there I want back." He slammed his knuckles on the box again. "Open it at once!"

"Sorry. Once it's in the box, I am required by law to deliver it."

The man kicked at the post holding up the box. Shadows cast by the building behind them concealed the man, reminding Stephen of a phrase he'd read from Dickens. Or was it Longfellow? "Cloak and dagger." The mysterious man reached for Stephen, but just as Stephen stepped backward, the fellow withdrew his arm, seemingly changing his mind about accosting a postal employee. "Open it. I won't report you."

"I will at the appointed hour, but I am honor-bound to deliver whatever has been mailed."

The man marched away, thankfully. Stephen wished more folks would understand how the US Post Office operated.

When Thursday came, Stephen at least had the Irish dance to look forward to. It did not seem to matter to those he'd met there that he was not Irish, and the fact that New York could house recent immigrants but consider them all Americans pleased him. He thought about his customers and how, though different, they were in some ways the same. Everyone struggled to earn a living, at least in this neighborhood. Stephen was thankful he even had a job. He greeted a family passing him on the sidewalk: a raggedly dressed mother, a sullen-faced father, and two little boys whose feet had grown through the ends of their shoes. He gazed down at his polished black leather shoes, government-issued. Indeed he was thankful. He did miss having family, though. Even a crowded city like New York could feel lonely when there was no one to sit around your supper table.

He whistled one of the Irish ballads from the dance as he continued his route. He was in an Irish neighborhood, after all. When he went to the Italian quarter, he ate long macaroni, and when on the odd occasion he picked up an extra delivery route and found himself in Chinatown, he purchased herbs and tea from the street vendors. Folks appreciated that he tried to be part of the community, and he wanted the people on his route to trust the postman, the man who brought mail right up to the steps of their private homes.

He stopped, blinked in the hot sun, and glanced ahead. He was a few blocks from his favorite stop, Hawkins House, with its cheerful hanging flower baskets—a sight to look forward to. What a kind woman Mrs. Hawkins was, taking in young immigrant girls to keep them out of the shabby tenements and away from shysters waiting to take advantage. If only she could save them all.

"Afternoon, Mr. Adams." A man in a linen duster coat tipped his hat.

"Good day to you, Mr. Parker. What business brings you out here during the week?"

Mr. Parker collected tithes at First Church, where Stephen had begun to attend. That was where Reverend Clarke served, the man who had helped Stephen cope right after his parents' deaths. Stephen liked to visit different neighborhood churches, but First Church was his favorite and also provided an opportunity to see the Hawkins House residents who attended there.

Mr. Parker lived uptown, but the man had dedicated his time to helping provide immigrant aid in Lower Manhattan.

"Grace left early, as she does every Thursday, and she forgot her new hat." He held up a box. "I'd say she's not used to wearing them, so not surprising. She bought it on a shopping trip with my sister."

Grace, a boarder at Hawkins House, worked for Mr. Parker and cared for his children. Stephen had heard at church that she and Sergeant McNulty were engaged to be married. Interesting how women with a beau attempted to enhance their beauty with fancy garments. "How kind of you to bring it to her. Would you like me to deliver it?"

"Very much appreciated, Mr. Adams. I'm stopping off at the church to help the reverend review some repair work that needs to be done. You say you don't mind?" He handed the box to Stephen.

"Not at all. Delivery is my business."

As he continued on, dropping mail into door slots and collecting letters from the locked boxes on his route, he thought about how many Irish immigrant girls were maids for middle-class families like the Parkers. Or else worked in boardinghouses like Annie did. He supposed it was the fact that they spoke English that made them good fits compared to other immigrants.

Ah, Annie Gallagher. If Stephen's mother were still alive, he was sure she would like Annie. She was friendly, soft-spoken, and obviously a good housekeeper.

He continued on, throwing back balls that spurted loose from kids playing in the alleys, tipping his hat to old women walking with canes, and watching in wonder whenever one of those newfangled horseless carriages happened by.

But all the while, Stephen Adams thought about Annie. Annie from Ireland. Annie with the beautiful curls that seemed to sparkle like gemstones in the sun. Her wide smile, intense green-brown eyes—the memory of her stayed with him all day long. Always Annie.

When he arrived at Hawkins House and twisted the door-bell ringer, it was not Annie who answered but Mrs. Hawkins. He explained his encounter with Mr. Parker.

The woman collected the hatbox from his arms. "A hat? I'm a bit perplexed she'd spend her money on one, but I suppose it's that handsome fiancé of hers she wants to look her best for."

"Yes indeed, I suppose so. Sergeant McNulty."

"The very one."

Stephen tried to peer past the sturdy woman to see if Annie might be standing nearby. Mrs. Hawkins must have guessed his intent. "My housekeeper has the afternoon off. It's those maid dances. Are you familiar with them?"

"I find the music splendid, Mrs. Hawkins. I try to pop in on them when I can."

"Superb idea, Mr. Adams. I suppose you should get along to your work now . . . so you have time to get there."

"Oh, why, yes. Good day."

The fact was, he just wasn't entirely comfortable around women since his mother passed away. Pleasantries he could handle, but not much more. He had never had a sister, not even any female cousins close by. Stephen Adams's family line through his parents would die with him if he never married, and he had no idea how to find a wife. He was an average-looking, hardworking fellow who was more comfortable reading about people in books than socializing with them. But he was trying to overcome that obstacle. Proper effort could move mountains.

He did remember what his mother had once said. *"Kindness is understood in all languages."* He was as nice as he could be, especially when visiting Hawkins House. Maybe one day that lass would notice. That had been his prayer, and Scripture said, "The effectual fervent prayer of a righteous man availeth much." He was doing his best to be a righteous, upstanding man.

He passed by a couple walking arm in arm. They barely noticed him because they were staring into each other's eyes. He thought about his parents as he dropped a few letters through a mail slot. He had no memory of his father courting his mother, of course. He could not recall the two of them ever gazing into each other's eyes. Other married folks he knew, from church and near where he lived, just seemed to go through life, working day after day, year after year. There did not seem to be any time for fun or romance. But those husbands had snared their wives somehow.

"Afternoon, Mr. Adams."

Stephen tipped his hat at the shoeshine boy he passed every day on that street. "Shouldn't you be in school?"

The lad only shrugged.

"You should be in school. School prepares you for the future."

"If you say so, Mr. Adams."

"You want a job that will support a family someday."

The boy smiled, tight-lipped, as though holding his tongue. Stephen didn't know what this boy's family life was like. Hopefully this lad had a father who kept his earnings safe. There were happy people in this neighborhood. Not everyone gave up as easily as Stephen's father had.

Stephen kept whistling as he walked. If there was one thing

you could say about the habit, it was that the cheery sound lifted spirits. Just the effort made him stick out his chest, pull back his shoulders, and push breath into his lungs. The endeavor usually made him feel better, and it was worth trying all the more in light of the president's death, the main topic on people's minds today.

After work Stephen rushed home to shave and put on a clean shirt in hopes of seeing Annie at the Irish dance. Davis heard him come in and met him before he could clamber up the steps.

Stephen hung his head. "I know I'm late this month, Davis. I've got the money for you, though. Let me go up and get it."

"Fine, fine. Terrible news about President McKinley. . . ."

"Indeed. A horrible, deplorable thing." The two of them stood quietly for a moment, a silent tribute to the dead president that seemed to be repeated countless times all over Manhattan that week.

"Before you go, Adams, I need to speak to you."

"About?" Stephen's feet hurt. He wanted to sit down.

"The rent."

"I'll get it."

"Yes, you said that." Davis cleared his throat and stared down at a cigar wedged between his fat thumb and index finger.

Most men Stephen had observed fiddling with unlit cigars did so out of agitation. He wondered what the trouble was with Davis.

Davis glanced up, his eyes intense. "Just gotta raise your rent is all. Sorry to do it, but I got no choice. My printing costs went up."

This was bad news indeed, but Stephen didn't think it ought to affect the rental property. "Well . . . er . . . not my fault precisely."

"Ah, but it's your luck you live over top of the offices of a publisher, now isn't it?" Davis shifted from one foot to the other. "You know, seeing as you like reading so much, you're probably good at judging what makes a book grand."

"Well, I suppose all the reading I do, or try to do, does make me a judge of sorts. Look, Davis, you don't really plan to increase—"

"That's right." He pointed the cigar at Stephen. "The more you read, the more discerning you are. Got my people searching for good material, but I declare they don't read enough. I need someone who is sensible yet imaginative enough to spot good work when he sees it. Anyone who enjoys Verne will know what I'm talking about." The man drew his posture straighter. "You could be the fellow, Adams. Young, connected with the public, unencumbered by traditional publishing parameters. Say, bring me a good manuscript, one I can sell ten thousand copies of, and I'll give you rent half-price." He said that as though he were doing Stephen a favor.

The man had to be desperate to think a postman could find him his next bestseller. "Now where on God's green earth would I find a manuscript? I don't know Verne personally, Davis."

"Of course not, and I'm not saying that exactly. Lots of folks talking about fanciful children's books. Something like that."

"You mean something like *The Wonderful Wizard of Oz*?"

Davis chuckled, rubbing the brown vest that barely stretched over his gut. "There's a new trend going round in children's publishing. Moving away from frightening fairy tales to new, lighter adventure stories kids are keen for."

"That so?" Stephen remembered *Grimms' Fairy Tales* and how the stories had frightened him when he was a child. Maybe there was something to this trend.

His landlord glanced over his shoulder to his open office

door. "Davis Publishing would love to be a part of that. Yes, we would. You talk to folks every day, seeing as you deliver mail. As many people as there are in New York City . . . well, got to be a writer or two on your route, I imagine." He patted his overstuffed vest.

"I wouldn't know."

"But you could find out, I'd guess."

"Look, Davis, I don't know anything about the book business. I'm afraid you've got me over a barrel."

"Not my intent, son. I just gotta pay my bills. Starting next month your rent is fifty cents more." He cast his gaze at the book in Stephen's hand. "What's the harm in trying? Ask around. And you do know a good story when you see it."

"Did you say fifty cents more?"

The man nodded as he backed into his office and closed the door. Stephen stared at the frosted glass that spelled out the name of the company. There were not many apartments in town that he could afford—not to mention any as close to the main post office, where Stephen picked up the mail he delivered, as this one was.

He did not want to move.

7

"*MUSIC SWEEPS AWAY the cobwebs in your mind,*" her da always said. Annie had missed the dance last night because of preparations she and Mrs. Hawkins were making for Aileen's arrival. Kirsten had been working long hours, so she hadn't been able to go either. Work came first, but as Annie swept the front steps, she appreciated this memory of her father's love of music, a memory she chose to keep. She sang the words to one of Da's favorite songs.

When she got to the chorus, she realized someone was humming along with her. She continued the song to see if he'd keep up.

"Those days in our hearts we will cherish
Contented although we were poor
And the songs that we sung in the days we were young
On the stone outside Dan Murphy's door."

The postman joined her on the stoop. "You know the words to that song, do you?"

Annie leaned against her broomstick. "I'm Irish, don't you know." Her da used to sing that song to her, but she didn't feel like saying so.

"True enough. I learned it recently and haven't gotten it out of my head."

Annie laughed. "I thought I'd heard you whistling it."

He tipped the bill of his hat toward her. "Tell me, Miss Gallagher, do you know this shop of Dan Murphy's that the song mentions?"

"Can't say as I do, Mr. Adams."

"Sounds like a jovial place."

Annie sighed and stared out at the brick and clapboard siding buildings and paved sidewalks. "Aye, it does."

The man fumbled through his bag. "Got the mail for you."

"I thought you might."

He smiled and handed her a stack. "Plenty of mail today. Keeps me employed and the bill collectors away."

Annie playfully shook her head at him. "Thank you, Mr. Adams."

"Quite welcome. Always good to see you, Miss Gallagher."

He had emphasized the word *always*. She knew she was blushing, so she bent her head down toward the bristles of her broom. She had not felt so comfortable around a man since . . . well, since her father. "And you, Mr. Adams."

She wasn't sure what made her look up just then, but she spotted a man on the street staring at them. A panic rose to her throat, an emotion she didn't anticipate. Puzzled by how a stranger could unnerve her, she supposed he must know the postman or maybe he was looking for an address.

The postman glanced over his shoulder and then back at her. "Miss Gallagher, do you ever—? I mean . . . Those Irish dances, the maid dances . . . Mrs. Hawkins mentioned that you have been there."

She struggled to draw her focus back. The stranger moved along. "Aye, I go when I can."

"I have been to a few myself."

"Is that so? I thought I saw you once."

"I was there yesterday, but I didn't see you."

"No, I could not go, but perhaps you were there two weeks ago. That was the last time I attended."

"I missed that one. I'm afraid my work kept me busy."

They both laughed, as though missing each other at the maids' dance were a comedy of errors.

"I suppose 'twas just someone who resembled you." Or someone like that stranger just now? Nay, her imagination wandered.

He stared at his shoes a moment, then smiled at her. "Hope to see you there in the future. Good day." He turned and hopped down the steps. "'There's a sweet garden spot in my memory.'" The postman turned the tune to a whistle and then hurried off down the street.

Clutching the broom in one hand and the letters in the other, Annie entered the house, thinking about how the music had helped to whisk away her sadness. And that song in particular. Memories. If only she could completely separate the good and the bad.

She set the letters down on the silver tray just as Mrs. Hawkins passed her with a basket of sheets. "Splendid day for washing," she said.

They sent most of their laundry out to be done, but the sheets and linens they did themselves. It had taken Annie several washing days to bury her fear of hot wash water stemming from her toil in the Magdalene Laundry. Even now the impression came rushing back against her wishes. . . .

"Not good enough," Sister Mary Martha said, plunging Annie's hands back into the scalding wash water.

Annie gasped and tried to pull her hands out, but the nun held them down.

"No, don't!" Sister Catherine, a novice, complained.

But no one listened to her. The punishment was meant to

wash away Annie's sins because, as the doctor had told her, she was a sinner of the worst kind. She didn't know what she had done. She still didn't. But she obviously was not good enough for God to want to keep her from that place.

Eventually she'd gotten past it. The effort had helped to bolster her will to share with unwanted girls the power of a story, the importance of keeping only good thoughts. This small victory, conquering her fear of washing, she had achieved without help. She could do even more. So long as she kept her wits about her.

Mrs. Hawkins had been patient with her slow washing, understanding that the Magdalene Laundry had bruised her soul. Even so, the Hawk had insisted she do the work.

"Nothing will help you heal faster than facing the very thing you hated," the woman had said.

She'd struggled to forget and in fact couldn't, but with practice the memory no longer made her hands sting.

Annie lifted her gaze to the ceiling to collect her thoughts and bring her mind back to the task before her. "Well, 'tis warm enough to dry the sheets in the air."

"That it is, love, warm. When you finish there, would you help me?"

"Of course."

That night Annie woke suddenly from a dream. She and her father were in a field with the mice of his stories. She'd gotten separated from everyone, and no matter which way she turned, she could not find her way out of the field. She heard their voices, but she was still utterly lost and unable to remember the way out. When she awakened, she threw her sweaty sheets off her legs. The hour seemed late, but she was wide awake and decided to go to the parlor and look at the stories again.

Once she had the box in her lap, she realized how very alone she was with everyone else sleeping. Deep in the box, under the loose writing paper, her father's stories rested. She pulled one out.

By the light of a candle she read the title. "Nolan the Nice Mouse." She remembered Nolan. He was a reluctant soldier in Omah's army. She smiled and set it aside. She was cold and needed the blanket from her bed. On her way back to her room, she glanced at the mail on the entry table. The top letter appeared to be from Kirsten's brother. She was right. He had replied promptly. She returned to the light of the candle in the parlor and her stories.

A tiny tapping noise came from outside the window. Annie nearly jumped out of her skin. "Who's there?"

"Me, Annie. Let me in. The door is locked."

"Kirsten? What are you doing outside?" Thinking she must have decided to use the toilet outside the kitchen and locked herself out, Annie hurried to the front door to let the girl in.

When Annie opened the door, she was surprised to find Kirsten not in a nightgown, but fully dressed. Her hair was a tangled mess over her face. "Where have you been?"

"At work. Hurry, shut the door, please."

Annie gazed past her into the night, then leaned her head out the door and looked in all directions. A hobo leaned against the lamppost at the corner, but that was not unusual. "What's wrong, so?"

"I just got home." The girl stumbled in and steadied herself by holding on to the banister.

"I don't understand. Why so late?"

Instead of answering, Kirsten picked up the letter. "This is like the other one. Has my brother answered, Annie?"

"I believe he has."

"Read it. Please."

"Now?"

"Please."

"Just be quiet. We'll go in here."

Annie led Kirsten into the parlor, and she sat on the dark corner of the sofa. Annie slid her fingernail under the seal.

Dear Kirstie,

Do not worry about me. I will be fine. I mailed a package to you. You understand? Please expect it shortly.

I am your loving brother,
Jonas Wagner

Kirsten sighed and moved toward the stairs. She lifted a foot onto the first step but then set it back down.

"Let me help you to bed." Annie hurriedly blew out the candle in the parlor and shoved the writing box back into the breakfront. Then she wrapped an arm around Kirsten and helped her to her room. The door was open across the hall, and sounds of heavy breathing told them Grace was fast asleep.

"Quiet," Annie warned. "I'll make sure you are up in time for work tomorrow. You leave about half five, that right?"

"That's right."

"You still going?"

Kirsten's eyes were round as robin eggs and just as blue. "I have to go. Please, Annie, make sure I catch the train." Kirsten collapsed on her bed.

"I don't understand your coming home so late. Does your boss work everyone this hard?"

Kirsten only moaned, too tired to respond.

Annie removed Kirsten's boots but left her otherwise dressed, pulling a light sheet over top of her.

She seemed far too fragile for such long hours.

Annie was about to return to her room and wind her alarm clock when yet another soft tapping came from the front of the house. She froze, hearing only the sound of her own breathing.

Then a voice. "Sergeant McNulty, making my rounds. Anyone up?"

Relieved, she rushed to her room to throw a coat over her nightgown, so as not to be immodest, and then went to the door. "Evening, Sergeant."

"I saw someone just come in. Everything all right, Miss Gallagher?"

"Everything is fine now. Thank you for your concern."

He tapped a finger on the brim of his gray hat.

She stopped him. "Sergeant? See anyone out there watching us?"

"What do you mean?"

"Well, our new boarder might be a wee bit . . . uh, unsettled by the city, and she seems to think someone is following her."

"Was she the one who just came in?"

Annie lowered her voice as much as she could. "She was, but do not worry. Mrs. Hawkins will see that she observes the curfew in the future. Her boss should not be allowed to keep her at work these late hours."

"I see. Well, I can tell you I saw no one just now. Miss Gallagher, you will inform me if you have trouble with your new boarder, won't you? There are plenty of people about who get themselves involved with the wrong sort of crowd in this neighborhood."

No one would know better about that than he. "I will. I am sure she is innocently unaware."

"All the same, do not hesitate to bring this to Mrs. Hawkins's attention. I can remove the girl if need be."

Remove? To a reformatory, the American version of a Magdalene Laundry. Certainly not! "I'm sure that won't be necessary."

Very early in the morning, Stephen neared Hawkins House on his first route of the day. He was happy that he had a mostly residential route and no other postman was required to service the area, like they had to do in business districts, where mail was delivered up to nine times a day. He selfishly wanted to be the only postman Hawkins House had. A few blocks before reaching the boardinghouse, he encountered Owen McNulty. They'd had a brief introduction at church.

"Good day, Sergeant."

The man dipped his chin in greeting. "Tell me, Mr. Adams. You deliver this route daily. Ever see any miscreants hanging about the boardinghouse?"

"Why, no. Is there trouble?"

"Anyone out of the ordinary?"

Stephen pulled on his heavy mailbag as he considered the question. "This is New York—all sorts of people from various origins. Hard to say what's ordinary these days. I'm not sure what you mean, Sergeant McNulty."

"My future bride lives there. You understand my concern." He placed his large hand on Stephen's shoulder, dwarfing him as though he were Stephen's older, much taller brother. "Always valuable to have folks like you be vigilant and report to us anything odd. We can't be everywhere."

"I understand. I will most certainly be watchful. Do you think they are in danger there?"

"Probably just the jitters of the newest immigrant girl boarder. Everyone's on edge with the news of the president's funeral and all."

"Perhaps so. Say, when is the wedding?"

The man lifted his hat and stroked his brow. "My Grace is quite attached to the children she cares for, and she's trying to find her own replacement. The wedding will take place nonetheless, mind you, in just a few weeks."

"So soon? Delightful. My congratulations."

"Thank you."

A broad grin bloomed across the policeman's face. He was obviously in love. Everyone at First Church spoke about Owen and Grace as the romance of the century, which was amusing because the century had just begun. Whether exaggerated or not, Stephen observed them and was just a bit envious.

Owen continued. "But yes, the time is approaching whether a replacement is found or not. The delay thus far has allowed me to save for all the superfluous things I believe she deserves."

Rumor was Owen McNulty came from a wealthy family but preferred to make his own way in life. So long as the man could do that, Stephen admired his industry and the fact that he wanted to give his bride all he could. Stephen wished to follow that example. If only he could take Davis up on his offer and stash away some funds for his own hoped-for nuptials.

"Carry on, Mr. Adams."

As Stephen made his way up the sidewalk, the presence of a man on horseback caught his attention. He wore a bolero tie, the type Westerners sported, and he sat so straight in the saddle that his slight build bore him no disadvantage. So confident was his pose, Stephen found him hard to ignore. The man glanced toward Hawkins House as he rode by, then caught Stephen's eye and gave him a nod. Dark curly hair and an attitude befitting the most determined lawman . . . or criminal thug. For some reason Stephen was reminded of the shadowy man who earlier had been pounding the letter box, but he had not gotten a good look at him. There were plenty of odd sorts on his route. No reason he should think those two might be one and the same. Stephen acknowledged the horseman and then gathered the mail for house number 503.

Out of the ordinary? Odd? Indeed. There was nothing mundane about the streets of New York.

8

ON THURSDAY MORNING, just as Annie finished trimming all the candlewicks on the main floor, a loud rapping erupted at the front door. She hurried to answer it.

A man dressed in dark-blue clothing and a string tie stood on the stoop.

"May I help you?"

He glanced to the candlewick trimmer in her hand. "The housekeeper, I assume?"

"I am. And you are?"

"Clayton Cooper of the Pinkerton National Detective Agency, miss." He pointed to a silver badge, official looking, but unlike the one Grace's betrothed wore. "I planned to come by earlier, but headquarters sent me off on an unrelated case." He cleared his throat. "Oh, never mind that. I am here now."

"Oh, aye . . . What do you want?" She started to slowly close the door a bit in case she needed to push him out. She had never seen a detective or whatever he claimed to be in the neighborhood before, and she wondered if this might be Kirsten's shadow.

He slipped a brogue against the doorjamb.

"I have duties to attend to, sir, so I must ask again what your business is here."

"Forgive me. I am here to inquire about a young lady, someone who has on occasion entered your house late at night."

"I don't know what you're talking about."

Thankfully Mrs. Hawkins arrived. "What business do you have with our boarders, sir?"

"Just asking questions."

The woman edged Annie away and strained her neck like a goose, showing her dominance at her own front door. "We will not betray the privacy of our boarders, sir, but you can be confident there is no unruliness here."

The man smirked. "I do not doubt that, madam, but I must leave you a warning. If for some reason we are both mistaken, it will be my duty to report your establishment to the city and have your boardinghouse closed."

"Closed? Mrs. Hawkins, what does he mean?"

"Let me handle this, love."

If Hawkins House were shut down and all the occupants scattered, where would Annie go? She had not yet saved enough of her own money.

Mrs. Hawkins huffed. "That cannot happen, sir."

"Oh, it can. There is enough evidence, I believe, to inform the committees that exist in this city to put an end to ill-reputable houses that your boardinghouse is one of them."

"I am well aware of the citizen committees, young man, and they have no cause to do such a thing."

The man clicked his tongue. "But perhaps we can avoid all that. I must speak to this newest boarder of yours."

Annie's knees went weak, and her stomach turned as her thoughts raced back to the laundry, where someone once wanted to "speak to her." The tone in this Pinkerton man's voice rang with the same malicious intent.

Mrs. Hawkins did not back down. "I do not see what business she has with you, sir."

"I am investigating a case, and I assure you I have only the best interest of the public at heart."

"Come back next week." Mrs. Hawkins nearly slammed the door in the man's face.

Annie followed the woman into the parlor. "What does he mean? What case?"

"I don't know. Men like that . . . they cannot be allowed to bully women," the Hawk said, stomping her thick-heeled shoe on the rug. "I cannot imagine why he decided to pay us a visit."

Annie's instincts about the rude man when she'd first opened the door to him must have been correct. "I . . . uh . . . I should have told you she came in late. I was going to—"

"I see. He observed Kirsten keeping late hours and assumed the worst. Well, I will deal with Kirsten, but that man! He is much more important in his own eyes than his station merits. He is one nosy neighbor I've never seen before. Did he introduce himself before I came to the door?"

"He did. He disturbed me, so I forgot his name. Connell or Crayton—I don't know. Said he was from a detective agency."

"Pinkerton's?"

"Aye, that is what he said."

Mrs. Hawkins chuckled sarcastically. "A Pinkerton? Dodgy, that is." She pointed a finger at Annie. "Those men think they are above the law. We'll have nothing to do with them."

"Who are they? Do they have authority?" Annie realized she probably didn't know enough about the laws in America to understand if they were truly in danger. If she thought God cared, she would have gotten down on her knees right then and prayed that there were no Magdalene Laundries in Manhattan for Pinkertons to send innocent girls to.

"Private detectives. They have an office in Manhattan, but according to the papers, they spend most of their time tracking down bank robbers and locomotive bandits. Surely he has better things to do than annoy us."

"Can he do that, Mrs. Hawkins? Can he get this house shut down?"

Tears came to the woman's eyes. "I do not want to turn anyone away, love. I asked God to send me those he wants me to provide for and encourage. It is not for me to decide who is worthy, but if the other aid societies suspect someone in this house is operating in an immoral capacity, it could possibly happen even without that Pinkerton sticking his nose in my business." She plopped down into her chair.

Annie didn't know what Kirsten might have done, but if the aid societies knew that the housekeeper had once been sent to a Magdalene Laundry, they might think ill enough of her to cause trouble. It was Neil's fault . . . Well, Aileen's truly, but the whole mess followed Annie, haunting her dreams. She could still remember that day clearly. . . .

"Oh, I'll send her. Don't think I won't, Cora."

Aileen was the cause of Neil's discontent, or at least she added fuel to it with her account of what happened after Da's burial. Annie wished she could have had a fair chance to explain what really took place.

A fisherman's son, Johnny Flynn, followed behind her as the mourning party left the grave. Annie had only met him a day earlier when folks stopped by her father's wake.

"Say, Annie, I'm awfully sorry."

She turned around. The lad's face drooped the way someone's does when they feel helpless trying to cheer you up. She forced a wee smile. The other mourners passed them by on the road to the O'Shannons'. Neil was expected to feed them all, and she knew he wasn't happy about it. She wanted to take her time getting back.

Johnny leaned against a standing stone and waved her over. He showed her the flask in his pocket. She shook her head.

"Aw, I wish I could make ye feel better, Annie Gallagher."

"I wish you could too." She hadn't meant to say it out loud, but she'd done it.

He pulled her close and pressed his lips hard against hers. She did not want to be kissed like that, but she felt so weak and hurt and limp that at first she did not push away. He dug his fingers so hard into her arms that even if she'd had the strength, she might not have been able to escape him. She leaned as far away from his clutch as she could when he suddenly let go. She gasped, feeling the need to pull her arms across her chest like a shield. He smirked. The smell of whiskey hung like a cloud. She stepped backward.

"Ye liked that, didn't ye, lass? Well, there's more—"

She spun around to see what had interrupted him. Aileen O'Shannon stood on the road glaring not at Johnny Flynn, whom she'd said was her sweetheart, but at her.

Annie pulled her cousin aside. "Your man is an *eejit*. What are you thinking taking up with him, Aileen?"

"Is that the way of it? You trying to force my lad to kiss you?"

"What?" Annie dropped Aileen's arm and took a step back to be sure it was Aileen herself she was looking at. "My poor da is fresh in the grave. Why would I do such a thing?"

But Aileen held tight to her story, saying Annie was a loose woman as her mother must have been. The pain of hearing those words still stabbed needles in Annie's heart.

Then, not long after her father's burial, Annie prepared to bring in the morning's milking and paused outside the front door, listening to shouting within the house.

"Not there, Neil. Say you won't. Poor Kate's daughter."

"Kate's daughter has got more than you know. Look here."

She peeked in the window. Her father's writing desk lay on the table. Neil clutched her accounting book. How dare he. There was only a wee bit of cash in there, but he had it in his grimy hands. She was about to barge in when Neil shouted again.

"Ever since I heard she was Kate's daughter, I knew this day would come. She and Johnny Flynn, right there in a sacred churchyard. No shame at all, that one. No telling how she let him touch her."

"Aw, Neil, have ye no mercy?"

"Mercy, ye say? For women like her? She's the spawn of my sister, and she'll be turning out to be just like her, mark my words. Don't ye know she's been on the road with that Protestant tinker father of hers, Cora?"

Annie shook her head in an attempt to dislodge the memory. Mrs. Hawkins was correct. Men should not be allowed to bully innocent women. Aileen might have been her accuser, but it was Neil who had stolen Annie's freedom. Who knows what folks might choose to believe, though she'd been innocent enough. A private detective could find out things. That's what they did.

Mrs. Hawkins tapped her fingers together. "Tonight I'll wait up for Kirsten. This is my fault for not being more heedful. She's been coming in after I've gone to bed, and I cannot allow that. I will speak to her boss if I must."

Annie returned to her chores. As she wiped down the kerosene lamp globes, her hands trembled. One Pinkerton man should not be allowed to make them turn Kirsten away. Not only was America a place where a leader could be assassinated; it was also a place where people could lose their homes over mere hearsay.

Seek your place of refuge.

"Did you say something, Mrs. Hawkins?"

"No. Why?"

She waved her hand in front of her face. "'Twas nothing." Just something she'd heard somewhere that had popped into her head. Worry does terrible things to the mind.

The message boy who sometimes ran errands for them knocked at the kitchen door wearing brown cotton knickers and matching jacket, the ragged uniform of a hardworking lad. Annie opened the door to speak to him. He bent at his waist to catch his breath. "Here to tell Mrs. Hawkins, miss, that the ship she's waiting fer just arrived on Ellis Island."

Mrs. Hawkins came up behind her. "Thank you, Jules." She reached around Annie and put a few coins in the lad's outstretched palm. "Now straight to your mum with that, you hear? You don't want to be walking about the streets with money in your pocket."

"No, ma'am. Thank you, ma'am." He bounded down the steps.

"And don't be stopping for lemon drops and licorice," she called after him.

Annie shut the door. "Aileen is here." Could things get any worse?

"Not quite here yet. She's at Ellis Island. You know how long that can take. We'll go down to the docks before supper. She will be expecting you, I suppose."

"She will be quite uninformed, Mrs. Hawkins."

"Well, I'm sure someone will explain things to her. Don't worry."

She wasn't worried, not about Aileen. As she stared out the window and watched Jules meld into the mass of New York pedestrians on the street, Annie thought about the characters in the book she'd been reading. No immigration station in Oz, but the shock of entering a whole new world was not very different, she supposed. Dorothy had realized Oz was far removed from Kansas, and likewise, Aileen would see that New York was nothing like the west of Ireland.

With hours to wait, she and Mrs. Hawkins returned to their chores. The lavender scent lingering on the sheets Annie folded reminded her of Irish meadows she and her da had traversed. Snowdrops in the spring, heather in the summer. If ever home had a fragrance, this was it. She breathed it in, wondering if once Aileen arrived, the place would reek of the damp rock walls of the Ireland she'd tried to forget.

When she finished with the laundry, she paused at her room and went to the desk by the window, where her father's tattered Bible lay. Father Weldon had rescued it from Neil along with the writing desk. She'd never asked how much he'd had to pay him for it. She opened it, remembering what the priest had told her. "There are some things that must be remembered always. The Bible tells us to do this with God's Word, you understand?" Perhaps God could speak to her that way. She had little hope of it, seeing as God had abandoned her in that Magdalene Laundry, but Da had loved the stories in the Bible, and for that reason she thought it worth trying.

She flipped to the New Testament and stopped at a verse in 1 Timothy. *"But if any provide not for his own, and specially for those of his own house, he hath denied the faith, and is worse than an infidel."* Such had been done to her. Angry tears stung her eyes. She'd wanted to hear God tell her she had a place with him. That he'd not turned from her. But all she heard was scolding about her attitude toward her cousin.

Annie wiped her eyes and laid her head down on the book. Truly, she knew that with no one to meet her at Ellis Island,

Aileen very well could end up in one of those horrible places, and as insufferable as that lass was, she did not deserve that.

It was late afternoon when she finished cleaning. As she was wringing out the rags in the scullery's utility sink, Mrs. Hawkins found her. "Go freshen up, love. We'll go down and see about your cousin. I've ordered a coach to take us to the ferry."

"Kind of you, Mrs. Hawkins. I could have taken the trolley to Battery Park and caught the ferry myself."

"Nonsense. She is family, is she not?" Without waiting for an answer, she added, "I would not hear of it. When you're ready, meet me in the garden. I've instructed the driver to wait out back."

Annie exited the scullery by the back door, a washing-up rag in one hand and a comb in the other. 'Twas the curse of the Irish to have so much hair.

She finished quickly, and soon Mrs. Hawkins and she were on their way. They passed businesses and massive buildings; their function she didn't know. A few newsboys shouted from street corners, and men in black bowler hats darted periodically across the carriage's path. It seemed to Annie everyone had a place to go.

Eventually they came to the docks. The driver stopped to let them disembark. You could see Lady Liberty from there. A green glint had begun to overcome the copper, but her majesty was no less diminished than when Annie had first seen her.

"Wait here," Mrs. Hawkins ordered the driver. "Remember, I've hired you for the evening. No in-between jobs while you wait."

"Yes, ma'am." The driver tipped his flat-topped hat.

As they scurried toward the crowd anxiously waiting for the government ferry, Mrs. Hawkins leaned in close to Annie. "What does she look like, love?"

"She's a wee lass with a contrary demeanor."

"Well, generally then, give me an idea."

"So, she's reddish-blonde hair—more yellow than not, much sunnier than my own—and a sprinkling of freckles across her nose. Her arms, too."

"Does she bear any family resemblance to you or your mother, perhaps?"

"My mother? Mrs. Hawkins, I told you I did not know my mother. Did I ever mention what she looked like?"

"Of course not. I'm sorry, love. Just trying to get an idea. Anything else you can tell me about her?"

"Pale eyes, green, I think. In any case, not as deep as my own color. My aunt and uncle are both short in stature, and so is she."

"Good heavens, love. That describes half a shipload of folks coming from Ireland. Good thing I am acquainted with several of the immigration officials. I'll inquire about her by name. Otherwise we'll be waiting quite a long while as they work their way through the list."

When the ferry arrived at Ellis Island, Annie sucked in her breath. Neil might have come too—to rip her away and cast her back to a solitary cell. She closed her eyes and tried to focus. She was in America. She could stand up to anyone now, the way she'd seen Mrs. Hawkins do with that Pinkerton.

Even so, her stomach flittered in anticipation. Annie tapped her lips with her gloved hand. Her imagination had just gotten the best of her, as it was wont to do. All they would do is collect Aileen and go back home. Annie would do her best to steer clear of her as much as possible, but what happened was in the past. Should Aileen decide to accuse Annie of wrongdoing again, who would now so easily believe her?

They filed in behind a crowd of bearded men and a few elderly women, everyone still whispering about the poor dead president, as though whispers could make things better.

When they stepped ashore and approached the massive brick-and-stone building, an impressive structure that had replaced the former building that burned before Annie had arrived, Annie sensed the optimism the travelers carried with them, the same timid hopefulness she'd had when she first came to America. She had been processed onshore because the island was still being rebuilt, but the uncertainty of what was going to happen before she was released and what this new country had to offer was surely the same for those on Ellis Island this day. There was opportunity in her new country, and she could still open her library, someday. She would not let wee Aileen spoil that ambition.

Mrs. Hawkins approached one of the officials and spoke to him. Annie realized she'd been gawking up at the peaks and corbels along the roof of the structure, lost in memories of her own passage to America. She hurried to catch up with the woman.

They waited. The idle time allowed Annie to once again relive in her mind her first day in America. She remembered hearing something that momentarily shook her confidence. She'd feared someone could send her away again. She'd overheard someone mention a reformatory, a description some folks used back in Ireland when referring to the Magdalene Laundry. When she heard the name of the place in America, she decided to inquire of a well-dressed woman in the room where passengers waited for family members to pick them up. This particular woman appeared to be American, and Annie guessed her to be better informed than she herself was.

"Excuse the bother, but can you tell me—do you know St. Anne's in Albany? What kind of place is that?"

"Oh yes. A home where the nuns rehabilitate young girls who have misbehaved. I hear they have great success with it, and the girls are ready to be responsible citizens by the time they turn twenty-one."

Nuns? "And there are doctors there?" She suddenly realized she'd been tugging on one sleeve.

"I expect so. But nice girls like you don't need to worry about such places, now." She smiled and walked away.

Nice girls? Smart girls, for certain. Annie was determined never to allow anyone to force her into such a place again, and she chided herself now for entertaining the thought that Aileen could have any influence over Annie here in America. She rubbed the spot between her eyes with her index finger. Not Aileen. But possibly Neil.

The hands on the wall clock moved forward, but still Aileen did not come. They were nearly alone in the vast waiting room. "She's not here," Annie said. "We should go."

"Let me inquire." The Hawk approached another official, who pulled a small pad of paper from his pocket.

"Give me her name and where you live, and I'll do my best to get information to you. There are many reasons for detainment: illness, inability to pass a cognitive test, confusion, likelihood of becoming a public charge . . . I will find out."

As he said this, Annie noticed a wad of banknotes peeking out from the inside breast pocket of his jacket. Mrs. Hawkins had paid him to find Aileen.

"Don't worry, love," Mrs. Hawkins said as they headed back to the mainland ferry. "The folks here don't mistreat people. I daresay we both know corruption in other lands. We are in America now." She lifted her head toward Lady Liberty's torch.

On the ride back home, the Hawk was quiet, perhaps waiting for Annie to speak. She reached for the woman's hand. "Why did you pay that man? You don't even know Aileen."

Mrs. Hawkins gazed out toward the gas streetlamps that cast a mellow glow across her face, lighting her forceful profile. "I know *you*, love. How could I not try to help? No harm will come to her while she's on Ellis Island, or they'll have Agnes Hawkins to deal with."

That was the spirit Annie admired, although she wasn't entirely sure Aileen was worth it.

9

FINISHED WITH VERNE'S *Facing the Flag*, Stephen reached for the journal where he recorded his expenses. When he had stopped by the dance earlier, a girl named Emma told him that Annie wasn't there, so he headed back home. The electric bulbs buzzed above his head, and he complained to himself about how those lights made his eyes especially weary. Electric lights were convenient generally, but there was something about reading by a kerosene lamp that he found comforting. Probably one of those childhood memories the modern alienists found so fascinating to study. Stephen had read some of their publications simply because he'd found nothing else to read.

Sighing, he looked over the numbers he had recorded, trying to determine where all his money had gone. He hadn't written everything down—just rent, groceries, and laundry expenses. The amount he dropped into the hands of newsboys that week probably totaled ten cents. Twice he'd paid for elderly citizens to ride the trolley because the men either couldn't find their wallets or truly had no money for the fare. He'd bought a girl an apple, and it seemed to brighten her day as she continued down the street hobbling on crutches. He had deposited a quarter into the collection box at St. Paul's when he stopped in to get out of the rain for a few minutes.

He ran a hand through his hair. God had not given him a mind for numbers, but he was determined to keep a better watch. If only he had studied mathematics with more vigor when he was in school, he might not have this trouble now. He considered the possibility that such things could be attributed to genetic failings. Numerous books had been written exploring the influence of inborn tendencies as opposed to the efforts of stern discipline. He would fight against his lot in life to avoid following his father's example and instead use his own intellect. Unlike his father, he would not trust the banks. He might have been only a teenager during the financial troubles of 1893, but he knew history. His father should have taken heed of that before he lost his money.

The only funds Stephen had risked thus far was the dollar he'd given to Minnie, and now she was saying it was worth more than she had anticipated. Good, but he needed even more. When he picked up his second round of deliveries that day, he had stopped by the board near the time clock where requests for extra help were listed. Nothing. Minnie had called out to him.

"Hey, Stephen Adams, how's your day been out there?"

"Oh, hi, Minnie. All fine. How about yourself?"

"Couldn't be better." She whispered, "Leonard has done it. He stopped by to take me to the lunch counter today, and he says he's made more money than he ever expected. Instead of a 10 percent gain this week, he's made that dollar of yours worth $1.50."

"Are you sure?"

"That's what he said. Want it back?"

"Uh, no. Just invest it again."

"Sure, but if you want to deposit any more, just let me know."

Minnie's words echoed in his mind as he worked. Leonard's scheme seemed like a much easier way to make extra cash than working overtime. He just hoped it wasn't ill-gotten. Stephen would plan his way through life rather than become a pauper, even if it took some creative thinking.

He rose and retrieved his money box from behind some cereal tins in his kitchen pantry. Counting what was left told him how much he had to spend far better than those numbers on a page. Oh yes. He'd need to pay the tailor who had mended his trousers. Better keep that in mind. Stephen rubbed his hand over his chin. His lack of remembering had never been intentional. A flaw in his mental makeup perhaps, but not in his character. *Please, God. Don't let me become my father.*

He set aside the money for that expense. All he had left was two dollars. Not enough for his rent. Not enough for the undertaker's bill this month. But he would make up for that on payday.

He found a dime in the bottom of the box. If he were a fan of dime novels, he might be tempted to purchase one. But no. He couldn't even spare that. Sticking the coin in his pocket, he scrambled out to head for the drugstore and purchase shaving soap.

Unfortunately he met Davis, who was coming into the building just as Stephen was going out. He had no answer for the question he knew the man would ask.

"Find anything yet, Adams?"

"Now just where do you think I'm going to find a children's book author?"

The man shrugged. "Ask around. Lots of people say they're gonna write a book."

"Yeah, sure thing. Look, I'm on my way out."

Davis backed away from the entrance, hands up in surrender. "Rent's due next week, remember."

"I am aware of that, Davis. I'll get it to you right after I get paid on Saturday. Is that satisfactory?"

"Sure."

All of a sudden even soap seemed like an extravagance. He could scrape by with what was left in his shaving cup. Stephen headed to the diner instead, where his buddy always poured him coffee for free.

A bell jingled on the door when he entered. He found an open red leather stool at the counter. Dexter, the owner, filled a white porcelain cup and shoved the sugar jar toward him. "Job wearing you out, Stephen?"

"Aw, no. I enjoy my job."

"Good thing, fella. Good thing." He leaned against the counter as Stephen sipped from his cup. "Whatcha reading these days?"

This was what continued to draw Stephen to the diner. Literature lovers must congregate to talk about books. Two people could read the same story and note totally different points of interest. He thoroughly enjoyed that kind of thing. "I ran out of material. How about you?"

Dexter plunked a book down on the counter. Stephen turned the spine up. "Longfellow? *The Song of Hiawatha*? Haven't you read this before?"

"Yep. Three times. Like you, I keep running out of good books. You live above a publisher. Can't you work out some kinda deal with him?"

"As a matter of fact, he thinks I might be able to help him find a new children's author. There's a fat chance I can."

Dexter shrugged as though the request were not exceptional in the least.

Stephen set the book down and picked up his cup. "Oh, I finished *Facing the Flag*. Forgot to bring it back with me. I'll drop it off on my way to work tomorrow."

"Fine, and what did you think? That Verne sure weaves

some remarkable tales. I liked it all right myself, but really, all that patriotism at the end for that European country. Didn't seem real to me. If it had been the good ole US of A, maybe."

"I thought it was pretty good. Say, Dexter, do your kids read?"

"Sure. In school. American history stuff." He stowed his book under the counter. "They've been begging for a copy of that *Wizard* book since it was published."

"*The Wonderful Wizard of Oz*, you mean? By Baum?"

"Yep. That's the one." Dexter wiped the counter with a white linen cloth while he talked. "I hear it's better than the Brothers Grimm and more entertaining than Mother Goose. Figure if business picks up a bit, I'll get 'em a copy for Christmas. I saw it in the bookshop. Copies are selling better than Harriet's creamed cabbage." He nodded at his wife through a small pass-through to the kitchen. "Imagine all the copies are gone by now, but they'll be printing more."

The mention of a home-cooked dish distracted Stephen. "You know I adore Harriet's cabbage. I'll have to stop in for the special next payday. Save me some."

"You got it."

Dexter's wife's cabbage sometimes sold out early in the day. People knew what they liked when it came to food and books. Stephen couldn't blame Davis for wanting a piece of that publishing pie.

Dexter lifted his black brows. "Last year I bought them Baum's *Father Goose*, and they've about worn out that book."

Davis was right. Parents *were* interested in those kinds of stories for their children. "Dexter, you don't happen to know any authors, do you? Anyone writing children's stories and talking it up here in the diner?"

"Can't say as I do." The door jingled, and he lifted his head and smiled at his newest customers. "Lots of people come by, though. You never know who you'll meet. Keep your eyes open, Stephen." He scurried away, coffeepot in hand.

Stephen hoped Dexter would be able to buy that book for his kids someday soon. He wondered if Annie Gallagher had read it yet. If he and Annie were both able to read the book, perhaps he could trade his book banter with Dexter for a Baum discussion with her.

When Annie and Mrs. Hawkins arrived back home from their unsuccessful trip to fetch Aileen, they found Grace sitting alone in the kitchen eating the soup they had left for her on the stove. She glanced up at them and nodded. She hadn't taken the time to hang up her shawl. The deep-red fabric lay across her lap. "Come eat with me. There's plenty more soup in the pot and I've warmed it, so 'tis ready."

"Kirsten has not returned from work yet?" Mrs. Hawkins asked.

Grace glanced toward the front door. "She has not."

Annie fetched two white bowls, the deep ones with painted pink roses around the edges, and proceeded to dish up bean soup while Mrs. Hawkins hung her own scarf on a hook near the back door. "Did you go to the dance, Grace?"

"Indeed. Owen got the night off work, and I do think he is warming up to them. A few more times and I'll have him step-dancing."

Annie smiled at that. It was the joviality of the gatherings that helped her view her birth country more positively, and what could be more amusing than a man, whose connection to Ireland went way back to his granny, dancing like the Irish, like her da . . .

Mrs. Hawkins handed Grace a bowl of bread slices she'd

covered with a linen napkin to keep the flies away. "We have readied the room for Annie's cousin, the companion we told you about, love."

Grace accepted a piece of bread and slid it into her steaming soup bowl. "Ah, when is she coming?"

Mrs. Hawkins took her own bowl of soup from Annie's hands. "Thank you, love. Indeed, Annie's cousin will be here tomorrow or the next day."

Annie pulled out a chair across from Grace and sat. "Her ship arrived today, but she has been detained."

Grace used the back of her hand to push away the lock of hair that always seemed to trouble her. "Oh, dear me. I remember my first day in America so well. Didn't they frighten me when I came over."

"I do remember," Mrs. Hawkins said. "You were so unnerved you couldn't even speak to Sergeant McNulty on the trolley."

They giggled about that. Now she was going to marry him.

Grace patted her lips with a blue cloth napkin. "Nothing ill happened to me. 'Twas just . . . you know, not knowing. I've come to understand more about America, Americans, and . . . well, I've learned that my security comes not from others but from God."

From a silent God? He had not stepped in and helped when Annie was in danger. Grace had seemed afraid, true, when she came over. Everyone is afraid of something. But Grace had worked to overcome her fears. That was how it was done. Still, if Annie were to say aloud that God had not helped them like they'd imagined, the women would surely chastise her. She kept those thoughts to herself.

Mrs. Hawkins smiled and patted Grace's hand. "You've done a wonderful job with the Parker children, love, teaching them a bit of what you've learned."

Grace let out a breath. "I'm trying." She glanced at Annie. "Better to move on from memories like buttonhook eye examinations by immigrant doctors, aye? I'm sure your cousin will get through fine, just like thousands of others have."

Annie swallowed hard, the soup stinging her throat. She remembered thinking that no matter what that immigrant doctor did, she couldn't be rejected and sent back. She just couldn't. Aye. Better to move on.

Mrs. Hawkins leaned her head to her shoulder, apparently noticing that Annie was lost in thought. "I understand there are health checks on Ellis Island. Indeed there must be more than what they did when I arrived. But the latest government regulations seem to be segregating more people for the purpose of deporting them. Tell me, what was that eye inspection like?"

Annie lifted her gaze to the plastered ceiling as she recalled. Back then Annie had prayed to God just in case he might be listening anew in America. *Please, God, remember Father Weldon's blessing and have mercy on me.* Standing in a line had helped save her before in the laundry. When she arrived in America, she had stood as close to the lass in front of her as she could. When it was her turn to lift her chin up toward the man doing the examination, sweat trickled down the back of her dress and a gray wooziness threatened to drop her to her knees. But then it was over. She had made it.

Annie shook away the memory and answered. "We stood stoically as the doctor used an instrument—a buttonhook as Grace said—to pull back our eyelids, looking for trachoma."

Mrs. Hawkins gasped. "They did nothing like that to me when I arrived at Castle Garden years ago. I've never heard folks talk about that. How horrible, love."

"Well, I just gritted my teeth and endured it. Then I was sent on. Suppose folks don't talk about it because they are eager to get admitted, and truly the screening is over quickly." She didn't like talking about doctors. There are some things a person doesn't talk about because bad fortune might follow if you do. Not to mention the erroneous conclusions folks could make. Mrs. Hawkins had been gracious not to tell anyone Annie had been in a Magdalene Laundry. She had to know because her brother had rescued Annie, but they didn't talk about it, thank the good Lord, or knock on wood, or whatever manner of luck that had been.

Annie tried not to contemplate, even in private, the details of her experience in the laundry. Why give life to the words that would bring it all back fresh in her mind?

When they finished eating and washing the bowls and utensils, they retired to the parlor.

Mrs. Hawkins handed Grace her paper for drawing, a hobby Grace liked to pursue in the evenings. "Tell me, Grace. A man has not been here snooping around, has he?"

"No one has been by. Who do you mean?"

"A Pinkerton. Says he's on a case, but for some reason he's chosen our Kirsten to spy on, and he's even threatened to report us as a disreputable house if I do not allow him to speak to her."

"What does he want?"

"I have no idea, but perhaps we ought to have Owen stop by."

"I will ring the station house." She hurried out to go to Mrs. Jenkins's house next door, where the closest telephone was located.

Annie's discomfort must have shown because Mrs. Hawkins tried to distract her. "Why don't you find something of interest in the *Times* to read aloud, Annie?" Mrs. Hawkins handed her the newspaper.

Distractions were usually helpful. Annie thumbed through the pages, looking for something besides reports on the aftermath of the president's death. The world was a scary place.

She searched for more local news. Perhaps something from the society pages.

She spotted a headline that looked promising. "Oh, J. Pierpont Morgan has a new collie dog."

Mrs. Hawkins looked up from her needlepoint. "Dogs are nice. What else does it say, Annie?"

Annie looked over the article a moment. "Oh, I see why 'tis news. He has a whole kennel of Scotch collie dogs valued at over forty thousand dollars."

Mrs. Hawkins clicked her tongue.

Annie ran a finger over the type. "It says the dog is a blue-ribbon winner imported from London at a cost of eight thousand dollars. He's going to enter the dog in shows and expects to win prizes. His daughter also has some expensive pets called Chinese spaniels. Hers cost two thousand apiece."

Mrs. Hawkins threw down her needlepoint. "Think of all the hungry people who could be fed with that money." She stared at the window. "I am not saying the businessmen should share all they make. They probably earn their money or else it was handed down. I don't know. Theirs just the same. But those poor children out there on the streets, no more than a few blocks away, begging for a nickel. This is not the time for fancy dog shows. As Shakespeare wrote, 'That thou mayst shake the superflux to them and show the heavens more just.'"

Annie let the paper fall to her lap. "Shakespeare? I did not know you were fond of him, Mrs. Hawkins. My father used to recite his plays aloud."

The Hawk smacked her lips. "Some people think Shakespeare is just for the university types, but just because a woman hasn't been to university doesn't mean she can't read, love." She pointed to the shelves in the breakfront, where books stood as thick as a birch forest.

Ah, books, aye. One had to amass as much knowledge and foresight as one could.

The woman fussed. "My mission here is to help immigrant girls like you and Grace and our newest arrival, Kirsten. I will do so until my dying breath."

"I'm sorry all this has distracted you from seeing to Kirsten's situation."

Aileen's imminent arrival had preoccupied the Hawk so that she hadn't yet quizzed Kirsten's boss about her long hours. Already Aileen was interfering.

Grace entered and handed Mrs. Hawkins something wrapped in a blue cloth napkin. "Mrs. Jenkins sent over some scones for your evening tea."

"How kind of her." She set the bundle on the tea tray. "Were you able to speak to Owen?"

"I was not able, but his captain promised to let him know you'd like to speak to him. He will probably come by after his shift, if that's all right with you."

"That will be fine, love. I don't think it's an urgent matter as yet."

"His shift ends fairly early."

"That young man can come by and visit anytime."

Grace returned to her place on the sofa. "That Mrs. Jenkins, she's quite . . . Well, how shall I put it? She's all ears, if you know what I mean."

"Oh, she's a friendly sort, is all," Mrs. Hawkins said as she put a morsel of the pastry in her mouth. "She's an excellent baker. Shall we get some clotted cream and jam to go with this, girls?"

Annie couldn't eat anything. With the Pinkerton business, and now Aileen being delayed, her stomach twisted in knots. She wasn't sure she could handle any more surprises.

10

"Annie, come here, love," Mrs. Hawkins called to her from the parlor on Monday. It was not the day for dusting or sweeping. With tidying up the boarders' rooms, cooking, planning the meals, and managing the household accounts, Annie was sufficiently employed. Hopefully the woman was not about to add another chore to the list just because Aileen would be arriving soon.

"Coming, Mrs. Hawkins."

When Annie got to the room, the woman waved a paper at her. "I dropped my embroidery needle and had to search around for it, and I found this under my chair. You must have dropped it, and with the skirt on this chair, it's no wonder you didn't notice it."

"I'm sorry, Mrs. Hawkins. I should have been sweeping under the furniture, but with all the preparations and all, I must have neglected that task."

"Never mind that." She gave the paper another flip in the air. "What is it?"

"A story your father wrote. His name is at the top. Marty Gallagher, correct? I hope you don't mind but I found it delightful. And what an interesting monogram at the end."

"Monogram?"

"Looks like the letters *L* and *R*. Quite an elaborate decoration he made underneath them." She put on her glasses and peered at the paper. "Looks like a cross inside a heart inside a rose enclosed within a circle and a little bishop's staff on top."

"Aye. He scribbled bits of pictures quite a lot. Suppose he had to occupy his time while he was ill, as used to traveling about as he had been." Annie took the paper from the woman's outstretched hand and carried it to the bookcase like the treasure it was. "My apologies. I must have forgotten to put it away and then it fell to the floor. I have not swept in here for far too long." She bit her lip. She would never have been that careless if it weren't for Kirsten coming in so late.

"I am not concerned with the quality of your housekeeping. I tell you, love, those little field mice wearing red knickers and carrying lanterns while they marched in their teeny army, trying to be brave all the while—I found it brilliantly endearing. And me, afraid of mice."

"Aye, 'tis a sweet story. I cherish these."

"And well you should. It is more than just a delightful story. It's superb. I've never read anything like it, and I do read quite a lot, you know. Your father's descriptions took me back to Ireland. He was a master painter of words."

"You really think so?"

"I do."

"I suppose I have attached so much emotional value to the story I did not realize it would entertain anyone else."

"I can tell you I was enchanted."

Annie's face grew warm. "Thank you for telling me so, Mrs. Hawkins."

Annie made sure the papers were snug in her desk. "No word yet about Aileen?"

"Nothing from Ellis Island thus far, love. I last rang over there a few moments ago, and there was no news."

"Perhaps I will have to go out to Ellis Island myself." As much as Annie didn't want to go, she could not abandon wee, naive Aileen, no matter what the girl had done to her.

"Most detainees are released within a week's time. I expect we will hear soon. You will be happy to know, though, that I've been informed she is not in the infirmary. Whatever has detained her, it was not illness."

Then it was ill behavior, Annie was sure. "I will be patient, although I am sure she is not."

"Who could blame her?"

"That's right, so."

"Annie, when I went over to use the telephone, whom should I meet but Sergeant McNulty. Coming to speak with me but detained by our neighbor."

"Is that so? Grace may have been right about Mrs. Jenkins."

"Yes. A busybody, it seems. Do you know I had to rescue him off her porch? I was headed over there to telephone out and inquire about your cousin, and there he was, unable to free himself from all her blabbering."

"I knew some women like that in Ireland."

"Well, that aside, I was pleased to learn that Owen promised to look into that Pinkerton's business and to suggest the man desist from visiting Hawkins House in the future."

What a relief, especially for Kirsten. Annie turned to leave.

"Love? One moment?"

"Yes?"

"Is anything worrying you, dear?"

Worries were never far away. "What do you mean, Mrs. Hawkins?"

"I try not to be a busybody myself, but you are such a dear. I want you to be happy here."

"I'm happy."

"Yes, well, you do seem a bit . . . reflective."

Annie plopped down on the piano stool. "Oh, Mrs. Hawkins, sometimes I wish I were in Oz." A place where dreams could actually be pursued.

"Where?"

"Nothing. I was just thinking about that book you gave me. You must think ill of me mithering on so."

"No indeed. The only reason I mentioned it was just to give you a bit of advice, in case you find it helpful."

Annie could not tell her that she found very little helpful these days. She just had to plow her way through troubles like the field mice in her father's stories. She grinned and nodded.

"Be faithful, love. You are God's child. Do not forget."

"I try not to." Still, she questioned why God would take her father away and leave her all alone. Why he allowed her to be in that stockade of a place where that doctor touched her and certainly would have done more given the chance. But most of all, she did not understand why God had ceased to direct her, even after she'd received Father Weldon's blessing. Not even a holy man had been able to intercede for one as unloved as Annie.

Barrels of unanswered queries made her head spin. More sleep and better attention to the reverend's teachings might be the only remedy she could hope for.

She returned to the ledger of Hawkins House expenses she had been studying.

Mrs. Hawkins patted her shoulder. "That is all of my motherly advice for today, Annie. I do hope you don't mind my indulgences."

"Not at all." Mrs. Hawkins's hovering might have been comforting if she had actually been her mother.

The Hawk looked down at what Annie had written. "See

there. You have saved twenty-five cents a month by switching our coal delivery to that other company. And earlier when you uncovered an error in the figures the laundress gave me, you saved us even more. Annie Gallagher, when I hired you on, I got much more than just an excellent housekeeper."

"You flatter me, Mrs. Hawkins. I am just doing my job."

"A fine job, that's what you're doing, love. I will be in the garden if you need me. I must tend to the waning herbs and harvest enough to dry for the season." The Hawk kept a corner of the fenced-in area behind the brownstone for a garden, a wee bit of green space. She said it reminded her of home. She toddled off toward the back door.

Annie put her pencil down, thinking she heard the postman. She met his whistling at the door. "Good day, Mr. Adams." The sun glinted off the metal buttons of his uniform jacket. Thinking he might be overheated since the day was rather humid, she asked him inside for a glass of lemonade.

"Very kind of you, Miss Gallagher." He rested his mailbag on the floor, placing his hat on top. He drained the glass while standing in the kitchen.

"Another?" She attempted to take the glass from his hand.

He held on to it for just a moment, and her fingers brushed his. A tingle ran through her hand and up her arm.

He let go. "Yes, please. If it's no trouble."

She refilled the glass from a sweating tin pitcher and handed it to him. "No trouble at all. Can't have you collapsing from the heat."

He drank slower this time. Stephen Adams was certainly a considerate man, and attractive. She admired the gleam of his coal-black hair, his square, strong chin, the firmness of his forearms from carrying that heavy mailbag every day. She had to look away lest he catch her staring. This American man seemed more like her father and less like some other men she had known and loathed.

He finally gave her the glass. "Miss Gallagher, I was wondering if you've gotten a copy of that book we spoke of, *The Wonderful Wizard of Oz*?"

"Oh, I have indeed. Mrs. Hawkins gave it to me. I am enjoying it quite a bit. How about you?"

"Uh, no. Not yet. But if I do, perhaps you and I . . . uh . . . we could discuss it."

"Discuss it?"

"I mean, talk about it—what you like, what you would change if you wrote it, what puzzles you about it, if anything."

"Oh, I see. Well . . . I would like that, Mr. Adams."

"That's fine, then. Uh . . . I better be going."

She nodded, but he seemed hesitant to go.

"I regret that I was unable to speak to you after church yesterday."

She shook her head. "We have been so busy we needed to get home straightaway. I hope we were not being rude."

"No. I understand. Perhaps I'll see you at the dance this week?" he called over his shoulder as he walked to the door.

Her palms began to perspire. "I'm not sure . . . I . . . I am not sure I'll be there this time."

He turned around. The smile dropped from his lips. He bobbed his head and went out the door without the usual whistle.

She was really beginning to like that man. Finally someone who did not present his gender as being superior to hers.

She stood in the open doorway for a moment as the postman departed. The messenger boy Jules came zigzagging down the street.

He waved one arm when he saw her. "Miss Annie, got a message for you from the island."

So today would be the day. The dreaded day.

He was out of breath when he reached her. He handed her a note, and she ushered him inside. "Just made some lemonade, Jules. Do you have time for a glass?"

"Thank you, Miss Annie."

He gulped his drink, thanked her for the nickel she'd handed him, and darted out the door.

Not a minute later Mrs. Hawkins came in from the yard with a basket full of herbs. She wiped her brow with the back of her garden glove. "The thyme has nearly taken over the patch. I've got enough of it weeded out now, I suppose." She glanced toward the front door when the lock clicked. "Was that Jules who just ran out? I thought I saw him come around to the front of the house. He must not have seen me in the garden."

"It was. I gave him some lemonade and a nickel."

"That's fine, love. So he brought a message?"

Annie tried to hand the paper to her, but the woman held up her soiled hands. "What does it say? Is it about Aileen?"

Annie unfolded it. "It says Aileen O'Shannon Moran has been released and is ready to be called for."

The Hawk set her basket down and hurried to the front door. She leaned out and let out a whistle. Annie came up behind her and watched as the wee messenger boy returned to the stoop. "Go get the carriage I hired last Thursday, love." She waved a hand toward the hall, and Annie knew she meant for her to hurry to the kitchen and get the lad another tip.

Annie collected another coin, and the woman pressed it into the youth's hand before he rushed off.

When Annie and Mrs. Hawkins reached the pier where the government ferry from Ellis Island docked, a man waved his arm frantically. "We are about to leave. Hurry, ladies."

They held on to their headpieces as they hustled toward him. "We are late," Annie breathed out. "Aileen will be furious. And she'll have no right to be, as generous as you've been, but she will be just the same. Just to warn you."

Mrs. Hawkins accepted the dockman's hand as she stepped onto the ferry. Annie was next, followed by their carriage driver. "Might as well come and help this time," he said. "Since I got to wait anyway." Clearly Mrs. Hawkins had overpaid him.

After taking a seat where they could look out on the water, Annie settled in to savor her last few moments of peace. Oh, how she did not look forward to having Aileen in the house.

After a short ride, the ferry pulled up to the island and the passengers crowded together, preparing to exit. Annie's stomach clenched with the thought of seeing the lass who had betrayed her. She would have to let bygones lie, but it would be difficult. *Must you send me such torment, God?*

No answer.

Mrs. Hawkins was wrong. God had not claimed Annie as his child.

When they got to the reception room, Annie spotted her. Aileen sat on a trunk, hands on her cheeks like a pouting child. When she saw Annie, she popped up and marched toward her. "That was miserable. Horrible. If Da had been here, he would have busted them, that he would. *Amadáin*, they are." Typical of her cousin to not even say hello before tearing into a tantrum.

Mrs. Hawkins leaned toward Annie. "Your cousin, I presume."

"I'm afraid so." Annie made introductions.

"Mrs. Moran is my mother-in-law," Aileen said. "I'll just be Miss O'Shannon here in America, if you don't mind."

The Hawk's chin wrinkled as she prepared to speak. "We do

not mind at all if that is what you wish. However, the officials are not idiots, child."

Annie was surprised Mrs. Hawkins had understood that Irish word.

Aileen balled her fists as though she'd bust someone herself. Even in her heeled shoes, she only reached Annie's chin. Annie gazed at her. "What did you do, Aileen?"

"I did nothing, Annie. They had no right. A buttonhook! They peeled my eyelids with a buttonhook. I've never been so humiliated in all my life. That is . . . until they put me in a cattle pen."

"A what?" Annie thought she must have gone crazy on the journey.

Mrs. Hawkins took Aileen by the arm. "Come along, love. I'm sure it could not have been as bad as all that."

Aileen pulled away. "'Twas, I tell you. Those waiting pens were no larger than a cattle stall. Smaller, really. They had no reason to detain me."

"And?" Annie asked.

"And what?"

"What did you say when they did all that?"

"You bet I said something, but 'twas not what I said, Annie lass. 'Twas what I did."

Annie massaged her temple as the hired driver hoisted Aileen's sizable trunk onto his shoulder and they strode back to the ferry. "Did you hit the man, Aileen? The health inspector?"

"Square in the jaw."

Annie rolled her eyes. "I'm surprised they let you go at all."

Mrs. Hawkins laughed and pulled the lass to her. "You'll be staying at my boardinghouse, but no boxing the staff."

Aileen, to her credit, blushed. "Pleased and delighted, ma'am. I'm sure you are more civilized over there."

Annie urged her toward the ramp to the ferry. "Just so you know, I'm the staff. Me and Mrs. Hawkins. Don't upset her, Aileen. She's been very kind."

"Annie, I never meant—"

Annie picked up the scarf Aileen had dropped and pushed it toward her, muffling whatever it was she was going to say.

11

WHEN THEY GOT to the house, Annie settled Aileen into her room. "Grace is another boarder, a very fine lass, and she's to be wed soon."

"How wonderful for her. Where is she now?"

"She is a nanny for the Parker family, four children. Most nights she comes home, but when Mr. Parker's sister is visiting, she often stays over."

"That sounds like so much fun. I love children."

You are one, Annie wanted to say. "Come on, I'll show you the bathtub." As she walked down the hall, she told herself that if Aileen didn't have the courtesy to apologize for the lie that sent Annie away, she wouldn't mention it either.

When they entered the bathroom, Aileen's eyes grew wide. "That is where you bathe?" She unlaced her shoes and hopped into the empty tub. "'Tis so deep. What a luxury, Annie."

"Indeed it is. A bit unlike the cattle troughs we used in Ireland. If you want hot water, we have to stoke the stove downstairs and wait for the water to heat up, and then it can be fairly slow to pump upstairs. We have to plan ahead and space out our turns." She showed her how the faucets worked once she got out. "But you'll be wanting a bath now, I suppose." She wrinkled her nose, regarding her cousin.

"I suppose I do."

"Ah, Mrs. Hawkins predicted so. The water should be ready to go." She turned the hot faucet and the pipes moaned. Finally water came out and she put the stopper in the bottom of the tub.

Annie drew in a long breath. "Time for me to help Mrs. Hawkins put the finishing touches on supper. Can you manage, Aileen?"

"I can, thank you."

"Aileen, tell me no one else is coming after you. Your parents, they're staying in Ireland, aye?"

Aileen sputtered. "Of course they are, but why would you care?"

"After the way your father treated me, you should not have to ask why I don't want him coming after me in America." She wanted to say more but bit her lip. Aileen would deny she'd carried any responsibility, as she'd done before Annie was taken away.

"Oh, Annie Gallagher. Afraid of your own shadow, you are. Da was not happy you hardly served your penance."

"My what? You listen to me, Aileen. I did nothing—"

"That's what he called it, not me, so. 'Tis all in the past. Johnny Flynn is as well, thanks be to God. Were you the one who called him an *eejit*? He was. Let's not argue, Annie. You're here. I'm here. They are not."

Forget it all as though it had never happened? Annie wanted nothing more, and she'd nearly accomplished it until Aileen tagged along to America after her. "Get comfortable with things here. I'm going to the kitchen. The back stairs are just beyond the bathroom."

Trying to calm herself, Annie left Aileen in the bathroom and unpacked her cousin's things, reminding herself that she was the housekeeper and she had to do her job. Among her cousin's clothes was a small linen bag that felt as though it had some coins inside, something only a pampered lass would have. Annie laid them on the windowsill closest to Aileen's bed.

She rubbed the back of her neck when she came downstairs to the kitchen. The aroma of freshly baked brown bread and Mrs. Hawkins's famous peas porridge made Annie's stomach rumble. The porridge—a combination of peas, a bit of mint from the garden, and fresh milk—was one of Annie's favorite meals. When Annie had first come to Hawkins House, Mrs. Hawkins had guessed she'd like it, saying it was what all mothers made for their wandering children when they made their way home. Annie didn't know about that, but she did enjoy it.

Annie wrapped a towel around her hand and removed the large pot from the stove by its swinging handle, setting it on an iron trivet on the kitchen table. Mrs. Hawkins began ladling the peas porridge into the sieve, and Annie used the wooden pusher to squeeze the mixture into a clean bowl. It was a difficult process because the porridge was so thick, but well worth the effort.

When they finished, Annie, arms aching, carried the cooking pot to the sink. She nearly dropped it when loud wails erupted from the hall.

"What is the matter, love?"

Annie turned to see Mrs. Hawkins waddling through the kitchen doorway into the hall, wringing her hands within the depths of her apron.

"I've been robbed. My wee money sack was in my trunk and now 'tis gone!" Aileen roared.

Annie bit the inside of her cheek. "Calm down, Cousin. I unpacked your trunk while you bathed. The sack is on the windowsill. No one has robbed you. You forget where you are." And a long time Aileen had been in that bath too. Annie had done all that and helped prepare peas porridge in that time.

Aileen sniffed. "I could go back if I've a mind to."

"Then go."

Annie's wee cousin scrunched up her face. "You'd like to go home, wouldn't you, Annie? But there is no one there who will have you."

Annie glared at her, ready to ignore the presence of her employer and show the lass where her place was. "I'll deal with you later," she mumbled. She turned and carried the pot of porridge to the dining room. Just as she got to the hall, Grace entered.

As if to answer Annie's silent question, Grace explained her presence while she hung up her coat. "Mr. Parker took the children on an outing to the park. Said they'd be having sausages and pretzels from the vendor for supper and didn't need me the rest of the day. He's been trying to spend more time with them since . . ."

Annie knew she meant since the children's mother had passed away. "Aye, I suppose so," Annie answered. "That's good."

"Aye, 'tis. And I'm happy for it today. I'm knackered. Interviewed five potential nannies, and either the children did not like them or the other way round."

"I do hope you can find a proper nanny to take your place, Grace."

"From your lips to God's ears, so."

God wasn't on speaking terms with Annie, it seemed.

Grace helped her set the table. Annie was thankful Aileen hadn't followed her. She seemed to be having a conversation with the Hawk back in the kitchen.

"'Twill need to be someone young with a lot of energy, so." Grace poured herself a glass of water. "But somehow all the applicants I've received are doddery and somber. The children need so much more than that."

Grace had been working long hours. Not even the children's

aunt's visit had shortened her days. Four children to care for. Annie could not imagine it. It was good Grace was getting some time off. "Go freshen up before dinner, Grace. We don't need help."

Aileen cleared her throat behind Annie. Annie took a step to the side. "This here is my cousin Aileen herself."

"Just come from Ireland, are you? You are very welcome here, Aileen." Grace greeted her as though they were friends already.

Aileen's face revealed a thin smile.

Annie tried to relax her shoulders as she walked back to fetch the rest of the supper. Aileen stopped her. "I apologize. My temper. I didn't mean no one wanted—"

Annie nodded. "Never mind." The sound of the front door opening and closing caused them both to turn in that direction. Kirsten marched in. Without comment, the lass climbed the stairs.

Mrs. Hawkins edged past Annie with a pot of tea. "She's home early and about time. I telephoned over to the factory and gave Mr. Watson, her boss, an earful."

"I'll get her."

Mrs. Hawkins shook her head. "We won't wait. The porridge will get cold. She'll come down if she's hungry, love."

It was true that peas porridge was not as good cold. Grace left her conversation with Aileen and helped carry in the last of the hot dishes, and they sat down, joining Aileen, who seemed to think she was to be served.

Mrs. Hawkins clicked her spoon against her glass, and Grace and Aileen finally ceased their chattering. "Let us thank God for our bounty." She bowed her head and proceeded. When she finished, she tapped her fingers together. "Now, let's eat. Who's hungry?"

The pipes overhead began to rattle. Annie looked up. "Is she taking a bath now?" Aileen had surely used all the water they had heated earlier.

Mrs. Hawkins put a hand on Annie's arm. "Perhaps you better go check, love. She might be ill."

Annie glanced down at her untouched porridge and pushed back her chair. When she got to the bathroom, the door was locked. She knocked. "Kirsten? Are you ill?" She held her ear to the door.

The reply was faint. "Go away."

"What is the matter?"

"Annie, go, please."

"At least let me get you some warm water. The bathwater must be terribly cold."

She heard the faucet squeal, and the banging pipes silenced. The smell of Vaseline wafted from within.

"What are you doing, Kirsten? Let me help you."

"You can't help."

The door suddenly opened and Kirsten stood there, hair dripping, a towel wrapped around her body.

"Let me go get some hot water."

Kirsten pulled her into the room and shut the door.

Although the girl's hair was flung over her face, Annie thought she noticed something amiss. She reached up and pushed away a few strands. She gasped. "What happened to you? Did someone attack you on the street?"

Kirsten turned away and cranked the faucet on. The pipes shook once again. Kirsten stuck both hands under the faucet and shivered. "I lost my job, Annie."

"Why? What happened?" Annie grabbed another towel from the stack she had earlier left on a shelf near the window. Wrapping it around Kirsten's shoulders, she urged the girl away from the water.

"I was bad."

"You are not bad. Tell me what happened."

Kirsten turned toward her and flipped her hair back, revealing several fresh bruises. "A good girl doesn't tempt men." She dropped to the linoleum floor beside the tub.

Her words sent Annie right back to Ireland and the doctor's office. *"A sinner of the worst kind."*

"What are you saying?"

"He . . . How do I say it? . . . He forced himself on me."

"Nay. Who? The fellow you thought was following you?"

"*Nein.* My boss."

"Mr. Watson . . . hurt you. Did he . . . did he violate you, Kirsten?" She gripped Kirsten's hands.

"*Ja.*" She sobbed into her towel.

"I am so sorry for this trouble, Kirsten." She thought about the man who had come around with questions. "The man you thought followed you earlier, Kirsten, was he a Pinkerton?"

"A what?"

"A detective. Those men . . . they conspired against you, I daresay. This was not your fault." Even as Annie said that, she fought the urge to sink back to the place she'd taken her mind to when she was in the Magdalene Laundry, but she was losing the battle. To escape to that dreamworld meant one could not control what was happening, and Kirsten needed Annie to have her wits about her now. She swallowed the salty taste in her mouth. "You . . . uh, Kirsten . . . you did not invite this attention, isn't that so?"

Kirsten nodded, sucking in her lower lip. "You will not want to be in my company anymore, Annie. Neither will the others. I am a bad influence on *gut* Christian women."

"You are here to cleanse your sins, child."

Annie's knees began to ache from the memory. She had to sit down on the floor. "We . . . we cannot allow this, Kirsten."

"It is done, Annie. I am a soiled woman. Without this job, Jonas and I . . . It was the only way . . ." She could not continue.

What had happened to Kirsten had nearly happened to Annie, and all her efforts to put it in the past failed in that moment.

"You listen to me, lass," Neil snarled. "Forget about your dead father. He left ye nothing. You're alone, see? I've no obligation to care for a Protestant."

She started to jump out of the wagon. He caught her around the waist and tugged her back. Then he kept one arm around her until they reached the laundry the nuns ran. "Your new home," he said.

Neil left her sitting in a hall with a handful of other girls. They stared, waiting for her explanation, the girls wearing identical slack, drab gowns. They'd already shared their reasons for being there: a petty theft, a pregnancy, a father who had knocked teeth out and might do worse next time. Now it was Annie's turn.

"I should not be here."

"And we should?" a dark-haired lass asked. "Why are you so special?"

"I don't mean that. I'm here because of a misunderstanding. My uncle brought me here because my cousin said . . . uh . . . a lad she courted, he kissed me against my will and Aileen said 'twas my fault. Vengeful, she was."

One of the girls shrugged. "Happens all the time, don't you know."

"But my uncle stole from me. As soon as I explain so, I'll be off."

The one expecting a babe looked away.

The toothless girl spoke up. "Maybe we'll all get out when we explain ourselves."

The girl with the full, round belly sighed.

"Shh. Here she comes."

The nun returned and bid Annie to follow her. The sound of an iron door scraping across the concrete floor sent shivers up Annie's spine. She hadn't thought the place would be this . . . this repugnant. Pink flowers bloomed outside the door, but not a ray of sun entered this hall. A shadowy evil dripped from every crevice of the stone tunnel the nun led her down. When they got to the end, another spine-curdling scraping of a door. They stood inside a room with a table, an open cabinet filled with metal objects and jars stuffed with cotton, and a desk where a man sat staring up at them.

"The doctor will see you now," the nun told her.

"I . . . uh, I don't need a doctor. There was a mistake."

"This one, is she unsoiled?" the doctor asked.

The nun shook her head and backed out of the room.

"Come here," the man said, holding out his hand like . . . like the caring father Annie had just lost. "You can explain yourself to me."

"I'm not to stay here long," she said, worrying about what kinds of things the instruments on the shelves had been used for. "My uncle . . . he doesn't want me, but I can take care of myself—"

"I won't hurt you," he said, still holding out his hand. "Let me take care of you."

She inched forward.

"Do you know why you are here?"

When she shook her head, she felt her whole body tremble.

"You are here to cleanse your sins, child. You do know you're a sinner—and of the worst kind."

She dared to speak. "What is the worst kind, sir?"

His fingers slid down her arm to her wrist. "The worst are girls who are so lovely, who have skin soft and smooth . . ."

The doctor pressed his face against her neck and she struggled to get free. The door squealed again and he broke from her. The nun reappeared, bringing in two more girls. "Wait," he ordered the nun.

"I demand you let me out of here," Annie said.

The back of the doctor's hand struck her face, sending shards of pain to her eyes. "You will not speak unless you are asked to. Is that understood?"

She nodded, her jaw aching. At that moment she realized what kind of place she had been taken to. She would have no rights. No one would listen to her. She watched as the others received a physical examination, unpleasant but not as frightening as hers had been. As they filed out to leave, Annie was last in line. She felt the doctor's hand along her back and then across her bottom. She moved to follow the others in time to escape him.

Annie had been lucky. Another day in the laundry and she would have surely suffered the same fate Kirsten had today. Folks didn't talk about it outside the laundry, but inside, the lasses did, and Annie knew most of them had been assaulted the way Kirsten was. A tremor ran down to Annie's chin as she forced herself to attend to the frightened girl. "We have to do something." She rubbed Kirsten's arms with a towel. The girl's chill seemed to seep right through her into Annie. Someone had to stand up for women like Kirsten. No one had done so for the women of the Magdalene Laundries. Now, here in America, Annie could not stand by. She could not, though where she'd find the strength for this she did not know.

12

STEPHEN GROANED when the bells clanged on his alarm clock. A postman's day started early, and today it seemed way too early.

Rising to visit the washroom down the hall, he first pulled on his wool slippers, then kicked them off. It was too warm. Sleepily, he clambered down the hall, tripping and sending an empty metal milk crate scooting across the floor.

"Quiet," someone called from the next room.

Stephen forgot who was living there now. New tenants came and went almost weekly. It was hard to keep up, and no wonder why. The other room was small, too small. He'd looked at it before he rented his own. Davis had told him Stephen's apartment used to be bigger but he'd put up a wall and created another apartment to bring in extra income.

"Times are tough all over," he'd said.

Davis was lucky he had a stable renter with a good job in Stephen. When he returned to his room, he clicked on the electric light and began whisking up shaving suds. When he was done with his razor, he splashed cold water on his face. As he gazed into the mirror and buttoned on his collar, he tried to remember the Irish tune he'd learned last week. After just a brief visit to the dance hall, he'd remembered the tune and tried to repeat it. Perhaps he should learn to play the pennywhistle. He'd heard it wasn't difficult. Maybe Annie would be impressed.

He paused to sit a moment and pray. His day always went better when he began that way. The times he had felt God with him the strongest, he'd been praying, holding the family Bible. His father had not taught him the ways of God, but Stephen's mother had been a faithful woman and encouraged Stephen and his brother to seek righteousness. When Stephen was the head of his own household, he would take on the role of spiritual leader like his father should have, not neglect it. He reached for the Bible and thought about the births, deaths, and marriages recorded there. *When will I find my family, Lord?*

Seek me.

Yes. Following God's laws, being obedient, reading the Bible. The answer would come. Someday.

The psalm he read did quiet his spirit, and he continued to prepare for his day.

He strolled outside just as the horizon brightened above the roofs. A rather warm day for the first of October, but thankfully summer's humidity had waned. Stephen could not remember a more sweltering summer during his lifetime. Despite snarling dogs and treacherous streets littered with piles of horse manure, he preferred his job to working inside a hot factory.

When he got to the post office to pick up his load, Minnie was waiting for him. "Stephen, great news! Leonard's got so many investors now, your dollar is worth two."

"Two dollars? How can that be?" He lowered his voice, feeling as though he shouldn't announce the profit like a theater barker.

"It's no secret there's a lot of money in America. My Leonard has learned how to earn some of it. Hardworking folks like ourselves deserve to join in the prosperity, wouldn't you say?"

"I can't argue." He could use that money now. "Say, Minnie,

how about—?" He halted when he saw the postmaster glaring at them. "Uh, never mind. Better get back to work."

Before he set out on his shift, he stopped by his apartment. He'd forgotten his lunch.

Davis saw him coming and waved him into the office. "Listen, son. There was a bill collector asking for you. He didn't think I knew his business, said he was a friend. But I know these types."

"I . . . I don't understand. I've kept up on my bills." He began to sweat, wondering if he could be absolutely certain he had. "Did he say who sent him?"

"He didn't. I told him it was cowardice to come snooping around after a man's left for the day."

"Well, I thank you for that." It had to be Murray's doing. What would it take to convince the man Stephen was doing his best?

"Adams, I've had tenants before who had thugs come collect from them. If the police come too, I can't deny entry to your apartment. Wherever you keep your cash up there—bankbooks, whatever—I'd suggest you bring it down here and put it in my safe."

"Uh, I don't know, Mr. Davis. I mean, I appreciate the offer. I don't want to trouble you."

Davis put a hand on Stephen's shoulder. "You can trust me. I run a business here. I'm not going to run off. This is where I live and work. And if your money is in my safe, no bill collectors can claim it. Always better safe than sorry."

"You're right. I'll be right back." A fellow had to trust somebody, and Davis was a good man.

Stephen dropped his mailbag inside Davis's door and then hurried upstairs. He grabbed an apple and wrapped a bit of cheese in the brown paper his neighbor Mrs. Jacobs had given him with some sweet rolls. Another reason for never wanting to leave his neighborhood was that woman, who lived a few buildings down from him. She baked for several restaurants and had made Stephen her taster. Stuffing his food into his coat pocket, he retrieved his money box. He paused and then opened his accounting ledger. When he ran his finger along the line for the undertaker, he realized his mistake. He had skipped that line and forgotten to pay. An honest mistake, but one that set his head to pounding. With his paycheck from last Saturday cashed, he could pay Murray, and he'd do it today.

He took the money box down to Davis, who wrote him a quick receipt.

"Just to make you feel better," he said. "You come here to get it anytime. I'll answer this bell. It rings in my apartment if you press the button down here. Ring it with two short taps, and then hold it down for a bit. That way I'll know it's you."

"All right. Thank you."

Stephen hurried back to work with the payment for the undertaker and a little extra bit of cash in his pocket. He hadn't left much in that box in Davis's safe. Not this time, anyway.

Later, as the noon hour drew near, Stephen approached the bookshop. He had dropped off the undertaker's payment and thought he could now indulge in a book. But even if he found none to buy, he wanted to browse a bit, see what this new trend in children's literature was that Davis spoke of. He turned onto Worth Street just as his pocket watch showed noon.

Two red- and white-striped awnings tented over the plate-glass windows of Bourne Booksellers. He paused a moment to admire the tomes on display. A book titled *Lives of the Hunted* with a green forest on the cover surrounded by gold-leaf decorative trim. Next to that stood a book with a brown leather cover. Not a new book, but *Pembroke*, a novel by Mary E. Wilkins, was still in demand. Being an avid reader of the *New York Times*,

Stephen had heard of both books and knew *Pembroke* would not be a choice for him. He was not taken by the other title enough to purchase it, either. The window did not hold a copy of H. G. Wells's *The First Men in the Moon*, which sounded like a good read. Alone in the other window stood the book everyone had been talking about: *The Wonderful Wizard of Oz* by L. Frank Baum. Despite being introduced last year, the story was still immensely popular. It had even been mentioned as a possible theater production. This book had a green cover and was more lushly illustrated than the others. In fact, the illustrator's name, W. W. Denslow, was prominently displayed on the cover along with the author's.

Stephen pushed open the door, sending a little bell jingling much like the one Dexter had at his diner. He greeted the proprietor, who stood behind a counter. "Here's your mail."

"Thank you. Care to browse a bit while you're here?"

"Certainly I would." Stephen proceeded to weave his way around the book stacks. Near the front, close to the display windows, he noticed two mothers in conversation. One held the hand of a pretty little girl with blonde ringlets, and the other cradled an infant in her arms.

"I wish there were more books like this one for children," the mother with the infant proclaimed. She held out a copy of Baum's book.

"I know what you mean. I perused it. You can read a chapter at a sitting and there are delightful illustrations. It's not just for children, it seems. I would say it's a story adults would enjoy as well. I might even persuade Mr. Bainbridge to read it to the older children."

They both laughed over the prospect of a father reading to his children. Stephen would read to his, if he had any, without coercion.

The first mother looked down at her daughter. "Stop pulling, Lucille. Mother is not ready to go yet."

The infant-toting mother rocked slightly with her bundle. She looked back to her friend. "And what's more, I tell you, those old-fashioned fairy tales gave me such a fright when I was a child. I'd rather read Dorothy's adventure in Oz to my own children even if my husband does not."

"Agreed," the other mother said.

They both took copies to the cash register counter to purchase them. As they moved away, Stephen noticed that he hadn't been the only one eavesdropping. Leaning against a bookcase opposite him stood Annie Gallagher. She gave him a slight smile.

He waved and approached her.

"Good day, Mr. Adams. I shouldn't be surprised to see you in here since you said you enjoyed reading."

"Indeed I do. Books provide great pleasure for me."

She wore a sapphire-blue dress with a cream-colored scarf wrapped around her shoulders. Her fair complexion and hazel eyes seemed to glow against the backdrop of brown and black book covers, even though her expression seemed strained.

"Are you feeling well, Miss Gallagher?" He reached for her hand and brushed his lips across the fabric of her glove.

"I am well, just a bit tired. We . . . uh, we are adjusting to having more boarders, is all."

"Oh, well, it's delightful you were able to get away and come to the bookshop."

"I adore books." She turned to the stack and drew a finger across the spines as though searching for a particular title among those in the children's literature section.

The cap he'd pressed under his arm as he entered the store grew heavier with each passing moment. The circulating ceiling fans did little to cool the air. Outside he'd noticed a crispness in the air, but in the bookshop it seemed rather warm.

Stephen had to say something soon or Annie Gallagher would walk right out of his day. "Say, did you notice they have copies of *The Wonderful Wizard of Oz*?"

She grinned and pointed toward the display in the window.

"Ah, yes. You are reading it, you mentioned. I'm thinking of purchasing a copy."

"I believe you'd like it, Mr. Adams. And I hope you do get your own copy someday." She breathed deeply as though just standing in the shop had renewed a weary heart.

Thank you, Lord, for this opportunity.

"Ah, indeed." He glanced for a moment at the women who were at that instant accepting their wrapped books from the bookseller. He turned back to Annie. "All of New York seems to be buzzing about that book. After I read a few chapters, I'd be delighted if you would have a conversation with me about it."

Her face reddened. "You did mention that, aye."

"I mean to say . . . my friend Dexter and I discuss books all the time . . . and I thought if you would like . . ." He was destroying his chance. "If you have the leisure, I mean."

"While that sounds delightful, I am afraid I have less and less leisure with each passing day. My cousin has come over from Ireland, so, and another boarder needs me—"

"I'm sorry, Miss Gallagher. I should not have imposed."

"Oh no. I'm delighted you asked me. 'Tis just . . . not the best time."

"I understand."

"I should be going, Mr. Adams. I have to finish my errands for Mrs. Hawkins, and I should not be away too long." Wrinkles formed across her brow. Something was occupying her thoughts.

She took a step toward the door, her skirts sweeping across

the floorboards like a ribbon of dragonflies. Never had he seen such enchanting elegance.

He remembered the concern the police sergeant had voiced earlier. "Is everything all right over at Hawkins House?"

His question seemed to unnerve her. "Of course. Why do you ask?"

"Uh . . . well, a houseful of ladies. Please do tell me if I can do anything to assist you."

She looked at him strangely, her expression changing as her facial muscles tightened. "This houseful of ladies, Mr. Adams, can take care of themselves."

"I did not mean—"

"Thank you for your concern." She softened a bit. "Very kind of you indeed. Good day, so."

He was still staring at the bell on the door when the young mothers exited after Annie. He was trying, wasn't he? He scratched his head. He didn't know how to act around women as beautiful as Annie Gallagher.

He did want to read that book. He snatched the copy from the window and then decided to take a copy of *The Master Key*, a new novel also by L. Frank Baum, to the counter.

When he stepped out onto the sidewalk, he stuffed the wrapped packages into his postal bag. He would read them at night before bed. One had to have something to talk about in social situations, and maybe one day he would actually have a conversation with someone other than Dexter and the publisher to whom he paid rent.

13

ANNIE FELT NEARLY as sick as Kirsten and only sipped at her soup after returning from her shopping trip. If the postman had suspected there was trouble at Hawkins House—not to mention a Pinkerton—they had to do something right away to ensure that Kirsten, and indeed all of them there, were safe. They had confided in Grace last night because she was sure to see Kirsten and would need an explanation. And Grace was a kind lass. She would keep it to herself for the moment. Annie needed time to determine how women in America could be spared from places like laundries or reformatories—whatever they called them on this side of the Atlantic.

During her entire outing, save for the brief conversation with the postman, she had been considering her options. Taking legal action against Kirsten's boss did not seem feasible. Judges didn't rule in a woman's favor, even if they would give them an audience. The best thing for Kirsten would be to start over somewhere.

Annie had to speak to the Hawk soon. The woman was lunching with a friend and would return at any time now. Annie pushed away her soup bowl and tried to concentrate.

She'd seen Mrs. Hawkins stand up for herself against that Pinkerton fellow. Thinking about that, she went to the back door but did not see anything unusual. She wondered if he'd seen Kirsten come home battered and bruised or if a neighbor would report it.

She paced the kitchen, worrying her lip. Perhaps she and Mrs. Hawkins could visit the police station and plead their case. Kirsten was innocent. The fact that Owen McNulty was taking so long to report what he'd learned about that man could mean bad news. Either there'd be no stopping the man or the police were not willing to help.

She stood over the sink, pulling at her sleeves. Her father had once told her not to borrow trouble. Easier to speak than follow, that.

After checking the coal supply, she set a kettle on. Most conversations went better over afternoon tea.

Mrs. Hawkins entered by the back kitchen door, seemingly drawn by the sound of the whistling teakettle. "How kind of you to ready tea, love. Are you well this afternoon? You didn't eat your soup there."

Annie picked up her bowl. That woman didn't miss much. "I'm sorry, Mrs. Hawkins. I am fine, so. Thank you. Did you enjoy your lunch?"

"I did. Clam chowder."

"Sounds delightful."

"What about our Kirsten? Did you see her off this morning?"

"She is not well."

"Poor dear. Should I send for the doctor?"

Annie reminded herself that not all doctors were evil. The doctor Mrs. Hawkins was referring to was the woman's close friend and confidant. Annie understood this but still could not dismiss the face of that horrid man in Ireland from her nightmares. Now, however, she had to be sensible. *Keep your wits, Annie. Stay calm.* "Perhaps you should. But, Mrs. Hawkins . . ." Annie searched her mind for the right words. She hemmed and hawed until the teakettle's blast overtook her voice. She pulled it from the stove and set it on a trivet. Kirsten had been sure no good Christian women would accept her now. What if Mrs. Hawkins had trouble understanding? "I . . . um . . . Aye, get the doctor."

The woman scrubbed her hands at the kitchen sink with Pears soap and then dried them on a white tea towel while Annie waited for her. "I'll hail Jules. I should get one of those telephones. You know, for emergencies. Mrs. Jenkins next door is out for the day or I would use hers. Does she have a fever, love?"

"I don't believe so."

"What about Grace? Did you see her today? She hasn't caught it yet, has she?"

"Uh, she has not."

"Good. We wouldn't want it passed along to the children. Aileen?"

"'Tis only Kirsten, Mrs. Hawkins."

"One cannot be too careful with infectious diseases. Thank the Lord nothing has spread. But poor girl. I should check on her." She ignored the tea Annie set in front of her and started for the back stairs.

"Wait."

The woman turned around.

"We need . . . the doctor. I mean . . . we need him to be . . . discreet." Annie stared at the floor tile. "'Tis not an infectious disease. She is not ill. Her boss did something to her."

"Oh, dear. I see."

Annie rushed to her side. "You don't understand. 'Twas not her fault. Her boss forced her."

Tears formed at the corners of the woman's eyes and rapidly spread down toward her hooked nose. "Oh, poor Kirsten."

"I know. I . . . I should have said something earlier."

Mrs. Hawkins raised her graying brows. "How long have you known about this . . . this assault, love?"

"She told me last night." Annie's face grew hot. "I have been trying to think of something . . . a way to keep her safe. Someone has to do something."

Aileen's chirpy voice resounded from the opposite end of the hall. "Do something about what?"

Annie had forgotten she'd tried to keep her occupied waxing the wainscoting. Unfortunately Hawkins House had thin walls and little privacy. Before long they would all know anyway. Kirsten's bruised face would take weeks to heal.

Annie trudged into the hall to hush Aileen and stopped short when a white envelope drifted through the mail drop in the door. Ignoring her cousin, she rushed to scoop it up, opened the door, and called to Mr. Adams. "Thank you."

He turned, smiled warmly, and waved.

Some days the postman came two or three times if there was something to deliver. She wished his visits were better timed. There was so much commotion at Hawkins House now, it probably didn't matter anyway. Previously she'd had leisure to chat with all the delivery folks who dropped by but not now. She shut the door to find Aileen staring. "Come now, Cousin. You didn't speak to your postman at home?"

"Not like that. I think you're sweet—"

"Nonsense."

The lass shrugged. "As you wish, Annie Gallagher. Now tell me, what is the matter with that boarder who rooms across the hall?"

Annie looked to the top of the stairs. "What do you mean?"

"Saw her run out her door and into the bathroom. I think she vomited in there."

"She did. She is sick."

Mrs. Hawkins hurried past her and up the stairs.

Aileen stomped her wee foot. "Would someone tell me what's going on? What's got the pint sour?"

"None of your business. How about you go . . . polish the silver in the dining room?"

Aileen pouted as she went to the scullery to fetch supplies. Annie would deal with her later.

As she began to ascend the stairs, Mrs. Hawkins marched down wearing her feathered hat. "I have to go out. Some matters are best handled in person. Annie, you and Aileen see to the sweeping up, will you?"

After the woman hurried out, Annie entered the dining room and glared at her cousin. "The broom closet is in the scullery. First salt the rugs; it will make the colors bright again. Sweep them thoroughly and then remove them and sweep the downstairs rooms. I will be in the garden sweeping the back stairs and waiting for the iceman. Kirsten should sleep for a while, but if she needs anything, you get it for her and . . ." She hesitated, realizing Aileen would likely see Kirsten's face. She should give some kind of explanation. "She's in a bad way, Aileen. Someone treated her ill. Her face . . . Well, she won't want to talk about it. Just allow her privacy. Understand?"

Aileen scowled back. "All right. Don't I know what a drunk's face looks like."

"What? I'm warning you, Aileen."

"I won't say a word. Off with you. We will be fine."

Annie glanced down at the letter in her hands. Another letter for Kirsten. What would they tell her brother when he arrived?

14

STEPHEN HAD INQUIRED all along his route, but so far he'd had no luck finding anyone who even came close to being a writer. It was a ridiculously hopeless endeavor. He met Dexter at his counter. "Salami sandwich and coffee, please, Dex."

"Coming right up. Didn't discover a bestseller, I take it?"

"Nah."

"Don't fret, Stephen. Something will come up."

Stephen swirled a sugar lump into his black coffee. "Thanks, friend. There's an automobile show over at the Madison Square Garden next week. I can get off early. Want to go?"

"A what, you say?"

"You know. Horseless carriages. It's a display of all the new machines soon to be produced in mass. Could never buy one myself, but it might be fun to look. What do you say?"

"Ah, sorry, fella. After I close up the diner, Harriet expects me at home. You understand."

Stephen said he understood. Annie Gallagher had been pleasant enough to him, but he wasn't quite ready to invite her on an outing. If she were willing, however, he'd give up the automobile show for paper dolls or hat shopping or whatever she wanted.

Dexter pointed to Stephen's mailbag. "You have so much mail to deliver today."

Stephen looked to his bulging sack. "Oh, that. I bought a couple of books at Bourne's and haven't taken them out of my bag yet."

"Wonderful. You get a raise?"

"No. I'll eat beans for a week to make up for it." Books were the escape of lonely men, although Stephen wouldn't admit that out loud. "I need to keep up so I can talk with people. You know."

"You mean that girl you have your eye on. I am sorry she did not come to that dance you talked about last week."

Stephen should not have told him he'd admired Annie since he couldn't be sure anything would come of it. "Don't worry about me, Dexter."

"Let me worry about who I should worry about."

Stephen shrugged, unable to hide his disappointment.

"So she likes books. You like books too. That's a start."

"She's not interested in being anything but friendly, like most folks when they pick up the mail delivery."

Dexter laughed and picked up a plate of food from the pass-through. "That did not stop me with Harriet, my friend. These things can be worked out. You woo her. She will pay attention."

"If you say so."

When Dexter returned from serving a table, he pointed to the sack. "Show me."

"You want to see what I purchased?"

"Why not?"

He pulled out the copy of *Wonderful Wizard.*

Dexter's eyes went wide. "You got one. Can I see it?" He opened the cover and smiled when he saw the illustration of the Scarecrow with the list of chapters. He turned the page and sighed as he silently read the dedication. Stephen had read it also and had responded similarly, but with a bit of wistfulness. *This book is dedicated to my good friend & comrade, My Wife. L.F.B.*

"Just as amazing as people are saying," Dexter stated, turning a few more pages.

"Say, after I'm done with it, I'll hand it off to you so you can give it to your kids."

Dexter shook his head. "Let's split the cost. What do you say? I know how much it set you back, so seventy-five cents apiece?"

"You don't mind that it's been read first?"

"Nah. After my kids get ahold of it, no one will know the difference anyway. You should see how ragged that *Father Goose* book is. Seems like a deal for us both."

"Thanks, Dex."

After delivering his route, Stephen dropped by the post office to see if he might speak to Minnie again. He could draw out some of the money he'd deposited with Leonard and make a bigger payment to the undertaker and prevent his man from dropping by his apartment again. But she wasn't there. He should have realized sorters didn't work all day.

"May I have a word, Mr. Adams?"

He turned to find the postmaster, Mr. Sturgis, standing by a mail bin at the other end of the room. "Uh, good afternoon, Mr. Sturgis. I . . . was just leaving for home."

"This will only take a moment. In my office, please?"

Stephen followed the man to his small work space, where the postmaster closed the door behind them. There was only one chair, so they both stood.

"Is there some trouble?"

"I am not sure. I've noticed you having several conversations with a mail sorter."

"Uh, well, I do like to talk to folks. Is that a problem?"

"Not usually. I'm a bit concerned about our newest employee, Minnie Draper. She has been talking to quite a few mail carriers lately. I just don't want her to interfere with our operations."

"Oh, I'm sure that's not happening, sir. Perhaps if I suggest to her that she not be quite so . . . socially engaging. Would that help?"

"Perhaps. I would prefer you not have long conversations."

"Understood." Stephen put his hand on the doorknob.

"Mr. Adams?"

"Yes?"

"You will tell me if this employee does anything out of the line of normal duties, won't you? I would rather find out about it than have the postal inspectors uncover something and escort her out."

"We would not want that, sir."

Stephen left the office sweating. The cooler air outside did not refresh him. Both he and Minnie could lose their jobs if the postmaster found out they'd been conducting business on the clock. He'd have to get all his money out and be done with it.

Late that afternoon he stopped at the grocer on the corner of Elm to pick up a few things after work. He examined the potatoes and apples in the bins outside the door, chose two of each, and then entered.

"Stephen, my boy. How's the world treating you?" The proprietor, Mr. Gorman, greeted him wearing a white apron and holding out a turnip.

"Fine and dandy. What's this?"

"Just delivered, son. Would make a lovely addition to your Sunday stew."

"I don't cook much, Mr. Gorman."

The man frowned and put the vegetable back on the carefully constructed mound next to the cash register. "I know, I know. Roasting potatoes is your limit. You've told me before. What you need is a young lady to—"

"What I need is coffee and canned milk." Stephen laid his produce on the counter and then wandered to the back of the store, where Mr. Gorman stocked odds and ends. He was leafing through an outdated literary magazine when someone called his name.

"You see there? You are a reader, Adams."

"Davis." Stephen dropped the magazine back to the pile on the floor. "I was just picking up a few things for supper."

Alan Davis retrieved the magazine and squinted at it. "Planning on reading this during your meal?"

"I . . . uh, I don't know. I have some books. . . ."

"Ah, fine then. You've moved on from Verne."

"I finished that novel."

The man rubbed his chin, but before he could say anything else, someone called to him from the front of the store. "Uncle Alan, we are ready now."

Davis grinned at Stephen. "My niece and her husband. Visiting from Syracuse."

"How delightful." It seemed everyone had a big family.

"Good evening, Adams." He was halfway down the aisle when he turned around. "Don't spend too much money here, son. Rent's due at the end of the week."

Stephen let out a breath as the man joined his family at the cash register. He couldn't spend too much now that he had exhausted all of his expendable income.

As he was leaving, he encountered Mrs. Jenkins, the woman who lived next door to Hawkins House. After they exchanged pleasantries, she asked him to check in on the women at

Hawkins House. "I'll be away a few days, leaving the day after tomorrow, and it seems there has been some disturbance over there. They are such nice people. Sergeant McNulty will keep an eye on them, but you can't fault a lady for her concern. You deliver on the street every day and sometimes morning and afternoon. Tell me that if you see anything amiss, you'll contact the police, Mr. Adams."

"Certainly."

"I'm probably fretting needlessly. It's my nature."

"Don't worry, Mrs. Jenkins. The women there have friends to look out for them. And I will pay attention to your residence while you are gone as well. Shall I hold your mail until you return?"

"Thank you kindly. I will be home next week, so only halt it through Saturday, dear boy. I won't be going far, just visiting relatives in New Jersey."

"My pleasure. Have a wonderful time."

"Thank you, Mr. Adams. There cannot be too many watchful eyes."

Whether or not the woman was overly concerned, Stephen couldn't help but wonder. Owen McNulty had also voiced some apprehension. Just what was going on over there?

15

THE NEXT MORNING, after Annie and Kirsten finished cleaning up the kitchen and the day's bread was rising, Annie read Kirsten's latest letter to her.

By the second week in October, I will already be aboard the train for Manhattan, Kirstie. The package should arrive soon.

Kirsten began to cough, not one of those hacks that splits the air or anything. Just a wee, persistent cough. Dust, perhaps, if the delicate lass was particularly sensitive. The rug could use a beating outdoors before the cooler weather came. Annie would get to the task as soon as she could.

There was nothing else but a closing, so Annie put the letter away.

"Thank you for reading, Annie."

"My pleasure." Annie supposed Kirsten was uneasy about her brother coming given her situation with her former boss, so Annie said no more about it. While Kirsten searched in a sewing box for a needle to mend a stocking, Annie read her book silently.

Kirsten stiffened when she pricked her thumb with the needle.

"What is the matter?" Annie rose to help her, but the girl waved her away, placing her thumb in her mouth.

"I love my brother. He is a *gut* man, as I said." Her tone was flat.

"Then you'll be happy to see him, aye? He is certainly looking forward to seeing you."

"I look forward to it, but . . ." She leaned into the back cushion of the sofa, and Annie realized the girl was experiencing some physical discomfort. She'd not been outside the house since the attack, but still she seemed so tired. The doctor had not been around to see her yet, but Kirsten insisted she was fine, and Mrs. Hawkins told him to come at his convenience. There was nothing he could do anyway. The vile act was over with.

But this cough was another concern. And the fact that Kirsten was so jittery. She didn't seem able to sit still, as though she had hives and was trying not to scratch.

"Annie." Kirsten glanced toward the hall. Seemingly satisfied they were alone, she lowered her voice anyway. "He worries too much about me. The package, Annie. It has not arrived?"

"It has not yet. What is the trouble?"

"Nothing."

The sound of Mrs. Hawkins's heels on the wooden floor came clattering down the hall toward the parlor. "Tea, girls?" As she entered the room, Annie rose to help. "Thank you, love. Just put it by the window as always." She perched in her favorite chair. "We have had our talk, haven't we, Kirsten?"

"*Ja*, Mrs. Hawkins." Kirsten closed her eyes, obviously fighting back tears.

Annie grimaced. "What happened was not her fault, Mrs. Hawkins. You could not possibly understand—"

"Indeed I do know this, Annie. I just wanted you to be aware that Kirsten won't be going back to the awful factory, and she's agreed to obey our curfew. Rules—fair ones—keep a home running smoothly."

A home. Annie considered this and believed she should have referred to the place as a house, a boardinghouse, not a home. Turning toward her employer, Annie brought the woman her tea. "Here is your cup. Just the way you like it, milk and a lump of sugar."

"Thank you, love. I must seem like a pampered woman to you, but my life was not always pleasant."

Kirsten glanced up, eyes wide.

"Uh, no, Mrs. Hawkins," Annie said. "I know you have had difficult times. 'Tis just that what Kirsten has suffered—there is nothing she could have . . . Well, she's innocent, yet many would not understand, so."

Kirsten coughed again. Annie brought her tea and joined the girl on the sofa. "I would like to open an extensive library one day, and I believe girls who have had troubles like Kirsten would find it a haven for learning and enjoyment."

Kirsten wiggled a bit as Annie spoke.

Mrs. Hawkins held up a finger. "Ah, admirable, Annie. Books are windows to a world we might never otherwise begin to comprehend. We have a good collection at Hawkins House, and that's an excellent place to start."

Annie didn't want a part of someone else's library. She wanted to provide the whole, be the entrepreneur, the one in charge, so that she would know all would be well. She wanted to do it for Da and for herself because . . . that would be her home; this was Agnes Hawkins's home. "I do enjoy working here, and I'm grateful you employed my services, Mrs. Hawkins. But what I'm suggesting is a bit . . . different."

"Even so, you are welcome to any of my books, Annie. Everyone here is. I would like all my girls to think of this as their—"

Kirsten began wheezing and clutching her throat.

"Are you all right?" Annie asked.

Kirsten waved her thin fingers in the air. "Fine, fine. Thank you. I rest in my room now." She rushed out of the parlor and up the stairs.

Annie started to follow, but the Hawk stopped her. "Let her retire, love. That's the best thing for her. In a bit you can take her some of my special parsley-and-lemon tea to ease her coughing."

As they sat in the parlor with the window open to let in a breeze, a practice that Annie believed was healthy and Mrs. Hawkins allowed with reservation, Annie wondered aloud, "Mrs. Hawkins, do you think Jonas's impending arrival is upsetting Kirsten?"

The woman smacked her lips. "My, no. It is possible, though, it's entirely something else."

"What?"

"Time will tell if she's been left with child."

"Oh, Mrs. Hawkins, you don't think . . ."

"We shall not consider it yet, love." She reached for the newspaper. "We certainly had an extremely hot summer. I do hope the new century doesn't continue to bring us such unseasonable weather." When Mrs. Hawkins decided a subject was closed, it was.

"Do you mind if I retire and read a bit, Mrs. Hawkins?"

"Heavens, no. The morning chores are done. Enjoy."

Annie added the figures in her savings book again. If she had her own building apart from the immigrant-aid sector, no one would question its purpose and she wouldn't be worrying some Pinkerton would evict her. Kirsten could live there and not be worried about her brother or whatever it was that concerned her. A small apartment above the library would not be unreasonable. Annie wasn't determined to leave her employment at Hawkins House, if indeed it was not shut down, but she was determined to have something of her own, something to prove she really wasn't a sinner of the worst kind.

She needed to find a way to make money faster. If there was something she could sell . . . well, she would never part with her writing desk, and that was all she had.

Patience, please God.

Words and phrases like that sprang from the lips of every Irish person—*thanks be to God; please, God;* and *God's blessing on this place, this travel, this harvest.* . . . If Annie was going to become a true American, she'd need to break the habit. That's all it was, truly. Certainly he was not listening. She would have to do this by her own ingenuity.

Annie opened her book. With its colorful illustrations, *The Wonderful Wizard of Oz* was quite the marvel. Most children's books were in black-and-white or inked in just one or two colors. She opened to the chapter titled "The Cowardly Lion" and soon came to a part that told her something more about the wee protagonist.

> . . . and the great beast had opened his mouth to
> bite the dog, when Dorothy . . . heedless of danger,
> rushed forward and slapped the Lion upon his
> nose. . . . "Don't you dare to bite Toto! You ought to
> be ashamed of yourself, a big beast like you, to bite
> a poor little dog!"

Annie loved how strong Dorothy was. Where such bravery came from, she wished she knew.

When she finished the short chapter, she closed the book and stored it back under her bed. She liked to ponder what she read, taking her time to slowly savor the story. If she moved through it too quickly, the discovery would end too soon. She could read it again, but the real delight in any tale was the first time through it. Stephen Adams had wanted to chat about the book, but Annie supposed she would not have the opportunity now. Her primary obligation was to the boarders of Hawkins House, and any book discussions she might have in the future should involve them. A proper businesswoman conducted her affairs thus, focusing on her obligations.

The novel seemed to call to her from the place she'd stowed it, though. Papers bearing words were never silent, not for her. Everything she read seemed to revisit her throughout the day.

Mr. Baum had certainly thought up some interesting characters. How easily Dorothy befriended them. Even the Lion, though she had first been so angry with the beast for scaring her dog, Toto. Annie suspected that the author was going to show that the Scarecrow really did have a brain and the Tin Woodman really did have a heart. After all, the Tin Woodman was worried about stepping on bugs, for heaven's sake. She wasn't sure about the Lion, but that would be revealed. Dorothy did need to get back home, or at least she thought she did. She sure didn't belong in that strange world she was in.

Annie lay down to stare up at the plaster molding in the corners of the ceiling as she contemplated how this story might mirror real life. Annie was certainly on a journey as well. In the old Irish tales, tragic endings were common, doling out warnings to listeners to apply to their own lives. But *The Wonderful Wizard of Oz* was a modern tale, with a fresh twist, she'd heard, so one could assume Dorothy would find her way home happily. Annie couldn't be sure she'd experience a happy ending herself, not if she didn't work for it.

Annie's eyes grew heavy as she reclined on her bed. Hundreds of people in New York alone must be reading this book. Nearly every time she stopped in at the bookshop, she heard someone talking about it. Even the postman. The paper said the tale was very popular, calling it a . . . What did they say? A phenomenon? She rolled over to face her pillow, wondering who decided what was a phenomenon and what wasn't. She couldn't imagine who would be wise enough. Wizards didn't exist in this world.

She rose from her bed and paused at her desk, looking down at her open Bible. She'd kept reading it, perhaps as a link to her father. Just like every other book she read, the words there stayed with her. Unlike most, though, this one puzzled her uncomfortably. So much did not make sense, yet what she read, especially the Psalms, seemed to keep reciting in her mind. If only God did care enough for her to direct her the way Father Weldon had wished, perhaps she would know the joy the psalmist had written about in chapter 84.

She remembered the first time she knew for certain she was in a place where not even God cared to dwell.

The girls had been led to wee cells and locked inside. Annie sat with her knees pressed up to her chin, the only way she could sit in that space, pulling her sleeves down to cover her skin. The realization of what the doctor had in mind nauseated her until that misery was temporarily replaced by the horrific sensation of rats running over her feet and out between the bars in the door. Only when she heard their squeaking from a distance away did she try to breathe again.

She should not have been there, but no one was there to hear her. She lived in no one's heart now. Even God had abandoned her.

Yea, the sparrow hath found an house, and the swallow a nest for herself.

But nothing was that easy. Not for her.

Blessed are they that dwell in thy house: they will be still praising thee.

She dug her fingers into her hair. Surely it was not madness for these passages to spring to mind, was it?

Annie heard footsteps at the front of the house, so she made her way to the parlor. Aileen was browsing the pages of a magazine.

Her cousin glanced up. "I'm to help you with the brown Betty when you came out of your room."

Annie walked past her as she moved toward the kitchen. She spoke over her shoulder. "Has the doctor been here?"

The sound of Aileen's boots clattered along behind. "Oh, he has. Been here and left."

"Mrs. Hawkins should have beckoned me. I didn't hear a thing. Did you speak to Kirsten?"

"I did not. I did peek into her room, and she was asleep. A short time later the Hawk arrived with Doc in tow."

Annie turned and grabbed her cousin's arm. "Don't let her hear you call her that."

"I heard you say it."

Annie didn't remember using the name in front of Aileen. If she had, it was a mistake. Aileen didn't pick up on the social cues everyone else observed. Annie drew in a deep breath, reminding herself the Johnny Flynn business was in the past and better left there, and now she needed to treat Aileen like any other boarder. "Thank you for minding what I told you about Kirsten."

Aileen put her small hand on her hip. "You mean thank you for not talking to anyone. Honestly, Annie, how am I going to get to know anyone here if you don't allow me some freedom?"

"You've only been here a few days, Aileen!"

Annie mumbled under her breath as she turned toward the

scullery to fetch a bag of sugar. She returned for the apples. Aileen held the basket of red fruit out for her. "Want me to peel these?"

"That would be good."

Annie pulled a tin of lard down from a shelf and returned to the kitchen. While Aileen peeled, Annie closed her eyes. When she opened them again, Aileen hadn't disappeared like she'd hoped. Everything about the lass, from the point of her nose to the cut of her dress, reminded Annie of being sent to the laundry, the place where God had abandoned her. She tried not to think of it because whenever she did, panic pounded at her chest. She had to constantly remind herself she was not in Ireland anymore, and that had become thorny at best now that Ireland stared back at her through that wee freckled face.

Annie pulled the wrist of her shirtwaist over the heel of her left hand and turned toward the stairs. Right now, she needed to check on Kirsten.

The girl sat drinking tea as Mrs. Hawkins looked on. They both glanced up at her.

Annie sat on the edge of the bed. "Feeling better, Kirsten?"

The girl nodded.

Mrs. Hawkins motioned to Annie to join her in the hall. "The doctor says her bruises will heal fine. Now we'll wait to see if she's gotten with child."

Annie sensed the worry in Mrs. Hawkins's voice. "I'm sorry I did not suspect this sooner."

"Don't blame yourself, love. We will take good care of that girl and see that she has whatever she needs. If we have to later find a home for unwed mothers, well . . . we will deal with that if need be."

"Nay, Mrs. Hawkins. She should not be sent away. There are doctors . . . and metal doors . . . rats and spiders . . ." She put her hands across her face, desperately trying to maintain her sensibilities.

"Calm down, love. Nothing like that will happen to our Kirsten. You need to trust me."

"But I wanted to . . . *I* have to help her, Mrs. Hawkins."

"Of course you do. We both do." The woman gave her a little squeeze. "I do only what I wish others had done when I was younger. Not that I was in Kirsten's predicament precisely, but I have been a victim of others' apathy, and I will not stand by and see another girl . . . uh . . . I do what I can." She tapped her hand on her forehead.

"If you only knew, Mrs. Hawkins, what those places are like."

"I do know, love. I have been there myself."

"What do you mean?"

They heard Kirsten coughing again.

"We will talk about this later." Mrs. Hawkins went back into the room. Annie followed.

Annie collected another pillow to lift Kirsten's head a bit, thinking about how Mrs. Hawkins had probably visited reformatories in America. Different, so. Even if the American institutions were as horrendous as the place Father Weldon had rescued Annie from, visiting such a place did not reveal the tribulation of those locked inside. Those within the walls did not know from one moment to the next if they would be abused by so-called doctors or gnawed on by rodents. Annie wished Mrs. Hawkins would listen to her rather than expect Annie to blindly follow her guidance. Annie knew things, and that knowledge led to empathy, which in turn could be called upon as a voice for those who could not speak out. All she needed was Dorothy-like resolve, but obviously the Hawk didn't think Annie possessed it.

After lunch and before Annie needed to visit the fishmonger to pick up mackerel for the evening meal, she returned to her book. She read about the great ditch Dorothy and her friends encountered on their way to the Emerald City. The Lion thought they could jump it, and he agreed to carry them across on his back.

The next moment it seemed as if she were flying through the air; and then, before she had time to think about it, she was safe on the other side.

Aye. Safe on the other side. That was the place to be, but someone had to do the carrying on his back.

Everyone was afraid of something. The Scarecrow was afraid of fire.

She squeezed her eyes tight. She was afraid that if she couldn't find something to hang on to, she would be completely lost. In America she had found shelter and a job, and even a couple of women she could call friends. But those things were not enough to bring her the sense of belonging she so desperately needed, what she'd had when her father was alive. Dorothy needed that in the story. Annie did too, and the only places she felt truly secure were in church, when she could hear Reverend Clarke preach, and when she lost herself in a fictional world—the stories her father had written for her, *The Wonderful Wizard of Oz*, the mythological sayings in her father's Bible. God did not speak, but words of others carried the wisdom she longed to hear. Treasure is often buried.

The fearful mouse Nolan and the brave leader Omah—they were hers. Their words lived in her. She remembered a line from one story.

"Wisdom cannot be borrowed from a neighboring field. When wisdom's rain and sun fall upon the dirt at your own feet, you will find truth. If you look."

Your own feet. Not Mrs. Hawkins's. Annie's.

Annie cocked her head to one side as an idea kindled in her mind. Like *The Wonderful Wizard of Oz*, stories could make money, even lots of it. She had no physical object she could sell, but she had words. Perhaps hearing these things over and over again in her head did not mean she was daft after all.

Thank you, Nolan and Omah.

16

STEPHEN HAD LEARNED to whistle a reel called "Finnegan's Wake," or at least part of it, from the dances he'd gone to, and he whistled as he approached Hawkins House. The day felt cool as he trekked his route, at least compared to how hot the summer had been. He welcomed the crisp October air as he was sure the tenement dwellers a few streets over did. Maybe Annie would hear him, but even if she didn't, he had a package to deliver that would not quite fit into the mail slot. It was just slightly larger than a letter. She'd have to open the door.

By his second knock he finally heard footsteps. Glad that he wouldn't have to leave the package on the stoop, Stephen bent his head to follow the slow, creaking opening of the wooden door.

"What is it?"

Not Annie's voice.

"Postman. I have a delivery. Is Miss Gallagher available?"

"Gone to the fishmonger."

"Mrs. Hawkins, then?"

"Out visiting. Leave it on the stoop, sir?"

"I would rather it was safe inside, if you don't mind."

The door pushed open then, and a thin girl with nearly translucent skin reached for the package.

"Uh . . . it's for Miss Kirsten Wagner."

"That is me."

"Oh. Very well. Here you go, miss."

He tried to be as chipper as he could, but she did not respond in kind. She licked her chapped lips and lowered her head as she ducked back into the house.

"Have a fine day," he hollered at the solid door.

No response. No Annie Gallagher.

The next day Stephen was so delighted when Annie met him at her door that he was sure his answer sounded garbled.

"A package? Oh yes, I did deliver one yesterday, a small one. Seemed as though it might have been a book."

"Did you leave it outside?"

"No. A girl, rather frail looking, answered my knock, Miss Gallagher. I did not recognize her, but she said she was the addressee."

"Kirsten?"

"Yes, that's right."

Annie Gallagher folded her arms across her crisp maid's apron. "I'm delighted to hear she received it promptly. 'Twas a package from her brother."

"Oh yes." He wanted to say more, but his brain seemed as stuck as the three o'clock Fifth Avenue el.

Annie raised a brow. "Well?"

Her question jolted him and he jumped. "Right. The mail. Not much this morning, I'm afraid. Just the electric bill."

She slowly shook her head. "We don't get electricity at Hawkins House. That must be for another residence."

He lowered his head and searched through his bag. "You are correct. I . . ." He came up empty. "I was mistaken. There is no mail for Hawkins House."

"Well, so, Mr. Adams, thank you for checking. Tell me, were you able to get a copy of *The Wonderful Wizard of Oz*?"

He could not hide his smile. "I did indeed. A fine story, isn't it?"

"Oh, aye, 'tis. Do you think Dorothy will ever get back home?"

"Well, Miss Gallagher, it has been my experience that in a story every character is after something, going somewhere, and if they don't make it, it's a tragedy. But this is a children's book, purported to be not at all as gruesome as some of the old fairy tales, so I suppose . . ." She was grinning at him. He'd been rambling. "Uh, what do you think?"

Annie sighed. "She has so many obstacles to overcome."

"Yes. Yes, she does."

"But she's a brave lass." She put a hand to her pink lips. "I might be further into the book than you are. I will say no more, Mr. Adams."

"Not a problem. I . . . uh . . . I should allow you to return to your work, Miss Gallagher."

"And I to yours. A fine day to you."

"And to you, Miss Gallagher." As Stephen stepped off the stoop, he began whistling just to console himself. He wished that encounter had been longer because only time would tell when he'd get another chance to speak to her again. He would not be the cause of her abandoning her duties, however. Still, she had wanted to talk, and that was something.

An idea hit him like a refreshing shower bath. He hopped back up the stoop and caught her attention before she fully shut the hefty door. "See you at the dance tonight, Miss Gallagher?"

"You do seem to like those, now, don't you?"

He smiled and so did she. "What sensible fellow would not delight in that merrymaking?"

"I agree. I'm afraid I've been occupied with my cousin arriving, and the boarder, Kirsten, has not been well, and—"

He held up a hand. "No need to explain. If I am blessed

with the pleasure of seeing you there, I will greet you earnestly."

Annie's cheeks reddened. "Mr. Adams, you are quite charming."

Stephen thanked the good Lord he had recovered from his miserable start. He continued on his way, sorry he lacked two dollars for a new shirt to wear when he saw her next.

By five o'clock Stephen was well into his meal when the bell jingled on the door of Dexter's diner as another customer entered. Even without creamed cabbage on the menu, the place was packed.

"There you are. Been looking for you, Adams."

Stephen's landlord stood next to his table, the evening paper in one hand and a cigar in the other. He helped himself to a chair. "Asked around and found out you eat here sometimes."

"What can I do for you, Davis?"

The plump man rested his elbows on the table, making it wobble. Stephen steadied his water glass.

"I'm glad you asked, Adams. I would like to discuss business."

"What business? Raising my rent again?"

The man thumped a fist on the table. "Look, I was hasty. You're a good tenant. I don't want to lose you. It's still true, however, that my printing costs have escalated. Got to bring in more income, know what I mean?"

Indeed Stephen did understand.

"Tell you what. You work for me, and we'll go back to the old rate."

"I already have a job, Davis."

"I mean on the side. You know, do this in addition to delivering the mail."

"As though I have time for anything else. Look, I probably

won't be able to find an author for you, if that's what this is about. Sorry."

"Oh, that. That would be dandy if you could pull it off. But I'm talking about something else."

"What? I'm busy as it is, like I said."

Davis tilted his head upward and let out a chortle. "Yeah, you got no woman as I can see." He turned his head from side to side for emphasis. "You should have plenty of liberty. Take it from a man who was married once. If you've got no wife, you've got time on your hands."

"What's your point?"

"You might like to have a girl on your arm, I bet. I'm guessing you could use some extra cash to start courting a little lady. Am I right? Young, handsome fellow like yourself."

"What are you getting at, Davis? I work long days already."

The man looked down at the table, where Stephen had left his copy of *The Wonderful Wizard of Oz* open. Not on the level of Dickens or even Verne, it was entertaining nonetheless. Even so, not wanting Davis to think less of him for reading a children's book, he pulled it into his lap before the publisher could read the title.

"Reading brings you pleasure, and you devour books, articles, short stories—all sorts. Right?"

"I suppose so. Been that way all my life, but that doesn't mean I have an aptitude for working in the book industry."

Davis slid a hand under his vest. "Hear me out." He leaned forward, finally seeming to get to the business he came to discuss. "I need a reader, someone to look at manuscripts that come in and tell me what's garbage and what ain't. Know what I mean? You can read through some before you turn the light off at night. That's all I'm asking. You could do that, now couldn't you, Adams?" He lifted both hands from the table in an exaggerated shrug.

"And for this all you do is not raise my rent?"

"I could throw in a free book or two a month."

Appealing. Books were expensive, and he'd nearly polished off the one in his lap. He was a quick reader and knew he'd soon finish *The Master Key* as well and pass them both off to Dexter. He had no more unread books and no money to purchase any. Just think of all the tomes he could share with his book-loving buddy if he did what Davis asked. Davis might not publish the more fashionable stories, but he'd stayed in business, so he must have something worthy.

Apparently the man took Stephen's silence as hesitation. He raised his voice to a cheerful pitch. "And a meal on me, in here, every month." He made a wide gesture with his cigar-toting hand.

Stephen cut his Salisbury steak and stuffed a forkful into his mouth as he considered Davis's offer. Stephen did love Harriet's cabbage, and if Davis paid for Stephen's meal once a month, Stephen could savor that dish often enough.

The man drummed his forefinger and thumb on the wooden tabletop. When Stephen figured he'd made Davis wait long enough, he answered, "Deal."

They shook hands. "I'll leave a stack outside your door." He stood and glanced down at Stephen's brown gravy–covered meal. "A bachelor's supper, son. Think about that." Then he left Stephen to eat alone.

Certainly Stephen was motivated to find that author Davis wanted and start stockpiling some savings. He did not wish to be a bachelor all his life, nor could he depend on Minnie's husband's scheme for long. But things were looking up with this opportunity. Books and his favorite meal. Better things were in store. All it would take was some determination and the will to never follow in his father's footsteps.

17

WHEN ANNIE RETURNED from the fishmonger late in the afternoon, Aileen darted down the front hall toward her. "A man is waiting, Annie. Someone let the cat out of the bag, and it weren't me."

"What are you talking about, Aileen? Where is this man?"

"In the parlor. Another fella is there too, from some Fifteen Committee or something. They are giving Mrs. Hawkins a talking, and she wants you to come."

Annie scurried along the hall, pausing briefly to smooth her disheveled hair back into place. She hesitated at the opening of the pocket door.

"There you are, Annie."

The two men rose.

"This is Mr. Clayton Cooper, from the Pinkerton Agency, and Mr. Taylor."

"How do you do?" the one named Cooper said, giving no indication they'd met before when Annie had not wanted to let him in.

"Bring tea straightaway, Annie."

The two men lowered themselves back to the sofa and stared at her. She realized from the look on their faces she had interrupted their conversation. Mrs. Hawkins should not even have let them in the door. The poor woman just did not understand why Kirsten could not be sent away. Annie wasn't sure how to convince her.

"Are you sure you want tea now, Mrs. Hawkins?"

"Tea, I said."

"Certainly."

Aileen kept jabbering while Annie filled the teakettle. "Is it true, so? Will they fill out a report based on Kirsten's behavior? That's what I heard them say. And you, having been in a laundry. Do they know that? Where will we go, Annie?"

Annie halted what she was doing and turned on her heel. "Might you have been talking to someone about Kirsten's unfortunate circumstances, lass? And think of her, upstairs as sick as a dog." She thought of Dorothy's admonishment to the Lion and spoke the words. "You ought to be ashamed of yourself."

"I have told no one, I tell you. I never leave the house."

She had not been outside, true. "Oh, all right, so." Annie stared at her sleeves, determined not to react. "I did not deserve to be in that laundry, as well you know, and this has nothing to do with it."

Aileen's lower lip quivered. "I didn't know. I never knew . . ."

Focus on the present. "I do not understand where men like that get information on folks."

"Well, not from me."

"Right, so."

She bid her cousin to hide out in the kitchen while she returned to the parlor. As she was entering, the man called Cooper, the Pinkerton, was speaking. "As I said, I am doing an investigation, and I have good reason to believe your German boarder has connections to a financial scheme. There are many such operations, you know. Not that I expect you to understand how Wall Street operates."

"And you think a German immigrant girl who barely speaks English would comprehend these operations, Mr. Cooper? You are tremendously mistaken. On both accounts."

The man's face paled as though he'd received a blow to the stomach. "Uh, well, she may not even be aware that she has gotten involved, or that she has information I need, but we have ways of uncovering these things, madam, and I must insist you allow me to question her."

As Annie handed the man a cup of tea, she glanced down at her chalky-white wrists, hoping he hadn't noticed her nervousness. She did want to order him out—and would have, she hoped, despite her trembling hands, if only Mrs. Hawkins would have allowed it. Men like this Pinkerton, ones who imposed their authority on vulnerable women, made Annie feel as wobbly as the Scarecrow. *I am not a sinner of the worst kind. I am not!*

The other man scribbled on a pad of paper. She tried to look at it when she served him tea, but she could not read his handwriting.

Cooper put a hand behind his head, drawing attention to a mass of dark curls much like Stephen Adams's. Annie had the distinct impression she'd seen him somewhere else, not just that day outside of Hawkins House when Mrs. Hawkins had asked him to leave. She wondered again if he was the one Kirsten thought was watching her. He might have been the stranger Annie had seen at the dance. The man was obviously misled, but once a man got a mistaken notion in his head, who could change it?

The Pinkerton stirred his tea as he spoke. "I urge you to consider my request because . . . well, we have learned from a credible source that your tenant has staggered home late at night on more than one occasion."

"Yes, because of her job. But her employer kept her late. She works hard. That does not make her a woman of questionable morals."

The Pinkerton leaned forward. "Your establishment is in danger of losing its good reputation." He exchanged glances with Mr. Taylor, who seemingly got the hint and continued to write.

Annie still wasn't sure if Aileen might have somehow mentioned this, even inadvertently. How else would he ever have known?

The Hawk pulled her chin downward and glared at the man. "I do not understand, gentlemen, why you would be watching my house at night. If you are concerned about my girls, that is considerate indeed, but we have friends to look out for us."

"We have not been watching you, Mrs. Hawkins," Mr. Cooper said.

Annie noticed his stare moved toward the far wall. She wondered what he was contemplating. "Someone else informed us."

Annie truly hoped it hadn't been Aileen. That lass just didn't know when it was wise to keep silent about things.

Mrs. Hawkins grunted. "We are very busy planning a wedding, gentlemen. I suggest you go about your investigation without our assistance, but as you do, you will discover Hawkins House is an upstanding establishment in the city, providing a much-needed service. You have the references I gave you." She nodded at the quieter man. "Reverend Clarke and Dr. Thorp top that list. It's a pity you are spending your valuable time on this, however. You would do well not to interrupt our work here and instead go about following up more serious leads."

The Pinkerton set his teacup down and tugged at his unusual tie. "If you will not send that girl out, madam, you will be making this matter more difficult than need be."

Send her out? Annie had to say something now. "Mr. Cooper, the lass is recovering from an illness. You should be asham—"

"Annie, please return to the kitchen. I will handle this."

Annie had no choice but to go, but this was why she needed her own establishment. She could handle it, and with experience Mrs. Hawkins did not have. Annie knew what these kinds of men were capable of. As she left, she heard the Pinkerton again. "If she's ill, it's no doubt due to her late hours, and Mr. Taylor here will take note of it."

Annie headed for the back stairs to make sure Kirsten stayed hidden.

When Annie went upstairs, the bathroom was occupied. She sat down on a chair in the hall to wait, bouncing her knees. She couldn't be sure how long the Hawk would be able to hold the men off. A gagging noise brought her to her feet.

"Are you all right in there?"

"Nein."

"Kirsten? You are sick again? Would you like towels? Some hot water?"

The door cracked open. Kirsten's normally golden hair hung sullen in front of her face.

"I fear . . . I think perhaps when the man hurt me, he . . ." She held her hands over her stomach.

"Oh, Kirsten, 'tis too soon to know." She handed a towel through the cracked door. "We will tell Mrs. Hawkins, darlin', but she has company right now and—"

"Nein. She won't want me here, Annie."

Well, Annie wanted her there. That man touching her had not been Kirsten's fault any more than it had been Annie's that the laundry's doctor had wanted to do the same to her. "No one here will ask you to leave. You can tell her later, if indeed there is a need to. Can you let me in, lass?"

"You should stay away, Annie Gallagher. Far away."

"I will check downstairs to see if those men have gone."

"Wait! What men?"

"Don't worry, Kirsten. No one will harm you. Stay here."
The door shut, and Annie scurried back downstairs to the
kitchen.

Aileen was washing the teacups. "They've left. You have to
stop thinking ill of me, Annie."

"Ah, you are my cross to bear, Aileen."

"Me? How?"

Annie heard Mrs. Hawkins plodding up the hall. She whispered, "We will talk later."

She met Mrs. Hawkins halfway. "Whatever will we do? We
can't let them shut the house—"

"Annie, be calm. When they investigate, they will not find
reason. As a female entrepreneur, I have experienced this kind
of prejudice before. It will pass."

But a pregnant boarder? Best not to borrow trouble where
none's yet due. Annie remembered something she'd read about
friendship: *"He that covers a transgression seeks love; but he that
repeats a matter separates very friends."* She would not mention
the possible pregnancy. Not yet. Oh, to have her own home
where everyone was accepted no matter their sin.

Later, she pulled Aileen into her room.

"I told no one Kirsten was sick. I haven't spoken to anyone
but you and the girls, Annie."

"All right. I am not accusing you, Aileen. But do you think
you might have mentioned it, to a deliveryman or the message
boy—just casually, not out of malice?"

"I did not."

"Then how could they know Kirsten came in late?"

"Saw her, I'd guess."

Annie plopped down on her bed. "None of you understand what this means."

"What are you talking about, Annie Gallagher? Gone loony, seems."

"Leave me, please." Thoughts . . . words . . . many things bounced around together in Annie's head, and she could not think straight.

"Gladly."

When Aileen shut her door, Annie pulled her knees up to her chest and covered her ears with her hands, sure that she'd heard the scraping noise of metal on concrete.

After supper Stephen Adams came calling. Aileen let him in and took his hat. Mrs. Hawkins came from the kitchen, wiping her hands on her napkin. "How delightful to have your company, love. Do come in. Annie, make him comfortable. Aileen and I will finish up in the kitchen and then come join you."

"I heard that there was some trouble here, Miss Gallagher, and I wanted to see if I may be of assistance."

"Trouble? Whatever do you mean? I hope my cousin has not been gossiping."

"Oh no. It's just that your neighbor asked me to check in. She says you've had several strangers coming and going."

"Oh, there were two men here earlier suggesting our newest boarder might be the corruptible type, which she is not, of course. I do not understand why folks think they have the right to make such judgments." She sucked in her breath.

"Of course they are mistaken. Who are these men?"

"A Pinkerton detective and someone from the Committee of Fifteen, I think. He took notes."

"I see. Has Sergeant McNulty been by?"

"He has, but he hasn't yet found out what they want. I believe we are being unjustly scrutinized."

"It will all work out, I'm sure."

Mrs. Hawkins returned. "I'm going out, lovies, but Aileen will see to your tea." She turned to Annie as she pulled on her white gloves. "Playing Nellie Bly at the Thorps'. You don't mind visiting with Mr. Adams, do you, Annie?"

"Of course not."

"Check on Kirsten in a bit. She's tucked in with my special tea."

"Certainly."

Stephen had stood when Mrs. Hawkins entered. He moved toward her. "I am sorry to hear your new boarder is ill, Mrs. Hawkins."

"Thank you. We are taking good care of her. She will be good as new."

"I am sure of it."

When the woman left, Annie knew she only had a few minutes before her annoying cousin would interrupt them. "'Tis Thursday, Mr. Adams. You did not go to the dance."

"No, I . . ." He turned his astonishing blue eyes on her. "I decided to call on you here instead."

"I haven't been going because . . . well, regardless of everything else, I promised to help Grace trim her wedding dress this evening."

"Oh." He slapped his knees. "You are busy. I won't keep you."

"Not busy at present. She has not returned home yet. Stay and have tea. Please."

He smiled and nodded.

"I know you wanted to discuss the book we're reading."

"Certainly."

"But, Mr. Adams, I'm curious what makes you such an

avid reader. I mean . . . if you don't mind me asking." Her father loved books. A love of reading set men apart, Annie thought.

"I do not mind at all. Besides the fact that I live over the offices of Davis Publishing, I've loved books since I was a child."

"Me as well."

He tipped his head to one side, regarding her.

"Tell me, Mr. Adams, what is it about stories that enthralls you?"

"I believe it is because a tale, properly spun, transports the reader to other places and adventures he or she would not otherwise experience. A book can take you anywhere."

She gazed toward the breakfront cabinet. "My father used to believe the same."

"He is a great reader too?"

"He was a storyteller. He's passed on."

"I am so sorry, Miss Gallagher. Did he create his own tales?"

"Besides an ability to recite Shakespeare and tell all the epic tales of ole Erin, he created many original works."

"How marvelous. Do you know any of his tales, by chance?"

She retrieved her writing desk. "I have some of the stories he told me as a child, in here." And she had them in her head, along with many other things often difficult to sort through. Her father had been wise to write these down.

His eyes grew wide. "May I see them?"

Delighted he was interested, she sat and pulled out the yellowing papers. "I will read a tale or two, if you would like."

Aileen brought the tea and did her best to serve them. Annie was astonished. Perhaps she was trying to atone for her meddling. When she was done, she sat in the chair opposite the sofa where Annie and Stephen sat. Annie had no choice but to read to them both.

When she finished, they both applauded.

"You liked them, so?"

Stephen bobbed his head. "Indeed. Wonderful tales. You could make money selling them, I would expect."

"Truly?"

"If you would allow me to show them to my landlord, Mr. Alan Davis, I think he'd be charmed by them."

"Oh. I will think about that."

Aileen piped up. "I had no idea, Annie. My da said—"

Annie held up her hand. "Never mind, Aileen. Best left unsaid."

The lass sighed heavily.

"Why don't you check on Kirsten, Aileen? She could probably use her tea warmed up."

The girl stomped off upstairs.

"Mr. Adams, I'm not inclined to allow these stories out of my hands. They are precious to me. You understand."

"I do. But they are tremendous. Would you consider bringing them around?"

"Perhaps. I will think about it." She had hoped such a thing might be possible, but she had to do it on her own, and she did not want to reveal too soon that this idea pleased her.

"Give me pencil and paper, and I will write down the address for you."

When he was done, she took the paper from his hand. "Lovely handwriting, Mr. Adams." She thought she saw him blush.

"May I take a look? There are drawings as well, I see."

She handed him one of the stories.

He studied the papers a moment. "Enjoyable." He turned them over. "This . . . mark . . . Quite unusual."

"Mrs. Hawkins thought so too. Just scribbling."

"No. I think . . ." He brought a page closer to his face. "This appears to be the mark of Luther Redmond."

"The British fiction writer? Certainly not. My father wrote these stories."

Stephen turned the paper back over. "I see. His name was Marty Gallagher."

"That's right, so."

"But this mark . . ."

"Perhaps he was just experimenting with Mr. Redmond's mark."

"I don't think so. No one except British publishers knew what it was."

"You know."

"Only because Davis—that's the publisher I was speaking of—told me about it when we were discussing the authors we've read. It's an industry secret, but he confided in me since Mr. Redmond is now deceased."

"Well, how did he know about this mark, or whatever 'tis? This Mr. Redmond. He lived in England, I think."

"Davis is familiar with British authors because he distributes in New York for a London publisher. Early in his writing life, Mr. Redmond sold his work in many places, and this told the publishers it was authentic. It was a secret they did not let out lest someone try to pass off writings as his. But now that he's deceased, Davis didn't mind talking about it. And this mark . . ."

She shook her head. "Just happenstance."

Aileen bolted down the stairs. "Come, Annie. Kirsten's got a fever."

"Excuse me, Mr. Adams." She hurried upstairs.

Annie felt the girl's cheek. "She's hot. We better see if we can call Mrs. Hawkins."

"She's out playing Nellie Bly, remember?"

Stephen called from the bottom of the stairs. "Ladies, is something the matter?"

The girl was all but unconscious.

Aileen put her hand on top of Kirsten's head. "She's with child, ain't she?"

Annie's heart raced and she bit back the words she longed to hurl at her cousin.

"May I assist?" Mr. Adams shouted from below.

Annie scrambled down the stairs. "I think Mrs. Jenkins is away."

"She is. She told me she would soon be traveling outside the city."

"We don't have a telephone."

"Would you like me to go to Dr. Thorp's house?"

"Could you?"

"Certainly." He turned and dashed out the door.

Annie scrambled toward the back of the house and prepared a fire in the stove. Then she trotted up the stairs. "If you can get her to her feet, I'll get a tub ready downstairs. That way we'll get her into a tepid bath much quicker than waiting on the water up here."

Some time later they were able to escort Kirsten downstairs.

Kirsten settled in, now alert and shivering in a galvanized tub full of water. They wrapped her shoulders in a green robe.

Not long after, Mrs. Hawkins came clattering down the hall. "What's happened? Stephen Adams said Kirsten was ill." She pushed past them and hovered over the girl. "Poor thing. We'll have you better in no time." She turned around. "Aileen, put coals in the bed warmer. It's frigid in those rooms upstairs. And make sure there is lavender under the sheets."

Aileen retreated and headed upstairs like an obedient soldier going to the front battle lines. Thankfully the lass was bearing up under these stressful conditions. Annie never would have expected as much.

Annie and Mrs. Hawkins turned their attention back to Kirsten, who began groaning and holding on to her middle. A stream of red swirled in the bathwater.

18

When Stephen finally arrived home, it was past midnight, rain had soaked his clothes, and an overwhelming cloud of disappointment over not being able to engage Annie hung on him like an eight-day cold. He hoped Mrs. Hawkins's German boarder would be all right, though. He had done all he could.

He gathered up the stack of manuscripts Davis had left outside his door. After all the excitement, he would not be able to go right to sleep, so perhaps he'd look at a few.

As he slid off his coat, he realized there was something in his pocket. He pulled some papers out. Oh, dear. When he and Annie were looking at the stories her father had written for her, they'd been interrupted by the medical emergency. He must have stuffed the papers containing one of the stories into his pocket in his hurry to summon the doctor.

He smoothed them out on his lap as he sat on the couch under the electric bulb. Now he had the luxury of fully studying the tale. As he began to read, the beauty of the language and the compelling morality lessons expertly woven in amazed him. Beautiful. Just beautiful.

The prose was so descriptive Stephen could almost hear the animals chatter and feel the dewy ground they scampered on.

The intense green grass, bubbling clear streams, lumpy tumble-down rock piles, and massive, looming cloud formations made him feel he'd actually visited Ireland. But what was more, the truths taught within the pages nearly brought him to tears. Not many authors could do that. Certainly these had been penned by Luther Redmond despite what Annie thought. Her father had written under a pen name, obviously. Who knew why, but he had, Stephen was sure. An author—an excellent one—had a unique voice, and these stories, despite being written for a child, bore Redmond's voice. Imitators of popular authors were easy to spot.

He glanced to the pile of manuscripts. Might as well take a look.

After Stephen had sloshed through pages of poor imitations of popular current novels, he began to wonder if the deal he'd made with his landlord had been worth it. Vampire stories that were nowhere near as compelling as Bram Stoker's book and weak characters that could not come close to those created by Charles Dickens or Mark Twain. Dickens was uniquely Dickens. Twain was unmistakably Twain, and the imitation Stephen had just read, while a gracious nod to the famous writer, was nowhere close to his quality. Likewise, the tales Annie had were Redmond. They were probably the only stories he wrote for children, tales for his little daughter. Tales that just might give the Chicago publisher who printed Baum's stories a run for his money.

Stephen used pages from the manuscripts Davis gave him to light his fire. The authors would get most of their stories back, of course, just minus a couple of the worst scenes. This, he thought, was doing them a favor.

No wonder Davis was frustrated. Stephen had found only one worth passing on to him, a romantic drama titled *Truth Dexter* by Sidney McCall.

But this Redmond tale . . . No, Annie made it clear she wasn't ready.

He lay down and shut his eyes tight, thinking hard. He might not have caught Annie's attention with his attempts to appear suave and gentlemanly, but what about those stories? He'd prayed for God to show him a way to get her attention, and he'd remembered that Scripture: *"The effectual fervent prayer of a righteous man availeth much."* Right after that, Alan Davis had told him he was looking for a manuscript. This could be God speaking to him, telling him Annie had the perfect stories. And if those stories became popular, like *The Wonderful Wizard of Oz*, with every mother in the country clamoring for a copy for her children, Annie Gallagher would thank him for it.

Before he turned out the light for the night, he thought about the postmaster. If these stories were what he thought they were, they'd make everyone plenty of money, and Stephen wouldn't have to keep investing with Leonard in order to get out of debt. With suspicions growing in the office, it would be best to step away. He'd been tempted, foolishly. He would tell Minnie as soon as possible that he would not continue to invest. He should have trusted God and not been pulled into a profit gamble.

Before work the next day he would leave the McCall manuscript on Davis's doorstep. He was sure he'd found a gem in Annie's stories; however, he would need to persuade her.

The doctor had come despite the late hour, and before he left in his lantern-bearing horse-drawn carriage, he confirmed that Kirsten had miscarried. Now Annie feared they would lose Kirsten. It happened all the time, women dying from miscarriages and childbirth. Annie had seen it in Ireland and on the ship to America. She'd heard about neighbors suffering such a fate in Manhattan. Grace's mistress, Alice Parker, had developed a blood clot. There were many perils.

Annie couldn't sleep, so she'd told Mrs. Hawkins and Aileen she would check on Kirsten throughout the night. She sat in the kitchen by the stove, her face in her hands. If Kirsten had only trusted her enough to tell her what had been happening with her boss, perhaps she could have done something. Women observed some kind of code of silence about these things, and that only led to bigger injustices like Magdalene Laundries.

Rubbing her face with her cold hands, she ached with the desire to feel her father's touch again and see him gazing at her. *Oh, Da, tell me what I am to do here. No one wants me.* She desperately longed to hear her father's voice, yet if she actually did, she would have no doubt she had gone mad. When she'd been locked in the laundry, she'd almost gone to that dire place where folks who have lost their minds dwell. Moving forward now, but still living as she did in a hollow place, had been only a wee improvement.

She laughed at her own folly. God wasn't speaking to her. Her father could not. Her own mind defied her at times, waving dark, ribbonlike fingers toward the path to derangement. Annie had tried to convince Kirsten she was not a bad person like the lass was given to thinking, but why should Kirsten listen to her? Sinners of the worst kind ended up in these sorts of situations, didn't they?

She returned in her mind to the place of despair.

She counted her breaths, in and out, in and out—measuring the fact that she was still alive despite the wee space she'd been confined to for some kind of mistake she must have made. And then she saw the doctor again. He strode down the hall holding a lamp. She sucked in her breath, praying he was not coming for her.

He bent low and held the flame in front of her face. "Oh, it's you, little one. You are a soiled girl, aren't you."

She pulled wildly at her sleeves, which were too short.

He poked at her through the bars. Like a caged animal, she could not get away. He laughed. Then he . . . he unlocked the door, reaching out his long fingers. Just before he could touch her, a noise in the hall made him pull away.

A pain pierced right through her as she thought about that girl in the cage, waiting day after day, watching for him, jumping at every screeching metal door sound she heard. She had worked as hard as she could scrubbing floors and laundering sheets in that place, trying to scrub away the blackness in her heart so God would answer her prayers.

Only one person had thought Annie was good. And he was gone. God was too. Going on alone, without so much as a yellow brick road to follow, was proving more difficult than she could have ever imagined. If she never again observed the impact of abuse, as she was seeing with Kirsten, she might be able to put the past behind her. But this brought it forward along with a chill that crept up inside her like the transgressing fingers of a demon she could not kill.

Annie patted her cheeks with her palms, reminding herself she was in Hawkins House now. She stood and stretched, determined not to give in to self-pity. The house was so quiet she heard her own heartbeat. Grace had sent word earlier that she would be staying at the Parkers' since she and Mr. Parker's sister were planning Grace's wedding trousseau. She did not need Annie's help with her wedding dress after all. Just as well Grace had not had to witness this.

Annie reached for her book, the only way she knew to free her mind.

Aileen padded in on stocking feet. "She's sleeping now. I'll watch over her. You go to bed."

An unusual gesture from her cousin, but perhaps this adversity had prompted a measure of kindness. "Thank you, Aileen. I know you don't know her well. You've been thoughtful to help nurse her like this."

Aileen shrugged and stoked the stove with a shovel of coal. "I know what 'tis like, I suppose."

"What do you mean?"

"To lose a child."

"Aileen, nay."

She turned to face Annie. "Oh, aye. It happened while Donald was at sea. I lost him and the child, likely on the same day, I suppose."

Annie rose and embraced her cousin. "I didn't know."

"Sure and you couldn't." Aileen wiggled away and began straightening the bowls on the shelf above the sink. "Didn't want anyone to know. Tried to forget it, I did. But then Kirsten . . ." Aileen spun to face her. "I often think I would have made a good mother, Annie. I do not know now if I will ever have the chance."

"I'm so sorry." Annie started to reach her hand out but then awkwardly pulled it back. Just because Aileen had revealed her pain, her cousin wouldn't want Annie's condolences. She had no reason to trust Annie with her raw emotions, and truly, trust was not something the two of them shared.

The lass began wiping the kitchen counter with a red-striped cloth. "Things happen in life. You know. You have to move on. Keep going. That's what's important."

"I suppose 'tis. I am sorry for your trouble. I know what 'tis like to need to move on, Aileen."

"I suppose you would, and 'tis a fine thing how you've started over here, Annie. I admire you for it."

"You do?"

"Aye, but me? Trouble? Nah. I fared fine, don't you know." She gazed downward. "Please forgive me for saying you started that business with Johnny, Annie. I was a stupid lass."

Annie took her hand. The irritation of having Aileen there began to cast away like falling autumn leaves. Annie never would have thought it possible, but she could see the sincerity on her cousin's face. Perhaps that old code of silence was coming to an end. "Foolish, perhaps, Aileen, but that is all over now. Of course I forgive you."

Aileen smiled, nodded, and returned to the mindless task of straightening crockery.

A quietness floated so long between them afterward that Annie didn't feel right interrupting it. She went to the parlor, retrieved her writing desk, and padded off to bed.

The only way Annie could hear the voice she longed to hear was through his words. She took out the stories. Something was amiss. She counted the pages, then examined the titles. Omah's story was missing.

Sighing, she slipped on her robe. She had been showing it to Stephen Adams when Aileen called for help. They had probably left it lying on the sofa.

With the mantel clock ticking through the silence, Annie searched the room. She even looked under Mrs. Hawkins's chair, where they'd found one of them before. Nothing.

Maybe she had overlooked it. She returned to her room, looked inside the desk, and then shuffled through the stack of papers. It positively was not there. She would have to seek Stephen out and ask him about it.

19

In the middle of his morning route, Stephen stopped by his apartment because he'd forgotten his lunch again. Davis met him at the door, waving some papers at him. "Nah. This won't do."

"What do you mean? It's a fine story."

"Maybe, but it's not what I'm looking for."

"Come on, Davis. With phrases like 'a nose like a can opener' and 'a mouth like a steel rattrap'?"

"Did you read the whole thing?"

"You know I can't do that. Just enough to know this one has merit, Davis."

"I do not agree."

"Fine, but I'm going to remember this title. *Truth Dexter* is going to make someone money."

"Right. Now you're an expert."

"Hey, you asked me."

"True, true. But I'm looking for something more in the league of L. Frank Baum."

Someday Stephen would remind Davis that he'd turned this down. "I'll keep looking."

As he turned to leave, Davis stopped him. "I have not been upstairs, but the police came by about an hour ago and asked for you. I told them you were at work. Then I had to go out. Maybe they left you a note or something. Hope everything's all right."

"Thanks, Davis. Probably had the wrong fella."

"Probably."

When Stephen got to his room, the door was ajar. He pushed it further open with his foot.

What the devil?

He turned on the electric light.

Completely empty! Everything that wasn't bolted to the floor or walls was gone. A note was pinned to the inside of the door.

> *In partial payment for your debt to Archibald Murray, undertaker, we have taken claim to your belongings. They are being held in storage until they can be auctioned on Thursday, October 31, at 9:00 a.m. at No. 105, 13th Street. You have until that time to reclaim your items by repaying your debt to Mr. Murray and the resulting rental storage fee. If payment is not made, your items will be auctioned and the proceeds applied to your debt.*

The note was written on the official letterhead of the New York City police. Stephen had delivered mail with the same logo. He knew it was legitimate.

Under the window he noticed something in the shadows. When he got closer, he realized it was his expenses ledger. They must have figured it wasn't worth taking. He had lost track, apparently. Just how behind had he been? He threw the book at the wall with all his strength. He should have been more mindful of why Davis thought it might be necessary to put his locked box in the safe. Those fellows meant business.

He went to his stove and opened it. Thankfully they had

not also taken the coal he had in there. He stoked it and then decided to borrow a blanket from Mrs. Jacobs while it was still daytime. The woman baked early, and he didn't want to disturb her by waiting until he got home from work.

Before he went to visit Mrs. Jacobs, Stephen paused to ring Davis's bell. He had Annie's little story in his pocket, ready to return it, but perhaps he should tell Davis about it first.

"Adams, has there been trouble?"

"I'll say. They took everything."

Davis clicked his tongue. "I believe I warned you about that."

"I know, I know. But I may have something here to solve all our financial troubles."

"Oh?" He opened the door wide and invited Stephen in. "Sit down, son. Show me what you have."

"I . . . uh . . . The owner of these stories, of which I have one here, doesn't exactly know I have it."

"What? You stole something? Adams, I never suspected you were a thief."

"No, no. It was purely accidental. But before I return it, I thought you should take a look, see if you come up with the same conclusion I have."

The man sat at his desk and wiggled his fingers, waiting for the papers. Stephen slowly pulled them out of his pocket. "They are old and fragile. Please be careful."

"All right. Let me see."

Stephen tapped his foot, waiting for Davis to finish reading or to get sight of that mark, whichever came first.

"Blessed be! Could that be what I think it is? Weren't you and I just talking about Redmond?"

"We were."

He let the papers fall to his desk. "You aren't trying to pull a prank now, are you?"

Stephen laughed. "No, I promise you. The young lady to whom these belong told me her father in Ireland wrote them for her."

"And she said Redmond was her father?"

"No. Marty Gallagher, like it says at the top. I suspect Luther Redmond was a pen name."

"And the daughter did not know?"

"She does not seem to have known."

"A stretch of our fortunes, I'd say, but it is a wonderful tale— and for children. And there are more of these, you say?" He carefully refolded the papers.

Stephen held out his hand. "There are several more. I need to get that back."

"I don't think so. Not yet. I'll keep it in my safe for now, and this afternoon I'll drop by the club and show it to the editor at *Harper's* magazine. This could be a gold mine if it's genuine."

"But Annie Gallagher will want it back. She did not intentionally give it to me."

"You explain it to her. In the meantime I'll find out if it's real." He shooed Stephen out of the office. He was late anyway.

꧁꧂

When she woke midmorning, Annie pulled on her robe and sought out Mrs. Hawkins. "How is Kirsten?"

"Up and drinking tea. Her fever broke. The doctor's been here again and left. She may have whooping cough."

Annie let out a breath. "Oh, my. After all she's been through. Where's Aileen?"

"Sawing logs, love. She was up half the night. Well, all night, I suppose."

"You should have awakened me sooner."

"You had a busy day yesterday, love. We'll take turns."

"Fine, so. I'll start the fire."

"Already done."

Annie reached out both hands as she tried to focus her thoughts. "I should . . . Breakfast. I'll make breakfast."

"We already ate, but there are buns on the stove. Help yourself."

"Mrs. Hawkins, you pamper me so. You did not have to let me sleep. I'm perfectly capable—"

"I suppose it is just my nature, love."

"I do not think that is the reason. You don't do for others what you do for me."

The Hawk patted Annie's cheek. "You remind me of your mother."

Her mother? Annie rubbed the spot between her eyes, wondering if the fog of sleep still lingered, causing her to misunderstand. "I thought you said my mother."

"Oh, well . . . I probably said *my* mother, or meant to. We've a busy day ahead. We must clean the house from ceiling to floorboards for the upcoming postwedding party. Don't tell me you've forgotten."

"I have not, of course." The Hawk had ended the conversation again. But Annie was still left with the feeling that Mrs. Hawkins was avoiding something. Didn't she trust Annie? She thought about how Mrs. Hawkins had seemed hesitant about Annie's idea to open a library. There was something a wee bit odd about that. Something about the woman and her brother, Father Weldon, that felt secretive somehow. For instance, how had they decided, far apart from each other, that Annie should come to live at Hawkins House? Annie was weary of secrets.

Later, as Annie swept the carpet on the stairs with a whisk broom, she heard the familiar whistle of the postman. She fetched the outgoing mail from the silver tray. When she opened the door, a brisk gale entered the house, sending a letter flying out onto the front steps.

"Get that!" Annie cried, lunging toward the threshold.

She nearly bumped heads with Stephen Adams, who was bundled up like a north woodsman with the collar of his raincoat turned up toward his chin.

He pulled off one mitten and snagged the letter before it blew off the top step.

"Hurrah!" Aileen cried from somewhere in the hall, clapping her hands.

Stephen's blue eyes shone in the cool air. "Letters are my business."

Mrs. Hawkins scrambled up behind them. "Stephen Adams, come inside, young man. A cup of hot tea will warm you up. Truly winter is knocking on our door already, and too soon. Last week it was warm, this week cool. Such is autumn in New York." She reached out one chubby arm and pulled him in off the stoop.

Annie closed the door and gathered up the man's wet mittens to dry by the stove in the kitchen. What a generous soul Stephen Adams had, to help Kirsten like that last night.

Mrs. Hawkins pointed to the front room. "The fire is stoked in the parlor, Mr. Adams. Please go on in. We'll put the kettle on."

He glanced to Annie and then back at the woman of the house. "That's very kind of you. Really, all this is not necessary."

"I'll get the tea," Annie said.

When Annie returned with a tray, she heard Mrs. Hawkins profusely thanking Stephen for helping out with Kirsten. "You've got time to visit awhile, haven't you, love? After what you did to help our poor Kirsten, it's the least we can do to give you a bit of respite from the dreary weather out there."

He shrugged. "Well, I do have only one block left to deliver."

The Hawk grinned. "Good. Annie will see to you until I get back. Come along, Aileen. You can help me in the kitchen." She gave Annie a nudge. "Make our guest comfortable, love."

Whatever that was about, Annie was glad to have the chance to speak to the man.

He lifted his dark brows. "How is Miss Wagner?"

"Much better. Please have some tea." She poured him a cup and then took the plump chair opposite Mrs. Hawkins's. "Kirsten is . . . recovering. My cousin Aileen sat up with her most of the night. We took good care of her."

He smiled, tight-lipped, as though trying not to speak.

"Mr. Adams, the story I showed you earlier—I'm afraid I've misplaced it."

"Uh, yes. I need to explain. It seems in all the rush, I inadvertently put the papers in my pocket. I did not mean to."

"Oh." She held out her hand. "You've brought them back, so."

"Miss Gallagher, remember what I told you about that mark?"

"I do. You thought it was some famous author's mark, but you were mistaken."

He sipped from his cup. "I hope you will forgive me, but I was prepared to return your story. I just wanted to show it to Alan Davis, the owner of Davis Publishing, first."

"I see. Well, you brought it back, didn't you?"

He closed his eyes.

"What is this about, Mr. Adams? I would like my story back."

"I know. And you shall have it. Miss Gallagher, allow me to explain my position with Davis Publishing."

"Position?"

"Indeed. My landlord observed my love of stories, and so he asked me to do some reading for him as a side job, to help him find a new author to publish. I've been looking through what people have sent him, and . . . I can tell you positively that your father's stories are far superior to anything else he's received."

"Truly?" She felt proud.

"In addition, you should know he agrees with me. He thinks those stories were actually written by Luther Redmond. Perhaps your father was using a pen name."

"Oh, nay. That's preposterous. He would have told me. But your publisher friend liked them, so?"

"He did very much. He wants to show the story to the editor at *Harper's* magazine."

"Truly? Well, that is splendid, but you did not think to ask me first?" She swallowed hard, suddenly realizing that Stephen Adams might not be interested in her at all. "Are you being compensated for this side job?"

"I am, for the time I put into it. But that does not negate the fact that these stories are excellent."

All this time he was searching for stories to publish, in cahoots with his landlord.

He stared at his shoelaces. "I am sorry, but I truly did not have the opportunity to consult with you prior to speaking with him. He lives in the same building, so we talked about it before I delivered your mail. I'm telling you now."

"Please continue."

"He insisted on keeping it temporarily, but don't worry. He's trustworthy. He thinks this story might be quite valuable. I assure you it is secure in Davis's safe."

She pinched her hands together. "And the two of you did not think I could handle such a transaction on my own."

"No. We weren't thinking anything of the sort. You have the wrong idea. There is no transaction. He is collecting information, opinions, you understand."

She stared at the roses on the carpet. Now was the time to stand up for herself, to be the woman no one thought she could be, with or without guidance. "I will have the story back by tomorrow, Mr. Adams, or I will go to Mr. Davis's office and get it myself. You gave me the address, as I recall."

"I did. Yes. I understand your concern. But you really need not fret. The papers are safe."

"Can you get them back before suppertime tomorrow?"

"I . . . uh, I'm not sure exactly. I give you my word no harm will come to them."

"I suppose I will have to trust your word, Mr. Adams. My father's stories are immensely important to me."

She was happy when Mrs. Hawkins joined them, bringing biscuits. She could think of nothing else to say to him.

Mrs. Hawkins offered Stephen a gingersnap. "Did I hear you talking about Annie's father's stories, love?"

For the love of St. Michael, there was no privacy within this house. "'Tis nothing, Mrs. Hawkins. I believe Mr. Adams needs to be on his way."

Mrs. Hawkins ignored her. "I read one of those stories. It was delightful. About a mouse in suspenders who rallies all the other mice in the field to send a message to the farmer."

Annie twisted the hem of her apron in her right hand. "Oh, I don't know. They are just my stories, Mrs. Hawkins." They were staring at her as though they had a right to demand she hand them over to Davis Publishing. She didn't like being told what she should do with something that was hers alone. "If you will excuse me, I'm going to check on Kirsten." She took her writing box with her.

When she had gone halfway up the stairs, she gazed down toward the parlor. Mr. Adams was preparing to leave.

She opened the door to Kirsten's room. "Are you all alone in here? It's freezing. The windows are open a bit too wide."

Kirsten sat up and held a handkerchief to her mouth as she coughed. "You should not get too close. Doctor says I may have whooping cough. There are masks outside the door."

Annie backed into the hallway. She hadn't noticed the chair in the hall, where two cotton masks lay. She set the box down on the floor, took a mask, and tied it over her mouth and nose, then scooped up her precious possession and went back into the room. The mask sucked in toward her mouth as she began to talk. "You're going to be better soon, Kirsten. Did I wake you?"

"*Nein.* I cannot sleep with all this coughing. You? You look as though something bothers you."

"Me? Oh, just some old turf on my barn."

"Old what?"

Annie jiggled her head. "An Irish expression. Never mind me. I am fine, so. But you? I'm so sorry you are ill, Kirsten. You have been through so many trials."

Kirsten's stare dropped to the object in Annie's arms. "I need to get a message to my brother. You will give it to him when he arrives. I am ill. I should not see him."

"Of course. You probably want to tell him you received that package." Shivering from a draft, Annie pulled the window almost closed and sat on the extra bed. It had been stripped of bedclothes.

When she was settled in to write, she nodded to Kirsten.

"My dearest brother, I am doing well at my job."

Annie lifted her head. "What?"

"Please write what I say. It will become clear."

"All right." Annie put the pen to the paper.

"I am doing so well that I am being transferred to a new plant in Massachusetts."

"Kirsten, you don't have to leave now. You'll get better. And your brother will be here very soon. You don't have to move out of state or to that home or anywhere." She wished she hadn't mentioned the home for unwed mothers that Kirsten no longer needed. "Uh, you are most welcome here."

The girl gathered her covers and pushed them underneath her legs. "You are right. I should not write a letter. You will just tell him, *ja*? I do not want to see him."

"But why, Kirsten? What are you afraid of?"

"Not afraid." She looked up with watery eyes. "I will do what is right, *ja*? For Jonas."

"Kirsten, if it's about the miscarriage . . . I won't tell him."

"*Nein.* Tell him nothing. He is stubborn. Would not listen to me before and will not now. The only thing I can do . . . Just do not tell him where I am. Promise me."

"He already knows where you are."

Kirsten shifted as though the sheets were sandpaper. She coughed forcefully. When she caught her breath, Annie handed her the glass of water on the bedside stand. Kirsten sighed. Talking stole her breath as though she'd been running a race.

Annie pitied her. "We don't have to discuss this right now, so."

"I told the doctor I will go to the infirmary. He is sending an ambulance coach in a few hours."

"Oh, nay. No matter what Mrs. Hawkins said, I will not allow it."

Kirsten slid down into the depths of her pillows. "She wanted me to stay, but the doctor agreed with me. I should be isolated. Do not tell Jonas, Annie." Kirsten lifted her head and sipped again from the glass. When she finished, she returned to her pillow, grimacing. "Send him away. That would be best."

"You can't mean that. He is your own brother."

She glared at Annie. "Do not tell me blood matters to you. I know you did not want your cousin here."

"'Tis different, Kirsten. There are things about my past you don't know."

"*Ja*. You do understand."

Annie gazed at the ceiling. "I'll try."

Kirsten stared past her as though contemplating something. "*Danke*. That is *gut* of you. And Annie, be careful."

"Careful? Why?"

"I cannot say."

"There is something you aren't telling us about why that Pinkerton is following you."

"I do not know this . . . Pinkerton."

"Some kind of detective that they have here in America. He believes you may have gotten involved in something without knowing it . . ." She searched her mind. "An ill financial deal of some kind. Gambling, is it?"

"*Nein*. Not gambling."

"Is it the package you received? You must tell me, Kirsten."

"You would not understand, Annie Gallagher. Jonas has always wanted more for us, but he is not involved. I am not involved. He just . . . he just needs a new start here."

"More, is it? Greed. If 'tis not greed, then power. Or maybe they are the same thing."

"*Nein*." She struggled for her next breath. When she recovered, she grunted, seemingly needing to say more. "I tell you, like I said before. He is a *gut* man. Not greedy. He will not get a new start for his life if he continues on . . . Ah, never mind, Annie. I just have to do this for him."

"You are trying to protect him."

"*Ja*. I will."

"Are you sure you know what you are doing, Kirsten?"

"I do what I can. If only I had not lost my job. Then we might . . ." She inhaled, gasped, and began another coughing fit. When she recovered, she said nothing new, just repeated that her brother needed a fresh start.

"I do understand that. Isn't that what we all want?"

"*Ja.* But some of us have more to repent of than others."

Annie felt that. The ache of wanting to atone but knowing that it could never be done. The terrifying feeling that when God turned his back on you, you were left in the desert wandering like a child of Israel. There were some stories Annie wished she could forget, like that one about God leaving his people because they were sinners. How did she think she could convince Kirsten there was hope when she was not convinced herself?

"You can't tell me what the trouble is exactly?"

"I cannot."

"Or why you must hide from him in order to protect him?"

"*Nein.*"

Annie dipped her head and turned toward the door. Before she slipped out to the hall, she turned to the whisper of a girl lying in the bed. "Be well, Kirsten Wagner." She'd avoided the usual Irish farewells, so the wish sounded deflated. She wanted to do much more.

Late in the afternoon, Mrs. Hawkins, noting that her neighbor had returned from her trip, borrowed Mrs. Jenkins's telephone, and shortly after, the doctor arrived as promised. Mrs. Hawkins paced the hall as they waited for the staff to carry Kirsten from her room. "It just does not seem right, love," she said to Annie. "I won't be able to check on her every morning. No, no." She wrung her chubby hands and worried her lip.

Annie patted her arm. "Dr. Thorp is your friend. He'll take

good care of her. And Kirsten wants to be there." All the while Annie reminded herself how different this was, how much safer this situation was than the place in Ireland where she had encountered a doctor.

"I just didn't realize how much I was going to dislike this." The woman halted and tipped her pointed chin upward. "If she had not wished it, I would never have made her go."

"I know."

"Of course." A tear came to her eye, and she dabbed at it with a handkerchief.

A clattering of feet upstairs told them they were on their way down. One man had Kirsten, still wrapped in Mrs. Hawkins's floral quilt, in his arms. Another carried a bag of her belongings. They said nothing as they whisked her outside. Mrs. Hawkins donned a white mask and prepared to join them in the ambulance.

Annie stepped out to the stoop, where the doctor was supervising. "The infirmary seems like an odd place to take her, Doctor. Why not a bigger hospital like Bellevue?"

"Her secondary ear infection qualifies her for care there, Miss Gallagher. I assure you I have her best interests at heart."

"Of course. I don't know about such things. Forgive me."

"Not at all. You're concerned. That's understandable."

Annie followed the doctor as the transporters lifted Kirsten into the ambulance.

Dr. Thorp used his walking stick to push up his top hat as he stood to the side of the open door of the carriage.

"Dr. Thorp?"

"Yes, Miss Gallagher?"

Annie whispered, "How will the bill be paid?"

He matched her tone of voice. "Lifetime subscribers, my dear. Folks pay a great sum of money to reserve private beds in the hospital, to be used either for themselves or for someone they designate. Upon their deaths, the beds are to be used for the poor. It was an ingenious strategy to encourage folks to contribute thousands of dollars to open the facility, but . . ." He cocked his head to one side. "It did benefit the poor in the end, and that's a very good thing."

"Kirsten got a bed like that?" Annie pulled her cloak to her chin as the brisk wind picked up.

"She did indeed."

"Whose bed is it? Or was it?"

Dr. Thorp shifted his walking stick to his left hand to free his right to rub his mustache. "That is confidential, my dear, but you know the names of New York's elite: Agnew, Astor, Dubois, Macy—folks like that."

Annie said good-bye and watched as the ambulance's horse pulled forward and set off down the street.

A benefactor? Mrs. Hawkins's name was never in the society pages along with those the doctor had mentioned, but no one else knew Kirsten well enough to do this for her. How had Mrs. Hawkins managed it? Another secret.

20

Stephen had another lengthy, blustery day ahead tomorrow. He dropped in at Dexter's, his last fifteen cents for a meal in his pocket. Payday tomorrow. Then Sunday, a day off. The counter was full, so he took a table near the door.

As someone from the corner table rose and came in his direction, he suddenly recognized Minnie Draper and stood.

"Mr. Adams, I was hoping to find you. You mentioned you ate here."

"You were looking for me? Why?"

"Leonard is with me. Mind if he comes to talk to you?"

"Not at all." Stephen waved at the gentleman sitting at her table. He waited for the Drapers to be seated before he returned to his own chair. "Pleased to meet you."

Leonard gazed at him with eyes the color of hot cocoa. "My wife, she asked you to deposit, that right?"

"She invited me to, yes. Look, I'm not really savvy about investing, so—"

Leonard lowered his voice. "We have struck gold, Mr. Adams. We're about to. I'm asking my investors, over fifty strong now, to each deposit ten dollars by tonight. I know which stock is about to rise from pennies to a fortune. With the money we make, I'll be able to buy big and keep rolling. It's how the prominent men in town keep getting richer, but with all of us joining together, we can play in their league. It's the American way." He held up his large hands in apology. "But if you'd rather withdraw, that's all right, now. You do what you're comfortable with. I just wanted to offer you the opportunity, seeing as you work with Minnie and you've been so kind to her. Wouldn't seem right to keep this deal from a good fella like you, Mr. Adams."

"I don't know. Are you sure your tip is a good one?"

"Know Lemings, the fella who used to sell oysters?"

"Yeah, the man who now owns a brownstone near Washington Park. He made some money in the stock market last year, I heard." Folks on the street had not stopped talking about it.

"My boss, the investor? Well, Lemings deposited with him. Lots of folks would have been a lot richer now if they had heeded the advice Lemings got."

"I see. Well, I'm afraid I haven't got ten dollars."

Leonard gripped Stephen's arm. "That's all right now." He stood.

Minnie smiled. "We can wait for you to get your paycheck tomorrow, if you'd like. Think about it."

Stephen really needed the money he'd invested now, and he thought about asking to withdraw it, but the possibility that Leonard's hunch was right was tempting to say the least. Who knew when he'd ever get a chance like this again?

"See you tomorrow," Minnie called, taking her husband's arm and hurrying out the door.

Stephen ordered fried ham and a hot roll from Dexter's eldest daughter, who, like her father, poured him a free cup of coffee. He grimaced as he realized his thoughts had caused him to forget the sugar. As he stirred a lump into the steaming cup, he continued to think about the Drapers. Say he kept just fifty cents from his paycheck tomorrow and deposited the remainder with Leonard. He'd meet the minimum deposit he'd asked for and by the following week, when Stephen got paid again, he'd have more than enough to get his things out of storage and pay Mr. Murray. And if the earnings from the stock were incredibly large, he would have more to boot. A one-time risk but probably smart considering Stephen's situation. With those problems behind him, he could work on being the kind of man a girl wants to marry.

The next day Stephen asked for his paycheck before lunch.

"For you," the postal accountant said. "Since it's a rare request. You do know I can't do this all the time?"

"I appreciate this." He asked Minnie to wait for him at the corner of Broadway and Rayburn while he cashed his check. "Will Leonard wait for me?"

Minnie smiled so smugly her cheeks grew round. "He will if I tell him to, but you'll have to hurry. Stock market closes soon. Shorter hours on Saturdays, he says. I'll be waiting at the corner."

Stephen hurried out to the crowded street and wove his way past newsboys, shoppers, and oyster vendors whose presence made him consider Lemings again. If he could do it, why not Stephen?

After he cashed out his paycheck, he stared down at the ten-dollar note. He'd never asked for so large a denomination before, preferring to deal with small notes and coins, but a single bill would be easier to hand off to Minnie. The image of the buffalo on the front seemed to scowl at him, speaking danger. Drawing in a deep breath, he told himself times like these tested a man's mettle. He would do what he had to.

When he approached the meeting place, he saw Minnie glance up at him from underneath a fur hood. He almost didn't recognize her. She seemed to notice him staring at her coat. "Chillier up north than I'm used to. Leonard said, 'A gal like you deserves a fur.' Now isn't that something? Like it?"

"Fine." He didn't think the weather quite merited such a cloak. He had not figured Minnie to be a show-off. The lure of money could make people behave strangely. "Here. Take this before I change my mind."

She accepted the money and they parted ways.

As he made his way up Broadway, he noticed a man standing astride the curb a few feet in front of him. As he got closer, he realized it was the postmaster, Mr. Sturgis. "Adams, we need to talk."

"I've never seen you in this neighborhood before, Mr. Sturgis."

"Yeah, yeah. I want to have a word with you."

"About?"

He put his hand on Stephen's shoulder. "About what just happened. Let's step over here."

They backed into an alley. Stephen's throat parched and his hands grew clammy. His mind bounced like a tennis ball in play as he pondered what excuse he could make to explain giving Minnie Draper money out on the street. An attempt to put the situation in perspective might deflect the inevitable question. "Uh, I am not at work, Mr. Sturgis. I'm on lunch break."

"I understand, but this is critical, Stephen. As you know, we are ever vigilant against mail fraud."

"What are you implying?"

"Not that. But hear me out."

They paused as a couple of newsboys pushed past them.

"You see, we are continually on the lookout. That is how we've uncovered the unscrupulous scheme Minnie Draper's husband has been luring some of our employees into."

"Unscrupulous?"

"Indeed. Mr. Draper does not buy stocks. He pays profits only when his depositors require it, and he does so with money obtained from other depositors. So long as everyone does not call their money in all at the same time, the Drapers are left with a lot of cash. We think Leonard Draper might be about to take a huge risk by investing a large portion of what he has right now, attempting to make himself a lot of money."

"That's insane. Minnie Draper is a nice woman."

"I agree. She's been duped like the rest."

Stephen hated feeling so foolish. He should have listened to his conscience.

"The postmaster general feels that married women should not be employed at the post office, and this bears witness. She should be caring for her family at home."

"I do not think this is her fault. Mr. Sturgis, you're not going to dismiss her, are you?"

"The first order of business is to put a stop to her husband's ploy. With your help, we can do that."

"My help? How?"

"Just go with me to the police station and file a report. That's all." He glanced toward the street. "Your money is long gone, but if you do that, you can still keep your job."

"I see." Stephen saw no alternative.

When he got to the police station, he was thankful Owen McNulty was not on duty. He felt ashamed and downright stupid enough without having someone he knew observe him making a statement. Before he went home, he made a stop at the undertaker's, knowing the office stayed open late on Saturdays.

He stomped into Mr. Murray's office, hurried past his secretary, and slung his mailbag down in front of the surprised man, who had been talking on the telephone. He hung up.

"Look, Adams, this is not personal. It's business."

"Sell it."

"What?"

"Sell it all. Then how much will I owe you?"

"Now don't be hasty, son. We hadn't received a payment from you in two weeks, and before that sporadically at best."

"Sell it."

"But it's all you own entirely, I'm told. Clothes, dishes, forks and spoons. Better that you just pay your debt and get those things back."

"You think I've been holding out on you, don't you? Well, I haven't. I was all set to make a large payment today."

"I see, and did you bring it?"

"I . . . No. I was not able."

The man shoved the mailbag off his desk. "You have a job, Adams. Get an advance, pay your debt, and get your stuff. You don't even have a pot to . . . Well, you know what I mean."

Stephen slung the heavy bag over his shoulder in one swoop, his anger giving him more strength than usual. He marched to the door and stopped. "Thank you for hearing me out, Murray."

Murray sputtered. "Indeed. Now go be a responsible citizen and make good on your obligations."

Stephen slept fitfully that night thinking about Minnie losing her income and all the money he'd lost. The fact that he had no mattress did not help matters. For the first time he understood the agony his father must have been under when he took his own life. He would never comprehend how it led to such destruction, however.

On Sunday, determined to bear up and continue on, Stephen straightened his bow tie, preparing to make the trip to Rayburn Street for services like he'd done most Sundays since he'd met

Annie Gallagher. When his parents were alive, they had attended St. Matthew's across the street from Bourne Booksellers. Surely God would forgive him for his ulterior motive in attending First Church instead. He was still in worship, as a righteous man should be on a Sabbath morning.

He stopped at Mrs. Jacobs's for a sweet bun to take to Annie. "You come any Sunday morning," his Jewish neighbor said. "I do my baking on this day, and I give you your fill."

"You are quite generous." He placed the bread, dripping with honey and safely wrapped in brown paper, in the inside pocket of his overcoat. It was all he could offer Annie at the moment. Davis had not answered his door the last two days, so Stephen didn't know about getting the story back yet.

The morning drizzle ceased just as he approached the church building. Removing his hat as he entered, he studied the crowd. Clusters of ladies in feathered bonnets filled the first half-dozen pews on the right, with only a few men sprinkled in between them. Annie was too practical to wear a feathered hat. He expected to find her on the other side of the sanctuary, where she usually sat. At last he spotted her about a dozen rows from the front on the far end of a pew. Mrs. Hawkins sat next to her, her prominent nose turned toward the altar, and the other Hawkins girls sat to her right. A seat was open behind them.

He scurried over, politely acknowledging the ushers, and sat down just as the pipe organ resounded with the processional.

When the service ended, Stephen was ready. He jumped to his feet and stood at the end of Annie's pew. He bowed slightly. "Mrs. Hawkins, Miss Gallagher." He nodded at the others. "Ladies. Lovely to see you."

The older woman, cheeks pasty with face powder, stuck out her hand. "Oh, Mr. Adams. What a delightful surprise." She turned to Annie. "Isn't it, love?"

The shortest girl, whom he knew to be Annie's cousin, reached out a long, white-gloved hand. "Lovely to see you."

Stephen grazed his lips over the girl's hand, as he had done for the older woman. Owen McNulty had been seated next to Grace, and he greeted them as well. Then he turned to Annie. "I was wondering if I might walk you home, Miss Gallagher."

Her employer replied. "Indeed you may. We are dropping by the Thorps' for our noontide meal, and Grace and Owen are lunching with the reverend—prenuptial planning, you understand. But I've need of the pie I baked yesterday, and it would be delightful if you and Annie fetched it for us."

"Certainly." He turned to the couple. "How wonderful for you both. The big day is almost upon us, isn't it?"

Grace blushed. Stephen shook Owen's hand.

Mrs. Hawkins tapped the fingers of her gloved hands together. "Indeed it is, Mr. Adams." She turned to her housekeeper. "Annie, you will pick up the pie we are to bring the Thorps, won't you?"

Annie knitted her brows and stared at the woman. "We have plenty of time to—"

"If you're so inclined, Mr. Adams, to walk Annie on this errand, I would be most appreciative."

"I would be honored."

Annie did not appear to appreciate her lack of choice in the matter. He would need to charm her as best he could. He must explain that he had not yet been able to get her story back.

"Now go along, lovies. I'm eager to see my friends. Ella Thorp is helping me plan my menu for Grace and Owen's wedding reception."

Stephen smiled. "May I extend my congratulations again." He bowed slightly in the couple's direction.

"Thank you," Grace answered. "If you would excuse us, we must make our way to Reverend Clarke's house."

When they all had gone separate ways, Annie sighed. "Oh, you have no idea what a major event she is planning, Mr. Adams."

"Indeed. You will have to tell me about it on the way." He offered Annie his arm and they left together. Thus far she didn't seem too miffed at him. Perhaps she had forgiven him for handing that story to Davis.

21

STEPHEN BEGAN WHISTLING "The Stone outside Dan Murphy's Door" again. It seemed to be his favorite.

Annie thought she might have reacted too strongly to Stephen's taking the story without permission. She didn't want to risk having the publisher dismiss her, because seeing her father's stories in print truly would be a great honor. She listened to the postman's whistling as she gathered her thoughts. If she could make it clear that she was the proper party to make the decisions about her stories without sounding too disturbed about his lack of good judgment in taking one of them to a publisher, perhaps this could work out. "Mr. Adams, about my father's stories—"

"I apologize. I have not been able to see Mr. Davis yet. But I promise you—"

"I've thought about this. You should not have taken one of them without permission."

"You are right, Miss Gallagher. I should not have. I'm sorry. It's just that I'm always trying to make things right for folks when perhaps I should not get involved. I know you want to do well here in America, and rightly so. These stories were your inheritance, weren't they?"

"Mr. Adams, whether they were or were not is not pertinent."

He glanced away like a scolded schoolboy, and she felt guilty. She needed to make her point, but perhaps she was going about it the wrong way. The publisher was not the only one she hoped would not reject her.

He turned back to her, eyelids half-closed. "I just thought, with my association with a publisher, I could . . . Well, I overstepped." He pinched his lips together a moment. "You understand, don't you?"

She smiled. "You understand I do not appreciate you trying to conduct business on my behalf?"

"Indeed I do."

"I admit your motives seem worthy enough. Seeing as you meant no harm . . ."

"I truly did not. Please believe me." His face softened. The curve of his smile was understated enough to convince Annie he was not overplaying his concern. Stephen was a man who could be trusted despite this error in judgment.

"I would like Mr. Davis to publish them, if he's so inclined."

"You would?"

"I have plans that the proceeds could assist me with."

"I see. This is a splendid opportunity."

"And for you as well?"

Stephen shook his head, his dark curls bouncing. "He sent me to look for something appropriate. Finding your father's stories was happenstance, but fortuitous for you both, wouldn't you say?"

"Indeed. While I admit I was miffed, I do in fact owe you my thanks. I don't think I could ever have found a way to publish them on my own."

The tight muscles in his face relaxed. "I want you to know, while I do receive pay for helping Davis, my main motivation is to see that you get what you should have, Miss Gallagher.

You want your father's memory to live on in the minds of the reading public, isn't that so?"

She liked how he expressed the sentiment. "'Tis. Like you said, a good opportunity."

"Yes." He rubbed his chin. "May I ask what your plans might involve, if you care to tell me?"

"You may. I'm to be the owner and chief administrator of a library, named in my father's honor. I will specifically welcome girls who need the services a library can provide."

"That is wonderful indeed. Is Mrs. Hawkins assisting you in this endeavor?"

"You don't think I can do this on my own?"

"I didn't mean to imply anything like that."

"She has been very kind, but this is my own undertaking."

As they neared Hawkins House, he paused and opened the iron gate for her. "I will speak to Mr. Davis right away. As a matter of fact, he did ask that you come by to see him if you are able."

"I would like that."

"I would be happy to escort you there."

"Will he see me today?"

"It's Sunday."

"I know 'tis Sunday, Mr. Adams. I would like you to arrange it, if you can. I am dutifully employed every other day. We do have a wedding to prepare for." She knew she sounded bad-tempered, but she could not help it. It was time to move forward with this.

"He might possibly make himself available."

"Good. Would you mind calling for me at the Thorps' in two hours?"

"Certainly."

They entered the house, and Stephen stood in the parlor while she fetched the pie. "You don't have to wait," she told him when she returned with the pie basket swinging on her arm.

"I would be without proper manners if I allowed a young lady to walk alone, Miss Gallagher. Please allow me to escort you. The Thorps live a block east of here, I believe. Three houses down from an apothecary."

He was most assuredly the postman.

On the way he told her the names of the people who lived in various houses. "The Millers have at least six cats wandering about that they feed. I've counted the bowls of milk. And the Olsons have a boxer named Wilmer. Normally I do not care for dogs, but he's a good fella. Of course in the tenements there is no counting the dogs and cats, but in this neighborhood it's different."

"How interesting."

"Mrs. Jacobs bakes outstanding hot rolls. Folks like to feed the postman at times, you know."

"Is that correct?"

He smiled again. "I have just finished *The Wonderful Wizard of Oz*. Are you done reading it?"

"You read quickly, Mr. Adams." She thought she saw him blush. "I am nearly finished. Don't tell me what happens, so."

"All right. Tell me, though, who is your favorite character?"

She did not hesitate. "Why, Dorothy, of course. She is quite brave, wouldn't you say?" Annie found she could not stay perturbed with him for long. His easy chatter so reminded her of her father.

"Dorothy? I suppose, although she depends upon her friends quite strongly. I am fond of Toto."

"The dog? I thought you didn't care for dogs."

He chuckled. "That dog won't bite me."

Annie gave a dismissive shake of her head. "In all seriousness, I do hope Dorothy gets home." She stopped walking and gazed at him. "But don't you dare tell me, Mr. Adams."

He laughed. "I wouldn't dream of it. I almost forgot. I brought you something." He reached into his jacket and produced a package. "It's a sweet bun baked by my neighbor."

A gift. Annie could not remember the last time someone other than her employer had given her anything. "How kind." She turned away to hide her flustered face and stuck the package into her basket. "How did you know you would see me today?"

He blushed and tripped over his words. "I . . . uh . . . I thought I might see you in church." His dark brows rose as though he'd made a huge error. "I did not intend to disturb you. I know where you attend because . . . Well, I know where you live because—"

She laughed. "You deliver our mail. Of course you know where I live. It was very kind of you, Mr. Adams, to think of me. I hope Mrs. Hawkins hasn't put you up to this."

"Mrs. Hawkins?"

She might have guessed wrong. "Oh, never mind. Sometimes that woman seems to want to live my life for me, all the while keeping me oblivious to some things. I thought she might have sent you."

"No. Not at all. I mean, she did not send me."

"She is a kind soul, of course—but she is, after all, my employer."

"Oh, she is kind. She has a heart for helping others."

"I did not mean to appear ungrateful."

"Of course not. You just want to make your own decisions, is that right?"

So very right. "I'm happy you understand."

They reached the brownstone with forest-green shutters and the shingle out front reading *Matthias Thorp, Physician*. This was where Stephen Adams had come the night Kirsten became ill.

"It was very thoughtful of you that night, fetching the doctor for Kirsten."

"I hope she's all right."

"She will be in time."

When the Thorps' maid answered the door, Stephen turned to leave.

"Thank you for walking me."

"I will return in two hours' time." He waved as he stepped away.

"Oh, Mr. Adams?"

He stopped.

She held up the brown package. "Thank you for the sweet bun."

His face lit up. Emma was right. He was dashing.

22

As soon as Stephen and Annie approached the glass door at Davis Publishing, it opened.

"I'm so delighted you came to see me, Miss Gallagher."

"Thank you for being available today, sir. I could not come any other time."

"The pleasure is all mine. My door is always open for you. When Stephen told me you wished to see me today, I could not refuse."

Refuse? Davis had been overly eager, Stephen thought. He'd even told him to get her there as soon as possible.

The man pulled out a chair for Annie and she sat. His eyes never left her as he circled around to sit at his desk. "I apologize for taking so long to be in touch about your stories, my dear."

Stephen saw Annie's shoulders stiffen. Davis should not be addressing her as though she were a child.

"Stephen couldn't find me earlier because I've been in several conferences with the men over at *Harper's* magazine."

"Truly?" She sat up straighter.

Stephen stood in front of the cast-iron heat radiator under the window, from where he could study both of their faces.

"Yes. The folks at *Harper's* would like very much to publish this story, if you would allow."

Stephen interrupted. "*Harper's*? I thought you wanted to publish them."

"I do, indeed. We've worked out a plan, and I would like to tell you about it and see if it is amenable to you, Miss Gallagher."

"I would like to hear it, Mr. Davis."

"You have more of these stories?"

"I have ten."

Davis seemed delighted enough to bounce right out of his office chair. "Good, good." He pulled some typewritten pages from a brown envelope. "We have taken the liberty to draw up an agreement. Allow me to explain."

She nodded.

"*Harper's* will publish one story every week for . . . eight weeks." He reached for a pen and made a mark on the paper. "I'm filling in that number since we didn't know how many there were. Then, once the public's interest has been stoked, we at Davis Publishing will publish all ten in a book. We will have the last two exclusively."

"The money, Mr. Davis? How much am I to be paid for this?"

"One hundred dollars for each story. And then we will negotiate again for the book."

Annie held a hand to her chest. "What?"

Stephen slapped his knee. So they were Redmond's. What a find. He couldn't allow Annie to be taken advantage of just because she did not understand who her father was. "Two hundred!"

Annie spun around. "Mr. Adams. I will discuss this, please, if you don't mind."

"I . . . uh . . . You should get more."

Davis spoke up. "He's right. Two hundred it is."

Obviously Davis had been given some negotiating power.

"And she will receive royalties from the book, in addition to some payment in advance," Davis added.

"Certainly she should," Stephen agreed.

Davis nodded in Stephen's direction. "And you, my boy, will receive a finder's fee."

Annie stood. "I implore you both to stop talking as though I'm not in the room."

Davis dipped his head. "My apologies, dear. We are positively giddy over these tales, and we only want the best publishing situation for them . . . and for you, of course."

"I . . . I'm grateful, but I don't understand how you can be so generous. They are just my wee tales."

Davis took a deep breath. "Your father, Miss Gallagher—it appears he wrote under a pen name. That is to say, he used a false name in the interest of privacy."

"Why would he do that? Why would he not tell me if this was true?"

Even as she spoke this argument, she seemed weakened by the idea that it might be the case and slumped in her chair. Stephen understood how she must be feeling, and he wished he could make it better. His father had also hidden things. When the truth is revealed, you're left to wonder how you could have been so gullible. Were you really so unworthy of the truth?

He pondered her posture and how moments ago she had held her head high. Annie Gallagher was a strong, determined, beautiful woman. He hated thinking she might have these doubts about herself. Hopefully, for her sake, there had been a sensible reason her father hadn't told her he was really Redmond.

Davis stood at her side and tapped his fat fingers together. "Perhaps he wanted to spare you all this, dear. He wanted to provide for you without you having to be burdened with the details of business and—"

Annie seemed to break free from her sadness as suddenly as

a hunted duck fleeing from cover. "I assure you I'm perfectly capable." She buttoned the neck of her cloak. "I will accept the offer of . . ." She cleared her throat. "Two hundred dollars per story, and when the time comes for a book, I will engage a solicitor to assist me. However, I will only sign the contract for one story at a time."

That was the Annie he knew.

Davis returned to his desk chair and fidgeted with his cigar. "As you wish. Thank you, Miss Gallagher. It is a privilege indeed. I'll just change the number here." Davis's recovery was on par with finding the proverbial golden goose egg. He knew when he had a good opportunity in front of him. The man pushed the papers forward on his desk and handed her a pen.

"Let me see." Stephen stepped in front of her.

"I know how to read, Mr. Adams. I appreciate your concern, but I can handle this."

Stunned by her reproach, Stephen stepped back. "No offense, Miss Gallagher."

"None taken."

Stephen sat at the diner's counter Monday after work and poured out his heart to Dexter.

"I thought I had broken ground with her, but then she made it clear she did not want my help. I only wanted to ensure she wasn't taken advantage of."

"Don't take it so hard, buddy. These things—courtships— they take time. She's just a bit independent, is all. You have to allow for that."

Stephen sipped his black coffee. "Got any milk?"

"Like, for kids?"

"Come on. Got any for my coffee or not?"

"Hey, take it easy." Dexter disappeared into the back room and returned with a glass bottle.

"Thanks. Look, I'm sorry."

Dexter held up his hands. "No harm done. You're one of the few fellas I know who puts milk in his coffee. I forgot."

"I'm just a bit jumpy."

"Say, why don't you come by tomorrow and have supper with us. My Harriet's cooking up creamed cabbage."

Stephen gave him a thumbs-up. "I'll be there with bells on."

A lanky fellow came in, out of breath, and took the stool next to Stephen. "There's a storm coming."

Stephen nodded to acknowledge him. "I had not heard."

"Down at the pier the fishermen are all coming in and tying up."

"Fine and dandy. Nothing worse than delivering mail in a storm."

"The mail must get through." The stranger chuckled.

Stephen wasn't sure if that had been a sarcastic remark or not.

Dexter returned after serving a customer an egg salad sandwich and received the newcomer's order for a roast beef special. After pouring the man a cup of coffee, he turned to Stephen and handed him a slice of pie on a white china plate. "On me."

Stephen grinned. "You're a good friend, Dex."

"I bet it will be no time before you're having pie with the ladies over at Hawkins House."

"That so?" the stranger asked. "I've heard of that place."

Dexter handed the man some silverware rolled in a cloth napkin. "Stephen here is the postman. He befriends everyone on his route."

The man unrolled the napkin and placed it across his lap. "Good. Then you have probably heard of a girl there named Kirsten Wagner."

Stephen caught a glimpse of the man's unusual tie. He'd seen a tie like that before, the other day on the street in front of Hawkins House . . . but maybe somewhere else too. He couldn't be completely sure, but that day a man had been banging on the letter box. What were the chances? "Why do you ask?"

The man pointed to a metal badge pinned to his lapel. "From the Pinkerton Detective Agency. Just asking some questions and doing my job."

Dexter frowned.

His wife called out from the kitchen. "Order up!"

He did not turn around. The Pinkerton man motioned toward the plate of food, but Dexter ignored him. "We don't serve folks that come here causing trouble."

The man smirked. "No trouble, friend. If this young man is the postman, then he'll know whether or not he's delivered a package at Hawkins House for Miss Kirsten Wagner." He turned to Stephen. "Have you?"

"I . . . uh . . . I deliver lots of mail. Why?"

"I am not one to answer questions, boy, just ask them."

Harriet marched around from the kitchen, grabbed the food from the pass-through window, and placed it in front of the man. Then she stomped back to the kitchen.

"I think I'll have my pie at the table over there," Stephen said, and Dexter nodded and followed him over.

"The nerve of some people, interrupting other folks' conversations," Dexter said when they sat. "Pinkertons! Everyone knows they break the law as much as the criminals they're tracking. Untrustworthy snakes."

"I never expected one of those fellas to sneak around here, Dexter."

"Me either. And Harriet wanted me to feed him anyway."

"I don't know what he's about, but I'll warn Ann—I mean, Miss Gallagher."

Dexter grinned. "Of course. Now, let's talk about something more pleasant. Like books . . ."

Stephen held up a finger. "I got a couple more to share with you."

"Oh? What are they? I hear H. G. Wells has a new one."

"No, sorry. Not that one. Later I'll have *The Master Key* to loan you, but today just a couple books of poetry that Davis is distributing for a publisher in Boston."

He groaned.

"They're not so bad, really."

"Right." He tossed his tidying-up rag into the air and caught it. "Hey, thanks for bringing the *Wizard* book by the other day. I have been reading it, just so I know how it is before I give it to my kids."

"Sure, that's why. I know you were eager to read it. Like it so far?" Stephen had hoped to have conversations like this with Annie.

"That's some story he wrote there. Just like folks have been saying. Davis ought to publish a book like that. It would make him a millionaire."

Stephen shook his head. "A millionaire just from a book? You've gone mad, Dex."

"Hey, I believe it. In the future that book's gonna prove to be even bigger than it is now. I hear he's writing more of them. Quite a talent, that Baum."

Stephen talked around a mouthful of pie. "Well, I agree with you. Davis needs a book like that." And he hoped it would be Annie's. Not just for his finder's fee, but for her. She had plans, and he wanted all her dreams to come true.

As Dexter chatted with other customers about ways to board

up their tenements against the growing storm, Stephen day-dreamed about how it had been his doing that Annie's stories were discovered and how that should eventually get him a spot at her supper table instead of Dexter's.

Annie missed the postman's arrival because she'd been out seeing to Mrs. Hawkins's order at the florist. Just as well after the way he'd tried to speak for her in Davis's office. He meant well, but she just couldn't tolerate it. She had to do this herself. She would be a successful American woman once she proved to herself and others she did not need to scrub away her shortcomings.

She found Mrs. Hawkins and asked about Kirsten.

"Dr. Thorp advises us to stay away for a few weeks to give her time to rest. We will go visit her as soon as the wedding is past us. That will give Kirsten time to recover without the added excitement visitors would bring."

"I do wish we could check up on her, though."

"I do every day, love. Since Mrs. Jenkins has returned, she has been gracious enough to offer the use of her telephone line. I've just come from there, in fact, and the news is Kirsten is breathing a bit more comfortably. In fact, the doctor now believes that she does not have whooping cough after all, just a severe lung infection. That is good news because whooping cough would have meant a much longer recovery. So try not to worry."

"I'm happy to hear that. Thank you." Annie climbed the stairs toward Kirsten's room. She would need to do a thorough cleaning. She shoved Kirsten's trunk into the closet and fluffed the pillows. Aileen should be helping. Where was she? When she stepped back into the hall, she noticed the other bedroom door slightly ajar. Pushing it open, she found Aileen sitting on her bed, weeping.

"Aileen?" Annie tapped the door with her fingertips.

Aileen looked up with watery eyes. "While you were away, a messenger came to the back door. Brought this telegram." She held up the paper.

"What does it say?"

"Don't know."

"Didn't you read it?"

Aileen sniffed loudly and looked away. "Can't read, Annie."

"What do you mean?" Annie marched into the room and took the paper.

"The letters make no sense to me. You were the smart one. You were the one who had a chance to make it in America. I can't even get a job, and now . . ." She stared at the paper in Annie's hand. "That could be bad news, couldn't it? Folks don't send telegrams otherwise. Is it from Ma?"

Annie unfolded the paper. At the top in black block letters were the words *The Western Union Telegraph Company*. On the line marked *To*, she read out loud, "'Miss Kirsten Wagner in care of Mrs. Agnes Hawkins.'" She glanced back at Aileen, who was trying to suck in sobs. "'Tis not for you. Dry your eyes."

Aileen let out a sigh and wiped her face with the backs of her hands.

"Get a backbone, Aileen, and come help. There are dresses to trim and decorations to assemble. The wedding's in just a wee bit more than one week, you know."

Later, after evening tea, Mrs. Hawkins stared at the telegram on the tea table. "Jonas Wagner seems to already be in the city."

Annie knew the woman was as sharp-witted as a hawk, but how could she know this? "Why do you think so, Mrs. Hawkins?"

"Telegrams state where the message originated, along with

where it is going. He must have sent it as soon as he got off the train. I don't know, of course, if he has other business to attend to before he comes, but I must drop in on that boardinghouse I had in mind for him. I should go now. When I return, I'll draw up a list of things that need to be done." The Hawk stood, calling out her mental list. "The dried apples need to be soaked for the compote. The herbs must be mixed for spiced cider . . ."

Annie sighed. "I will attend to it, Mrs. Hawkins. Trust me."

"I know, love." She patted Annie's cheek as though she were a child. "We will work on those things when I return."

So she didn't want Annie to mix herbs without her supervising. Soon, very soon, Annie would tell her what a businesswoman she was becoming. Annie crept toward her room to read more of the *Wizard* book.

When she got to the part where Dorothy and her friends were falling asleep due to poisonous poppies, she wondered if the author might actually cause harm to come to one of the characters.

"If we leave her here she will die," said the Lion. "The smell of the flowers is killing us all. I myself can scarcely keep my eyes open, and the dog is asleep already."

Perhaps this book was not really much better than the Grimm brothers' "Hansel and Gretel."

"If we leave her here she will die."

Annie thought about Kirsten. She did not want to abandon anyone the way she had been . . . Well, Da hadn't meant to leave her, but he had.

She found it hard to concentrate on the book with the wind whipping so loudly outside her window. She met Aileen in the hall.

Aileen shouted to be heard over the howling wind. "'Tis a

storm we'll be having," she said. "I'll check to see the windows
are locked up."

Mrs. Hawkins burst through the front door. Annie helped
her inside and took her dripping garments. "We are headed to
the third floor now, lovies."

"What do you mean? What's happening?" It took all of
Annie's strength to push the heavy door shut against the wind.

The woman hurried to the kitchen and returned with a
lamp and a box of matches. "When I got to Miss Hall's to
inquire about a room for Mr. Wagner, she admonished me for
not telephoning and sent me right back home. It seems there's a
storm coming, and folks fear flooding. The peril of living at the
tip of Manhattan, I suppose. Now, girls, gather all the reading
material and other valuables you find near the floor and bring
them upstairs."

Annie rushed to her room. She had left both the writing
desk and *The Wonderful Wizard of Oz* on the mahogany desk.
Gathering up the book and placing it on top of her stories, she
glanced at her father's Bible. She couldn't leave it behind and
risk something happening to it. It might not be of much importance to her for its content, but it had been to her father. She
grabbed the Bible, her book, and the writing desk and hurried
toward the stairs, where she and Aileen followed the Hawk up
through a door that had been previously locked.

"Aren't there bats up here, Mrs. Hawkins? That's what you've
always said." Annie ducked her head just in case.

"Perhaps. We'll see."

"What?" Aileen froze in her tracks.

"Come on," Annie urged. "Didn't I tell you to get a backbone, lass?" In truth the creatures made Annie jittery, but she
was determined not to let anyone see.

An aroma of musty wood met them when they climbed the

stairs that were normally hidden behind a wooden plank door at the end of the hall. Once they stood on the drafty third floor, Mrs. Hawkins went to a trunk and pulled out a couple of quilts. Then she tugged a wooden cask across the floor. "Water," she explained. "In case we're stuck up here awhile."

"My, you are prepared," Aileen said, wrapping an entire quilt around her small frame, leaving just one other for Annie and the Hawk to share.

"There's no need to fear the wind if your haystacks are tied down," the Hawk replied.

Such an Irish adage coming from a British lady. "Where did you hear that?" Annie asked.

"Oh, it's a common expression."

"'Tis as Irish as shamrocks," Annie insisted.

"Is it?"

"Mrs. Hawkins, surely you've been to Ireland."

"Indeed. Come on, girls. Get settled in. Thank the good Lord Grace is secure at the Parkers' and Kirsten is well looked after on an upper floor of the infirmary."

With the wind wailing so, it was not the time for conversation. But Annie would raise questions later. There was something the Hawk was keeping to herself.

Rain pounded against the side of the building. While Mrs. Hawkins examined her own tattered Bible, Annie held her book toward the glow of the lamp to read. It seemed Dorothy had awakened from the poppy field to quite a surprise. An army of field mice were so grateful the Tin Woodman had rescued their queen from a wildcat that they were teaming together to pull the still-sleeping Lion to safety.

Annie sucked in a breath. Her father had also written about the valiant efforts of field mice. The smallest creatures, who alone could do nothing, had joined together to accomplish something. There must be a lesson to be learned from that.

"If ever you need us again," she said, "come out into the field and call, and we shall hear you and come to your assistance."

Oh, Da, if only I could call to you!

Annie closed her eyes and imagined her library. A massive brick structure because books must be protected from fire and flood. There would be rows and rows of volumes. Novels and inspirational tomes. Maps and dictionaries. But most of all, her books would hold stories from Ireland—especially her father's, now that they were to be published. Sad that Da had not lived to see his fame. He did know Irish folks enjoyed his tales, but even he could not have imagined how many readers there were in America.

A loud crash came from one of the eaves. The small window there had shattered.

"Watch out!" Aileen cried, throwing her quilt over Annie as shards of glass flung toward them.

Moments later Annie scrambled to her feet. "Mrs. Hawkins, are you all right?"

The woman's hand was streaked with blood. "I am fine. Just a cut. Oh, dear. We should stack up this old furniture against the wind coming in."

Aileen pushed against a tall chest with more force than a wee one like her ought to have. Annie scooted the lamp and blankets behind it, and then the three of them squeezed in close.

"Much better, girls." The Hawk had wrapped her hand in her apron.

"We'd better see to that cut." Annie slowly unwrapped it.

Aileen ladled up some water from the cask. Not waiting for

Annie to tell her what to do, she gently dabbed the woman's hand.

"Like I said, it's not bad," Mrs. Hawkins said. "After the storm my homemade ointment will heal it in no time."

Annie stared at her cousin. In the frenzy of the moment she had responded with amazing calmness, not complaining once about her discomfort. Annie never would have predicted such behavior.

Eventually Aileen noticed her staring. "What is it?"

"Nothing. Uh, you really helped, Aileen."

The girl smiled and began sweeping away the glass shards with a whisk broom.

A few hours later, when the wind died down, Mrs. Hawkins declared it safe to retire to their beds. Descending to the second floor just as Mrs. Hawkins was coming up from checking below, Annie heard a noise in the kitchen.

"Rodents, I'll bet," Mrs. Hawkins said. "Floodwaters send them scurrying into the houses."

Aileen took the oil lamp from her. "I'll go see."

Astonished at her wee cousin's bravery, Annie followed her downstairs in case she needed help. Aileen held the lamp low, and Annie retrieved a broom from the scullery. Thankfully the house had not flooded, but as Aileen directed the lamp toward the table, she jumped back. A stranger sat in one of the chairs.

23

As MORNING DAWNED, Stephen was relieved to find the rain had ceased. Walking home from the diner had been an adventure, holding on to lampposts and fences the best he could against the gale. A glance outside told him this day would be quiet, and he was thankful.

A newsboy on the corner shouted out the headlines. "Scenes of Destruction at Old Coney Island!"

Stephen glanced at the paper. "What happened?"

The boy pointed at a large photograph on the cover page. "Coney Island's all flooded out."

"Do you know about the streets in Lower Manhattan and Battery Park?"

"Aw, they're wet is all. Last night the waters rose, but they went back before dawn."

He knew the boy would not be wrong. Stephen had been one of them once, sleeping in alleys and basement wells. Stephen had been able to go home when he wanted to but, like most newsboys, preferred the streets because it felt safer there. Stephen's father, when he bothered to leave the pub, tore into a rage the moment Stephen's mother asked for money. He never used his fists, but the shouting and slamming of doors pierced Stephen's young heart and sent him to seek solace on the crowded streets. He knew it was that way and worse for those boys he saw every day on his route, and that's why he did whatever he could for them. The most dedicated charity workers could not get them into a home. "You stay safe, son."

"You bet, mister."

Stephen would knock when he got to Hawkins House, whether he had a delivery or not. Between the storm and the stranger asking about Kirsten Wagner, he needed to be sure they were safe. He rearranged his route to get there early.

The little cousin opened the door, looking as if she'd seen the devil.

"What's wrong?"

"Last night. That storm? Someone got in the house."

He pushed past her. "Where are the others?" Not waiting for her to answer, he made his way to the kitchen. The window in the rear door was smashed. He turned back to Aileen. Dropping his mailbag on the floor, he gently shook her by the arm. "Miss O'Shannon. Where is everyone? Tell me."

Her head tilted to look at him.

He turned toward the back staircase, where Annie was descending. His knees went weak. "Annie! Uh, Miss Gallagher. Are you all right?"

She dabbed at a scratch on her face. "Sit down. I'll tell you what happened."

They each took a chair at the kitchen table. "Where is Mrs. Hawkins? Is she all right?"

"She is. She is at the police station this moment trying to get this resolved."

"How did you . . . ?" He stretched out a hand but knew it wouldn't be proper to touch Annie's face.

She shook her head. "I'm fine. When I ordered that man out, I slammed the door and the glass shattered. Probably weakened by all the wind we had."

"What man? Are you sure you're all right?"

"Really I am fine. Aileen, however, is a bit shaken up. She and I encountered the intruder, and it scared the life out of her."

"Oh, and not you?" Aileen screwed up her face.

"Never mind, Aileen. 'Tis over now." She turned back to Stephen. "All's well. Thank you for your concern."

"I'm so sorry. A burglar?"

"We thought so at first."

"I should have been more vigilant. Sergeant McNulty asked me to be." He put a fist to his mouth. He'd failed again.

"We are fine, just faced with a terrible dilemma."

Again she didn't want his help. Stephen wasn't sure what to do. Aileen sighed loudly and rose to fill a teakettle.

Annie grimaced from the scratch across her cheek when she tried to smile. "This man, this Pinkerton, has been demanding that we allow him to see Kirsten. Something about a case he's working on, and Kirsten has something he wants."

"And he thought he'd drop by during a horrendous rainstorm?"

"Oh, he said something about getting in out of the rain and no one heard his knocking, but I think he's trying to scare us into giving him what he wants."

"Any idea what that might be?"

She blew out a breath. "That package you delivered to her. He didn't say what he was after, but I would suppose that's it. She wouldn't reveal what the package contained, but I can't imagine she would have anything someone would want—not money or jewels or anything. She is just an unpretentious immigrant. She has been mysterious about her brother and all, but the Pinkerton has never mentioned him."

Aileen spoke up. "He just sat there in the chair you're sitting in now, plain as the nose on your face. Said he was aware Kirsten was not in the house. 'Twas as though he'd been spying on us. Mrs. Hawkins wants him charged for trespassing."

Stephen drew in a long breath while he thought about this. "Why was he here if he knew Kirsten was not? Did he say?"

Aileen grunted. "I believe he thought he could bully us into telling him where she is."

Annie nodded. "This Pinkerton was warned to leave us alone." She motioned for Stephen to take a toast triangle from a plate on the table. "We haven't had time to bake this morning."

He accepted the bread. "This is fine. Thank you. Now, what about Kirsten?"

"Somehow he knows Kirsten was taken away somewhere." Annie's gaze drifted to the baseboards as though she were talking to herself. "I suppose he might have seen the ambulance, but if he had, surely he would have followed it."

The man he'd run into at the diner. Stephen should have checked on the women right then. He recalled some time ago Annie telling him about some men nosing about and accusing their newest boarder of impropriety. He should have known something like this might happen. How could he ever become the kind of man Annie would be drawn to if he wasn't smart enough to put clues together and protect her?

Annie wagged her head. "I don't understand it all, but he says he will have our house shut down for harboring women of ill repute."

"Preposterous! Does Sergeant McNulty know about this?"

Aileen spoke up. "Mrs. Hawkins is going to speak to him again."

Stephen was outraged. "How dare this man insinuate such

a thing and threaten you this way. Mrs. Hawkins runs a fine
Christian outreach here."

Annie agreed. "She does, but Kirsten—although she's done
nothing wrong—has given some people reason to wonder. 'Tis
all a misunderstanding."

"I am sorry, Miss Gallagher." He turned to Aileen. "Miss
O'Shannon. But it must be more than that for the man to come
into your house in the middle of a terrible storm. The package you mentioned. Earlier in the day a man asked me about
something I delivered here for Miss Wagner. I didn't tell him
anything. It must have been this Pinkerton."

"From Jonas Wagner," Annie said. "That's what I was talking
about earlier."

Stephen couldn't sit by. "How can I help?"

"Find out what that Pinkerton wants," Aileen snapped.

Annie stood. "No matter what it is he wants, Cousin, we
won't turn Kirsten over to him."

The younger girl shook a tea towel at Annie. "But how can
we get rid of him if we do not know what he is after, Annie?"

Stephen felt he had to stand too. "Well, if that man is both-
ering you . . . I think Aileen is correct. I will see what I can do."
He retrieved his mailbag and headed to the front door. "Would
you like me to send a carpenter by to fix the door?"

"Very kind of you, but I will wait to see what Mrs. Hawkins
would like to do. We covered it with blankets last night."

"Would you like me to help with that?" He glanced around,
looking for something to use.

"Thank you, no. We've swept up the glass and we will take
care of it. You are very kind to ask, though." Annie's expression
softened. He might have stood in the glow of her gazing all
morning if Aileen had not cleared her throat loudly. He excused
himself and went out the front door.

Instead of finishing his route, Stephen headed straight for the neighborhood police precinct.

"McNulty's off duty," the man behind the desk told him. "He works nights, and what a night we had too with that weather."

"I imagine. When did he depart?"

"I don't know exactly. They had a meeting this morning. Not sure if he's left from that."

Impatient, Stephen carefully measured his words. "How might I find out if he's still here?"

The officer nodded to some chairs lined up in the hall. "Wait there, and when the police chief's door opens, you can see if he comes out or not."

And these are the folks protecting our city? They can't even keep track of each other. He did not sit, but on his second pacing past the chairs, the door opened and Owen McNulty stepped out.

"Mr. Adams? What brings you here? No trouble, I hope."

After Stephen told him what he'd learned at Hawkins House, Owen escorted him outside. "Mrs. Hawkins has been in. We should talk about this, you and me. I'll explain what I know. Coffee?"

They made their way to Dexter's.

Owen McNulty wearily clutched his coffee cup as they sat at a corner table, away from eavesdroppers.

Stephen smacked his fist on the table. "That man was in their home in the middle of the night!"

"I know that is disturbing. I'm happy no one was harmed, but this fella, he just likes to intimidate people, as though scaring them to death can help him get what he's after. Thankfully Clayton Cooper—that's his name—is not a common criminal, even if he is rude and irksome. And I hear Annie Gallagher gave him what for and he took off, tail between his legs."

Stephen chuckled. "Yes, Annie Gallagher has made it clear she can handle all sorts of matters on her own." He stirred another sugar cube into his coffee. "Has anyone questioned Miss Wagner about this object she is accused of having?"

"It's a delicate matter, considering her health, but I trust that has been done."

"I think it's a book of some sort. Something I delivered from her brother." Stephen told Owen about his conversation with the Pinkerton the night before.

"I see. Well, try not to worry. My father, Mr. Parker, and Dr. Thorp are all with Mrs. Hawkins at the police chief's office on Mulberry as we speak. My father and the others support her in such matters. They have a committee of sorts they call the Benevolents. It seems this Pinkerton has a lot of pull, but together these Benevolents have quite a bit of influence in the neighborhood themselves."

"So has the Pinkerton explained what he's after or who he might be working for?"

"It would seem Kirsten has something—likely the object you delivered to her—pertaining to an investigation into a stock market investment scheme, and not a legitimate one." He tapped his fist on the tabletop. "If you ask me, the man should have just been up-front about it. Scaring all those women the way he has. Pinkertons don't know how to conduct themselves. These are not bank robbers he's dealing with." He stared out the window as though considering what he'd just said. "You know, I would not put it past this Cooper fellow to be working *for* the schemers and not in pursuit of them." He pulled a photograph out of his coat pocket. "Not a mug shot, but we do have a few images of the agents at headquarters."

"This is the man I met in the diner." *Wait a minute!* His earlier hunch may have been right. That day he'd encountered a man demanding to have something that had been deposited in a letter box . . . Could it be that he'd been following Jonas? "I don't know for certain, but a while ago a man about my height, wavy black hair . . . I didn't know about the Pinkerton then, but it could have been the Cooper fellow I saw pounding on the side of a letter box. He wanted something back, but I was not at liberty to give it to him."

"Would not surprise me at all. Pinkertons don't care about the law. If there weren't any people around, he would have blown the top off it to get what he wanted. These financial schemers are relentless."

Oh, my. "I have been helping with an investigation of the sort at the post office as well. Could they be connected?"

The man wagged his head. "I don't think so. I read your report. What the Drapers were doing was small-scale. They did not even buy stocks, just used new deposits to pay withdrawals."

"Borrowing from Peter to pay Paul, so to speak."

"That's right. A small operation and easily shut down. This, however, is more than that."

Stephen remembered what the postmaster had said. The US Post Office was primarily concerned with mail fraud, and since this package the Pinkerton was so keen to find had been delivered in the US mail . . . "I have some checking to do of my own. Thank you, Sergeant, for telling me about this."

They stood. "Certainly, but, Stephen, you do realize this is a matter for the police?"

"I understand."

24

ANNIE AND HER COUSIN sat in the parlor while they waited for Mrs. Hawkins to return. "I wonder if the postman will be coming back today," Aileen said.

"I don't know. You and I can handle things, so. Sergeant McNulty has said the Pinkerton is cleared off our block, so we know he won't be back."

Aileen brushed the lace curtain aside and gazed out. "This may be the postman right now."

Annie charged toward the front door and opened it quickly so she could speak to Stephen first.

"*Ja*, what a welcome that is. Are you Annie Gallagher, the housekeeper?"

A knot formed in Annie's stomach. Instead of the postman, a tall man wearing a gray felt hat with a black band and a long charcoal overcoat stood in front of her. Aileen came to her side.

After glancing around him as though someone might be watching, he removed his hat. "Jonas Wagner. I believe my sister is expecting me."

Annie's throat went dry.

Aileen spoke up. "Oh, Kirsten is not—"

Annie pushed her back with her shoulder. "She means she

is not in at the moment, Mr. Wagner. Won't you come in out of the cold?"

"Not until you tell me which one of you Irish ladies wrote to me. The housekeeper wrote on my sister's behalf, *ja*? When I was . . . uh . . . upstate, as they say."

"Her," Aileen cried out, rubbing her collarbone where Annie had shoved her.

"Miss Gallagher?" He took her hand like a gentleman.

"I am happy to finally meet you, Mr. Wagner."

"And you."

"Please be seated in the parlor." She and Aileen followed him in.

"Where is my sister?" His copper eyes held hers. "Tell me there is no bad news." He turned and parted the lace curtain with one finger, then shrugged and let it fall back.

"Not bad news precisely. But she is not here, Mr. Wagner. She's found . . . housing elsewhere."

"Where?" He spun around to face Annie. "Tell me no harm has come to her. Did someone come looking for her?"

Annie glared at him. "Someone like a Pinkerton?"

His wide-eyed look told her she'd guessed correctly. "Where did they take her?"

"No Pinkerton has taken her anywhere, just inquired is all."

"Did you tell him I was coming?" He balled his fist.

Aileen gasped and Annie gave her a stern glance. Looking back at the man, she knew she had to think of something. She let out the breath she'd been holding. "We did not. Please, won't you sit?"

Aileen patted the back of one of the chairs.

His face flushed, as though he'd realized his rudeness. "Thank you." He sat.

Annie moved gingerly as though the roses on the carpet

might sprout real thorns. "Please, have some tea. 'Tis Mrs. Hawkins's special recipe."

He fidgeted with a button on his vest. "She is safe, my sister?"

"She is." Annie smiled as she lifted the cup from the tray. "May I say that your English is superb?"

Jonas accepted the cup and returned to his chair by the window. *"Danke schön,"* he said, as though to remind her of his nationality. He took a sip of the warm drink and then smiled. "I have been unkind. Please forgive me." He seemed to stare at those roses on the floor.

"No apologies necessary," Annie said, exchanging glances with Aileen.

Her cousin got the hint. "I will go next door and have Mrs. Jenkins telephone the . . . Uh, we will let Mrs. Hawkins know you've arrived, Mr. Wagner."

"Very well. But my sister?"

Annie handed him a plate of biscuits. "I prefer to let Mrs. Hawkins answer your query, Mr. Wagner."

He stood until Aileen exited. Then he turned back to Annie. "Ah, *gut*. You were right, Miss Gallagher. It is a pleasant drink." Still, he did not look directly at her. "Tell me where my sister is . . . please."

Annie followed his gaze and began studying the pattern on the rug herself. This man seemed nothing like his letters. Even fatigue should not cause someone to be so brash. If she could just get him to tell her what kind of business he was up to . . .

He finally glanced up. The smoothness of his face, the lack of mature stubble, showed him to be much younger than she had imagined.

"Who is the elder, you or your sister?" Small talk might give Mrs. Hawkins more time to hurry back.

"We are separated by just one year. I was born a week after Kirsten's first birthday. We are like twins. We are very close."

"I imagine you are, the way Kirsten speaks of you."

He tapped his foot with unspent nervousness. "The package I sent. It arrived, *ja*?"

"Indeed." She willed Mrs. Hawkins to arrive with haste.

"I am happy to hear this." He pursed his lips and nodded.

Minutes of silence passed. They glanced at each other a few times, awkwardly.

Jonas set his teacup down. "She should be at work, no? The shirtwaist factory. She is not there. I checked first." He stood.

"Uh . . . you are correct." She rose to stop him. Somehow. "She is not there. Please, won't you wait for Mrs. Hawkins? She has secured you a room at a very nice boardinghouse."

Aileen returned. "Mrs. Hawkins left the . . . I am told she is on her way home this very minute."

Annie relaxed a bit. "Have some more tea, Mr. Wagner."

A half hour later Mrs. Hawkins entered. After introductions she clasped her hands together. "Well, now. Aileen has gone to find the messenger. A cab will be here soon to take you to the boardinghouse."

"I appreciate that." He glanced out the window again. "You will tell no one where I am staying, Mrs. Hawkins."

Annie couldn't keep quiet. "The Pinkerton, you mean."

Mrs. Hawkins gave her a sharp look.

"I will explain when I can." He smiled tightly. "I am not a criminal."

Agnes Hawkins narrowed her eyes. "Mr. Wagner, whatever business you have, I must insist you leave your sister out of it. She has been under my supervision, and I assure you she is fine."

"You don't understand. Why don't you just tell me where—?"

The woman stepped closer to him, a display of dominance. "We do not know what kind of family argument you might have with your sister, Mr. Wagner, but we will not be party to it. She asked us not to tell you where she is." She took a breath and relaxed her shoulders. "I would like this matter resolved so that we can focus on planning a wedding for one of my girls. She is marrying a police sergeant, and he's in line to become a detective one day."

Jonas's eyes grew wide. "I need to speak to my sister. I promise you I'll cause no harm. She is my only family. She must think she is doing this for the best, but she is mistaken."

The Hawk sighed. "I am willing to arrange a meeting if she consents. If you wish to see her, you will follow our instructions. Otherwise, we have nothing more to discuss and you may leave."

Annie longed to know what had been discussed at the police station and how this woman found her bravado.

"I do not need your cab, Frau Hawkins. I will be on my way."

When he'd gone, Annie questioned her. "How did you know he'd back down?" When Annie had ordered the Pinkerton out of the house, it had probably been the loony tone of her shouting that had made him flee, not a strong, confident demeanor like her employer's.

"I learned a long time ago, Annie, not to allow others to strong-arm me." She pulled out her handkerchief. "And that poor girl in that condition. It was not her fault. He won't make her a victim if I have anything to say about it." She plopped down on her favorite chair and turned to her open Bible. As though the man had intentionally interrupted her study, Mrs. Hawkins closed the book forcefully and tapped her fingers on the weathered leather cover.

Concern for the boarders was understandable—deeds like

making peas porridge and putting lavender under the sheets. But the way Mrs. Hawkins had stood up to that man just now? She seemed to carry a righteous sword against him. There was something more personal about this.

They heard a wee knock on the kitchen door. Mrs. Hawkins rose from her chair but motioned to Aileen. "That's Jules, love. Tell him we no longer need the cab but to go and fetch the punch bowl I'm borrowing from his mother for the party. Would you mind? And remember his nickel."

Aileen nodded and hurried to meet him.

Annie stared at the cover of Mrs. Hawkins's Bible. She hadn't noticed it before, perhaps because the woman kept it open most of the time, but there on the cover were embossed two gold letters: *K. G.* Annie blinked. This was the Hawk's Bible. The initials should be A. H. or perhaps her late husband's, H. H. But K. G.? Like Kate Gallagher? Surely not. But as unlikely as it seemed, there had been too many coincidences with Annie coming directly to Hawkins House and then being accepted as housekeeper so eagerly. Mrs. Hawkins seemed to know the idiosyncrasies of the Irish as though she'd been among them. And she had inadvertently mentioned Annie's mother as if she knew her.

Tread lightly.

The words from her father's wise rabbit character suddenly popped into her head, though she didn't know why.

Annie turned back to the Hawk. "I would like it very much if you would do me the favor of being honest with me, Mrs. Hawkins."

"Honest? Whatever do you mean?"

Annie tapped the back of the woman's chair. "Come, sit."

When she was settled in, Annie poured her some tea. "There is something more than mere charity going on here. You spoke as though you'd been personally affronted."

"We must all stand up against aggressors, love."

"But there is something you aren't telling me, so. Isn't there? Ireland. My mother." She swept her arm around the room. "Hawkins House and where your support comes from. You've been very mysterious."

The woman's eyes were bug-like.

"And while we are at it, the reason I'm here at all is the biggest conundrum of all. Am I to believe Father Weldon just happened to feel compelled to send me to his sister? Me, and not any of the other poor lasses in that laundry?" She couldn't stop herself now. "And then there's your Bible . . ."

The Hawk flipped the pages back open, concealing the personalized cover. Tears came to her eyes. "You are right, love. You are a grown woman of strong character. I shall tell you everything and pray that you do not despise me for not telling you sooner."

25

STEPHEN DELIVERED most of his route as quickly as he could, deciding to finish the rest tomorrow. When he rushed toward the door of the post office, determined to speak to Mr. Sturgis before he left for the day, he met Minnie Draper. She clutched the nameplate from her sorting station. She obviously had been dismissed.

He held the door as she came out. "I am so sorry, Minnie. I hope you understand I had no choice."

She smiled. "No, no, Mr. Adams. I am the one who owes you an apology. If I had used the smarts God gave me, I would never have urged you to deposit so much money. Leonard deceived me. I have been a fool." She swung her head side to side. "My mother tried to tell me I didn't know Leonard well enough to marry him. I had to learn the hard way. Can you ever forgive me?"

Losing the money smarted, but he had not lost his job, and that was most important. "It's not your fault I lost that money, Minnie. Sometimes we put our trust in the wrong places." He heard the words as though he had not spoken them but received them from somewhere else, the words of an understanding, righteous man. "I let greed get the best of me, I'm afraid."

"As did I. Leonard deserves to be in jail. I'm still a blessed woman, you know. They let me go."

He walked with her down the steps toward the street. "Will you find another job?"

"Mrs. Waters says I can help her with her fish cart on Saturdays, and my cousin is letting me sleep in her kitchen. I will be all right."

"Which fish cart?"

"Corner of Mulberry and Worth."

"I'll come by and purchase some . . . as soon as I can, Minnie."

"Bless you."

When Stephen got to Sturgis's office, the door was open. "Oh, good. You are still here."

"Adams, what can I do for you?" Mr. Sturgis put the pen he'd been using back in an inkwell.

"There is a matter I believe the postal inspectors will be interested in."

When he was done explaining the situation, Sturgis called to his secretary. "Get the inspector on the telephone line immediately, Shirley."

While they waited, Stephen used another phone line to let Dexter know he would have to miss dinner at his place.

When Stephen finally neared the door of his apartment building at the end of the long day, it was not Davis waiting for him but Archibald Murray, the undertaker. Stephen tried to collect his thoughts.

The man tipped his top hat and then placed his hands behind him, waiting for Stephen to come closer. Wearing an English-style double-breasted morning coat that met his perfectly pressed striped trousers just below the knees, Mr. Murray presented the image of a refined, genteel elder gentleman of wealth, not a bill collector.

"Mr. Murray, I am aware of what my options are concerning my belongings. You have made your point clear. What brings you to my neighborhood this evening?"

"Mr. Adams, I do regret that proceeding was necessary, but I am not without compassion." He wrinkled his aquiline nose. "Even if we auction your belongings, there will be remaining debt, son. I owe you at least that explanation."

Stephen did not want to invite him in. He had nowhere for him to sit. And besides, Murray's smug, condescending attitude was irritating.

"Seeing as I was in the neighborhood getting my horses shod—the best stables and grooms are just a block from here, you know." He cleared his throat. "Or maybe you don't know. No matter. I made up my mind to pay you a visit. Your parents were fine people, Stephen. Down on their luck, true, but fine souls. I owe them the courtesy of seeing you myself."

Stephen bit his lip. He had no more than fifty cents to his name at the moment and would like to eat next week and put coal in his stove. Did the man presume to squeeze the life out of the son of those "fine souls"? "You know I have a good job, Mr. Murray. I . . . made some unwise investments, however, and . . . if you would care to speak to Mr. Davis, he will tell you that I'm due some wages for some side work I recently did for him. I could ring him for you right now."

Mr. Murray held up a gloved hand. "No, not necessary."

"I just need a little more time."

He stroked his gray mustache. "I cannot begin to suppose what you are spending your paycheck on, my boy, but I told you I would not be patient forever. It is just business, you understand."

"I do. I will pay you."

"Like I said, even the auction will not be enough. I thought I should alert you to the fact." He chuckled sardonically. "Come now. We both know you have proven over time that you pay intermittently. This is a big city, Stephen. People are dying every day, and I'm afraid the space to bury them all is vanishing at an incredible rate. The demand for suitable ground has risen. If you don't pay me for those burial plots, someone else will, and . . . I will have no other choice but to add another grave atop. I must be paid. This is my livelihood, and I have kin to care for." He grunted. "I don't expect you to understand that."

A cruel remark. The man knew Stephen's parents and his brother had been his only family. Stephen did not anger easily, despite his outburst at the undertaker's office earlier. Most times Stephen was fairly tolerant of all kinds of folks. But now he was vexed. He'd heard enough. "I will pay you. Somehow. And soon. You have my word." He turned to put his key in the lock. "What you are suggesting—is it even legal, Mr. Murray? The . . . shared burial plots, I mean."

"Think of it like subletting an apartment."

Stephen had to juggle his key in the air to keep from losing it. "But my parents' graves. How could you violate such a sacred place?"

Archibald Murray's stance indicated that he would not be dissuaded. "Like the notice said, you have until the end of the month. It's just business, son. But I did feel compelled to give you this warning in person. It's the least I can do. For your parents."

If he wanted Stephen to thank him, he was misguided.

"Better to know now so that you might avoid these steps. The bill must be paid in full. Good evening." He marched away with his head held high as though he truly believed his words carried no insult.

Stephen could not let that happen to his parents, especially his mother, who had had no will to leave this world when she did.

He let himself into the dark hallway and paused for a moment in front of the door stenciled with Davis's name. A finder's fee would certainly help.

26

"THAT'S WHY I BROUGHT you home to live with me, love. So nothing ill like this Kirsten business would befall you."

"I don't understand, Mrs. Hawkins. I was in a Magdalene Laundry, and I tell you what befell me there was at least as bad as what Kirsten is going through."

The Hawk took a deep breath, and for a brief moment Annie dreaded whatever she might say. What if it were something ugly? Annie's teeth hit her lip as she pondered this. People had been talking about her without her knowledge. She rubbed her suddenly chilly arms. Was this the way good people dealt with the worst of God's children, the ones taken away to Magdalene Laundries? Did they feel driven to hide the truth from the discarded lasses? Trust them with nothing? Could people know where she'd been, what she'd endured, even without her telling them? Or was it something about her? Something so unpleasant that she reeked of it? Even before she'd been taken away, when her father was still living, he hadn't told her the truth of his publishing ventures, as she was now beginning to realize. Mr. Davis, the publisher, believed her father was the author Redmond, and he presumably knew about such things. Her father had written under that pen name and chosen to keep it from her. And now Stephen hadn't thought to ask her if she wanted her stories published before he carted them away. Even Mrs. Hawkins was hiding something. Annie sat straighter, gathering her courage. It should not be this way. The truth, no matter how horrible, must be faced.

Mrs. Hawkins smacked her lips, ready to begin. "You have wondered about my connection with my brother in Ireland, Annie."

"I have. Shall we start there?"

"Indeed. And I think you should understand why girls like Kirsten, like you, tug at my heartstrings. I, too, was a victim when I was a young girl."

"You mean someone did to you what Mr. Watson did to Kirsten? Oh, Mrs. Hawkins."

"A long time ago, love. My family was living in Ireland at the time. My father was in the British navy and was away quite a bit. He had visited many places, and he thought the Irish countryside would be a healthy choice for us. He thought a boarding school would benefit me, the only girl in the family."

"Why did you not tell me you lived in Ireland? I had just supposed the church sent your brother over, but then those Irish phrases and the like. It seemed you had been there."

"I . . . I was unsure how to tell you. I should have known better than to keep it from you. The truth, no matter how terrible, must be faced sooner or later."

Annie shook her head. She'd just told herself as much, hadn't she? Or had she? Bits from her father's tales kept popping up in her mind, and she'd been thinking about wise phrases and sayings. Out of thin air, it seemed. Now this.

Concentrate.

Mrs. Hawkins's face began to blur. Annie blinked hard, then shifted in her seat. She would not give in to her mind's betrayal.

Listen.

"My brother, love? He stayed on in Ireland after his schooling, hoping to find me."

"Find you?"

"You see, in Ireland if a man shows too much interest in you, or if you are deemed too pretty, or—God forbid—the temptations of the flesh overtook you and you committed some kind of indiscretion, folks put you away."

Annie began to perspire and her head grew light and foggy. She bit the inside of her cheek to draw her attention back to what the woman was saying, which was more unpleasant for Annie than Mrs. Hawkins probably realized.

"For some, like me, these indiscretions came against our will. But we were blamed all the same and sent off." She dabbed at her eyes with a napkin. "My parents, God rest their souls, thought they were doing the best for me. They didn't know anything was amiss until they came for me and I was not where they had left me. I had been moved and my name changed."

"You don't mean . . . Mrs. Hawkins, were you in the Magdalene Laundry?"

"I was, for twelve long years. Magdalene was everyone's name, which meant you had no identity any longer. I suppose it was the same for you. Not much has changed."

"Oh, Mrs. Hawkins." Suddenly Annie needed to talk about it. Finally someone understood. "I remember a poor old lady we said prayers over before she died. They ordered us to a room where the woman lay on a bed. Her skin was wrinkled and bluish, her breathing shallow." Annie's heart ached as she thought about how Mrs. Hawkins, who had been there so long, might have once thought she would die in the laundry too.

"I know, love. We buried many unfortunate women." Tears dripped down her face.

Annie would never forget the smell of that room—mildew and human waste.

"On your knees," the nuns had ordered all the girls.

They prayed for the old lady's soul. She had been given the name Magdalene Ruth, although that was not her birth name. When she died, she was buried not in the churchyard but in a patch of ground next to the laundry.

As they stood around her grave, admonished to continue praying for the woman's soul, a girl next to Annie whispered, "She was brought here when she was eleven years old. Was raped, I heard. Spent the next fifty years here."

Annie remembered what she'd whispered then: *Help me, God.*

But God didn't answer.

The same could have happened to Mrs. Hawkins. Twelve years!

She leaned over the woman and embraced her. They cried softly for all the women who had not been freed. After a moment Annie breathed in deeply and poured them both more tea. "You . . . you must have felt . . . as though no one wanted you? You had no home, just a penal nightmare, 'twas." Annie could barely choke out the words.

"There was no forgiveness of your sins, love. Not from those people. You worked them off, along with the skin on your knuckles, and I expect it was the same for you, poor Kathleen's child."

"You knew my mother, so. How did you meet her if you were in such a place for so long?"

The sound of laughter came from the kitchen. Jules was still in there with Aileen.

Mrs. Hawkins blew her nose. "You can understand, I suppose, why it was so hard for me to tell you this, Annie."

"I do. I have more questions, though."

"Ah yes. Your mother, Kathleen." She took Annie's hand.

"Let's sit together on the sofa." The woman stared into Annie's eyes. "Your coming here was no coincidence, as you supposed. Your father confided in my brother, and when he told him the circumstances of your birth, Joseph knew you had to be the girl I had hoped to find for two decades."

"I don't understand. You were looking for me? Why?"

Mrs. Hawkins reached out and patted Annie's shoulder. "You're a good girl, Annie Gallagher. And so was your mother, despite what the Magdalene nuns told her. I was always telling her she was good, myself as well. We had to counteract the bad messages spoken to us over and over."

"Us? You must be confused, Mrs. Hawkins. I was the one in the laundry, not my mother."

The woman shook her head and reached for the handkerchief stuffed in her sleeve. "I wish it were not so, but the truth is your mother and I were in there together."

"That's not right. My father would have . . ." Ah, well, now Annie could no longer assume her father had told her everything.

"He did not want you burdened by the fact that you were born in such a place, love."

"Born there?" She rubbed her forehead. She'd been born on the road, her father said, while he and her mother traveled. He'd always been evasive about the location. Between here and there, he'd said. It had all been mistruth.

"He only found you after Kate had died."

Annie thought about what he'd told her. Her mother's family had not approved. They had run away to get married. They found an Anglican minister in Dublin willing to officiate. But was that true? "Were they in fact married, Mrs. Hawkins? You must tell me."

"Your mother came from a Catholic family, Marty a Protestant one. You know how that has divided people in Ireland for centuries. It was just the way things were, still are, even more than here in America. They ran away to Dublin, where they found a minister willing to perform the ceremony. They were married, and very much in love." She shook her head. "The pity is your mother's family came after her and brought her back to the west. Your father spent the better part of a summer looking for Kate. You know how it is, love. The secrecy. No one wanted to talk. He found it difficult to uncover . . . the truth of it. The sad truth." She began to cry.

"Please. Try to continue, Mrs. Hawkins. I must know. My father never said my mother was in the laundry."

"He finally did meet some folks willing to tell him what had happened to Kate, and he did discover where she'd been taken, but he was too late."

Annie shook her head. "Are you sure? You might be mistaking me for some other poor lass."

"Your father was Marty Gallagher. I remember him well. Medium build, dark-brown hair, blue eyes. He was quite the singer, Kate told me. And a storyteller as well. Kate said he knew everything from Shakespeare to 'The Children of Lir.' That was your father, now wasn't it, love?"

Annie nodded.

"I don't suppose there were two Marty Gallaghers who were both storytellers and looked just the same."

"I don't suppose so. But all this does not make sense, Mrs. Hawkins."

"I know, love, but I imagine he never felt attached to any place after that, and that's why he took you all over."

Annie gasped as the full weight of what Mrs. Hawkins was saying sank in. "You knew my mother, and not just as a child. What was my mother like? My father told me she had a lilting lightness to her voice, like doves, he said."

CINDY THOMSON

"True enough. It was the hope of the life she would give birth to that kept her going. She never doubted her love would come for her, although some days were easier than others, you know."

"I wish you had known her before the laundry."

"I wish I had too. I do know she loved you even before you were born."

"'Thou hast covered me in my mother's womb.'" Annie could not recall where those words came from, but she found them comforting somehow.

"I helped her deliver her baby . . . you, love. The nuns allowed her to keep you, to nurse, but something went wrong after that, as so often happens to new mothers." The Hawk gulped and reached for her handkerchief.

"Please, Mrs. Hawkins. You have to tell me."

She pursed her lips together, drew in a breath, and continued. "A doctor visited, but that did not help. As she grew worse and it was clear she was not long for this world . . ." She sucked in a sob, swallowed hard, and then went on. "The priest visited, but afterward a large delivery of laundry came from an estate and everyone was too busy to notice at first that your mother had passed on. I kept your mother's death from the nuns for several hours, hoping they would not take you away before I came up with a plan for your escape. Somehow I had to keep my promise to Kate and make sure you were fine. I even thought of smuggling you out in a load of sheets, but I realized that would not help. You needed someone on the outside to care for you. I prayed as hard then as ever I have in my life, and by a miracle, it was just then your father traced your mother to the laundry. He pretended to be a government inspector and planned to whisk Kate away with him. When I heard him asking the other girls about your mother, I snuck him in long enough to get you. You were a good baby, didn't make a whimper."

"How did a man posing as a government worker walk out of there with a baby? I cannot imagine such a thing."

"Oh, what's hard for man God can do easily. Your father tucked the quiet child—you, Annie—into a crate, said he had to repair some equipment, and took you away. Then I wrapped up a bundle of sheets and told the nuns I was going to bury a dead baby. They never questioned me."

Annie had been rescued from a Magdalene Laundry twice. She could scarcely believe what she was hearing.

"And my father thought it best I did not know this?"

"I suppose so, love. He made my brother promise not to tell you after he died, but God arranges these things so that you will question and search and find the truth."

"I don't know about that. It just hurts so much that my father didn't care to tell me this."

Mrs. Hawkins put an arm around Annie's shoulders. "I do not think he meant it the way you are perceiving things. Think for a moment. This was a horrible occurrence in the man's life. He wanted to move on and make your childhood happy. He did not want you to be scarred from the experience."

Annie sniffed. "And he achieved his goal. I was a happy child." *Put the old behind.* "Thank you for telling me." She stared into the woman's eyes, eyes that had gazed on Annie's own mother long ago.

"You deserved to know this." Mrs. Hawkins stood. "I promised Kate Gallagher I would look out for her child, and she gave me the only thing the nuns had allowed her to keep, her Bible. Praise the good Lord he's finally allowed me to do what your mother wanted. I should have told you sooner. I am so sorry, Annie. But God is good, and you are here now." The Hawk rose and crossed the room. "Here. This is rightfully yours." She handed Annie her mother's Bible like an award.

It truly was a treasure. Annie rubbed her thumbs over the initials on the cover. "I have a Bible, Mrs. Hawkins. The one my father used. This one . . ." She held it out toward the woman. "This one is yours. You truly knew my mother and loved her, and she wanted you to have it."

Just as she thought would happen, Agnes Hawkins dabbed at her moist eyes as she cradled the Bible.

After they sat in silence a moment, Annie thought it best to focus on her future. "Maybe 'tis time I moved on, the way my father wanted."

Agnes Hawkins looked as though she might cry again. "Your library. I understand. And we will help you, love, to honor your father that way."

"I'm not sure that can happen, not the way I hoped."

"Now don't be hasty. I can . . . I mean, we don't yet know how this publishing venture will turn out, Annie."

"I still don't understand why you are so generous to me, Mrs. Hawkins, unless it's because you owed my mother a debt."

"No, no."

"If it's about paying for being in the laundry, that was not your fault. If anyone owes anyone anything, it's me."

"You?"

"You saved me from that place. Twice, for heaven's sake!"

"Oh, Annie, love." She put a hand to Annie's cheek. "I do not care for you or do any of my charity work out of a sense that I must wash away my sins. God truly has given me his heart for others, and that brings me joy. And you?" She lowered her hand and blinked back tears. "You are a special girl, Annie Gallagher."

27

ANNIE GLANCED to the hall when she heard laughter.

"Let us talk more later, love. Why don't you go see what they are up to. I am expecting Mrs. Jenkins to stop by to give me her deviled egg recipe, and as nosy as she is, I would rather not be all red-faced when she gets here. Do you mind terribly much?"

"I do not mind, Mrs. Hawkins. Thank you for speaking to me about this. I know it was painful."

"No need to thank me, love." She dabbed at moist eyes and tipped her head to motion Annie on.

Annie sighed, took another glance at the Bible, and moved toward the kitchen.

When she entered, she found Aileen and Jules sitting at the table, her copy of *The Wonderful Wizard of Oz* open between them.

"See here, Jules? This is a windstorm lifting a house clear off the ground."

"I'm glad that storm we had didn't take our house like that," he said.

Aileen patted the boy's shoulder. "I am pretty glad about that too."

They both leaned in and turned some more pages.

"Look at that dog," Jules said. "I know a little black-and-brown dog like that. The girl he belongs to says he sleeps next to her just like this picture."

They turned a couple more pages. Jules laughed. "Look, he's sitting up and begging. Don't you like dogs, Miss Aileen?"

Aileen laughed. "Sure I do." She looked up. "Oh, Annie. I hope you don't mind. You left your book on the table and Jules and I were looking at the pictures."

"Not at all." Aileen was right. She would have made a wonderful mother.

Annie sat with them. She was about to rise to answer a knock at the front door when she heard Mrs. Hawkins and the neighbor chatting about the proper way to boil eggs. "I'll make a fresh pot of tea."

But before the water boiled, she heard Mrs. Jenkins depart. She handed Jules a biscuit before he left, and when Mrs. Hawkins came into the kitchen, she, Aileen, and Annie chatted around the kitchen table like . . . like family.

Stephen wanted to check on things at Hawkins House, and since he had a package to deliver from a printer—probably something for Grace's wedding—he went there early. Mrs. Hawkins would appreciate having it right away.

When Stephen delivered next door to Hawkins House, Mrs. Jenkins met him. "Such a pity the trouble those women are suffering," she said.

"Have you seen anyone today? I do hope they are getting things worked out for the best."

"Not today, no. I did drop by yesterday to give Agnes my deviled eggs recipe, and I can tell you, something upset the dear woman. She didn't let on, and in fact said everything was very well, but . . . did you know . . . ?" She leaned forward like the gossiping homemakers Stephen had witnessed in other neighborhoods. "Did you know, Mr. Adams, their newest boarder was taken away in an ambulance?"

"I had heard. I hope she's getting well."

"I don't know if one gets well from that kind of thing."

"What do you mean?"

She arched her brows and lifted her chin. "I'll say no more. I am a Christian woman." She crossed her arms firmly across her middle. "Oh, and then a tall, distinguished gentleman visited yesterday, quite early. Now, why would a man call on them at such a time of day?"

"I . . . I don't know. Mrs. Jenkins, did you not tell me you would be traveling? I held your mail for three days last week."

"Quite right. I left the very same day I saw some peculiar visitors next door. I returned last Sunday. Mrs. Blevins across the way told me about the ambulance. And I did happen to notice the man yesterday. I was not looking, you understand, I just happened to be on the stoop sweeping up."

"I see." He reached into his bag. "Here is your mail, Mrs. Jenkins." He spotted Grace walking up to Hawkins House. "Excuse me." He called to Grace and held up the package. She waited for him.

"Is that for us?"

"It is. I thought it might pertain to your upcoming wedding, so I wanted to deliver it right away."

She studied the brown ink writing. "Ah, 'tis something I needed indeed. Thank you so much, Mr. Adams."

"Delivery is my business." He tipped his hat and began to whistle as he went on his way. He silenced his tune when he realized his encounter with Grace meant he would not see Annie anymore that day since Hawkins House did not normally get enough mail to merit multiple visits in a day.

As he proceeded, he thought about Annie. If he were able to woo her, as Dexter phrased it, and perhaps even marry her one day, he'd be better able to protect her within his own household and see to her needs. But he'd done a poor job of taking care of his own needs. Repentance would be a part of his prayers from now on.

A thought came to him, gentle but firm: *I require obedience, son.*

Show me, Lord.

As he moved on toward the docks, the buildings rose over his head like a thundercloud. Numerous clotheslines strung with white undergarments and shirts flapping in the cold wind absorbed what sunlight did manage to penetrate. It seemed to him there was not a breath of fresh air to be had for several blocks.

He took his mittens out of his pocket and handed them to a shivering boy, no older than six, huddled on one of the building's stone steps. The lad didn't respond as quickly as boys like Matty did and, in fact, refused.

"Go on. It's okay, now. I know what it's like, being out here on the streets."

The boy turned a sooty face toward him. "How would you know that, mister?"

"I was a newsboy once."

The kid puffed up his cheeks. "I don't know what you did, but I do all right, almost a quarter dollar a day and nobody I have to give it to."

"Fine. You're a businessman, then. Got a keen sense of a square deal, I imagine."

The kid grinned. "You bet."

"Then you'll know a free gift to keep your hands warm while you hold the papers is a good deal. It's not too bad out now, but you do know winter's coming."

He shrugged and took them from Stephen's outstretched hands.

When Stephen walked away, he felt the chill against his bare hands but dismissed it. A quote from a book by Jacob Riis came to mind: "It is the tenement that gives up the child to the street in tender years to find there the home it denied him." He'd remembered it because it had been true for him. In the streets he had danced to "London Bridge Is Falling Down" played on a hand organ. He had moved about freely without enduring the hollowed-out stares and abrupt reprimands from his parents. Life on the streets was not the best, but it wasn't the worst, either. These kids had to find their own way, like Stephen had. No harm in helping them out when he was able.

"For a man's life consisteth not in the abundance of the things which he possesseth."

Possessions didn't define him. Perhaps, he thought, he was finally understanding. So long as he was working to help meet someone else's needs, his work would have meaning. And Annie needed him right now.

28

WHEN THE BENEVOLENTS assembled for Mrs. Hawkins's hastily called meeting, Annie was surprised to see the committee present consisted only of Mrs. Hawkins, Dr. Thorp, Reverend Clarke, and Mr. George Parker, Grace's employer. She had imagined Mrs. Hawkins's financial supporters to be either extremely wealthy folks—which these were not—or many in number.

"How is Kirsten?" Annie whispered to the doctor before he took his seat.

"A bit better. Now don't worry. She'll be fine."

Mrs. Hawkins caught her eye. "Please close the pocket doors, love."

Annie did as she was told, but she hated being shut out like that. She found Aileen in the kitchen. "Where did Grace get off to?"

"Ah, she's knackered. Said she had more wedding planning to do at her desk upstairs. I'm taking the laundry out now. Mrs. Hawkins said the laundress will accept it late in the day and do the work in the morn."

"Jules is gone?" Annie had seen him in the kitchen shortly before the committee meeting began.

"He is. Brought by his mother's boiled cider pie recipe."

Annie laughed. "The Hawk is determined that Grace and Owen will have a truly American menu at the party, aye?"

Aileen shook her head. "I suppose so. I will help make it, but that doesn't mean I'll eat it."

Annie shrugged. "Where was Jules off to so quickly?"

"To deliver messages, he said."

"You were wonderful with him yesterday, Aileen. Sometimes 'tis easy to forget those working boys are still children."

"He's a fine lad."

"Are you sure you're comfortable going out with the laundry?"

She rolled her eyes. "I am capable, Annie."

"I know you are."

Annie gathered what she needed for tea.

When she returned to the parlor, the doctor was speaking. "Sorry Mr. McNulty could not be here, Agnes, but it could not be helped. Owen reports that his father is traveling for his business. Even so, I believe there are enough of us to make a decision."

The room fell quiet as she served tea. Each one thanked her in turn, and then she left, balancing the tea tray on her hip so she could close the doors again.

"Annie," Mrs. Hawkins called to her. "Please stay."

Stunned, she entered and then shut the doors behind her, standing in front of them.

Mrs. Hawkins cleared her throat. "Gentlemen, I want you to know my housekeeper is not merely my servant. She is a wonderful girl, as you know, with a heart for helping those less fortunate, which is something we all have in common."

"Hear, hear," someone said.

Annie's face grew warm.

"She is planning an undertaking I think we could all champion."

Reverend Clarke raised his arm into the air. "In the interest of time, Agnes, could we discuss this at a later date? We have assembled for an emergency vote."

"Indeed, Ronald. But just allow me to mention one thing."

There was a mumbling of agreement. Mrs. Hawkins swiveled in her chair to face Annie. "Annie is going to open a library."

"Wonderful," Dr. Thorp said. "There aren't enough of them. Tell us about it, would you, Annie?"

She licked her lips. "My father was a great storyteller. I'm going to sell some of his stories and make a lot of money. I've already signed a contract with *Harper's* magazine."

A round of applause rang out.

"I'm going to name the library after him."

Mrs. Hawkins waved her hand in the air to bring the room to order. "So you see, she will need books. I say we start a drive to collect the dusty, unused titles sitting on the bookshelves of so many of New York's wealthier families and put them to good use in Annie's library."

"An excellent idea," Mr. Parker said. "I know I have a few."

Mrs. Hawkins pointed toward her breakfront. "As do I."

"Thank you. Thank you, all," Annie said. When she closed the doors behind her, her mood was buoyed with the thought of having others help her with her plans. She had never dreamed that would happen. Annie had wanted to do everything for herself, believing one must grow one's own dreams. But perhaps a solitary effort was not the proper approach after all. The mice in *The Wonderful Wizard of Oz* certainly showed what camaraderie could do. And so did Dorothy's friends.

After the men left, Mrs. Hawkins called Annie into the parlor. "We have decided the time has come to ask Kirsten for the ledger."

"The what?"

"The package she received from her brother. Owen has discovered the Pinkerton has been employed by a group of schemers, and the ledger is what these men want him to recover."

"I don't understand."

"All that matters is it's an illegal operation milking folks out of their savings, pretending to be legitimate brokerage firms. We don't know how Jonas came to have this ledger. No one—including, we believe, the Pinkerton—thinks these men would have brought a newly arrived immigrant into their inner circle, but somehow he has the accounting of their activities."

"But why would he send it to Kirsten, here at Hawkins House?"

"The doctor postulated a theory on that, love. He supposes that these men were hot on Mr. Wagner's trail, and he mailed it in the hopes that he could slip by them and retrieve it when they weren't looking."

"But they were looking."

"Yes, that is the fly in the soup."

"So will Kirsten surrender it, knowing her brother might get in trouble?"

"That is the dilemma, I'm afraid. He's likely to be deported."

"Haven't the police asked Kirsten for it?"

"Dr. Thorp hasn't allowed her to be questioned yet. She's been resting quite well and should be ready to cooperate now. It is best to let the authorities handle this from this point forward."

"Mrs. Hawkins, if you were going to tell me anyway, why did you ask me to leave the room?"

"It's the policy of our group, love."

Annie still didn't understand. "Well, I do thank you for supporting my library." She was still reveling in the honor.

"My pleasure. We were interrupted before. Would you like to continue our talk now?"

"Please." Annie sat on the rocking chair.

"You must be wondering how I came to leave the laundry and Ireland."

She was most interested in hearing about her mother, but she let the woman continue, hoping the story would lead her there.

"My brother never found me, although he tried. A handsome American solicitor on holiday did. He came to the convent quite innocently, but when he saw what was happening, he was appalled. He used his knowledge of the law to get some of us out. He talked the priest into allowing him to take me back to England. We were married and soon came back to his home in America."

"Your Harold?"

She smiled, the loose skin on her cheeks growing more taut. "Yes, my Harold. Later I found my brother. Once I learned he was a priest, it wasn't hard to track him down. We still write to each other after all these years."

"I am so happy you got away."

"Yes. Thank the good Lord for the mercy he showed us—me and you. I just wanted you to understand my heart, love. And to trust me in matters with our Kirsten. We will work through this as a unified collaborate."

"Aye, Mrs. Hawkins. I can't stop thinking about you knowing my mother."

"And may I say, you look so much like her."

Annie's father had always said so, but it was a delight to hear it from someone else.

29

The following Saturday Stephen answered a knock on the door. "Davis. I'd invite you in, but I don't have any furniture."

The man rose to his toes to look over Stephen's head. "I see that. Well, I brought you something that might help." He held a check up in front of his face.

"Twenty dollars? What is that for?"

"Compliments of *Harper's*. They are over the moon to have some of Redmond's stories."

He took the check. "That's incredibly generous."

"It's adequate."

"Is that right? I had no idea there was so much money in publishing."

"There can be, if you find the right author." He held up a copy of the magazine. "Here it is."

"You don't say. Already?" Stephen saw "The Lost Stories of Luther Redmond" on the cover.

Davis handed it to him.

"Annie will be pleased."

"They have sent her funds to her bank as she requested."

Stephen grumbled to himself, "Why do people trust banks?"

Davis pointed into his vacant room. "When will you get your things back?"

"I . . . uh, I hope soon. I have to pay the undertaker in addition to the rental charge."

"I don't mean to pry, but would you care to tell me what the trouble is, Stephen?"

"I still owe for my parents' funerals."

"Oh, you poor boy. Why didn't you say so? I can lend you the money to pay him off."

"I can't ask you to do that."

"I'm going to make a bundle on the book rights, son. I can do this. How much do you need?"

Stephen told him.

"I'll have a check waiting for you on Monday."

"Are you sure about this?"

"Absolutely. It's not every day a publisher lands a miracle like the one you brought me."

Stephen rose early, ran a comb through his cowlick-cursed hair, and dressed for church.

He got to First Church a bit later than he intended and did not have time to speak to anyone before the organ began playing "Christ Is Made the Sure Foundation" and the processional began.

Churchgoing folks were creatures of habit, always taking the same seats, Sunday after Sunday. In the old days families rented pews, so perhaps that was where the practice started. Knowing this, he wandered toward the left side of the church. Sure enough, he spotted Annie's curly copper hair peeking from beneath a hat.

As the sermon was delivered, Stephen contemplated the message but heard only what God had been speaking to him over and over.

Obedience is pleasing. Listen.

He was trying, wasn't he?

When the basket was passed for the offering, Annie spotted him. Her cheeks flushed and she nodded.

After the recessional he rose to allow those sitting next to him to exit the pew. But he did not leave. He waited for Annie. The women filed out, Grace last and Owen close behind. A rush of cold air assaulted them as they neared the exit, and Annie held on to her hat, although with the reserved height and adornment of her headpiece, she'd have less trouble than her cousin, whose hat was piled high with satin ribbons.

"May I walk you home?" Stephen asked Annie.

"Thank you, but with the wedding just a few days away, I'm afraid I have no leisure."

"I'd be happy to walk with you, nonetheless." He wanted to surprise her with the *Harper's* edition.

Mrs. Hawkins said she'd be along soon, after a chat with her friends on the church steps. The Hawkins House girls chatted the entire way about bouquets and ferns and lace—he didn't know what all. Stephen eventually fell back to the rear of the procession, where Owen was. Owen leaned down to speak to him. "The detectives are meeting with the doctor at the infirmary today. Once they have the ledger, we can all put this behind us."

"Think Miss Wagner will give it to them?"

"I don't know why not."

"Where is her brother? Hasn't the Pinkerton found him?"

"Not as far as I can tell. Some of those German immigrants come from a place where they learned to trust no one, and they can be pretty evasive, even for a so-called detective like Clayton Cooper."

"Lovies, wait for me."

They all stopped. Mrs. Hawkins waddled up to them as fast as her short legs could carry her. She held her hand to her hat to keep it from falling in her hurry. When she caught up, she struggled to catch her breath. "Terrible news. Ella Thorp just told me. Our Kirsten has gone missing."

Annie wasn't certain just how many people hurried along with them to catch the elevated train near city hall. Once they were headed north toward Second Avenue and Thirteenth Street, she glanced around. Even Stephen Adams had come. "What will we do when we get there?" she asked Mrs. Hawkins.

"Find out what happened. Poor Kirsten."

When they exited the train and stood in front of the Eye and Ear Infirmary, Annie thought about how someone could get utterly lost in this vast city.

They stepped up two stairs and entered the door under a green canopy. A nurse sitting behind a wide oak desk greeted them. After explaining their mission, they followed her to a stairway. "Go to the third floor and speak to the nurse on duty." She stepped out of the stairway, leaving them to find their way.

They clambered up, the whole lot of them, their stomping echoing against the concrete walls.

The windows were smaller on the third floor, casting slats of sunbeams across the wooden floor. There were no curtains or carpets to soften the sound, and the nurse sitting at the lone desk looked up at the clattering sound of their footsteps.

"May I help you?" She appeared stoic in her long pinafore and lace-trimmed hat. She laid aside her pencil as Mrs. Hawkins approached her.

"We have been informed that Kirsten Wagner, a patient here, has gone missing."

The nurse pressed her lips together and then reached for her telephone. "Just a moment."

Soon Dr. Thorp entered from the left side of the hall. "Agnes, there was no need to come down here."

"Ella told me our Kirsten is missing." She wrung her hands. "I must know what this is all about."

Grace and Aileen scooted close to Annie. The men stood behind them. Someone else entered from the stairs.

"You!" Mrs. Hawkins yelled.

Clayton Cooper, the Pinkerton, clenched his jaw. "Doctor, I demand to know where that girl is."

The doctor held up his arms. "I will tell you all the same thing. I do not know. She sneaked out in the middle of the night. We must all accept the explanation that the girl does not want to be found and leave it like that."

Stephen Adams made his way to the front of the group. "Someone frightened her off." He stood close to Clayton Cooper, though his nose only reached the man's top coat buttons. "I tell you, mister, the US Post Office handles these cases in a much more professional manner."

Owen came and stood next to Stephen, his size and rank lending importance to Stephen's words.

The detective shrugged and rushed out and down the stairs.

"What do you mean?" Annie whispered to Stephen.

"Mail fraud. To criminals, the postal inspectors are some of the most feared men in government. Even the bank robbers believe so. They avoid the mail cars when they rob trains." He appeared to be incredibly proud of his profession as he spoke with a clear, confident voice. "And the reason they are so revered is the postal inspectors are successful at catching the perpetrators." He turned to look at them all. "I assure you, since this ledger was delivered through the mail, the inspectors are on the case. They will find Kirsten." He reached for Annie's hands. "I will do all that is in my power to be sure your friend is found safe and sound."

Annie didn't think such a thing was in his power, not in that crowded city, but she admired his determination.

"Come along, ladies," Owen said, reaching out his long arms to usher them to the stairs. "The doctor has his duties to attend to, and Mr. Adams is correct. If the mail inspectors are on the case, they will do the best job possible."

Mrs. Hawkins sniffed. "I so wanted to help that girl, but some people are beyond my reach. May God protect her."

Annie hurried to her side. "She did tell me, Mrs. Hawkins, that she wished to protect her brother in some way. I should have known she'd sneak off with whatever it was he sent her. I should have warned someone."

"You cannot be expected to have anticipated all this, Annie. What's done is done, love. If she did not wish to stay here, or at Hawkins House for that matter, no one could have forced her. Pray for her."

Annie didn't think her prayers had helped the dying Magdalene woman or that they could now help Kirsten. Hopefully Kirsten was smart enough to ensure her own safety.

When they were all finally assembled back at Hawkins House, Stephen stood in the middle of the parlor holding something up in the air. "Ladies and Sergeant McNulty, may I present the first serial publication of the stories Annie brought over from Ireland."

Everyone clapped.

Annie reached out her hand. "Let me see that, please." She flipped through it a few times before realizing the story she was looking for listed the author as Luther Redmond. She glanced up. "Why would you do that?"

"Excuse me?"

"Use that name on my father's story?"

"Miss Gallagher, they are one and the same. Mr. Davis mentioned it in his office, and it was on the contract."

"Perhaps it was. I should have been more careful at the time, but seeing this in print now makes me realize it's not fitting. With him gone, there is no need to use a pseudonym." She dropped the magazine on the sofa and Aileen picked it up.

"Now, now, love. Surely these publishing executives know about these things."

"Mrs. Hawkins, my father writing as Luther Redmond was wrong." She glared at each face. "Don't you all believe in truth?" She could not keep tears from burning at her eyes. She held a fist to her mouth.

"I believe such things are customary in publishing—" The Hawk snapped her lips shut when Annie looked at her incredulously.

Aileen tapped her hand on the open pages of the magazine. "'Tis a wonderful story, Cousin. I hope they paid you well for this."

They had. She should be grateful. But to have her father's name, his real name, honored in print would have been wonderful. "Well." She sat straighter. "At least my library will have my father's name above the door."

Stephen cleared his throat. "Well . . . yes . . . uh, Mr. Davis tells me these issues are selling rapidly. Folks are eager to hear once again from their favorite author."

Annie stood. "I will get tea." She paused before she left the room. "I just might have to write to the editor of *Harper's* and tell them they should not have used a false name."

"Certainly you could," Stephen said, holding her gaze with his. "The tales might then cease to be as extensively read if folks begin to believe they were not written by Redmond. However . . . the truth matters. Miss Gallagher, I implore you to think about the repercussions before you make such an announcement."

She took a deep breath and left the room. There was much to consider, and much she wanted to know about both of her parents.

30

On Monday Stephen left work early enough to get home and collect the information he needed to get his belongings out of storage now that Davis had lent him money. He had already settled up with Murray, feeling only partially relieved because he'd paid him off with borrowed funds. He closed the door to his apartment and locked it. Once outside, he plunged his hands deep into his pockets. He missed his mittens, but on the next payday he'd stop by Mrs. Jacobs's and ask her to knit a pair for him. He would pay her, of course, but right now he needed all the money he had to pay the storage fee, so that would have to wait.

He started for the Broadway trolley.

"Adams, one moment!"

Stephen turned and waited for Davis to catch up to him.

"Is something wrong?" It was chilly out on the front steps.

"Wrong? No, my boy." He walked alongside Stephen. "*Harper's* telephoned. They want the rest of the stories right away. Do you know that issue sold out in two days? The whole city, maybe the whole world, is all atwitter over these long-lost stories, son. This is big. Huge. Better get all nine of the remaining stories to me as soon as possible."

"I don't know, Davis. She is not happy Redmond's name is on them."

He chuckled. "They would not sell nearly as well under a Gallagher fella's name."

"I know. I'll talk to her."

"Right away. Get me those stories today." He reached out and pulled on Stephen's collar, bringing him to a stop. "Do I need to remind you I did you a favor with that undertaker's bill?"

"No, you don't. I am well aware of my indebtedness, believe me." He wiggled free. "I'm grateful. But you don't understand, Davis. The postmaster needs my help with something, an important case for the government. I haven't even had time to pick up my belongings yet, I'm so consumed. I was just on my way to arrange that."

Davis yanked on Stephen's arm a bit harder. "I must have those stories, Adams. This is the biggest publishing event since . . . well, since that *Oz* book. This is bigger than your needs. We are serving the public, son. And besides, if I don't deliver, I won't get the book rights, and what a fool I'll look like to the fellas at the club." He spoke through his teeth. "Remember, if I don't get the book rights, that money I lent you, I'll need it back to pay my own bills. Do you understand?"

"I do."

"Go get them now."

When Stephen knocked at Hawkins House, Aileen answered. "Mrs. Hawkins and my cousin Annie . . . They are not here, Mr. Adams."

"Oh, I see. When do you expect them back?"

Grace pushed past the little Irish girl. "Come in here, Mr. Adams. You'll catch your death out there, the wind is blowing so."

He stepped inside and shut the door behind him. "I can come back later."

"Absolutely not. They had an errand of some sort to attend

to. I've got a pot of potatoes and stew on the stove. Won't you stay for supper?"

This sounded much better than anything he might cook for himself. He lifted his nose. "Is that corn bread I smell?"

"It is. I make it whenever Mrs. Hawkins allows me and whenever I'm here and not at the Parkers'. Mrs. Hawkins says 'tis too American for her tastes, but the children love that kind of bread. And I've got lamb stew. Sound all right to you?"

"Sounds delicious." Owen was indeed a lucky man.

Aileen took his hat and coat. "Annie and Mrs. Hawkins didn't say where they were going, but I'm sure they'll be back for supper. They are planning so much food for the party, they're probably visiting every butcher and grocer in the city."

"I see. I really do need to speak to Annie right away about the rest of the stories."

Grace motioned to the sofa. "Come in and rest a bit." She took the rocker by the window. "You are American. You must be as fond of corn bread as is my Owen."

"I enjoy all kinds of food." He got to his feet. "Please, do not think you have to entertain me if you are busy in the kitchen, Miss McCaffery."

"Grace. I do hope you feel as though we are friends. I would like you to come to the wedding."

"Thank you. That is very kind."

"I have a few moments until the bread needs to come out of the oven. Sit down, please."

He bowed his head and returned to the sofa.

She wrinkled her pale nose and struggled to push back a strand of hair that had plunged loose from her top bun.

Aileen popped back into the room and motioned to some papers lying on the tea table. "Speaking of stories, won't you look at my drawings? Grace has been teaching me and I'm making a story for the Parker children, all from pictures. I will visit them as much as I can once Grace gets married. I so enjoy them and they seem to like hearing the tales of ole Erin. See what you think. I need to get back to the kitchen."

He had begun to thumb through them when Aileen called from down the hall. "Grace, please come check on this, won't you?"

"Excuse me. Please, make yourself at home."

He rose as she left the room. The drawings were charming enough, but what intrigued him more was to hear that children liked Irish stories. Annie's father's were going to be outrageously popular, he was certain. He stood in the middle of the parlor, not sure what to do next. He perused the book collection and chose a volume written by Arthur Conan Doyle.

Moments later he returned the book to the shelf and noticed Annie's writing desk. Before he realized it, he had the desk in his hands. He carried it to the sofa. With the desk in his lap, he felt a bit like a burglar. He would just take a look.

He raised the lid. There were several sheets of unused paper on top. He lifted those out. Underneath lay a stack of papers softened as though they had been folded and unfolded many times. Now they lay open and flat with visible creases. The brown ink was interrupted here and there with line drawings of animals wearing overalls or dresses, much like the Omah story. He pulled out the pages to bring them closer to the light.

"We'll be back in a few moments," Grace called from the kitchen.

He rose and stepped into the hall. "Please take your time. I'm just reading."

By the time he finished the last page of one of the tales, he was more than delighted. He carefully folded them and tucked the fat bundle into his interior coat pocket and then replaced the other papers.

"What's going on in here?"

He spun around to find Annie glaring at him. "I . . . uh . . . Hello, Annie. I didn't hear you return."

"We came in the kitchen door, and Grace told me you were waiting in here. Did she suggest you entertain yourself by reading those?"

"No. I was just admiring this desk. I hope you don't mind."

"Not at all." She took it from him and put it back on the shelf as though she minded very much.

"I heard you were staying for supper. 'Tis almost ready."

"Uh, Annie, Mr. Davis would like to receive the other stories immediately. It's good news. *Harper's* wants to publish them as soon as possible."

She sighed and dropped to the sofa. "I don't know, Mr. Adams."

"Stephen, please."

"Stephen. I mean, I'm pleased, but I don't want that Redmond name on them."

"Please, Annie. You must consider the widespread interest in—"

"Ridiculous, that is. My father should have told me. I think I'm going to get some legal advice first."

"Oh, uh, I see. That does seem prudent." He had the stories in his pocket. He couldn't just hand them back now. He hesitated to follow her. Perhaps if he did what Davis asked and delivered them, Davis would not yet ask for the money Stephen borrowed. Of course, he'd tell him to hold off printing them until Annie signed a contract, and Davis was a businessman. He'd know that. And then with just a bit of wooing, he'd convince Annie and they would be all set to proceed. Annie would thank him in the end, certainly.

"Are you coming, Mr. Adams?"

"Thank you for the invitation. I'm afraid I've just remembered something of great importance I must attend to. Give Mrs. Hawkins my regrets. I will see myself out."

"Well, all right. Here, I'll get your things."

His stomach turned as he waited. He wanted to bolt out of there. A great weight hung on his shoulders as he knew he'd chosen to secure his financial situation over Annie's wishes. He'd had good reason, though. He could not allow himself to end up poor and broken like his father. He was doing what was best for them all in the long run. She would come to understand that. He just had to be quick about it.

31

KIRSTEN WAS A GROWN WOMAN, the doctor had stated. No one could keep her in the infirmary if she wanted to leave, and she was under no obligation to contact Hawkins House. That made Annie sad, but she knew people walked in and out of her life with frequency, and she would have to accept it.

After washing up the supper dishes—and noting that the potato bin needed filling already, probably due to Aileen's presence in the house now—Annie went to her room to relax. Reclining on her bed, she closed her eyes and imagined the soft green grass of Ireland, the ancient stones blue with age, the towering castle ruins, the glowing turf fires that engulfed every town with a sweet smell. She could still see the tumbledown abbeys where she and her father entertained townsfolk with stories of old under a canopy of ever-changing clouds.

She could almost smell the fresh rain-misted air. She could almost dip her fingers in the blades of grass. She could almost hear her father's lilting laughter.

Almost.

But like those mist-covered islands a younger Annie had thought she saw in the lough, none of it was real. A mirage. A long-ago memory.

The past was gone.

Her father was gone.

She had been young and naive while her father was alive, but the more she thought about it now, it made sense that her father had additional income. They'd always had what they needed, despite the fact his storytelling had been paid for with bartered goods on fortunate days and just a slap on the back during hunger seasons. Marty Gallagher's mysterious family never showed their faces, and if he'd had money from an inheritance, surely there would be more kin coming to lay claim.

Why didn't you tell me, Da?

She hated that she would never know with certainty why he hadn't trusted her with the truth.

"Mine enemies would daily swallow me up."

Annie had been reading in Psalms where David continually asked God to protect him from his enemies. Could it be that was exactly what her father was trying to do for her? Protect her from Neil's greediness? *If you had only told me, Da, I never would have gone to the O'Shannons.*

His illness must have skewed his good sense. How could she blame him, as ravaged by fever and sickness as he was?

Annie sat at her desk and rubbed her hands over the ragged pages open to the book of Psalms. Of course! He'd worked so hard through his illness to give her the stories, knowing they'd be valuable one day, the last works of a famous writer. He'd made sure of it by adding that hallmark. And then he'd hidden them in the desk's secret compartment and confided in the priest. All that had been necessary because the stories were immensely valuable, as it seemed the New York publishers understood. Tears dripped down her face as she realized how her father had provided for her.

She lifted the Bible to her forehead, wondering if it was

possible that someday this hurt might heal. She didn't want to think about it right now and open her raw heart.

She returned to her bed and fumbled around underneath until she found the *Wizard* book and flipped to the last page she had read. She laughed at herself for having hidden it there. There was no reason to keep it under her bed, but folks hide things when they're valuable.

She lifted the book to her nose. A book had a smell more soothing than any of Mrs. Hawkins's herbs. There was nothing like a good story to take her out of a world she didn't much like. Sighing, she closed her eyes a moment, focusing her mind on the imaginary world described within those pages until she was ready to reread them.

Ah, the Emerald City. Dorothy was waiting to see the Terrible Oz, and she was beautifully dressed, of course, in green silk. Dorothy entered the throne room to talk to Oz, who appeared as a mysterious talking head.

"Why should I do this for you?" asked Oz.

"Because you are strong and I am weak; because you are a Great Wizard and I am only a little girl."

Oh, she knew how Dorothy felt!

Annie knew what came next. Dorothy and her friends would be given a monumental assignment, the one thing they were terribly fearful of doing. Oz wanted them to kill the Wicked Witch. None of them could have what they wanted until they did that. Dorothy told her friends there was no hope. She couldn't kill the witch. Dorothy would never get home, or so she thought.

Someone knocked on the door.

"Who is it?"

"Aileen. Annie, I want to show you something."

"Come in."

They sat on Annie's bed.

"I showed these to the postman too, but he did not stay long enough to tell me what he thought of them." She spread some drawings on the bed.

"Very nice."

"I made them for the Parker children. Grace is taking me over there tomorrow. She needs someone to watch them while she finishes sewing lace on her wedding veil."

"Oh. I'm sure they'll like them."

"They tell a story."

"Truly?"

"They do. Here, let me show you. 'Tis pretty simple, but Grace thinks they'll like it and might even want to create their own. Even wee Linden can do it because you don't have to know how to read."

"Wonderful."

"'Twas that book of yours that gave me the idea. This one first. See the bears?"

"Oh, is this 'The Story of the Three Bears'?"

"'Tis, and I can tell the story this way."

Annie realized how much people who couldn't read were lacking when they couldn't enjoy a book.

"Aileen, you have given me a stupendous idea."

Annie rushed out of the room to find Mrs. Hawkins and Grace. They were discussing Grace's new home that was two blocks over, so Annie waited. Finally they looked up at her.

"Aileen has given me an idea."

Aileen shuffled up behind her. "I wish you would tell me what it is."

"Sit down."

She waited until everyone was assembled. "As you know,

with my profits from the publishers, I'm going to purchase a building and open a library, or at least I was."

Mrs. Hawkins raised her brows. "Oh? What are you planning now, love?"

Annie thoroughly enjoyed the freedom to make her own plans. "Aileen helped me to see that stories are told in many ways. Truly my father understood that. He brought stories to the people, many of whom could not have read them if they indeed had a book."

The three women smiled, waiting. Annie paced around the room, lifting a finger into the air as each thought rushed through her mind. "More people need to know how to read. That's one thing. I can teach them."

"A worthy undertaking, love." Mrs. Hawkins looked charmed.

"Hear me out. There is something else. Grace, you read stories to the children you care for, don't you?"

"Indeed I do."

"Have you told them some of the ancient tales, the stories only the Irish know?"

"I have. Why do you ask?"

Annie clapped her hands together. "Who will tell these stories in future generations? I mean, if the Irish stop coming to America, who will share them?"

"We can write them down," Grace said.

"True, we can, but wouldn't you say something is lost that way? Don't children in particular enjoy stories better that are told aloud? In acts and voices and gestures?" She turned to Aileen. "The way you and Jules were enjoying talking about the Oz drawings. The way you intend to use the drawings you made."

Aileen held her papers to her heart. "'Tis true enough. What is the lovely idea, Annie?"

"I will teach others. You can help, all of you. If you would like."

"I would like," Aileen said.

Grace and Mrs. Hawkins bobbed their heads.

"We will teach interested folks the art of telling a story, how to become *seanchaithe*, and thus continue what my father did."

Mrs. Hawkins applauded. "A lovely tribute to your father."

Someone knocked on the door.

Annie answered it. A man stood before her. "Forgive me for calling so late. Your neighbor was outside and I inquired. She said the lights are usually burning in your parlor this time of the evening, and she told me you wouldn't mind."

The Irish brogue, the umbrella he carried, the way he dipped his head, all seemed strangely familiar.

"You may not remember me, Miss Gallagher. I am Mr. Barrows. We met at your father's wake."

32

STEPHEN RUSHED BACK HOME. There was a light on in the publishing office. He rapped on the door.

"Adams, my boy! I did not expect to see you so soon." Davis led him into the office and pointed to a scarred leather chair. "You must have come with something."

"I have." Stephen pulled the bundle from his pocket and handed it over.

Much later Davis laid the final page on his desk and tapped the papers as though stroking a pet kitten.

Stephen stood. The ticking of the huge wall clock made him jittery. "I have to return these as soon as possible." He stuck out his arm and frantically wriggled his hand.

"What's the hurry? I'll guard them with my life." Davis grinned wide, his mouth absent of the usual cigar.

"I . . . um . . . I have to ask her first."

Davis's mouth dropped open. "Huh? You telling me she doesn't know you brought them to me?"

"I . . . couldn't . . . Look, I gotta return them. They have sentimental value. She'll want them back without delay."

"Of course they have sentimental meaning to her. I'm not an insensitive muttonhead." Davis carefully stacked the papers.

He lifted them from his desk and held them up in both hands. Then he let them fall back to the desk. "Be that as it may, I don't want to take a chance on losing this, Adams."

"You won't. You might have to publish them under the name Gallagher, is all."

"What? Why would I do that?"

"I'm still trying to convince her. In time, I'm sure she'll come around."

"Perhaps so."

"How about I take them back now and bring her in the morning. I shouldn't have brought them." He began to pace. "This was a bad idea."

Davis hung his head. "No, no. I'll take good care of them, like I said. If I let these go . . . if I allow them out of my sight for a minute . . . Things happen, Adams. I realize you do not know the world of publishing. Trust me on this. These stories could end up in the hands of another publisher. You brought them to me. I will guard them. That way we will both know our future success is secure."

"Uh . . . I don't know."

"Remember that empty apartment of yours." He held up the yellowing papers. "These, my boy, could make those troubles go away." He grabbed a newspaper from his desk and held it up. "Do you know what this is?"

"The *Times*?"

"That's right. And a mention of Luther Redmond's lost stories. The whole world knows about this now. Do you know how publicity like that profits us? This is tremendous, bigger than I had dared to imagine."

"Bully for you, Davis. Now, make a copy of these pages if you must, but give them back, and soon."

"I suppose we can type it up. I must have your word you will take these papers directly to the owner and safely deliver them. We can't risk them falling into other hands."

"I will. I don't want anyone but her to have them."

Davis tapped his fat fingers together. "In fact, if I have my own copies, I'll be ready to roll out the book all the quicker. After my boys type it up, I'll give it a once-over before the type-setting stage. Looks like pretty clean copy to me, but I'll need to change a word here and there for today's American reader. We will decide on the illustrations later."

The man was already moving ahead in his mind. "Do you have a worker here who can type quickly?" Stephen asked.

"I do, as a matter of fact. He's working overtime on another project, but we'll make this a higher priority. He'll get it done."

"Thank you."

Davis switched on a couple of electric lights. "You better be right about this. Disputes can delay publishing for years. We don't want that."

Stephen put an open hand on top of the papers and leaned forward. "Wait."

"What? Now you got a conscience?"

"Yeah . . . I mean . . . we won't do anything with the copies unless she agrees, right?"

"Right."

33

"From Dublin?" Annie asked.

"That is correct," the man said, tapping his black umbrella on the stoop.

"Won't you come in?"

Mrs. Hawkins came to the door. "How may we help you, sir?"

"Madam." He dipped his head. "I have come to speak to Miss Gallagher. I was a business associate of her father's."

She glanced at Annie and narrowed her eyes. Annie could not hide her apprehension. Anyone from Ireland could send her mind slithering back to screeching metal doors and deep, dark passageways.

"You will excuse me, sir, but as proprietor of this house, I look out for my girls. I must be certain you are who you say you are."

He pinched his lips a moment. "Forgive me. My popping around like this must appear unorthodox."

"'Tis all right, Mrs. Hawkins." Annie reached for the man's coat. "I do remember Mr. Barrows."

After introductions, they invited him into the parlor.

"I must say I'm surprised to see you, sir," Annie said.

"I know I must seem like a bolt from the blue. I had thought

287

to find you at your uncle's farm, but he said you had gone away and he didn't know where."

Annie tried to stay calm. "I am afraid he was not honest about that, Mr. Barrows."

"Indeed, as I was to learn. When I first inquired, just days after your father's death, even Father Weldon did not know where you had gone. My business called me back to Dublin, but although I inquired from time to time, I could not discern your whereabouts."

Annie remembered what Mrs. Hawkins had told her about the trouble her father had had finding her mother. The Irish didn't speak about another's trouble for fear it may be visited upon them. And especially when it involved a woman. Women were dispensable.

Mr. Barrows shifted uncomfortably in his seat. "I do apologize I did not find you earlier, Miss Gallagher. My failure was an injustice to your father. I am pleased to see you looking so well now and living in America. It must have been quite a journey for you."

"Thank you. It was." She wanted to ask why he'd been looking for her, but she decided to wait until he explained himself.

"I regret that I was not the one to arrange your journey. If I had only known, you would have had better accommodations on the ship."

His concern was puzzling. Annie knew many people held her father in high regard, but this seemed beyond the duties of friendship.

"I want to tell you why I am here. I have been in New York on business. I travel here quite a bit. I picked up a copy of the *Times* and was surprised to see that Luther Redmond's lost stories are being published. I immediately sent a telegram to Father

Weldon. He told me where to find you. I do regret not finding you sooner, Miss Gallagher."

Mrs. Hawkins reached for her newspaper. "The *Times*? I didn't realize."

"The piece came out a few days ago. It seems to say that there are more stories than the one that has been published."

Suddenly Annie remembered what Mr. Barrows had said at Da's graveside. *"The entire world will mourn his passing."* If she'd had trouble believing it before, the pieces were falling together now as though dropped from heaven by her father. Annie interrupted Mrs. Hawkins. "Mr. Barrows, can you confirm that my father really did write under the name Luther Redmond?"

"Yes, my dear. I regret I was unaware he had taken ill. We were waiting to hear of his latest whereabouts and did not know where he was until news of his death reached us."

"The decision to publish the one tale under Redmond's name was not my own. If that is the reason for your visit, I suggest you speak with the editors at *Harper's*."

"I have. Your father's stories, whether under the name Gallagher or Redmond, fall under the same copyright."

Copyright? Truly she didn't understand these things.

"Did everyone know this but me?" She rushed to the breakfront and retrieved her writing desk, wondering if all the stories had that mark Stephen had insisted belonged to the author Luther Redmond. She pulled open the lid and felt inside. She took out some writing paper, but that was all it contained. "My stories! They've been stolen!" She popped up the hidden compartment just in case, but it was empty too.

"This is quite disturbing," Mr. Barrows said. "Are you sure you haven't laid them aside somewhere?"

"They were here and now they're not." She suddenly

remembered Stephen Adams sitting alone in the parlor with the writing desk in his lap. He had left quickly, not even staying for supper. He'd taken one story already, but he apparently thought he was entitled to them all!

"I think I know what may have happened," she said, an ache forming in her head. "I will see to it in the morning." She turned to Mr. Barrows. "Thank you for your concern. I will handle my own affairs, however. I'm sorry to have taken up your time."

He stood as Aileen brought him his coat. "I'm afraid I have not explained myself fully. Please allow me." He slung his coat over his arm and took his umbrella. "I published Luther Redmond's work. His true name was Marty Gallagher. I have legal rights to all of his work, even after his death, Miss Gallagher. As I explained to your uncle, who I must say was extremely vexed to learn he had no claim, you are the only surviving heir; thus my agreement with your father falls to you. But you understand, I still hold the copyright. *Harper's* violated this copyright, although without malice. But I will not agree to have any more of these stories published in America, if indeed you recover them."

Mrs. Hawkins strode forward. "This is preposterous, Mr. Barrows. Surely you understand how much that income means to this young girl. She has plans. Her father would have wanted—"

"You cannot presume what her father wanted, Mrs. Hawkins. I will work with Miss Gallagher now that I have uncovered her whereabouts, but the courts will support me in this. The executives at *Harper's* magazine suggested I pay a visit to a man who is planning on publishing the stories in book format. His name is Alan Davis. Have you met?"

Annie felt affronted. They were her stories! She crossed her arms. "We have indeed met."

"It would be appropriate, I believe, for you to be there too,

Miss Gallagher. We have business to attend to, you and I. Say eight o'clock tomorrow morning at Davis Publishing?"

"Indeed. I will be there." Annie opened the door for him. They would not discuss her business without her if she had anything to say about it.

Early the next morning Annie prepared to leave the house. "I want to go alone, Mrs. Hawkins. Please."

"All right, love. But you telephone over to Mrs. Jenkins if you need me."

"I will. And I'll stop at the market and pick up potatoes and turnips."

"We don't need them yet, Annie."

"Oh, we do. I just checked."

"Hmm. I thought for certain . . . Better pick up some more cheese as well, since you'll be out anyway. I can't say for sure, but I think one of the delivery boys must have stolen a few things."

"Truly? I will have to watch closer."

"I don't mind as long as it's only a bit, and it has been. If I catch him, I'll give him a lecture, certainly, but I do understand hunger."

Annie grabbed her pocket purse and hurried to the door, wanting to arrive before Mr. Barrows got there. Mr. Davis and Stephen, if she could get there before he left for work, had better explain themselves. If she couldn't save the publishing agreement, all her hopes of honoring her father were in vain. She had told Stephen she wanted to wait, get legal advice, perhaps have the stories published under her father's real name. But she did want them published in the not-too-distant future so she could open that library. Mr. Barrows had an unfair hold on the stories, and she had no idea how long it took to resolve such publishing disputes. She should have control over *her* stories, not some man from Dublin or the postman, both of whom obviously thought she needed their help. She did not.

Only the newsboys were out on the street when she arrived. No businessmen commuting to their offices yet. She gazed into the plate-glass window of Davis Publishing. Someone tugged at the hem of her cloak. She looked down to see a wee lad. "Oh, hello."

"Swell, huh?"

"Excuse me?"

"How they make books. Mr. Adams showed me once. Want to go in and see yourself?"

"I would. Thank you."

She followed the lad inside. The first man they saw greeted them. "Hello, Matty. Miss. Come for another look-see, son?"

"You bet, Mr. Keaton."

"Excuse me, Mr. Keaton. My name is Annie Gallagher. Would you be kind enough to tell me if Mr. Davis is in?"

"I expect he will be soon, Miss Gallagher. I've been working extra hours on a special project, so I opened up early. I will alert him you are here to see him."

"Thank you."

"In the meantime, if you don't mind, our buddy Matty here will show you around if you've a mind to see the workings of our office, miss. Mr. Adams brought him in one day and he's stuck around, sweeping up and all. Thinks he wants to be a bookman one day, don't you, Matty?"

"Yep."

"Very kind of you." Annie smiled at the man and then allowed Matty to take her on a tour. "How nice of Mr. Adams and Mr. Davis to teach you things, young man."

"Yeah. They're swell." He pointed to a massive metal machine that was uniquely connected to some kind of typewriter. "They just typeset here. They pay other folks to print the books." He pointed to a tray just above the keyboard, where a piece of paper with typed words on it rested.

Mr. Keaton paused from his work and leaned to one side so they could see what he was working on.

Annie pointed to the paper. "Is this going to be in a book?"

"Yes, Miss Gallagher."

She gazed in amazement at the paper until she made out the words. *"Omah was the leader of a great clan of mice."* She gasped. Looking down, she saw the yellowed papers the typesetter had been working from. She considered snatching up her stories right then but thought better of it. The worker would not understand and would probably escort her out. She needed to confront the publisher. "How long have you had this . . . book, if I may ask?"

"Got it last night." He pointed to a stack of papers in a bin behind him. "Those stories have been waiting much longer, but sometimes one jumps to the front of the line, like this one."

She touched her jaw to keep from stammering. "Thank you." She rushed outside and let the cold air fill her lungs. Stephen had stolen the stories, and they were about to manufacture them into a printed volume when she hadn't even signed a contract with Davis Publishing yet, bypassing her completely. Not to mention the trouble they'd be in with Mr. Barrows.

She heard the door behind her open and close. She cringed. She was not yet ready to face Stephen Adams.

"Hey, Miss Gallagher." Matty bumped up against her leg. "You leaving already?"

"Aye. Uh, I mean no. I am waiting for Mr. Davis."

"Want me to go find out if he's here yet?"

She pulled up the boy's coat collar to keep out the wind. "You should get on home, so. 'Tis awfully cold out."

The boy frowned. "Nothing but chores." He dashed off toward a group of boys who were playing with a broomstick and a ball in the alley.

She entered again and noticed a light on in a room behind a door that had *Mr. Alan Davis* stamped on the nameplate. She knocked loudly. The door opened. "Miss Gallagher. Keaton told me you were here. I'm sorry to have kept you waiting. I was just tidying up a bit. Please, come in. Sit down. I'll get you some coffee."

"No thank you. I won't be staying."

He kept his hands on the back of a chair as though she might change her mind. "We—that is, Stephen Adams has the contract for you to sign. I'm sorry you made the trip in here. He's supposed to bring the contract to you."

"I bet you are sorry I stopped in."

His eyes widened. He wiggled his neck, sending his jowls wobbling. "Oh no. Not sorry. Always a pleasure to see you."

"Is that right? I stopped in the workroom. Had a look at what the typesetter was working on."

The man's face turned paler than new snow. "Uh, well, Stephen assured me you were going to sign the contract. And I wanted to get the ball rolling." He pulled at his shirt collar. "Your father's stories are already very popular, Miss Gallagher. They are going to earn you a lot of money."

Annie felt tears bubbling to the surface. She blinked her eyes. "All of you went on with this without so much as asking me. . . ." She struggled to keep her voice from rising to an irritated pitch. "You do not understand. I want Stephen Adams to have nothing to do with Omah."

She bolted out the door just as her chest heaved and her eyes burned with tears. Stephen pretended he cared for her. He only wanted to get the stories. That had been his plan all along. She had been an *eejit* for not trusting her instincts. He had been a very good actor.

She raced toward the trolley stop. Matty tried to stop her, but she brushed him away and kept going. Suddenly a hulking figure in a trench coat stepped into her path. She couldn't stop and slammed right into his chest.

"Hey there, Irish *Fräulein*."

34

Stephen rubbed his hands over his face as he sat in Davis's office. "We can't use the stories if she won't give permission. I'm afraid I've mucked it all up. She's angry with me."

Someone knocked on the office door.

"Come in," Davis hollered.

Stephen turned to see a tall man in a navy overcoat. The man removed his hat. "Mr. Alan Davis?"

"That's right. How can I help you?"

"I am sorry to intrude."

Stephen stood. "Not at all. I was just leaving. I have to get to work." He pointed to Davis. "We will talk about this tonight." He had his hand on the doorknob but halted when he heard the visitor say Annie's name.

"I am Barton Barrows from Dublin. I represent Blackton House Publishing. I was expecting to meet Miss Gallagher here this morning."

Stephen decided to stay.

"You just missed her. Maybe you can tell me what this is all about, Mr. Barrows. Please, sit down." Davis began twiddling his cold cigar.

When the man finished speaking, Stephen realized he and Davis had been trying to play chess with masters when they hadn't even understood the rules. "But Annie needs the money," he blurted.

Mr. Barrows tapped the end of his umbrella on the floor as he spoke. "Indeed, money is an issue. That is the reason Mr. Gallagher wanted to protect his daughter from all this business. It had been his hope that she would enjoy his earnings and not deal with these kinds of complicated matters."

Davis slumped in his wheeled office chair. "I will be ruined."

Mr. Barrows stood. "I suspect you have the stories since Miss Gallagher does not."

"In my safe."

"Give them to me, if you would."

"I don't think I better do that just yet."

The man tapped his fingers on the handle of his black umbrella. "I will have to appeal to the courts then. I warn you, Mr. Davis, this could be a long affair." He studied the confines of the office a moment. "One that I do not believe you can afford. I will be in touch." He exited the room, leaving Stephen and Davis stunned.

Stephen glanced down at Davis's desk at a ledger where the man was keeping track of what Stephen owed him. Then he stepped out of the room.

Perhaps there was no solution to this matter. Perhaps all his trying to be righteous had not been enough for God.

He continued on his route whistling no tune, taking no quick steps, and mumbling to himself. He'd tried to be a good son, a good person, a good friend. And still things were falling apart as though he hadn't even made an effort. He'd awakened that day with sore joints and hoped he'd have time soon to retrieve his belongings. Sleeping on the floor was for dogs. He'd feel the consequences all day, not to mention the misery of failure. Annie had no reason to appreciate why he'd taken her stories now.

I require obedience, son.

True, it had been wrong to take those stories. Stephen had been impatient and tried to work things out in a way that would benefit his own situation. He needed to forget about whether or not he could impress Annie and instead do what was right for her. He seemed to have lost sight of his original intent.

Put others before yourself.

Stephen could not deny God was instructing him.

The sky was dreary and gray. If it weren't for a few autumn chrysanthemums planted in front of some of the residences, the day would have no color at all. The chill in the air made his knuckles ache. Turning down an alley to take a shortcut, he noted several people gathered around a burning trash bin, warming their hands. He fingered the few pennies he had left in his pocket, planning to offer them.

He stopped before he got too close. A large man wearing a fine coat stood in the middle. There were some encounters a man should avoid. He planned to back out the way he'd come when someone yelled to him.

"Hey, mister! Got a penny for a fellow who just lost his job?"

He turned and nodded, and three of the men trotted toward him, leaving the larger man. When he'd given them what they wanted, they scurried away like rats.

Stephen saw the man was not alone. "Annie Gallagher? Is everything all right?" He hurried toward them.

Annie drew in her breath, as though irritated by his arrival.

"I . . . uh, I needed to make sure . . . I mean, I wanted to know if everything's all right here."

"It is, Mr. Adams." She turned her hand palm up and indicated the large man. "This is Kirsten Wagner's brother, Jonas. I've just invited him to come by sometime after the wedding this week and try to resolve things with his sister."

"Oh, I see." He grunted, then offered his hand. "Pleasure to meet you."

The man did not return the greeting. "You know my sister?"

"Well, not in a manner of speaking. I deliver the mail and I know she lived at Hawkins House." He turned to Annie. "It's about to rain. Perhaps I should walk you home now."

"Really, Mr. Adams. I am fine on my own. You do not have to hover over me as though I am a new hatchling."

"I meant no offense, Miss Gallagher." Stephen stood facing Annie, intentionally ignoring the man.

The large man briskly pulled Stephen's shoulder back toward him. Stephen gripped the strap of his mailbag with both hands. If only the postal inspectors were there to apprehend him.

Kirsten's brother glared. "Postman—my sister. I am looking for her. If she is not at Hawkins House, where? Miss Gallagher tells me she was in a hospital, but she left and no one knows where she is now. Do you maybe deliver mail for her somewhere else in this neighborhood?"

"I do not believe I have."

The man acknowledged this with a nod of his chin, but Stephen felt as though he was not satisfied. Thugs on the streets got what they wanted with force. If this fellow got a notion that he and Annie were withholding information, he might get violent. What had she been thinking, speaking to this man in the shadows of a Lower Manhattan alley?

Stephen turned back toward Annie. "Perhaps you are right. You know your way home. You go on." He gave her as urgent a look as he could, hoping she'd get the hint. If this man meant them harm, Stephen would take the brunt of it and be satisfied that Annie got off all right.

But Annie wrinkled her nose and didn't step away. "This man is worried about his sister."

Stephen exhaled. "I see that. I will speak to him. You go on."

When she didn't take his advice, Stephen turned his back on her, standing between them. "I delivered something you sent your sister, though. When she was still at Hawkins House. You deposited it in a letter box. That right?"

Annie patted Stephen's shoulder. When he twisted his neck to look at her, she wriggled her chin as though he should not have mentioned it. He tried to recover. "At least I believe I did. I deliver a lot of mail. And I should inform you . . ."

The man grabbed Stephen by the lapels, heavy mailbag and all. "*Ja*. Do you have it?"

"Of course not." He whispered toward Annie. "Go now." He heard the patter of her steps and waited until the echo sounded far enough away. Then he spoke as loudly as he could. "I tell you, sir, that when you send something illegal by the US mail, you may suffer extreme consequences."

Jonas pushed Stephen away, causing Stephen to trip over a discarded produce crate.

"I warn you, sir, the postal inspectors are on to you!"

The man hurried away. Stephen hefted his bag and started to move on. At the end of the alley, he saw Annie Gallagher staring at him.

She frowned. "There was no need to speak so harshly to him."

"You don't understand."

"I don't." Annie bolted across the street and disappeared in the midst of a group of pedestrians. He'd been trying to help. Why did she glower at him so?

35

"But, Mrs. Hawkins, Mr. Wagner meant no harm. Stephen Adams threatened him."

"You don't know that, Annie. He's likely mixed up in something sordid. What were you thinking, speaking alone to him? We should thank Mr. Adams for interceding. I'm sure you misunderstood."

"I did not. Stephen was going to get something called a finder's fee because of my stories. Mr. Davis was already preparing to publish the book of stories without my final consent. Their motives are questionable, to say the least. And after what he said to Jonas . . . you have misjudged his character, Mrs. Hawkins." She should have gathered up her stories when she found them in the workroom.

"Before you tell me about the stories, let me warn you. You must be more careful out there, love. After what our dear Grace went through, you cannot blame me for handing out this advice. Be friendly, of course, but ever cautious if you must speak to men out on the streets."

"I know. And I will be. 'Tis just that when I talked to Mr. Wagner, I discovered how concerned he is about Kirsten. Mr. Adams did not bother to ask any questions before he threatened him."

"I see. Like I said, he was right to be concerned."

Annie blew out a breath.

"Now then, it seems you did not work out the business with Mr. Barrows."

"I did not see him, but 'tis hopeless if he had an agreement with my father. And I understand now that my father was writing under the name of Luther Redmond to spare me all this, but . . ." She could not control the quiver in her voice. "He wasn't able to protect me from any of it."

"Now, now, love. This will all work out. And don't forget you have my full support."

"Thank you, Mrs. Hawkins."

"What did Mr. Davis say about your stories?"

"He has them in his office. It seems Mr. Adams thought he should take them from me and deliver them."

"Ah, well. Good that they are safe. At least you know they were not truly stolen."

"Just taken without permission, if there is a difference."

"There is, love. The postman was trying to help. I agree he should not have stepped in that way, but he did not mean harm."

"I don't know what to believe, Mrs. Hawkins. In any case, Mr. Barrows said he owns the rights to my father's stories. I can't allow anyone else to publish them."

"Is he going to do it, then? Surely now that he has found you, you'll receive some portion of your father's earnings."

"I cannot imagine there were any more earnings than what my father carried with him, and my uncle has that. Mr. Barrows seemed adamant about the stories not being published, I'm afraid."

"Annie, you have the entire committee of the Benevolents at your disposal." She handed her a cup of tea.

"Thank you. I just wanted to do this, Mrs. Hawkins. I wanted to prove I could."

"Of course you can, love. You rest a bit. And think about this. I will tend to the baking."

"Think? I have done nothing but. My father's tales of talking mice and learned rabbits represented home to me, Mrs. Hawkins. A joyful place I had to leave when they closed my father's coffin."

"Oh, dear child. Storms, like the one we had the other night, for example, don't last forever. I believe the Irish have a saying about it: 'There's no flood that doesn't subside.' Sorrows last for the moment, but joy comes in the morning. Remember these wise words. My Harold used to repeat them whenever I fretted about something."

This was more than simple fretting. There was no way back to that happier time. Her childhood didn't exist anymore. Those days were lost like ashes rising up a chimney, impossible to retrieve. The thought sat on her shoulders like a twenty-pound sack of potatoes.

Seeing the stories in print might have brought some measure of it back, but now that could not happen. She would never be able to publish them, never make money from them, never open her father's library or start a storytellers' academy. Or find anyone as kind as her father, as she'd thought Stephen Adams was. When she'd realized God didn't want her, she'd dared to hope she could still find happiness. A witless idea that had been.

"I will keep that in mind, Mrs. Hawkins." Although she knew it wouldn't help, it was thoughtful of the woman to try.

Annie returned to her room and held a hand to her chest. How she wished for a heart of stone that could not be wounded. Or to be like the Tin Woodman and believe that she had no heart at all. The continual ache from not finding a place to call home made Annie fully aware that she did indeed have a heart.

She mindlessly flipped through the pages of the Bible lying on her desk.

"For his anger endureth but a moment; in his favour is life: weeping may endure for a night, but joy cometh in the morning."

She slammed the book shut and covered her mouth with her hand. Some kind of demon must have possessed her. She'd imagined Mrs. Hawkins had just said the same thing to her.

As she sat at her desk, willing the storm in her soul to subside, a sunbeam bathed her face and she lifted her head toward it. "Oh, God, am I going crazy? I want to be with you in the light and not under these black clouds." She lay her head down on the desk and emptied her thoughts until she dozed off.

The next thing she knew, Mrs. Hawkins was tapping on her shoulder, holding out a plate of warm scones topped with honey. The sun still came in through her curtains, and a feeling of peace drifted to her senses along with the scents of mint tea and yeasty bread.

Mrs. Hawkins set the plate on the desk in front of her. "Are you feeling better now?"

"I am." She kissed the woman on the cheek, making her chuckle.

"Take your time. We have all evening to finish our preparations for the wedding." Mrs. Hawkins handed her a napkin.

Annie licked the honey from her fingers. Something about sweets always seemed to help her think more clearly.

"I was thinking about you running into Jonas. You said he has not found Kirsten yet?"

"He has not, although he is desperate to find her."

"I assume he has been in the city all along."

"Oh, aye." She tasted the warm scone. "But how would you know that?"

"A few things. One, the telegram he sent from New York. That could have been explained, but when coupled with something else, I suspected as much."

"What else?"

"Remember I had a boardinghouse for him? He left that day without asking the address or name. He obviously already had a place to stay."

"Oh, that's right, so."

"Also, those letters arrived so quickly. Letters take a while to get here, even from upstate New York, so I suspected they were mailed locally. A package takes a bit longer. He probably did not know that, and that's what prompted his worry and kept him asking about it."

Mrs. Hawkins's keen senses were a result of careful observation. Annie could learn from that.

"I don't know why he decided to confide in me when he saw me on the street, Mrs. Hawkins. But I'm glad I heard his story."

"Me as well. Sometimes folks have to have nowhere to turn before they'll reach out. Men, especially, let their pride keep them from accepting help. But when they are at the bottom of a well, they reach for whatever hand is there. I believe God placed you in his path at that time because he knew you'd give Jonas a sympathetic ear. Won't you tell me what he told you? Perhaps we can find a way to help."

Annie blew out a breath before continuing. "Aye, of course. He met the Pinkerton at some pub called McSorley's."

"I've heard of it. Women aren't permitted." She rolled her eyes, making Annie laugh. In America those public houses were rowdy places, not the cozy establishments entire families visited in Ireland. Mrs. Hawkins would not have gone to McSorley's if they'd welcomed her with arms wide.

"It was an untruth that he was ever up north working."

"Why were they not honest about that? I would have tried to help him find a job. What has he been doing?"

"He said he picked up odd jobs here and there and ate at various charity soup suppers. He's slept in different shelters and alleys. Anyway, feeling down on his luck and embarrassed that his sister was the only wage earner, he'd dropped in to drown his worries in a mug of dark ale. 'Twas there he overheard some men talking about a financial scheme."

"And he became involved. If only we could speak sense into these young people. I'm always seeing advertisements about how quick money can supposedly be made. There are swindlers everywhere. Too many people think that in America money can be picked off trees like leaves."

"Not exactly like that, Mrs. Hawkins. He was interested, aye, but the men moved away from him to another table. One was balancing his full mug, some envelopes, and whatnot, when he left behind a ledger. Jonas picked it up and looked at it. Suddenly they charged at him, as though he meant them harm. He dashed out of there and managed to escape. They were German like him, and the details in the book were written in his native tongue. He said there was a draft of a letter and addresses. He didn't know what to make of it, but he did know he'd looked at it and that made him a target—and soon Kirsten, also, because they followed him somehow and learned where she worked."

"Oh, dear. I guess the Pinkertons are effective at what they do. Those men must have hired Mr. Cooper."

"That would seem to make sense, Mrs. Hawkins."

"So Jonas put her here to be safe."

"It seems so. Some people take a long time to put their trust in anyone, especially immigrants like the Wagners, who have escaped unpleasantries in their homelands."

The woman crossed her arms across her bosom. "Is that so?"

"I'm not speaking about myself."

"Um-hum."

"He never would have given the ledger to Kirsten if they hadn't been watching him so closely. To escape his pursuer, presumably the Pinkerton, Jonas wrapped up the ledger, wrote Kirsten's name and Hawkins House on the outside, and dropped it into a letter box just in time."

Mrs. Hawkins pinched her hands together in her lap. "I don't suppose he thought the police would help him. I wish more people knew our Owen."

Annie agreed.

The Hawk clicked her tongue. "Kirsten hid to protect them both. I understand that now. She probably thinks keeping the ledger hidden is their only safeguard. Without it, those bad men would have no reason not to assassinate them like the poor president."

"I'm afraid so. Jonas said Kirsten feared for his life. Not being able to read, she might not have known what to believe. I'm sure she thought Jonas's involvement might cause him to be deported at the very least."

"She is right to be concerned about that, Annie."

"He says he doesn't care about that now. He only wants to find his sister and make sure she is safe." Annie popped a morsel of the scone into her mouth.

"So the Pinkerton thought he could force Kirsten to hand it over. The poor dear was probably so confused."

"I asked Jonas to come here after the wedding, Mrs. Hawkins. I don't know how we can help, but I thought perhaps we'd come up with something."

"Good thinking, my dear girl. You certainly have God's heart for the downtrodden."

God's heart? She wanted to do something, not sit by while others suffered, never again after the misery she'd been put through. She smiled. "I may never get my library or my story-telling school, but if we can do something to help those poor people get a new start . . . it would mean so much."

Mrs. Hawkins sighed, looking out the window. "I would like to help, and maybe there is yet something we can do for Jonas, but Kirsten may be far away from here by now."

While she waited for Mrs. Hawkins to finish her tea, Annie pulled the *Wizard* book out from under the Bible. Thumbing aimlessly through the pages, she stopped at the illustration of Dorothy sitting in a field surrounded by attentive black mice as the Tin Woodman introduced her to the Queen of Mice. If fairy tales were true, there would be a mouse queen who would make things right. If the Bible were true, calling on God, as Annie had, would pull her into the light.

Mrs. Hawkins's teacup clinked as she abruptly stood and gathered up the things she'd brought to Annie's room, including Annie's half-eaten scone.

Annie snatched back her snack. "What are you doing?"

"You and I are going somewhere, right now. I was just con-templating something, and I believe the best illustration would be to take you there."

"Where?"

"No questions. Let's go."

After they had gotten on the Ninth Avenue el and Annie could see the treetops of Central Park, she asked again. "Please, Mrs. Hawkins. Where are we going?" She had only been as far as Central Park, and only on one occasion, when Grace had insisted she go skating there with her.

"It will become clear, love. Patience."

She was still baffled, so she sat quietly. When they got off the train, she thought perhaps they were going to the park, but Mrs. Hawkins hired a cab.

"To Trinity Church Cemetery," she said.

"What are we doing?"

The Hawk said nothing.

They entered through an iron gate. Towering obelisks stretched toward the treetops and multiple tombs. Marble statues and more lushly green bushes than were found in Battery Park spoke to the affluence of the place. "Who is buried here?"

"The wealthy, love. The Astors, Audubon, mayors, statesmen . . ."

She followed the woman down a path between graves until she stopped suddenly in front of a limestone set of stairs guarded on each side by two massive stone urns. A weary rosebush sprang toward the steps on the left. The stairs led to a framed lot of graves where a handful of tombstones rested. Mrs. Hawkins leaned against the wall. "This is the Hawkins family plot."

Annie's heart began to ache. She knew the pain of loss as much as anyone. Standing there where surely numerous tears had been shed over many generations, it seemed as though the sorrow might seep right into her. "Your Harold is buried here, so."

"That's right. Among the wealthy, love. The extremely wealthy." Mrs. Hawkins turned to her. "I brought you here to show you that the Hawkinses have a place in high-society Manhattan, but this cemetery is the only part of that I'm willing to showcase. I have inherited, through my Harold, a great sum of money." She laughed nervously. "Me, without electricity. You must find that amusing."

"I don't mind it, Mrs. Hawkins, but what do you do with all your money?"

"The Benevolents, remember?"

"Aye, I know they help you with your outreach to immigrant girls."

"They support me, that much is true. They help me make decisions. But I fund everything."

"Kirsten's medical care?"

"Yes. And your passage to America. I never wanted anyone beyond the Benevolents to know about this. Harold and I kept an inconspicuous public image. We never attended the wealthy balls or other events, even if they benefited charity. Once his parents passed on and his siblings moved to California, folks tended to forget who we were, and we quite liked that. Therefore, the people in our neighborhood have no idea how well off he left me. Folks treat you differently if they know you own grave plots next to the Astors, love."

"I suppose not many would understand you turning your back on your wealth."

The Hawk approached a headstone and tenderly laid her hand on top. "Oh, I didn't turn my back on the money. I just put it to good use. All the blessings we have are God's anyway."

God wasn't blessing Annie, but it was good Mrs. Hawkins had God's favor and had in turn blessed others, like Annie.

"I brought you here not to boast about what I do at Hawkins House, but to show you I do trust you. This is not something I want just anyone to know." She kissed her fingers and then patted her husband's tombstone. Turning with watery eyes, she walked forward and reached for Annie's hand. "But there is something else. I want to ask you, love, if you would become the second female member of the Benevolents."

"Me?"

"If you would like. And I promise you I have no more secrets and do not plan to keep any from you ever again."

Annie nodded, and the woman embraced her.

36

Early on the morning of Grace and Owen's wedding, Stephen met with the postmaster. Mr. Sturgis's office chair squealed as he leaned back. "So the man is still in town. There may be hope yet this ledger will still show up."

"I don't know, sir. He said he's been looking for his sister everywhere and she's the one who has it."

"Nonetheless, bring this man in to speak to me. He may have helpful information."

"Bring him in?"

"That's why you came to speak to me, yes?"

"Well, I'm not sure where he is, but I will inquire at Hawkins House. I just thought you'd like to know Jonas Wagner has not left town."

"Better get on it, Adams. Remember you owe me for getting you out of that other mess."

Stephen stood. "Yes, sir." He had another matter to see to before he continued his mail delivery.

A half hour later Stephen arrived at No. 105 Thirteenth Street. The gray block building bore no lettering or advertisement of any kind. He hoped he was in the right place. He knocked on the metal door.

A few minutes later he tried the doorknob. Finding it unlocked, he went inside. A mountain of crates, carriage wheels, and cast-off items rose before him, but he did not see any people. "Hello?" he called out.

A moment later he heard footsteps. A wisp of a man appeared wearing no suit coat over his shirt and suspenders. His trousers were soiled and in need of mending. "Come to claim something?" he chirped.

Stephen handed over the letter he'd found pinned to his door. He wasn't thinking about getting his furniture back, though. He hadn't even brought a wagon.

The man chewed on a toothpick as he spoke. "Got the rental fee, have ya?"

"I do have it, along with a statement of settlement from Mr. Archibald Murray." He handed the document to the attendant. The finder's fee Davis had given him waited in his pocket. "However, I would like to know, do you ever purchase the items stowed here?"

The man scratched his back. "So ya don't have it." He handed the papers back. "We don't usually, no."

"But sometimes?"

"Only if it's good stuff. Adams, right? I'll go take a look."

"Wait."

The man retraced his steps.

"There is one thing I do want back." He held his hands apart in front of him. "A box. About this wide. Not valuable particularly, but of great sentimental value."

"I will check." The man disappeared down a row of bins marked with metal numbers.

He returned some time later with a clipboard in one hand and Stephen's prized box in the other. "A bed with linens, a small dresser, a box of dishes, a box of clothing, a small table and a chair, a well-used sofa, a lamp, matches, and a rug. That sound about right, Mr. Adams?"

"Yes, about right." He claimed his box and opened it. Everything seemed in order, although obviously rummaged through.

The man studied Stephen. "Think I'd take anything? Against my duties."

"Perhaps not, but you looked."

"If I was gonna steal—and on my mother's grave I would not—ya got nothing I'd want. 'Cept maybe that bed."

"Come on. You could resell all that stuff."

"The rug, perhaps."

The man was bluffing. "How much would you give me for the lot?"

"Fifteen dollars."

"I'll sell it myself, then. You know it's worth twice that, and I'll throw in the books you didn't account for."

"Ah." He tossed his hand the way Stephen had seen Italians do when they were dismissing what had been said. "All right. A deal." He pulled some bills from his pocket and waved them in the air. "Here you go, minus the rental fee."

Stephen shoved the box into his mailbag, accepted the money, signed a paper on the man's clipboard, and departed the building the way he'd come. Slinging his mailbag over his shoulder, he headed down the street. He would spare two dollars to purchase one of Mrs. Jacobs's woven blankets as a wedding gift and then use the rest of his proceeds along with his finder's fee to enable Annie to hire an attorney. Delaying settling up with Davis, going without a hot lunch, polish for his shoes, a train ride—those sacrifices would be inconsequential if he could actually help Annie Gallagher get what she wanted.

37

ANNIE, AILEEN, and Mrs. Hawkins sat in a pew near the front.
The wedding ceremony would be small, and then they would
proceed to Hawkins House for the celebration. Annie was
pleased for Grace, but her mind wandered. Her thoughts kept
turning to her father's stories. The night before, Annie had studied the design on the ceiling—a mindless activity she hoped
would wash away the sense of loss from the failure of her dream,
and the turmoil over finding out her mother had suffered in a
laundry, freed only by death. But her mind had kept working.
The design resembled wee paths leading in and out of circular
shapes, and she was reminded of the carved circles on standing
stones near where she played as a girl. She had almost forgotten
that her father's fictional animals trod circles in the dirt of the
farmers' fields. He had probably used those stones as inspiration
when he created the tales. She closed her eyes, remembering.

Omah, one of the mice, said he furrowed those circles in
order to remind the farmers of the spiritual significance of the
land they plowed. The mouse's name was a form of Omagh, a
wee Irish town in the north. She remembered that *Omagh* meant
fertile plain. She wondered if there was any other symbolism in
the stories, anything else her father might have been trying to tell

her. Stories, especially Irish ones, often hold a deeper meaning than what first appears. Her father might have had more reasons to conceal the truth about Luther Redmond. There were many things she did not understand, but one thing she knew when he had been alive and she still believed—he loved her without condition. She was eager to recover the stories and look for meaning that she might have missed before. Spiritual truths. Perhaps like the farmers, she needed some reminders.

She stared at the stained-glass window. The setting sun backlit the colors, giving off their true hues. The window, the Hawk had once told her, had been commissioned from Louis Comfort Tiffany, a master glassmaker. It entranced her as she studied it in detail. Down in the far left corner appeared the figure of a mouse. She had never noticed it before. A mouse, of all things.

She turned her head to the front as the organ began. Earlier she had placed a pillar candle on the altar, sent all the way from Ireland by Grace's mother.

"'Twas on the church altar when I was baptized," she told Annie. "A tradition from home."

Grace was also far from her homeland, but wee reminders like this kept home alive in her heart as she prepared to make a new home with Owen, she'd said. There were traditions observed in weddings that signified the mixing of the past with the present, like wearing something old and something new. Annie wondered if starting over in America did not mean turning one's back on everything past. Father Weldon had said to keep the good memories.

Grace, Owen, and Reverend Clarke entered from a side door. There would be no processional like some of the larger weddings at Trinity Church she'd read about. Grace and Owen had not seen a need. Grace was represented by Hawkins House in the pew where Annie sat, and Owen's parents, looking like

Buckingham Palace guards, stoic and regal, occupied a pew on the opposite side of the aisle.

Behind Annie the pew was filled with the Parker family. Aileen flung an arm back to tickle the children. She'd enjoyed spending the day with them.

"On this auspicious occasion," Reverend Clarke began, "we are gathered here to celebrate the union of this man and this woman."

Annie didn't hear the rest. That wee mouse in the window distracted her. Why would the window maker put a mouse there? Had she been so occupied with mice lately that she'd imagined it? What seemed like only moments later, the church organ rang out again and Grace and Owen marched down the aisle. Annie scrambled to keep up with the others. She stole a glimpse backward, wondering if she was not only dreaming up hearing things in church that had not been said, and recalling bits of stories she had not been specifically thinking about, but now seeing things as well. The mouse was no longer visible. A shadow had descended behind the window. She had to hurry to keep up.

Earlier the silver had been polished and the table set. Biscuits and scones had been placed on platters, and frosty pitchers of cider waited in the icebox. The ham had been sliced and the bread baked. All the table linens had been ironed and positioned, and the floors were swept, the furniture dusted, and the candlewicks trimmed. Perhaps the bustle of readying the house had made Annie so weary she imagined she saw mice in the church stained glass.

As Owen and Grace took their places in the parlor to greet guests as they arrived, Annie pulled Aileen aside. "Tell me, am I mad or does the church window, the one next to our pew, have a wee mouse in the corner of it?"

"What?"

"You heard me. I want to know."

Aileen shrieked playfully. "Surely not. A church mouse? I thought only the stone churches in Ireland had those."

Annie tented her hands and shook them in front of her. "Not a real mouse, Aileen."

"I do understand how the mind can wander during services."

Annie leaned against the kitchen wall. "I . . . well . . ." She couldn't deny it entirely. She had been too wrapped up in her thoughts of late. She gave up and stomped off to open the door for guests.

Aileen joined her. After collecting coats, she whispered to Annie. "I saw it too. The mouse in the church window. I saw it."

Annie released a breath. "Fine, so."

"I saw them in the graveyard in Ireland too," Aileen said.

"Mice are all over Ireland, Aileen. Just like they are in New York."

"We are not talking about real mice now, are we?"

"We are not. Why are they there, I wonder?"

"I saw a mouse carved at the foot of a high cross. I heard, though I don't know if 'tis true, that the monks drew mice in the Book of Kells—you know, that illuminated manuscript they have at Trinity College."

"That's very interesting, Aileen. I thought you didn't do well with your lessons."

"I listened. I might not have been able to read, but I was not lame-headed, Annie."

"Of course you weren't. I'm sorry."

At the next knock, Annie was surprised to see Mr. Barrows. "I see you are having a party, Miss Gallagher. I had hoped you and I could discuss matters before I leave for Dublin."

"Come in. We are celebrating a wedding."

He took off his hat. "I won't detain you. Until we can talk longer, please take this." He handed her an envelope.

"What's this?"

"Mail from Mr. Redmond's readers. Please, humor me. Examine a few of these. I will call again in a few days." His face softened. "I would like you to understand why we cannot allow those children's stories to be published by just anyone. I'm a businessman, true. But I do care about your father's legacy."

He glanced to the crowd in the parlor. "Later, when you have time." He replaced his hat and turned toward the door. "Please excuse my intrusion."

38

STEPHEN THOUGHT he was late when he got to the gate outside Hawkins House, but a couple was just entering ahead of him. After they were admitted, Aileen greeted him.

"Fancy seeing you here, Stephen Adams."

He took a step backward. "I was invited."

She pulled on his arm. "'Tis frightfully cold out. Get inside. Of course you were invited." She winked and took the wrapped gift he brought.

Embarrassed, he kept his gaze on the entry rug as he removed his coat. He didn't think Annie would have been so glad to see him had she answered the door, but he hoped to remedy that soon.

The doorbell chimed behind him. He scooted farther down the hall to allow the newcomers to enter.

"Hard to hear that thing. Most folks just knock." Aileen opened the door. "Welcome, Dr. Thorp, Mrs. Thorp."

The house was stuffed with merry folks chattering in clusters. He tipped his head toward the parlor but could not see as much as a foot-sized empty spot on the floral rug. He turned at the sound of his name.

"Ah, Mr. Adams. So good of you to join us."

The hostess held out a tray of cookies. "Please, have one. I used my own coriander from my summer garden."

"Delightful. Thank you, Mrs. Hawkins." He took two.

"Annie is here somewhere. Please be sure to speak to her, love. She has had quite a day." She moved on, wiggling between guests.

He made his way down to the kitchen, where there was a bit more unoccupied space. Annie was bent over a pot on the stove. He waited, wiping cookie crumbs from his lips.

When she turned, he pulled some banknotes from his pocket and laid them down on the table. "I want to make a donation, Ann . . . I mean, Miss Gallagher. To your library. Or perhaps to assist with getting your stories published." He was about to explain that the stories were in his coat pocket out in the hall, but she seemed rather employed at the moment and unable to accept them just then.

She pushed the tray of meatballs toward him, mumbling something about how fast they were disappearing. She glanced down at his offering and then met his gaze. "What a kind gesture. I . . . I don't think that is possible now. Mr. Barrows, a man from Dublin . . ." She bit her lip as though trying not to say more.

"Yes, I know. I was in Davis's office when he dropped by, and I heard about the copyright issue. Don't give up. I know how much it means to you."

"I imagine you are concerned about your dividends . . . what you might have received from the arrangement as well." She picked up the money. After a moment's hesitation, she handed it back.

"No, that's not how it is at all."

"It's all right. I'm sure you need this, and as I said, it's very nice of you to offer. However, it seems neither you nor I will be making any money with those stories."

Reluctantly he put the banknotes back in his pocket, telling himself he'd find a way to help her even if he had to do it anonymously.

She pointed to the tray.

He speared a meatball with the fork she handed him. "I'm afraid you have misjudged me."

"And Jonas Wagner as well? You think I've misjudged him?" she whispered. "You threatened Kirsten's brother."

"It's complicated. I do hope you will let me explain."

Aileen entered and tugged on Annie's arm. "I can't do all the work myself. Come."

Annie smiled tight-lipped as if to say there was nothing she could do, and the two women dashed off.

Stephen picked up the tray and followed after them. The hall was still filled with guests. Someone called to him.

"Ah, Stephen!"

"Dex. What a surprise."

"The police sergeant has been a great friend to many of the shop owners in the neighborhood. He invited us."

Stephen lost sight of the women just short of the parlor.

Dexter took a meatball from the tray. "Keeping these for yourself, fella?"

"Oh no. Please." He held the tray out. When Dexter took hold of it with both hands, Stephen let go. As he wove through the crowd of black coats and evening dresses topped with pearl necklaces, he heard Dexter calling after him.

"I need this recipe for the diner," he said.

Stephen held a hand up over the crowd to let his friend know he'd heard.

The piano music paused just then, and even though a fiddler Stephen recognized from the dances had not yet begun playing, the house was anything but quiet. The din of chatter made it hard to concentrate. If he were only a few inches taller. He dipped low, then rose up on his toes. Finally he spotted the women standing near the doctor, who was seated by the window.

The bespectacled man lifted his head to look at Mrs. Hawkins. "Your German girl has gotten away from the trouble that plagued her. So it seems this matter is finished for all of you. And what a fine party and delicious food you have prepared. My warmest congratulations," he said to Grace and Owen. He motioned toward the center of the room. "If you'll excuse me, I'll join Ella now."

The matter wasn't over for Jonas Wagner. Stephen didn't know if they realized that.

A few hours later the crowd thinned as celebrants began departing. Stephen retrieved his overcoat from among the pile on a hall coat tree. Annie found him there. "Leaving?"

He glanced over his shoulder. "Everyone else seems to be."

Mrs. Hawkins called from the parlor. "Annie, come sit. Grace and Owen are going to open some of their gifts."

Annie did not seem willing to break the gaze they held. Stephen blinked but did not move.

"I shouldn't intrude," he finally said.

"Nonsense." She nodded toward the room.

"Come in, love," Mrs. Hawkins said to him.

He stood awkwardly in front of the window, sending the candle holding watch there fluttering.

The couple opened boxes containing silver platters and linen tablecloths. The Parker children reclined near the hearth, where Aileen sat in a rocking chair holding the youngest, who slumbered peacefully.

"Thank you, Mr. Adams. What a well-made woven blanket,"

Grace said, pulling his thoughts back to the purpose of the gathering.

He smiled.

As the others chatted, he whispered to Annie, "I have something in my coat pocket for you. Let me get it." He hurried to the coat tree, found the fat envelope containing her stories, and handed it to her. He'd gotten them back from Davis that afternoon, after Davis had finished making copies.

Aileen came into the hall as the Parkers prepared to leave. Mr. Parker's sister took the toddler from Aileen and they handed coats around. Annie helped, so Stephen sat quietly on one of the floral chairs. Grace and Owen began to pack up their presents. "Allow me to help." He grabbed his coat again and started gathering boxes and baskets.

By the time he finished loading up a wagon parked in the rear alley, the hour was very late. But Mrs. Hawkins asked him not to leave yet. "Annie would like to thank you."

"For what?"

She urged him inside. He sat in the parlor with the woman and Annie, who was still wearing a coat after having helped to carry gifts. Aileen had gone with the Parkers, the newlyweds had departed for their new house, and all the guests had left.

"I do thank you for returning these, Mr. Adams."

"I apologize sincerely. I'm afraid my enthusiasm—"

Annie held up a hand. "Do not speak of it. What's done is done."

He bit his lip.

Annie gently lifted the yellowed pages to put them away in the writing desk she held in her lap, but as she did, a puzzled look passed over her. "The desk feels weighty." She dug her hand around inside. "Hmm." She slid her hand along the back and Stephen heard a click. Then she opened what appeared to be a hidden compartment and pulled out a small black leather book. "Who put this in here?"

"What is it, love?" Mrs. Hawkins asked, settling into a chair by the tea table.

Annie opened the cover, and Stephen gazed over her shoulder. The writing was peculiar, not in English. Being a postman, he'd seen foreign writing before. "This looks like German to me."

"Oh, Mrs. Hawkins, I think I found Jonas's ledger."

Indeed it would have barely fit inside a letter box.

A noise on the stair made them all turn to look. Stocking feet appeared and then a long, thin hand as someone bent low to gaze into the parlor. Finally a face peered from between the balusters. Miss Kirsten Wagner!

A clatter erupted as the women gathered around the girl. Stephen picked up the ledger so many people had been clamoring to get. He wanted to take it, but after what he'd done with the stories, he thought better of it. He would trust Mrs. Hawkins to guard it, but he'd have to let the postmaster know it had been found.

With all the hubbub over the reappearance of the missing girl, Stephen felt like someone who had sneaked into a theater without paying. His pounding heart accused him of intruding. He shouldn't be there. Even when he'd slipped a gift into Annie's coat pocket as they sat together on the sofa, she had not noticed. He hoped when she found it, she would finally understand where his heart truly was.

As both women fussed over Kirsten Wagner where she stood on the stairs, he went to the front door. "I should be going." No one looked at him. "Good-bye."

He opened the door and stepped out into the frosty night. Glancing up and down the sidewalk, he did not see Jonas anywhere. His sister had returned; the ledger was found.

He shoved his hands into his pockets and then remembered he'd forgotten the new mittens Mrs. Jacobs had made for him. He'd taken them off to return the papers to Annie.

He turned and looked back at the house, its windows glowing with candlelight. He'd sent his heart down a sledding hill for a woman who lived there, but she wouldn't even hear him out.

He opened and shut the gate, letting himself out like he always did when he delivered mail. He walked toward First Church.

When he rounded the corner of Rayburn Street, he saw lights on in the windows. He pulled off his hat, entered the building, and sat in a rear pew.

Someone put a hand on his shoulder.

"Reverend Clarke. I hope you don't mind."

"Mind? This is God's house, son. Stay as long as you like. If you need me, I'm right here. Just wanted to let you know that."

Stephen glanced up toward the altar, tears blurring his sight. Reverend Clarke was one of the few he'd told about the circumstances surrounding his father's death. "I have tried not to be a failure like my father was."

"Oh, son, your father was a troubled man who made a poor decision that he likely didn't foresee the consequences of. What he did has injured you, but it need not destroy you. The very fact that you are struggling proves you are not defeated."

"What do you mean?"

"It's dealing with our troubles that wearies us and causes us to come into the sanctuary late at night. And that's good, in fact. Someone who runs away from strife is not someone who will prevail when all is said and done. What your father did was give up. I don't see you surrendering. And if you're not, then you must be trying. And so long as you do, you will never be a failure. There is always a new beginning waiting for you."

Stephen took a long deep breath. They sat in silence a good while. Finally Stephen turned to him. "Sometimes I'm just so angry." The muscles in his jaw tightened. He hated the feeling.

"Being angry is understandable. I can't say how you should be feeling. It was an awful thing."

Stephen pounded his fists together, frustrated. "I don't like how it makes me feel."

"That is an important thing to consider. All your anger is doing is hurting you inside."

"How do I stop it?"

"Forgive him."

"I . . . I did not realize . . . That's a hard thing, Reverend."

"And that's the very thing you are struggling with. It taints every aspect of your life, I imagine. True, it's hard, but if you cannot do it, it's you alone who suffers."

Stephen thought about this. "How do I ensure that my life turns out better? How can I know I'm not destined for the same fate? I've tried to be nice to everyone. I've never said a harsh word to anyone on my mail route. I've tried to maintain a good financial standing, even though I've not done well thus far. But I've improved my situation. I've worked so hard, and still . . ." He put his head in his hands. "I'm alone."

"There you're wrong. You most certainly are not alone."

"I mean . . . I have no family, Reverend."

"I believe God intends for everyone to be in a family. You are God's child."

"I know. But I have no earthly family, despite how I've tried. I feel . . . unlovable. What it is about me that makes people want to leave me?"

The reverend gripped Stephen's shoulder with more force. "I do not believe your father wanted to leave you, son. He was so caught up in his own grief, he probably could not even remember he had a family."

"Is that possible?"

"It is, unfortunately. I have counseled many people over the years. Feelings of despair so overshadow some folks, they cannot think outside of themselves. They forget to eat, forget they have a job, fail to even get out of bed sometimes. So certainly they don't think about their families. It is not within their ability during those moments, not because they don't care about their loved ones, but because they cannot perceive anything besides the pain they feel."

"Truly I never thought of that. So he might not have even thought about me when he took his life."

"Anguish can consume people, son. They are in a place where they do not even allow the light of God to shine through. That is not the family's fault. Now for you, there are many standing with you, Stephen. You are not alone. You are a child of God and a member of the saints. I baptized you myself, just after your father died. Have you forgotten?"

"No, Reverend, I haven't forgotten. I was desperate then and seeking peace."

"And God brought peace, but he does not promise you will not have trouble again. He offers refuge and shows you the way to walk through hard times. We all stumble, but we rise again because of the hope he gives."

Stephen tapped his chest with a closed fist. "I know these things, but somehow . . . knowing doesn't help here. Where it hurts the most."

"I believe I see the errancy in your thinking."

Stephen swiveled in the pew to better face the man.

"You are trying hard, you said?"

"I think I am. I'm doing all I can."

"And that is the problem. You are trying to drive your own fate. Give that up. Allow God to steer you, and be confident that he never fails and never leaves you."

Relief washed over Stephen like a wellspring. If he trusted that God would lead, how could he ever expect failure?

The reverend tapped his open palms on the back of the pew. "Setbacks may happen. You may still make wrong choices, get off the path at times. But with God there is forgiveness and second chances—assurance that, in the end, all will be well." He lightly tapped Stephen's chest with his index finger. "Allow him to fill that ache."

"Thank you."

The reverend stood and motioned toward the altar, shrugging his shoulders in a questioning gesture.

Stephen nodded, and the two of them knelt before the altar and prayed.

39

Kirsten sat on the sofa, a quilt around her shoulders and a cup of Mrs. Hawkins's special chamomile tea in her hands. "I didn't know where else to go. I have nowhere to go. I've been hiding on your third floor ever since I left the infirmary."

Annie exchanged glances with Mrs. Hawkins. "The potatoes and turnips."

"The missing cheese," Mrs. Hawkins added.

"I did not take much."

"That's all right, love."

Annie held Kirsten's thin hand. The way the lass moved so lightly on her feet and slipped in and out of rooms oftentimes unnoticed had apparently helped her hide there, right under their noses. "Tell us the story."

Kirsten sighed. "Every day I asked myself, should I go tell them now? I feared what you would think of me, a German girl, bringing trouble to you. But finally, tonight as I thought about the wedding and how you, Mrs. Hawkins, have welcomed other immigrants with troubles into your home, I tell myself, *ja. Ja,* Kirsten, you go tell them. I waited until the party was over and you were loading up Grace's gifts. Then I came downstairs and slipped the ledger into the lap desk, that secret compartment you showed us. I thought it would be safe there until the time was right. Even if the Pinkerton caught me, he would not get the ledger, because you, Annie Gallagher, would not betray me if you found it. I know now, but I take a long time to understand this. And with the ledger still hidden, the men who hunt Jonas would not hurt him or me because they would be afraid they would never find it."

"Oh, Kirsten. We all would have helped you, if only you would have let us."

Mrs. Hawkins agreed.

Kirsten rubbed the back of her neck. "But the postman was here. I was going to wait for longer, and then I heard you saying you found the ledger."

The Hawk paced in front of her. "You did the right thing coming here, love." She slapped the ledger from one hand to the other. "Pity you didn't give this to the doctor while he was here. He can read the language."

"Nein!" Her eyes widened. "I don't want him to know I am here. If those bad men get this ledger . . . I fear they will kill my brother. It is an accounting of all the ill they have caused, I believe. I could not convince Jonas to listen to me and just forget this."

"He is worried about you," Annie said. "I encountered him on the street."

Her eyes reddened as tears dripped down her face. She wiped them with the heel of her hand. "Jonas and me. We planned to . . . save money and move to the fields . . . uh, the country, a farm. Jonas could not find work. I tell him I do not mind working, but he hated that. We were going to save money, even after he sent me to live here, where I would be safe from the bad men who own the ledger. But then . . ." She caught a sob in her fist. "I lose my job. We cannot get away. I think perhaps if Jonas does not worry about me and does not have the ledger, he can leave the city and be safe."

"You should talk to him, love."

"You do not understand, Mrs. Hawkins, Annie. That ledger. He wrote to me, telling me he mailed it. I do not know why he did that, except to escape those men. His hot temper caused trouble before. I would have burned it, but then I thought perhaps these men could be stopped because of the information it held. But if I gave the ledger to the authorities, what would happen to my brother? I thought if I just hid . . . if he does not have this book . . . then he will move west and find work and be free of all this and then perhaps I could give it to someone. But he is a stubborn one, *ja*? He would not leave. I have seen him from the third-floor window wandering past the house at night."

Mrs. Hawkins blew out the candle in the window and turned down the gas lamp. "This scheme to take other people's money. God only knows what makes people do things like that. We will get all this straightened out tomorrow, love. You will return to your old bed. No more sleeping on quilts on that drafty third floor."

"I understand, so, Kirsten, what 'tis like to feel alone and uncertain," Annie said.

"I understand too, love. You are an innocent, caring child." Mrs. Hawkins waved a paper fan in front of her face. "I wish you had confided in us."

"You are *gut* people, and I did not want to bring this trouble to you." Tears dripped down Kirsten's cheeks again. "But I did not know where else to go."

"This was too big a burden for you to bear alone," Annie said. "I wonder . . . Kirsten, how can you know your brother is not part of this fraud?"

Anger flashed in her eyes. "I told you he is a *gut* man. Deep down, people are who they are. And I know who he is. He would try to help me if I was the one in trouble."

Mrs. Hawkins snapped her fingers. "The police will know what action to take. By the time I summon them, you two can certainly be on a train west, but wouldn't it be best if you resolved this and did not have to think of it ever again?"

"I do not think some things have this . . . resolution, Mrs. Hawkins. In Germany we learned not all is fair." Kirsten turned to Annie. "You don't think your young man will tell anyone, do you?"

"Who?"

"The man you talked about your stories with, the postman."

Stephen! Annie ran to the hall. "Where is he?"

"I expect he left in all the confusion." Mrs. Hawkins handed her his mittens. "He even forgot these."

Annie wondered what he'd do. He had threatened Jonas in the alley, and from what she'd heard, having the US Post Office Department authorities after you was far worse than the law. She had asked Jonas to come to Hawkins House, and now that Kirsten was here, they could work things out. But if Stephen made trouble . . .

"I will go speak to Mr. Adams." She buttoned her coat.

"Oh, love, it's late. Why don't we all just get a good night's sleep?"

Annie rushed out the door despite the woman's protests. The trolley had stopped running for the night. So had the train. She had no money to hire a driver. She sat on the front stoop. The Hawk was correct. There was nothing to be done tonight. But if Stephen Adams thought he could wedge his way into this situation just because he was a postman and the ledger had been delivered through the mail . . . well, she would stand up to him the way she hadn't stood up to Uncle Neil or to that horrid Magdalene doctor. She tried to have as much courage as the Lion in Oz, hoping she'd acquired it in the manner he had in the story. Not through something that someone awarded her, but through the process of traveling a journey.

She placed her hand into her coat pocket as she studied the dark shadows of a few people moving slowly down the opposite side of the street. Her fingers touched something unfamiliar, something she hadn't put into her pocket—a small box. Probably a gift for Grace and Owen that Annie had absentmindedly stuck there while gathering up their things.

When she went back in, she glanced briefly at Mrs. Hawkins and Kirsten, who were headed upstairs, and then hung her coat back in the closet, placing the box on the silver mail tray.

40

THE DAYLIGHT HOURS were dwindling as the calendar inched toward the solstice, and now when Stephen readied for work, it was still quite dark. He turned up the wick on the lamp Mrs. Jacobs had lent him. He had mentioned missing his for reading, and she had insisted he take this one. All he had at the moment was the old black family Bible that had been in the box of belongings he'd kept, but that was all he needed just then.

He read from the book of Proverbs: *"Trust in the Lord with all thine heart; and lean not unto thine own understanding. In all thy ways acknowledge him, and he shall direct thy paths."*

He asked God to speak to him through those words.

This is obedience.

Now he understood. God had been speaking to him all along, but Stephen had applied what he'd heard according to his own will. Forgiving his father for his calamitous action had freed Stephen's heart to lean instead on God's leading.

As he prepared for his day, Stephen whistled that Irish tune he loved and thought about Annie. Annie with the gorgeous hair. Annie with the big heart. He tried to imagine her surprise when she found the gift in her pocket. Whatever she thought of it, he would be satisfied. She either understood his sincerity or she did not. God either planned for Stephen to win her heart or he did not.

And she would either approve of his plan to speak to the postmaster about that ledger or she would not. Either way, he would do the right thing, the thing God had impressed upon him to do, and it was a splendid plan, he knew.

Mr. Sturgis was just unlocking his office door when Stephen arrived. "Come in, Adams. I do hope you have something to tell me."

"I do, sir."

The man glanced around. "I do not see that Wagner fellow with you."

"No, but I believe we can work something out that will allow you to have all the information you seek, including the ledger."

"Ah, that is indeed what I hoped to hear, Adams."

Annie finally had time to look at the letters Mr. Barrows had given her. She slipped the first one out and began reading.

> *Dear Mr. Redmond,*
>
> *I found your story "Dallying at the Stone Wall" to be supremely interesting and enlightening. Never before had I fully considered the truths you wrote about, but now they have changed my life. To read about your character finding the inscription NOTHING IS EVER WRITTEN IN STONE indeed written in stone helped me to realize nothing I have done is unforgivable because we have a loving God who allows us to repent and start over.*

She put the note down and read another. And then another. By the time she was done, she realized how her father had affected so many lives. His stories were special and deserved the utmost care, like Mr. Barrows had suggested.

While Annie prepared breakfast, Grace came for Aileen. "I will show Aileen how to ride the trolley and where the landmarks are. I think once I show her, she'll be fine on her own, Annie."

"Very well, so. And you say the children like her?"

"They adore her. Having her replace me has eased my heart beyond measure. Those children are dear."

Aileen came bounding down the stairs. "Am I late?"

"We have time to spare, Aileen. Allow me to greet Mrs. Hawkins before we leave."

"Where is Kirsten?" Annie asked Aileen.

"Still sleeping. I do think she is relishing the comfort of that bed."

The Hawk entered from the kitchen door, wearing her gardening boots. "Well, if it isn't Mrs. McNulty paying us a visit."

Grace went to her and kissed her on the cheek. "Thank you for the delightful celebration, Mrs. Hawkins."

"And why aren't you with your new husband this morning?"

"He is shopping for a carriage. After I see Aileen safely to the Parkers', he will meet me there. We are going to Delmonico's for lunch."

Mrs. Hawkins clapped her garden-gloved hands. "How perfectly romantic!"

"Oh!" Annie hurried to the hall table and picked up the small box. "I think there was yet one more gift. I seem to have neglected to give it to you."

Grace cradled it in her palm. "'Tis a wee box, isn't it?"

The women sat at the table while Grace slipped off the thin yellow ribbon that held it shut. Inside was a cotton cloud. Grace removed a small piece of paper that stuck to the underside of the lid. She wrinkled her nose and then handed the box to Annie. "'Tis not for me, lass. Was meant for you."

Annie took the gold paper–covered box and pulled out the cotton. Underneath was a small heart-shaped brooch made of silver filigree with a tiny red enameled heart in the center. The pendant was suspended by a silver bar where the pin was attached. She held it up to the weak morning light. "Where did this come from?"

"Read the note," Aileen said, impatiently tapping her foot.

Belonged to my mother. She had a good heart like you, Annie. Fondly, Stephen

The women gasped and aahed.

Annie was stunned. "I truly don't know why he would give me this."

"Let me catch you on," Grace said. "At first, you may remember, I was not keen on Sergeant McNulty's attentions. Now, I know things are different for you, but perhaps Mr. Adams has had some trouble gaining your favor, so he chose to reveal his feelings in this manner."

"Perhaps." Stephen thought she had a good heart. Annie pondered that. What made one's heart good? She would not trade her friendship with Kirsten for this bribery, if that's what it was. The words of the Wizard to the Tin Woodman came to mind.

"I think you are wrong to want a heart. It makes most people unhappy."

Her heart longed for this man, hoped that he could love her, while her head told her how unlikely that was and how thinking so would only end up in hurt. *Home is the place where people love you.* Aye, having a heart was a painful thing. She slipped the note back under the cotton, placed the pin back in the box, and then rose from the kitchen table, choosing to stuff away her pondering as easily as she'd hidden away that gift. "I will check on Kirsten." She kissed Grace and wished Aileen well with her new position. "There will be more work around here for me now," she kidded Aileen.

Later she came downstairs to find Mrs. Hawkins feeding the cooking stove.

"How is Kirsten?"

"She's sleeping like a baby." Annie kept glancing toward the front door. She did not want to miss the postman today. She needed to find out what he had planned.

"I'll get the teakettle on. We don't know when Mr. Wagner will arrive, and we should have a chat first, Annie. You did not tell Kirsten you asked him to come?"

"I did not. I followed your wishes."

"Excellent. We don't want to risk her running off again."

"I know we will be busier than squirrels today, cleaning up and all. I don't mind skipping tea."

"There is always time for conversation over a cup, love."

"That may be, but let's talk now. I need to watch for Mr. Adams."

"Very well." She sighed and stared past Annie. "I believe that your desire to help people, as noble as it is, comes from a broken heart, one that you don't think you will have to try to mend if you keep focusing on others."

"Broken, is it?"

"Yes. Now I know we all have things in our past that we'd rather leave there. Quite understandable. But there is good as well as bad, and to throw out one need not mean discarding the other, even if they are woven together like jungle vines. You seldom talk about your life in Ireland, love. It may seem I'm the pot calling the kettle black, seeing as I've kept some things to myself as well, but we've learned, you and I. Look how long it took for you to talk about your father's writing desk."

"I know, but I don't see why I should dwell on it, Mrs. Hawkins. I'm starting over."

"I'm pleased that you are, but sometimes visiting the past is the only way to embrace the future, as my Harold used to say."

"What wonderful deeds you have done, Mrs. Hawkins. You are the one with the truly good heart. Kirsten's bed in the infirmary—did you purchase that? Dr. Thorp told me wealthy people purchase beds in case they need them someday, and they often allow the poor to have use of their facility."

She leaned forward. "One day I'll be feeble and I'll need extra care. That seemed like prudent use of my Harold's money, and little Kirsten needed it. God provides. 'Home is where your treasure is'—something else my Harold used to say. And God's Word says, 'For where your treasure is, there will your heart be also.'"

"Very noble. You've a blessed soul, Mrs. Hawkins."

"These things I've done for my God. He is all that is good."

Goodness. Annie had wondered where it came from. "And is anything good outside of God?"

"He is the source, love. To fully embrace life, to be free, he is the only way."

Annie had been born in the Magdalene Laundry, and she'd ended up back there despite her father's warning to leave the O'Shannons as soon as she could. When her father was gone, so was her shield against evil. Aye, she'd gotten away and come to America, but in her heart, she had never left her imprisoned state. The iron gates still squealed across the floor in her mind. The rats still roamed. Danger still lurked because there was no one to protect her. She might not be in physical danger any longer, thanks to Father Weldon and Mrs. Hawkins, but her soul felt very much in peril. She was still alone. How could a dark heart like that be good? She'd asked God, pleaded really, to allow her to walk in the light. But she wasn't sure he'd heard.

"I sit in church every Sunday, Mrs. Hawkins. I read my Bible. I have tried to appeal to God, but . . ." She hid her trembling hands by fumbling for a spoon in the kitchen cupboard drawer. "He doesn't speak to me, Mrs. Hawkins. He must have decided I'm not worth the trouble."

"What?" The woman came and wrapped her arms around Annie. "God loves you, Annie Gallagher. He made you. You most certainly are worth the trouble. Have you not heard the stories? Read them? He came down from heaven to be with all mankind, and he gave up his life for us on the cross, you included."

"I have heard the stories. But I do not think they are for me."

"Not for you? Why would you think that?"

She gritted her teeth and was about to blurt out the truth—that she was a sinner of the worst kind—but the bell at the front door chimed.

41

STEPHEN HAD MUCH to say to Annie. He hoped he would soon be able, but with his companion along, the conversation would lead to other places.

He rang the bell and waited, the other man standing behind him.

When Annie opened the door, he noticed the gold-foil box in her hands. "Mr. Adams, I . . . I believe you have made a mistake giving this to me."

"No mistake, Miss Gallagher. I meant it." He cleared his throat. "At the moment I need to speak to Miss Wagner. I have brought news. I believe this can all be worked out."

She swallowed hard. "I don't know."

"Please trust me. There is a solution."

She frowned.

"I never meant any harm. When you saw me in the alley, I was . . . Well, I spoke out of uncertainty about the situation. But the truth is, the postal inspectors *are* very interested in that ledger. Not so much Mr. Wagner himself, although they would like to speak to him."

"Come in, love." Mrs. Hawkins opened the door wide,

causing Annie to step to one side. That enabled them to see who stood behind him.

The man bowed. "William Sturgis, ladies. Postmaster."

"How do you do?" Mrs. Hawkins furrowed her brow and leaned toward Stephen. "What is this all about?"

"Compromise. May we come in?"

The woman agreed, and Annie took their coats.

Stephen stepped into the parlor and then turned to Mrs. Hawkins. "Are the Wagners here? We must speak to them as soon as possible."

The woman crossed her arms against her bosom. "I insist on knowing why."

Sturgis interrupted. "I would like to inform you, Mrs. Hawkins, that Clayton Cooper, the Pinkerton agent who troubled you earlier, has dropped this case and moved on. The Post Office Department has convinced the Pinkerton Detective Agency that working for criminals is not in their best interest. They are smart enough to know when the game is up."

Mrs. Hawkins smiled. "I am happy to hear that. And our house? Has he filed a petition with the police, do you know?"

"No, madam, he has not. I regret that he attempted to use the kind of persuasion that his kind have found so helpful in western cities. He forgot where he was, in New York City at a fine lady's place of business. I do hope you can dismiss that disturbing episode."

Stephen spoke up. "The postal inspectors explained to Cooper that he was pursuing a case contrary to our investigation, and he could be considered an accessory to this crime and be arrested. You see, even the Pinkertons understand it's not wise to interfere with the United States Post Office Department." He felt gratified just saying that.

She huffed. "All that disturbance he caused for naught.

Those Pinkertons," she mumbled. "Sit down, gentlemen. Kirsten is upstairs. Her brother is not here."

Stephen saw Annie place the box in her apron pocket before she headed back to the kitchen.

A few moments later Kirsten came down the stairs. He and Sturgis stood as she stepped into the room as though there were needles on the floor. "The . . . uh . . . ledger is not in my possession."

"Where is it?" Sturgis bellowed, seeming also to have forgotten he was in a fine lady's parlor.

"Now, now," Mrs. Hawkins said. "The ledger is safe."

Stephen would wait for the women to give it up rather than tell his boss where it was. "You can trust her, Mr. Sturgis, as I said."

Mrs. Hawkins folded her hands. "We must discuss the consequences of Jonas Wagner handing this ledger over to . . . well, to whomever we decide must have it. I have sent my housekeeper next door to telephone the police."

"We have already spoken to a detective," Stephen said. "You must allow me to explain."

She lowered herself onto the sofa. Sturgis had taken her chair. Stephen should have warned him he was in her place. That would win no favor for him in her eyes, and thus they were off to a bad start. Stephen turned to the German girl. "If you will allow Mr. Sturgis to simply look at the ledger, he will determine if it is what we think it is. He is fluent in German."

The postmaster tapped his long fingers together. "Indeed. Our investigation has led to one of the investors, and a cursory glance will tell me if his name is in the ledger. Even if I'm wrong, we will track down the true culprits eventually. We always do."

Kirsten stood just as Annie returned to the room and whispered something into Mrs. Hawkins's ear. Kirsten joined their huddle and then Annie went to the breakfront cabinet and took down her writing desk. She retrieved the ledger and handed it to the postmaster.

He thumbed through it, stopping halfway. He licked his thumb and turned a few more pages. Then he tapped his finger on one of the pages. He drew a small notebook from his vest pocket and held it against the ledger page, studying them both. Then he abruptly slammed the book shut. "Thank you." He stood and glanced at Annie. "My coat, if you please." He turned back to the room. "This is so much more than I had thought, Adams. Addresses and even a draft of what they were sending out. This was a mail scam." He still had the ledger in his hand.

"I think it's best if he takes it," Stephen said, noting the worry on Mrs. Hawkins's face.

"We would not think of it," she said.

Kirsten burst into tears. "My brother. He should have the freedom he seeks. Go west and find work. He means no one harm."

"Of course he doesn't," Stephen said.

Annie had not moved to fetch Sturgis's coat.

"A compromise, remember?" Stephen seemed to be losing this battle.

The postmaster handed the black book to Kirsten. "I daresay your brother is in more peril if you keep it. But if that's what you want."

She shook her head and dropped the book to the floor. Annie picked it up. Stephen glanced out the window, and just like he hoped, the man he'd been waiting for was standing on the sidewalk, his coat collar pulled up to his ears. Annie had mentioned she'd asked him to come. "One moment, please." He waved his arm at the furniture. "All of you sit. There is more to talk about. I will return shortly."

"I'll make tea," Annie offered.

"Yes, yes, tea." He put a hand on Sturgis's chest. "Go sit. It will all become clear in a moment."

"It had better. I have work to do, Adams."

Stephen stepped outside to speak to the man he had seen in the alley. Kirsten's brother bore just as imposing a posture as he had then. Stephen drew in a calming breath. *Help me trust you, Lord.*

When he was done explaining that inside Hawkins House they would all sit down and work things out, thankfully Jonas was cooperative. Stephen motioned for the man to follow him inside.

When Jonas entered, his sister sprang to her feet.

"Kirstie!" He embraced her, then kissed her, then hugged her again.

She was so small, especially next to him, she seemed to disappear in his arms. When they finally sat down, Kirsten's face was streaked with tears. "Do not do it, Jonas. Please, I beg of you. Do not confront those men."

"Indeed do not," Sturgis said.

Jonas turned to Stephen. "Mr. Postman? Why are you here? I came not at your invitation." Jonas motioned toward Annie. "You, Irish lass, you betrayed me?"

"No, no." Stephen waved both arms as though he held a flag at a finish line. "Hear me out. I think you will consider my plan advantageous."

The man put an arm around his sister. "Speak it."

Stephen tugged at his coat collar. "Uh, yes." He cleared his throat. "Mr. Sturgis, the postmaster here, asks that you come to the office with the ledger and give him your testimony about these phony investors. Some of the scheme has been carried out through the US mail, perhaps all of it, so he believes he has the authority to see those men prosecuted."

"That is correct," Sturgis said. "And soon. These things can't wait."

Jonas closed his eyes. "You are asking me to turn myself in." He squeezed Kirsten's hand. "I will do it if you tell me my sister will be safe."

Now the postmaster stood. "No, Mr. Wagner. What I'm asking you to do is go with me to meet with the postal inspectors, and after you tell them what you know and turn over the ledger, you can collect your immunity papers and go on your way."

Kirsten hugged Jonas. "He will be free?"

"Indeed. Adams here has worked this out in advance."

Stephen noted Annie smiling at him.

An hour after the men had left, Kirsten paced the room. "He should have let me go too."

Mrs. Hawkins clicked her tongue. "You can trust Stephen, love. He has bargained in order to free your brother, and the bad men will be punished in the end."

Annie gazed again at the heart brooch, then put it back in her pocket.

"Annie, whom did you speak with on the telephone over at Mrs. Jenkins's house?"

"A police detective. I thought it was odd at the time. They knew the postmaster was here, and he told me to hear the postman out. I was doubtful, but it seems it had been all arranged."

"We will have to bring Mrs. Jenkins some cake for allowing us to use her telephone so often."

"Mrs. Hawkins, she knew the postmaster was here as well. She seems to know a lot. I think she had been informing the Pinkerton of our comings and goings."

"Oh, dear. Grace thought she was a busybody too. I try to

always assume the best of people, but I think we will call a meeting of the Benevolents and discuss putting in our own telephone line at Hawkins House."

Kirsten settled down on the sofa to examine Annie's copy of *The Wonderful Wizard of Oz.*

"I will be in the kitchen, Mrs. Hawkins, if you need me."

"Very well, love. I will be in the garden. Got to prepare to put the plants to bed for the season."

Kirsten would be fine now. Grace was happy. Even Aileen seemed delighted to have found a position with the Parkers. Annie should be satisfied too. She had Mrs. Hawkins and employment there. She was even trusted to become a Benevolent member. But none of that filled the hole that seemed to sink deeper inside with every passing day.

When she finished her work in the kitchen, she joined Kirsten on the sofa with the book.

"Can you read this part, Annie? The monkeys with wings."

"Sure. There is nothing like the power of story to calm one's worries." She smoothed her hand over the page and began.

"'We dare not harm this little girl,' the winged monkey said, 'for she is protected by the Power of Good, and that is greater than the Power of Evil.'"

Annie set the book down on her lap. "This is a truth I seem to have forgotten in my own life."

"*Ja,* me too."

"My father used symbolism in his stories, but in the form of the earth—the soil that nourished. That was good, and there is nothing good apart from God. That is what Mrs. Hawkins says."

"No wonder people enjoy your father's stories."

"Excuse me a moment." Annie went to her room and picked

up her father's Bible. Searching the book of Psalms, she finally found it—the message she somehow felt her father wanted her to embrace.

"There be many that say, Who will shew us any good? Lord, lift thou up the light of thy countenance upon us."

When she placed the Bible back down on her desk, a sunbeam filtered through her curtains and bathed her face in warm light, just like it had before, but this time she did not cover her head and shut it out. Annie let the sunshine cover her for a moment and then returned to the parlor where Kirsten waited.

"It is raining," Kirsten said, parting the curtains.

Mrs. Hawkins came down the hall, sputtering about how muddy her wee garden out back was becoming.

"But the sun was just shining," Annie said.

"Oh yes, in another part of the world. I have not seen such a dreary October since I came to New York, love."

Annie turned her face heavenward. The things she'd been seeing, hearing, remembering that no one else experienced . . . Those things were not her mind playing games with her after all. They were messages, like a story behind the story. Just as the author of the *Wizard* book had noted that Dorothy had the power to get back home all along in the form of the magical silver slippers on her feet. That had been a message for children: they had all they needed if they had the will to try, and no adventure in Oz could give them what they didn't already possess. The Scarecrow just had to learn how to use his brain, and it had been the same for all the characters. Her father had been speaking to her through his stories as well, and now she knew. Those odd occurrences weren't odd at all. God had not abandoned her. He'd been speaking to her, and she had needed to learn how to listen.

It seemed Annie heard messages in duplicate, perhaps because she had been stubborn, stubborn the way Grace had admitted she'd been before allowing Owen into her life. God was good. God was light, the light she'd asked for. God really was speaking to her!

She retrieved her writing box and took out her father's stories. She was not supposed to forget the Power of Good—the hope that was always rewarded. That was the message her father left for her and what she had considered the last time she looked at these stories.

She smoothed a hand over the crumpled page and returned to the sofa. Kirsten looked over her shoulder.

"This is about Omah, Kirsten. He used what ability he had to remind the farmer, as the wise rabbit explained, that the land had a purpose beyond his own. The soil was there for him to grow his food and be nourished by it, but so it had been for others for hundreds of years. Everything they needed God provided. They just had to learn to use it."

"*Ja.* I would like to hear more. Do you know some people say there is a deeper meaning in children's stories? A moral to learn from. I have heard that about Aesop's fables. It seems in your book . . ." She picked up Baum's tale. "He said what that meaning is. The part you read to me, *ja*? Good defeats evil, and good is right here for us to have if we will."

"I think you are right. My father used the soil, the body of the land of Erin, as a symbol of God's provision. I see that now. Even the lowly field mouse understood. The rabbit told the story to his children so they would understand. But my father might have had something else in mind when he wrote the tales."

"What is that, love?" Mrs. Hawkins entered carrying herbal sachets for Annie to put in the drawers.

She collected the wee scented pillows. "My father must have

known what I would need to hear someday. Or . . . God knew. He speaks to me in ways I never would have imagined, and now that I think back on things, I believe he has been speaking all along."

"Marvelous. All we must do is listen." She whispered in Annie's ear. "Certainly God, through my brother, rescued you from that laundry, wouldn't you say?"

Annie thought about the day Father Weldon had showed up.

Sister Anna Grace, a stern nun who frightened Annie yet had never struck her, beckoned her to the chapel when the other girls went to the dining hall.

When she entered, the doctor greeted her. "I hear you'd like to leave us," he said, turning his lips into a frown.

Annie said nothing.

"You may go, Sister," he said to the nun.

"I'll wait, if you don't mind," she said, crossing her bulky arms in front of her.

He rolled his eyes and led Annie to the front pew.

The nun stood in the back.

"Kneel."

Annie lowered her aching body to the rail.

He inched closer to her. "Be a good girl now."

She squeezed her hands together and brought them to her lips. "Our Father, who art . . ."

"I did not bring you here to pray. Do you think I'm a priest?" He pulled her hair.

She continued to pray aloud. Maybe God would hear her that way. ". . . in heaven, hallowed be . . ."

"Stop that. We know why you are here, little Miss Magdalene." He put a hand around her head.

". . . thy name . . ." She groaned as she felt him closer to her, felt the tweed of his trousers against her cheek.

A grunt came from the rear. "There!" Sister Anna Grace called out.

The doctor let go of her.

Annie kept her eyes closed and continued praying.

"Why, Dr. Stewart, I did not realize you were so devout as to come to chapel to pray with this young girl."

Annie looked up. Angels? An army from heaven to her rescue?

Father Weldon.

"I've obtained permission to take you out of here, Annie. Shall we go now?"

She could barely feel her legs when she rose. The doctor scrambled out of the room like a water beetle.

"It took some time for me to discover where Neil O'Shannon had taken you. I suspected a laundry, but this one I was not aware of. I would have come sooner if I could have."

Annie had been so angry with God, she had denied that he actually had rescued her.

Forgive my unbelief!

"Annie?"

"Oh, I'm sorry, Mrs. Hawkins. I was just remembering, and you are correct. While I was in the laundry, before God sent your brother to rescue me, I believed God was not there but rather was a light at the end of a tunnel that I could not see. All the while, if I had just reached out my hand, I would have found him right there beside me in that dark tunnel."

The woman smiled. "Ah, so you see why remembering everything can help you find the good. Find God, in fact."

Annie did see.

"And it seems to me you ought to be sharing those stories your father wrote you." She pressed her hands together like an opera singer.

"Well, I cannot, not in a large way."

"Oh, certainly you can. In that library you want to open."

Annie told Kirsten what she'd had in mind. "But I can no longer afford to purchase a building. I thought I was to be a businesswoman." She tried to shake the idea from her mind.

Kirsten pointed toward the stairs. "Why don't you use the third floor?"

Mrs. Hawkins clapped her hands. "An excellent idea, Kirsten. We can all help."

"All?"

"I've got the whole third floor of this house we could fix up for a temporary school for misplaced immigrant girls, until they get jobs and move out. The library could be set up there as well. What do you think, girls?"

"Oh, the extra housework," Annie said. "I don't know if this is the best idea."

"I could help," Kirsten said.

"Your brother?" Annie asked.

"He can find work. I know he can. And . . . since you all say you will have me . . ."

Mrs. Hawkins hugged her. "Of course, love. You are always welcome here."

"And the girls who come," Kirsten said. "While they are living here, they can do work, *ja*?"

"Perhaps we can add another housekeeper. You will be the director, Annie. You won't have time to keep house for us." The Hawk smiled at Annie and nodded as she waited for an answer.

Annie rubbed her temples with her fingertips. Perhaps this was the best she could hope for. It was a hard thing to let go of one's dreams, but this plan seemed feasible enough.

The Hawk touched her shoulder. "And Mr. Adams, perhaps he could help. He enjoys reading, I believe."

Annie sighed. "As nice as he has been, the truth is, he be-trayed my trust. He took those stories without permission."

"Did he print them?"

"He did not, but—"

"And he apologized?"

"He did."

"So no harm was done, was it?"

"Trust, Mrs. Hawkins. I have a difficult time with it."

"Oh, I know."

The woman folded linen napkins as they spoke, rubbing each crease meticulously as she seemed to consider each word. "Let me see. You were fully prepared to allow Davis Publishing to publish your stories. Then you found out that Stephen Adams and Mr. Davis had anticipated your approval, perhaps because Stephen understood your heart for people and the power of a story—he knows you that well. And he prepared for but did not proceed with the printing. Because of that you decided to shut him out of your life."

"I . . . uh . . . well." Annie slumped down on the rocking chair.

The Hawk pointed a perfectly folded napkin at her. "Listen, love, when you find a special man, don't let him go. When God sends a man into your life to bring you to a place of happiness, it's best not to look the other way."

"Like your Harold?"

"Absolutely. Thank the Lord he showed up. I had many wonderful years with my Harold."

Annie smiled at her.

The Hawk stood and removed her apron. "Think about giving Stephen another chance, love."

Kirsten spoke up. "Like Jonas has . . . a second chance."

God's wisdom presented itself in many forms, it seemed. Annie should start paying better attention.

42

STEPHEN LEFT THE POST OFFICE feeling somewhat relieved. Not only would Jonas now be able to move on with his life, but Annie would be satisfied as well. Even so, there was another person on his mind. But first, he stopped in to see Mrs. Jacobs.

"A dozen sweet buns, Stephen? Are you sure so many?"

"I am. And I won't pay you a penny less than the restaurant does for them."

She tapped a hand to the top of her silver-streaked black hair and then bid him to follow her into her kitchen. The yeasty smell reminded him of his mother's baking.

"I will make it a baker's dozen then, just for you."

He waited while she placed the round rolls into a box. "I will eat that extra one myself. How can I resist?"

The kitchen was tiny and poorly illuminated but clean and smelling so good he could almost taste the dough. She waved her hands toward a table pushed up against a window where, outside, a fire escape formed a metal Z shape. "You eat this." She handed him a twisted confection. "*Rugelach*. You will like. I make these for Hanukkah but I practice early. Go on." She flipped her fingers at him.

He bit into the sweet, flaky dough and savored the walnut, cinnamon, and raisin filling. "You treat me well, Mrs. Jacobs.

I've never tasted anything so wonderful." The sugar and butter these must have required made them indulgent treats. "I will buy one."

She shook her head. "Not these. Tomorrow you stop on your way to work and I will have the perfect one for you. For someone special?"

"Perhaps." He licked his fingers.

When he arrived home, he knocked on Alan Davis's door to bring him out from his office. A few moments later the man appeared, looking ragged.

"Crickets, Davis. You don't look so good."

"Down on my luck, is all. What do you need?"

"I brought you something."

The man lifted his nose in the air. "Smells delightful."

"Perhaps you can share these with your staff."

Davis lifted the lid on the box. "Maybe, or maybe not." He smiled. "What did I do to deserve such a gift?"

"Nothing."

Davis shrugged. "True enough. Come in. I've got coffee."

Stephen sat at Davis's desk. "Look, Davis, I got to thinking . . ."

"Oh, just remembered." Davis turned his attention to the coffeepot. "Got a bed for you."

"A bed?"

"That's right. I know you didn't get your things back, and I'm truly sorry about that. My niece is moving upstate to join her sister and had to dispose of a few things. The bed's in the hall upstairs."

"Incredible. And you didn't even know I would be bringing sweet rolls."

Davis licked his fingers. He'd already sampled one.

"Well, what I was thinking about was that Barrows fellow."

"Yeah, one of the paramount men in this business. I had

hoped I'd find a big book and be able to play ball. Maybe I will one day yet."

"Yes. I mean he's a British publisher."

"He is. Lots of great authors have come out of the British Isles."

Stephen leaned back in his chair. "True, and many have been published on both sides of the pond."

"Hold on, Adams. You know the man said he would not allow me to publish the stories."

"Not without an agreement."

"What are you getting at?" Davis handed him a steaming cup.

"I wish I knew. There has to be a way. I'm looking to retain an attorney to help Miss Gallagher."

"You? With what funds?"

Stephen leaned forward. "You are correct that I don't own a stick of furniture. I've sold it all. And I don't mind it a bit, although I'm surely grateful for the bed. And don't worry. I'll pay you back. I do have a job."

"Not worried about that, Adams, although if things don't pick up, I will have to raise the rent, like I said."

"I'll get by. If I can use the proceeds to get someone to help Annie, it will all be worth it."

Davis chuckled. "Well, son, you've got it bad, struck by Cupid's arrow."

Later that day Stephen called for Annie at Hawkins House, explaining his plan to hire an attorney.

"You've done this for me?" Annie put her fingers over her mouth.

"Mr. Davis recommended someone." He held up his hands in surrender. "I know you don't want us interfering, but I hope you'll realize the wisdom in getting sound advice on this matter."

"I am astounded."

"Shall we?" He held out his arm. "It's not far, only a four-block walk, and I've told the man to expect us."

Mrs. Hawkins gazed at them, patting her fingers together in front of her face.

"Well, all right." Annie took his arm and stepped out the door. "Just to have questions answered. I'm not sure this matter needs to become a battle in the courts. All I want . . . Well, let me just say money is not of primary concern."

That was why he'd fallen for Annie Gallagher. She was independent and confident but also considerate of what really mattered in life—people, not money.

Stephen sat quietly by as Annie battered the poor man with questions.

She scooted to the edge of her chair as though she were preparing to rise. "In conclusion, are you saying, Mr. Dirksen, that I may be able to negotiate with Mr. Barrows for the legal right to publish my father's stories?"

The man, obviously unsettled by a woman's inquiry into the business, placed a closed fist on top of his polished desk. "Miss Gallagher, I said no such thing. I proposed that I, as your attorney, may be able to negotiate for the rights to publish your father's stories. It's my job. What your . . . your friend there has hired me to do."

She turned and smiled at Stephen. "Aye, and I am grateful. So much so that I feel compelled to treat his generosity with extreme care. I plan to do the negotiating on my own and employ you to draw up the appropriate contract or whatever legal papers are necessary."

The man grunted. "As you wish."

She stood and Stephen followed.

"Therefore, I trust you will refund some of the cost of your services, Mr. Dirksen?"

The man looked none too happy. "Indeed." He accepted her outstretched hand as they said good-bye.

The next morning Stephen at last felt like whistling "The Stone outside Dan Murphy's Door" as he approached Hawkins House with a mail delivery. He did not have to be loud to get attention, however. The door swung open to meet him. Jonas Wagner stepped out on the stoop.

"Ah, Mr. Postman. How can I ever thank you?"

Stephen stepped up to the man he had once found imposing. "No need at all. What are your plans, Mr. Wagner?"

"I found work building a railroad. I leave today. Mrs. Hawkins arranged a room for me nearby last night, and she invited me to come for breakfast this morning. I was just about to go hail a carriage, and when I opened the door, there you were."

"Excellent. I wish you God's blessing and a safe journey."

"*Danke*. I will tell the housekeeper, Annie, you have brought the mail."

"Thank you." Stephen began whistling as he waited, Mrs. Jacobs's *rugelach* resting in his pocket.

Annie appeared and waved him inside. "Stay for tea, won't you?"

"Certainly. Thank you." She did not seem to be miffed any longer.

When she returned, the gold box lay on the tea tray.

"I . . . I brought you something from my neighbor."

"Oh?" The copper in her hair seemed to reflect in her eyes.

"You do like her sweets, don't you, Miss Gallagher?"

She perched on the edge of Mrs. Hawkins's chair. "You have found my weakness, Mr. Adams." When she pulled the twist from the brown paper sack, her expression told him he'd done well. She set it down on a small white china plate and then sprang to her feet when the doorbell chimed.

Stephen stood as Mr. Barrows entered the parlor. Annie was called away after she saw him in, so the two men sat in awkward silence. Stephen had hoped for this opportunity, but now that he had it, he struggled to form his thoughts into words.

"Mr. Barrows, you represent a large British publisher; is that correct?"

"It is." He crossed his legs at the knees. "I am here to speak with Miss Gallagher about her father's estate."

"Estate? There is one?"

The man raised his graying brows.

"I don't mean to . . . I would never presume to invade Miss Gallagher's privacy; it's just that she supposed . . . well, she thought she had no inheritance save for those stories."

"I see."

He had to plunge in. Annie would return shortly, and at Hawkins House you never knew how many people might become part of your conversation at any moment. "Mr. Barrows, might I ask, out of consideration for my landlord and Davis Publishing, if you have considered granting the rights to publish those children's stories to an American publisher?"

"Certainly not."

"Why?"

"First of all, Mr. . . ."

"Adams. Stephen Adams."

"Mr. Adams, I guard carefully Luther Redmond's reputation among readers. I would not publish those tales merely because they would make a lot of money."

"Oh? Might there be another reason to prompt you, Mr. Barrows?"

"Yes. Miss Gallagher. She speaks on behalf of her father now."

"If she were amenable to a meeting at Davis Publishing, would you come, today perhaps?"

"I am at Miss Gallagher's disposal."

"I don't think she realizes that."

Annie returned with Mrs. Hawkins on her heels.

"Good day, gentlemen." Mrs. Hawkins turned to the man from Dublin. "Mr. Barrows, what can we do for you?"

"I would like to speak to Miss Gallagher. We have business concerning her father's estate."

"She is not responsible for that tale being published in that magazine. She didn't know it was forbidden. She did not even know her father wrote under a pen name. Surely you cannot blame—"

"No, madam." He turned to Annie, who had begun serving tea. "Miss Gallagher, Mr. Adams has suggested a meeting at Davis Publishing. Is this something that interests you? Perhaps an office would be the best place to discuss this matter." He gave Mrs. Hawkins a quick glance.

"I would be interested," Annie said, handing the man a cup of tea.

He grabbed the pastry twist and popped it into his mouth. Stephen and Annie exchanged surprised looks. Stephen mouthed the word *sorry*, and she smiled.

Annie brought her employer a cup. "Can you spare me an hour from my duties, Mrs. Hawkins?"

"Of course. Would you like me to come, love?"

"I can handle this."

Stephen knew she could.

When they arrived at Davis's office, Stephen held the door for Annie.

She lowered her voice. "Do you think we might publish the stories still?"

"We might," he whispered into her hair. "And I will not take a penny."

After some back-and-forth, during which Annie referenced some letters her father had received from readers, she stood confidently to address them.

"My father's stories must be handled with great care and consideration for the legacy he has left behind. For that reason, Mr. Barrows, I must insist Davis Publishing produce them, and as soon as possible. This is a neighborhood business, small but efficient. I have visited the premises, and I have come to realize . . ." She looked at Stephen. "Just recently I've learned I can trust them. As you have already noted, you do not hold that kind of confidence in the publishers you have been in contact with."

The man stood. "Very well, Miss Gallagher."

"And I would like the rights . . . That is to say . . ." She glanced at Stephen, and he nodded. "I would like to retain the American copyright to my father's work."

Mr. Barrows licked a finger sticky with pastry sugar from the leftover buns Davis had served him. "As it should be. I never meant to imply that you, as heir, do not have that right. I have just felt obliged to ensure that Mr. Gallagher's bequest is protected. I do hope you understand that I felt it necessary to protect your father's interest until I discerned whether his heir was ready to assume his business dealings. And you appear to be more than capable, Miss Gallagher."

Annie blushed.

"I will have the contracts written up." The Dubliner pulled something from his pocket. "With that settled, I have funds to deposit into your bank account." He gave her a small notebook.

When she looked inside, she brought a hand to her lips. "My father had this much money?"

"Indeed he did, but, Miss Gallagher, I feel it is my responsibility to inform you that your father did not enjoy having wealth. He said money never brought him what he truly wanted . . . your mother."

Tears dripped down Annie's face. Stephen handed her his handkerchief.

"And there is this." He handed Annie a paper. "The explanation of your father's seal. I have no need of it now, but I thought you might want it."

43

ANNIE WENT STRAIGHT HOME, telling Stephen they would talk later. When she arrived at Hawkins House, she was not sure how to break the news to Mrs. Hawkins. It was good news, but so incredible she didn't know where to start. The front door was locked. She let herself in with the skeleton key Mrs. Hawkins insisted she always keep in her pocket purse.

"Hello? Anyone home?"

She heard only the ticking of the mantel clock. A note on the silver tray in the hall told her Mrs. Hawkins had gone to deliver invitations for the next meeting of the Benevolents.

After hanging up her cloak, she climbed the stairs to the third level. Sun filtered through the repaired window, and specks of dust danced like wee fairies. She had enough money to purchase her own building now and wouldn't need to renovate Mrs. Hawkins's third floor. She sat on an old steamer trunk and opened the paper Mr. Barrows had given her.

Dear Barton,

I have decided on my mark. This seal will validate my writings. Without it, you should be dubious of anything you receive purporting to be from me. That should help alleviate your fears that my constant travel could make receiving stories from me problematic.

I do hope you understand. I do not want my dear lass Annie to grow up so privileged that she doesn't appreciate the simple life God has given us. I don't want her to have to conceal the truth about who her father is, so I have not told her about our arrangement. But neither do I want her to be a pauper. So in writing under this name I will keep my anonymity.

Now, to the explanation of why I have chosen the name Luther Redmond. What caused my dear wife and I to be separated was prejudice due to different religious backgrounds. Therefore, to represent the fact that we are all God's children, I chose Luther in reference to Martin Luther, the father of Protestantism. Redmond is the name of a Catholic bishop from the sixteenth century. Redmond O'Gallagher was bishop of Killala and perhaps an ancestor of mine, something the O'Shannon family would be surprised to learn. I thought it fitting to marry the religions through this pseudonym.

The seal is in fact one belonging to Martin Luther. I have added initials and a bishop's staff, and there you have it. The official mark of the author Luther Redmond.

All the best,
Marty Gallagher
aka Luther Redmond

Annie rubbed her hand over her father's handwriting. She might not agree with his hiding this part of his life from her, but she forgave him. He did what he deemed best. And he had indeed made sure she wasn't a pauper.

She glanced around the chilly attic. Her father had not

wanted wealth to corrupt her, and she'd seen in New York how money had done that to people. The funds she would soon have did not somehow feel hers. A school with many books would be a great legacy, but what was it if she could not share it? The power of story is meant for all.

A scene from *The Wonderful Wizard of Oz* played in her mind, one she had been thinking of earlier. Glinda the Good Witch told Dorothy she had always been able to get back home, using her silver shoes.

> "If you had known their power you could have gone back to your Aunt Em the very first day you came to this country."

How often do we think we are lacking what we need when it has been with us all the while? If Annie had fully understood what power she could have been calling on all along—the power of God—she could have avoided the long, lonely, dark trek she'd traveled up until she felt God's light shining on her face at her bedroom window.

She would not buy a building. She would not leave Hawkins House.

"Are you home, love?"

"I'm up here, Mrs. Hawkins."

Annie scrambled down the steps and met the woman on the second-floor landing.

"What were you doing up there, love?"

"Oh, Mrs. Hawkins. My father has left me a fortune."

The woman grabbed Annie's hands. "How wonderful. You can see all your dreams come true."

"When is the meeting of the Benevolents?"

"Two o'clock."

"Good. I have much to say."

Dr. Thorp cleared his throat. "Let it be known that on this day—add the date, George—the Benevolents admitted Miss Annie Gallagher to their ranks."

George Parker scribbled in a diary as the doctor spoke.

Dr. Thorp held up a finger. "And due to the recommendation of Mr. Stephen Adams, Hawkins House will employ a new housekeeper by the name of Minnie Draper."

"Who?" Annie asked.

The Hawk waved her fingers in Annie's direction. "A former coworker of Mr. Adams's. He says she lost her job, and he believes her to be a hardworking Christian woman. This will help free you for your work, Annie."

"That sounds wonderful."

The doctor grunted. "Now, I believe there is just one more order of business to attend to."

Annie raised her hand.

"Just a moment, Miss Gallagher." The doctor pointed toward the door. "I believe something has arrived for you."

Mrs. Hawkins went to the door. "Come see, love."

Annie hurried to the stoop. A horse-drawn flatbed wagon stood in front, loaded with books. "What is this?"

Reverend Clarke stood at her shoulder. "That, my dear, is your library."

She scrambled down the steps and pulled a couple of books off the stack. "Dickens and Twain." She looked at some others. "Histories and biographies . . . and some are brand-new."

The reverend whispered in her ear. "There are even some Baum volumes for the children—or the young at heart."

She spun around to look at her friends. "How did you do this?"

The doctor pulled at his lapel. "You have no idea how persuasive Agnes Hawkins can be, child."

The Hawk winked at her. "The men who delivered them will bring them in now, to store on the third floor until you purchase your property."

"Oh no. The books will stay there. This library and school will not be mine, but all of ours. And I can think of no better home for them, or for me, than Hawkins House."

She had reduced Mrs. Hawkins to tears, again.

EPILOGUE

THAT EVENING STEPHEN invited the Hawkins House ladies to a celebratory dinner at his favorite Italian restaurant. Before they were to leave, Annie slipped into her room to think. Her eyes went right to her writing desk, where she had laid the heart pin. She had planned to give it back but hadn't yet had a chance. Cupping it in her hands, she contemplated the fact that she had attached more to this heart than what Stephen Adams had intended. She didn't really want to give it back, but he said it had belonged to his mother. It wasn't right to keep it. The sooner she returned it, the better.

Carefully placing it in her pocket, she hurried to the closet and grabbed her cloak. "I'm coming."

Along the way she asked Mrs. Hawkins for a favor. "Could I speak to him alone for a moment when we get there?"

"I understand, love. I'll assemble the others outside until you are ready."

"I need to find out if he was only interested in me for those stories."

"I'm sure that's not true, Annie. You've put up a wall to protect your heart. I did that too when I was your age."

"I don't know if I can trust his affections. I . . . He seems to mean well, but I am not sure. I want to talk to him in private."

When they arrived, Mrs. Hawkins made her wait with the others while she went inside first. "I'll make sure everything's in order."

Annie stomped her feet to keep warm.

"Why are we waiting?" Aileen complained.

Annie clicked her tongue. "She's checking on things."

Mrs. Hawkins came out a moment later. "He is waiting at a table in the corner. We'll come in in a few minutes, love."

"But, Mrs. Hawkins, if I find out . . . if I think he doesn't really . . . well, I'm going to leave."

"We will deal with that if it happens, love. Now go in. He's waiting. And see if they can find me some tea, will you?"

Stephen looked up as the door opened. Annie stepped inside and inhaled. The place smelled delicious—onions, garlic, and the doughy scent of pasta. No wonder he liked coming here. She joined Stephen at the corner table and stared into his bright eyes. The candlelight made his silky dark hair glisten.

"Hi."

"Nice to see you, Annie, at last. Is it still all right if I call you by your Christian name?"

"Please do." She touched her velvet hat. She normally didn't wear such finery, but it had felt like an important occasion.

"You look lovely." He did not seem to be able to take his eyes off her headpiece. "I hope you wore that hat for me."

"I . . . I thought it would be appropriate."

"It is." The muscles in his face relaxed.

"Thank you for arranging that meeting with Mr. Davis and Mr. Barrows."

"I was happy to, for you and for your father's legacy."

Laughter erupted from another long table, and they both turned to look at the same time.

"Do you know Joey Falcone?" he asked.

"Aye, he likes to come to the dances. For Emma, I'm sure. He's Italian. I've seen them together often."

"They're from different neighborhoods. Things are changing, I believe. Folks from all backgrounds are finding common ground as Americans."

"I hope so." She frowned a moment, thinking of her parents' sad love story. She focused on the candle on the table as she tried to summon the courage to say what must be said. "I don't think . . . I mean, I don't know if I'll stay. I'm sure you all will have a good time."

"Oh no. I hope you will. I need to talk to you, Annie. We've had so little time alone. I brought you another *rugelach*."

"What?"

He pointed to a small plate in front of him, where a twisted roll like the one Mr. Barrows had eaten lay.

She laughed. "I was looking forward to that. Thank you."

"Please tell me you'll stay."

"All right, if you insist. How can I refuse that gift? But I need to return this. It isn't right that I have it." She held a closed fist over the table, the heart pin inside. "Here."

He slid his hand under hers, and she dropped the pin and then pulled away. "I realize that you gave this to me as an incentive, and 'tis your own mother's, so. You should keep it."

"I gave this to you. It's a gift, not an incentive."

"I shouldn't keep it."

"Don't you like it?"

"I do. But . . ."

He handed it back. "Please keep it, Annie."

She shook her head. The candle on the table reflected moisture in his eyes.

"Promise me you won't leave here until I've said everything I want to say. Please."

She agreed.

He laid his arm on the table. A gesture to reach for her hand? She wasn't sure.

"I want to help people, and sometimes I try too hard, try to do too much." He pulled a pair of mittens from his suit-coat pocket with his free arm. "Like this, for example."

"Oh, good. You got them. Did Mrs. Hawkins bring them to you?"

"Yes, she did. This is a new pair. I went without for a long time. I meant to replace them, but I kept putting it off."

"What happened to your first pair?"

He glanced toward the window that was thickly covered in drapes. "It makes me sick to see some of the people out on the streets. Kids, no more than five years old, out there hawking goods. They should be playing stickball or chase or reading books." He looked back at her and smiled. "I was one of them once, a poor boy on the streets looking for a penny here and there because my folks had no jobs. I gave my other pair of mittens to one of those boys."

Tears began to drip down her cheeks, and she took off her gloves and wiped them.

"Oh, don't cry." He handed her a thick white napkin. "I gave away those mittens without thinking about having to go without. I don't mind it, but that's an example of how I go ahead and do things without thinking of the consequences."

"That is admirable, actually."

"Perhaps that is not a good example. This leaping before I think things out sometimes gets me in trouble. Like what I did with your stories."

"I understand."

"I have been motivated by the fact that my father did not provide for me. He took his own life."

"Oh, Stephen. I'm so sorry."

He smiled, his handsome face focused on her alone. "I have learned a lot lately about forgiveness. I have forgiven my father for not being a provider. For leaving us instead of fighting for us."

The pain of her own past made her feel his all the more acutely. "I forgave my father for not telling me he was Luther Redmond."

He wrinkled his dimpled chin. "So you see. I suppose we would have made different choices if we were in their shoes, but we weren't."

"I suppose so."

She looked at the heart pin he still held in his open palm. "Mr. Adams?"

"Stephen."

"Stephen, I thought I was Dorothy, but I'm not."

"What do you mean?"

"I can't go home, like Dorothy did. She wound up landing in a field on her aunt and uncle's farm in Kansas. That can't happen to me. I can't be the child again, the one whose father loves her." She gulped air before she spoke again. "I can't go home, because my father isn't there."

"My father isn't here either, but there is One who is."

"Oh, aye. I feel my heavenly Father with me now, providing for me."

"A blessing. A gift."

"That's right."

He leaned forward. "I'm here, Annie. I'll always be here."

Annie tried to slow her breathing. The last thing she wanted was to faint right there in front of Stephen Adams. He held out his heart to her even as he still offered his mother's brooch. As though a spotlight beamed on the table between them, she began to see the truth. She did have a home. "I asked God to give me his heart, and it seems he has also opened my eyes."

She turned and looked as her friends began filing in. The woman who had truly been a mother to her, the one Kate Gallagher had chosen to look out for her. The giggling girls who were like the sisters she never had, even Aileen. You could be annoyed with sisters but still love them with all your heart. She turned back to Stephen. "If there is no place like home, like Dorothy said, then I'm sure I've found my home because there is no place that feels as good as this."

Stephen's smile grew so large, wee crinkles formed under his eyes. "I've always thought life was a journey like that yellow brick road. And I've always longed for friends to travel it with me."

She knew what he meant. He wanted her to be with him. Having someone want her, love her, was what she had been longing for. And now . . . now she could see that clearly.

The room, though dim, suddenly became vibrant with color. Sure, the red-painted walls and gold-framed floral prints were there when she walked in, but she only now noticed them.

She put a hand against her cloak, feeling her pounding heart. The things she'd been longing for had been in front of her all along.

She turned back to Stephen and put her hand in his, clutching the heart pin. His eyes were as blue as the Irish Sea. His hair, as dark and shiny as coal. The astounding color she now saw made her gasp. "I accept," she said. "I accept your heart."

Just then a trio of men began to play concertinas and flutes in the back of the room. The sound lifted her spirits.

Stephen rose and pinned the heart on the outside of her cloak. Then he leaned close and whispered in her ear. "You have my heart, Annie Gallagher. My true heart. Forever."

A Note from the Author

IRELAND HAS A long history of storytelling from ancient times that continues today. The *seanchaithe* were important and well-respected members of society. As keepers of historical lore and genealogies, they brought both information and entertainment to the people. I based the character of Annie's father on this storytelling tradition. Frank Delaney's novel *Ireland* is a good place to learn more about the Irish storytellers.

When *The Wonderful Wizard of Oz* released in 1900, it definitely took the country by storm. Long before MGM turned it into the beloved movie, people were snatching the story from bookstore shelves. Several stage productions predated the movie, including some silent films. What is sometimes overlooked today is that the illustrations were part of the appeal. As a package, the book was remarkable in its day. If you compare children's books before and after L. Frank Baum's publications, you will immediately notice the impact they made. Baum wrote other books, such as *Father Goose*, which my character Dexter refers to, and more books in the Oz series.

Magdalene Laundries existed in Ireland from the eighteenth century until recent times. The last one closed in 1996.

They were institutions for unwed mothers, reformatories, and sometimes places for women when their families didn't want them. I would not presume that all of them were abusive, but many firsthand accounts indicate that abuse, including holding women against their will and not compensating them for their labor, was widespread. I know that there are some who argue against this contention, and so the debate continues. The experience of my characters is fictional and not based on any one story in particular. When Father Weldon tells Annie that the church is not evil, he means that there are caring people within it, and I believe that has been true since the church first began. But a code of secrecy has allowed injustice to continue. History has lessons to teach us, and I pray our society learns from this awful episode.

I have found the early twentieth century a fascinating time to write about, in part because of the changing role of women. As Annie realizes in the story, American women were beginning to take roles as business leaders and heads of organizations. Mrs. Hawkins is an example of how women were working within their limitations to accomplish much.

The Post Office Department, as it was called at the time, did strike fear into the hearts of criminals who, when robbing a train, would avoid the mail car because of the penalties involved. The Pinkerton National Detective Agency was established in 1850 by Allan Pinkerton, who later claimed to have averted an assassination attempt against President Lincoln. During the time of *Annie's Stories*, Pinkertons were mostly employed during labor strikes and to track down railroad bandits. They sought outlaws Jesse James, Butch Cassidy, and the Sundance Kid. They were hired privately and had a reputation for being unscrupulous. As I portrayed in *Grace's Pictures*, the New York Police Department was ill equipped and, it could be said, frequently ineffective in solving the many cases the city dealt with at the time, so I sent the post office to the rescue.

When the immigrants of this era came to America, they still faced some of the hardships they had tried to leave behind. Yet they embraced their new country because the ability to improve their situations was for the first time within their grasp. I believe those of us who descend from such immigrants owe them our gratitude and respect. Most of us today enjoy a standard of living free from oppression that our ancestors never dreamed of.

Annie Gallagher, like Dorothy Gale, sought a home and in the end discovered it right in front of her. I believe sometimes all we need to do to find what we seek is open our eyes to what is already around us. As they say, "There is no place like home."

Please turn the page for an exciting preview from

GRACE'S PICTURES

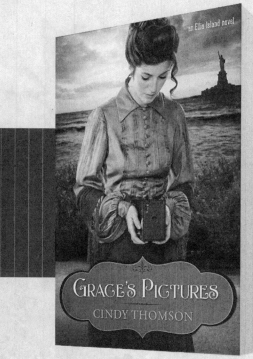

an Ellis Island novel

GRACE'S PICTURES
CINDY THOMSON

"A delightful story of overcoming obstacles.
Lynn Austin fans will savor this historical series debut."
LIBRARY JOURNAL

1

DECEMBER 1900

"May I take your photograph, miss?"

Grace McCaffery spun around. She had passed through the inspections without a problem and was on her way downstairs, where she would meet the aid society worker. What now?

"A photograph?" A man stood smiling at her, next to a large camera. She'd only seen one of these machines before, and that was on the ship.

"Why?" She bit her lip. Was everything about to fall apart now?

"For prosperity. It's your first day in America." He handed her a small piece of paper. "My name and address, should you later wish to see it. It will only take a moment of your time, and then you are free to continue on."

Free sounded good. "What do I do?"

"Stand under that window—" he pointed toward one of the massive windows—"and look this way." Streams of late-afternoon sun shone in through the ornamental ironwork, tracing odd shapes on the tiled floor.

She did as he asked.

"Now look up, miss." He snapped his fingers. "Look toward the camera."

Her eyelids were iron weights, but she forced herself to look his way, wanting to get it over with.

After she heard a slight pop coming from the camera, he dismissed her. "Welcome to America!"

America! Ma should see Ellis Island and all the people milling about. Grace sat down on a bench just to the right of the stairs to collect the thoughts rambling around in her head like loose marbles. Imagine, a girl like her, now free in America. She would not have envisioned it herself a few weeks ago. Exhausted, she dropped her face to her hands as she relived what had led her here.

"Must go to the workhouse." Huge hands snatched wee Grace from her bed. "Your da is dead. Behind in your rent and got no means."

Grace kicked with all her might. "Ma!"

An elbow to her belly. Burning. She heaved.

"Blasted kid!" The policeman tossed her onto a wagon like garbage.

"Ma!"

"I'm here, Grace. Don't cry." Her mother cradled her as the wagon jolted forward. "Oh, my heart. You are special, wee one. So special to God."

Heat emanated from the burning cottage, the temperature torturing Grace's face. She hid against her mother's shoulder.

Later, they were pulled apart and herded into a building.

A dark hallway. The sound of water dripping.

Stairs. Up the stairs. Following other children. So many children. Was her mother dead?

The sound of heels clacking down steps brought Grace back to the present. She sat up straight and watched hordes of people march down the stairs. They were divided into three groups according to destination.

She knew her mother had loved her, but God? Her mother had been wrong about that. God loved good people like Ma. Not Grace. Grace knew she was not good enough for God.

So many of the people passing in front of her were mere children, most with parents but some without. Grace wondered if they were as afraid as she had been when she was separated from her mother in the workhouse, the place Irish folks were taken to when they had nowhere else to go. All these people now seemed to have a destination, though. A new start. Like her. In America she hoped she could mend her fumbling ways and merit favor.

A wee lass approached the stairs with her hand over her mouth, the registration card pinned to her coat wrinkled and stained with tears. Grace was about to go to her and tell her everything would be fine. After all, this great hall, this massive building, was not in Ireland. They were in the land of the free. They'd just seen Lady Liberty's glowing copper figure in the harbor, hadn't they?

But the lass, obviously having mustered her courage, scrambled down the steps and into the mass of people. Would the child be all right? No mother. No parents at all. It had happened to Grace. Free one day, sentenced by poverty the next.

She pulled her hand away from her own mouth. In the workhouse she'd had this nightmare and cried out. She'd been whipped.

Not now.

Not ever again.

She struggled to remember the song her mother sang to her at bedtime. *"Thou my best thought by day or by night . . ."* She couldn't remember any more of it. She'd forgotten. The truth was, she didn't know if everything would be all right.

She rose and followed the orders she'd been given right before the photographer had approached her. Down the steps to the large room where the lady from the charity would meet her.

She rubbed her free hand along the handrail as she walked, barely able to believe she was in another country now, far across the Atlantic Ocean. If it hadn't been for the miserable voyage in steerage, the stench from sweaty, sick passengers that remained even now, and wobbling knees weak from too little food, she might believe she was dreaming. Had it really been just a few weeks ago when she'd sat opposite the workhouse master's desk and twisted the edge of her apron between the fingers of her right hand as he spoke to her?

"Eight years you've been here, Grace," he'd said.

"Aye." She'd stopped counting.

"You are a young woman now, with some potential to be productive. Yet there is no employment in this country of yours. Nothing you can do." He was British and had little patience for the Irish.

She'd held her head low.

"And so, Grace, you've been sponsored to leave the workhouse and go to America." He dipped the nib of his pen in an inkwell and scribbled, not looking up.

"What do you mean, sir?"

"America. You leave from Dublin in two days. I've got your papers in order. And this." He pushed an envelope toward her.

She remembered that at the time she'd worried about her fingernails when she'd held out her hand. She looked at them now. Grime on the ship had taken its toll. The master would not like that.

He is not here.

She touched that very same envelope now, crinkled in her apron pocket. It contained the name of the ship, the destination, and at the bottom, *Sponsored by S. P. Feeny.*

She mumbled under her breath. "Ma married him for this." To provide a future for Grace.

The line of people moved slowly. Grace sucked in her breath. Not long now.

"Mama!"

She turned and watched a red-faced lad scurry down the steps and into the open arms of his mother, who reprimanded him for wandering away.

Grace had begged to speak to her own mother the day the workhouse master told her she was going to America. He hadn't sent for her because her mother was no longer an inmate, but a free woman married to that lawman, that peeler named Sean Patrick Feeny.

But Grace's mother had come anyway, not to the workhouse but to the docks.

"Hurry along," the immigration worker urged her now.

Grace thought about S. P. Feeny's note again as she entered a room packed with people. Not knowing whether the charity lady would need to see it, she reached into her pocket and pulled it out. She glanced around and found a vacant spot on a bench.

"Wait until you hear your name called," a man in a brown suit said to the crowd.

There were more workers in that place than she expected. In Ireland only a handful of employees kept the inmates in line. She reminded herself again that she was in America. *People care about folks here, now, don't they?*

She opened the note and reread the part at the end, the words her mother's husband had scrawled there.

Your mother wants you out of the workhouse. With no other options, I have arranged for you to go to America, where you will find work and no doubt prosper. Pin this to your dress for the journey. It is the name of a man my connections say will take good care of you in New York and arrange a job. I have written him to let him know when you will arrive.

S. P.

The immigration official upstairs had told her not to expect this man to meet her, but rather someone who worked for him, mostly likely a woman from an immigrant aide society. "Don't worry," he'd told her. "They'll have your name."

As much as Grace wanted to crumple up the paper and toss it away, she dared not. Following directions had been essential to getting along in the workhouse, and she had no reason to abandon that thinking now. She had managed to survive back there, even though she was apart from her mother, who had worked out of Grace's sight until she got married and left the workhouse altogether. Surviving was a victory and perhaps the best she could have hoped for then.

She glanced down at the writing again. S. P. Feeny was a peeler, a policeman, like those who tore Grace and her mother from their home when Grace was but ten years old. Grace had thought her life was as good as over when she heard about the marriage. But now she was in America.

She blinked back tears as she thought about her unknown future. What if her father had been right when, so long ago, he'd told her she needed him to survive, could not do it alone? His death had forced them into the workhouse, and she had survived without him then, hadn't she? But now? Now she really was alone and she was not sure she could endure. And yet, she must.

She mentally rehearsed her instructions, the ones Feeny had written down. She'd done what she'd been told so far.

Now she was supposed to wait. But how long?

Running her fingers down her skirt to wipe away perspiration, she hoped she would not say the wrong thing when this stranger claimed her. Would they understand her in America? Did she speak proper English well enough? As much as her stomach churned, she mustn't appear sick, even though the doctor had already hurriedly examined her along with her fellow passengers. She'd heard stories. They sent sick people to a hospital and often they were never heard from again. Perhaps they executed the ones who didn't die. Or they put them back on the ship to return to Ireland. As bad as it was facing an unknown future in America, at least there was hope here that could not be found in the workhouse. So long as they let her stay.

She glanced over at a family. Mother, father, son, and daughter clung to each other. They would make it. Together they had strength. Grace had no one.

Soon a crowd of tall men jabbering in a language she didn't understand entered the room. Grace squeezed the note in her hand. As much as she didn't want S. P. Feeny's help, she'd needed a sponsor to start this new life. She had no choice but to trust his instruction. *If there is one thing a policeman like Feeny knows, it's the rules. Whether or not they abide by them is another matter.*

"Where you from?" a tawny-haired lass sitting next to her asked.

"County Louth." She thought it best not to mention the workhouse.

The girl nodded.

Good. She didn't seem to want to ask anything else.

After a few moments, sensing the girl's nervousness, not unlike her own, Grace gave in. "And you? Where are you from?"

The girl sat up straight. "County Down."

"Oh. Not far." Grace swallowed hard. They were both far from home.

An attendant stood on a box and raised his voice. "Mary Montgomery? Miss Mary Montgomery, please."

The girl next to Grace stood and went to him.

"I'm afraid there's been a mistake, miss."

A brief moment later the lass was gone from the room. Escorted off somewhere. Grace turned to the men seated behind her. "Where are they taking her?"

They shrugged. Only one of them met her gaze. "Don't be worrying, lass. Could be she's in the wrong place. Could be her family didn't come to claim her. Could be 'bout anything, don't you know?"

Grace tried to breathe, but the room felt hot and noisy. *You can do this,* she heard her mother say from the recesses of her mind.

In the workhouse, everyone was the same—wore matching gray uniforms, used identical spoons, slurped the same watery stirabout, marched together from dining hall to dormitory at the same exact time day after day, month after month, year after year. It was a routine she could count on.

She glanced around at the faces near her. Square jaws, rounded chins. Black hair, locks the color of spun flax. Brightly colored clothing, suits the color of mud. So many differences. And so many tongues. Where she'd come from, there had been no question of how to act, what to say, who to look at. But here?

She turned and kept her eyes on her feet and the trim of the red petticoat her mother had given her to travel in when she'd met her at the docks.

Oh, Ma! When Grace had been able to look into her mother's green-gray eyes, she found assurance. On the ship, Grace had tried to emblazon her mother's face on her memory so it would always be there when she needed to see it. She'd even sketched her mother on some paper with a charcoal pencil another passenger gave her. She had the sketch in her bag with her meager belongings. Not much, but all she had now.

"Thanks be to God." "God have mercy." "God bless our souls." "The grace of God on all who enter." . . . Her mother never failed to acknowledge God. She was a good woman. The best. Grace was so far away now from that umbrella of assurance.

She focused on the immigration official calling out names. Survival was human instinct, and humans adapted. She'd learned to do it once before. Perhaps she could manage to exorcise her father's voice from her head, the one that told her she was incapable, and actually make a life, a good life, for herself in America.

Grace's mother had held her at arm's length when they said good-bye on the docks in Dublin. She'd rubbed Grace's cheeks with her thumbs. "The best thing for you is to go to America. You are not a child anymore. I could not let you stay in the workhouse. Don't I know how hard it is for a grown woman to keep her dignity there."

Grace had tried pleading with her. "Take me home with you. I'll be polite to S. P. . . . I promise."

But her mother wouldn't hear of it. "There's no life here for you, Grace. Fly free, Daughter. Find your way. 'Tis a blessing you can go."

Grace had told her mother she couldn't do it. Not alone. Not without her.

"Listen to me," her mother had said, tugging Grace's chin

upward with her finger. "I don't care what lies your father once spoke to you, darlin'. To us both. Pity his departed soul that he left us with no choice but the workhouse. But promise me you will not think of the things he said to you. Remember instead this: You are smart. You are important. You are able."

If she could prosper as her mother had asked her to, then perhaps her mother might choose to come to America too, a place where she would not need S. P. Feeny. Grace would make it happen. Somehow. She had to. Her hands trembled as she held tight to her traveling bag.

About the Author

CINDY THOMSON has been making up stories for as long as she can remember. Her first novel, *Brigid of Ireland*, was published by Monarch Books, and she is a coauthor of *Three Finger: The Mordecai Brown Story*, the only full-length biography of baseball Hall of Famer Mordecai "Three Finger" Brown. *Annie's Stories* is the second book, following *Grace's Pictures*, in the Ellis Island series. Set in New York City at the turn of the twentieth century, the novels follow the lives of new immigrants as they struggle to find their place in America. Along the way they will find friendship and love and renew their faith in God.

Cindy is a mentor in the Jerry B. Jenkins Christian Writers Guild. She and her husband have three grown sons and make their home in central Ohio, where they enjoy rooting for the Cincinnati Reds.

Her greatest wish is that her writing will encourage, enlighten, and entertain her readers.

Visit her online at www.cindyswriting.com.

Discussion Questions

1. Though Mrs. Hawkins offers Annie a good job and a place to live, she still seems to be searching for "home." Why is that? Have you ever experienced a desire for home like Annie does?

2. Why does Stephen Adams whistle Irish tunes on his route, eat Italian food, and visit his Jewish neighbor? How does this reflect the culture and atmosphere of Lower Manhattan at the time?

3. Why is Mrs. Hawkins at first reluctant to tell Annie about her past in Ireland? How well can you relate to the women of this time period, and what do you struggle to understand about them?

4. At the beginning of the story, Annie believes God was not present in the Magdalene Laundry. In what ways was he active there even though she did not notice?

5. Why do you think Annie wants to help Kirsten Wagner so badly? Is there someone in your life to whom you can extend a helping hand?

6. In this era, serial stories in magazines were extremely popular. What can you equate that to today?

7. Why do you think the Irish are known as wonderful storytellers? How has the history of the Irish people influenced this?

8. What novels published in the early twentieth century have you read or would you like to read? Would you read any of the books Stephen and Dexter enjoy?

9. How does Stephen's tragic past affect his ability to build the future he's always dreamed of for himself? What message does the reverend have for Stephen that helps him move forward?

10. If you were Annie, would you forgive Aileen or would you insist she find her own place to live in America? What reasons can you find that influence Annie's ultimate decision?

11. Why might Stephen be drawn to the false investment scheme? Why do people fall victim to similar schemes today? What steps can you take to ensure you're making sound investments?

12. If you were to assign Oz roles to the characters in this story, and Annie is Dorothy, who would you cast as the Tin Woodman, the Scarecrow, and the Lion? What other parallels can you draw between the stories?